Hillsbor
Hill
A member of
COOPERATIVE

By Kristin Hannah
Published by Ballantine Books:

When Lightning Strikes

Kristin Hannah

BALLANTINE BOOKS • NEW YORK

A Ballantine Book
Published by The Random House Publishing Group
Copyright © 1994 by Kristin Hannah

Excerpt from *Between Sisters* by Kristin Hannah copyright © 2003 by Kristin Hannah.

Published in the United States by Ballantine Books, an imprint of The Random House Publishing Group, a division of Random House, Inc., New York, and simultaneously in Canada by Random House of Canada Limited, Toronto.

Ballantine and colophon are registered trademarks of Random House, Inc.

www.ballantinebooks.com

Library of Congress Catalog Card Number: 94-94404

ISBN 0-449-14908-0   33614082788596

Manufactured in the United States of America

First Edition: November 1994

OPM 30

To my father-in-law, Fred, who wanted a western,

To my sister, Laura, for all her help and
    encouragement, and

To my own everyday heroes, Benjamin and Tucker.

Love makes believers of us all.

Dear Reader:

Welcome to my world. It's a place of myth and magic and impossibility, where fact has an unpredictable way of becoming fiction. So put your feet up and suspend your disbelief, and come with me to a realm of sheer imagination.

Oh, and one more thing. Ask yourself what you would do—what you would think—if tomorrow you woke up in a different time, in a world that couldn't possibly exist. Ask yourself what you would do if you stood beneath the lightning and nothing was ever quite the same again. . . .

DOWN THE RABBIT HOLE

All this time the guard was looking at her,
first through a telescope,
then through a microscope,
and then through an opera glass,
at last he said, "You're traveling the wrong way,"
and shut up the window. . . .

"No, no, the adventures first,"
said the Gryphon in an impatient tone.
"The explanations take such a dreadful time."

—from the works of Lewis Carroll

Chapter One

NEW YORK
PRESENT DAY

"So, Ms. Costanza, how much sexual research do you do?"

Even now, almost four hours after the Geraldo interview, Lainie winced at the offensive question.

She played and replayed it in her mind, every time coming up with a witty, stinging retort. *So, Geraldo, how much research did you do before you blasted Capone's basement on prime time?*

Of course, she hadn't said anything that clever or intelligent. Oh, no. Not her. She'd let anger get the best of her—again—and spoken without thinking. "Could you ask a stupider question, Geraldo? Really, inquiring minds want to know."

She winced at the memory. She should have known better than to respond so bluntly. He was much too skilled an interviewer to let some historical romance author make a fool of him on national television. He'd seen right off that she was hostile, so he'd adroitly cut her off in midsentence and gone on to another guest. A woman who did as she was supposed to—blush and squirm and apologize for the books she worked so hard to create.

He'd also been smart enough not to come back to Lainie. He hadn't asked her another question for the remainder of the hour. She'd sat there, pinned to her uncomfortable chair like a dead insect, barely listening to what was going on around her, waiting desperately to be let loose.

God, it had been awful. It wasn't until now, hours later, in the anonymous, vast open space of John F. Kennedy International Airport, that she'd finally begun to relax.

She glanced sideways at the woman beside her. Judith gave her a tense, irritated smile, and Lainie knew immediately that she shouldn't have made eye contact. Her editor was still spitting mad.

"Did you have to look at your watch so often?" Judith snapped.

Lainie lit up a Marlboro. Dropping her purse on the pile of cheap powder blue luggage heaped beside her left ankle, she glanced at her editor. "I only take that kind of shit from men I'm in love with."

Judith shoved a well-manicured hand through her blunt-cut, Clairol-blond hair. Behind her, a steady stream of people pushed through the security checkpoint. "But it was so ... hostile. You practically *told* America you thought you were wasting your time."

"I was."

"The publicity director worked damned hard to get you on that show. National exposure isn't easy."

Lainie rolled her eyes. "The next time someone says the words 'national media tour,' I'm going to projectile-vomit. Maybe that'll get my point across."

Judith almost smiled in spite of herself and shook her head. "I knew I shouldn't have picked your manuscript out of the slush pile. I should have taken that one about the cross-dressing pirate. Now, *that* was a book."

Lainie smiled at the familiar complaint. It was the same thing her friend had been saying for ten years. Back then, Judith had been a hungry young editorial assistant, and Lainie a dreamer. Now Jude had her own imprint, and Lainie was a *New York Times* best-selling author. "And especially relevant for today's readers."

"I don't think you're cut out for television interviews. You were so ... testy."

Lainie laughed. "I'm a testy kind of gal. Ask anyone."

Judith snatched the cigarette from Lainie and took a long drag, blowing the smoke out in a hurried puff. "Why should I bother to verify the obvious? You spend more time alone than anyone I know. If I hadn't personally seen you in the daylight, I'd swear you were a vampire."

Lainie shrugged. "I *like* being alone. I don't need anyone besides Kelly."

Judith took another drag and handed the cigarette back. "Your daughter's a nice kid—in a prepubescent coil of hormones sort of way—but she's not enough, Lainie. You've got to get out of the house."

Lainie snorted. "Who do you think I am ... Madonna? I get out of the house every day. I go to the grocery store, the mailbox, the ..."

Judith gave her a knowing look. "Uh-huh."

Lainie extinguished her cigarette in a nearby ash can. "I'm fine, Jude. Don't worry about me. Okay?"

"I wouldn't waste my time worrying about an author. You're all a bunch of self-absorbed, undisciplined media hogs."

Lainie cracked a smile. "Yeah, be sure and book me on the Howard Stern show as quickly as possible. I'm on a roll."

Judith gave her an arch, knowing look. "You *need* a roll . . . in the hay, if you get my drift."

"It would be hard to miss, Jude. But there's not a lot of hay in Seattle. Especially not healthy, heterosexual, single hay. But if I find a bale, I'll give it a good roll."

Jude hesitated. "I mean it, Lainie. You know how you get when Kelly's gone."

Lainie flinched. "She'll be back in two weeks."

Judith started to reach out to Lainie, then checked the impulse. Reluctantly she drew her hand back and pressed it to her side. "Why don't you stick around for a while? Les and I would love to have you over."

Lainie looked into her friend's eyes, wishing, just this once, she could relax enough to let someone care for her. "Thanks, Jude." Her voice was embarrassingly husky. "But I've got to learn how to cope with this. Kelly's getting older. She'll be leaving . . . more."

"I know, hon."

Lainie cleared her throat and reached down for her mismatched luggage. "Well, I better run or I'll miss the plane."

Judith gave her a sad, understanding smile. A look that said too much from a woman who never would. "Don't forget, kiddo, if anyone asks you who you are on the plane, make up a name. We don't want your readers to know that Alaina Costanza is a foulmouthed, spike-haired, tattooed slob with a carton of Marlboro Lights sticking out of her handbag."

Lainie grinned at the familiar advice, knowing it was only half a joke. Her downtown, tough-girl look was a far cry from the media image of a romance writer. Oversized sweaters, holey Levi's, and cowboy boots weren't exactly the outfit du jour. " 'Bye, Jude."

Jude's smile dipped a fraction; her gaze turned serious, maybe even a little sad. " 'Bye, hon. I'll be waiting for the *Lightning* manuscript."

The two friends stared at each other for longer than they should have; perhaps it was only a second too long, but Lainie knew instantly that it was a mistake. She sighed. Christ, she hated good-byes. She stiffened and tossed Jude a half-assed smile. "Not long, you won't."

"Safe flight. Don't . . . drink too much."

Lainie made a harsh, defiant sound that was meant to be laughter, but even to her own ears sounded more like a snarl. "Is that possible?"

Jude's attempt at a smile made Lainie feel even worse. "Take care of yourself these next two weeks. Don't fall so deeply into your book that you don't have a life."

"I wish to hell I *could* fall that deeply in, Jude."

Judith reached for her. "Oh, Alaina . . ."

Lainie lurched backward before Judith could touch her. Resettling the garment bag's wide nylon strap on her narrow shoulder, she gave Jude a cocky grin. "Well, gotta run. 'Bye, Jude."

" 'Bye, Lainie."

Lainie straightened and headed toward her gate.

Judith watched Lainie walk away. The younger woman's body was perfectly erect, her back ramrod-stiff, her legs pumping in that no-nonsense, ground-gobbling march that was her usual gait. Her narrow shoulders were drawn up high and held stiff, her left elbow was pressed protectively against her waist, as if she were afraid to accidentally touch or be touched. Somehow, even as she moved through the sea of hurried travelers, she was a woman distant and alone.

For years, Jude had watched her friend contain real life within the parameters of a blue screen. Except for motherhood, writing was all Lainie had, all she claimed to want. The work was a refuge for Alaina, a safe place where she could control fate.

"Please ..." She mouthed the single word, wondering what she could ask of the God with whom she so rarely spoke. "Watch out for Alaina. Let the book take care of her until Kelly gets back."

The book. Jude shook her head, frowning. It was so little, so damned little. But without Kelly, it was all Lainie had.

Bainbridge Island, Washington

Lainie stood at her bedroom window, staring out at the dark, rain-drenched night, trying to be brave and failing miserably. Water hammered the pane in an endless, pounding heartbeat. Wind howled through the huddled, quaking stand of dogwood trees that bordered her small lot. Every new gust wrenched off another fistful of summer-green leaves, sending the tender branches tumbling through the stormy night. Beside her window, a maple tree shuddered at the onslaught, tapping a long, gnarled wooden finger against the glass.

Lainie brought the cigarette to her lips and took a drag. The sharp, unpleasant taste of the smoke scalded her throat and lungs. When she drew her hand back it was shaking so badly, it sent a spray of fluttering ashes across the hardwood floor.

"Damn," she cursed, glancing quickly around for her ashtray. She found it, overflowing, on the piano, and stabbed the cigarette out.

A drink, she thought suddenly. She needed a good, strong drink. She stumbled through her living room and reached for the bottle of Jack Daniel's she kept stashed behind the stereo. She wrenched off the top and took a long gulp. The liquor burned a path down her throat and puddled, hot and pulsing, in her stomach. For a second, a brief, fitful heartbeat, she felt almost warm. Then the cold began to creep in again, curling around her heart, chilling her deeper than her bones, chilling her to her soul.

She took another huge swallow and wiped her mouth with her sleeve. After about three more drinks, a pleasant, familiar lethargy stole through her bloodstream, easing the cold burden of fear.

She set the bottle down with a sloshing clank and padded to her bedroom, sitting on the edge of her unmade bed and pulling the pile of blue flannel sheeting around her body. She hugged herself and slumped forward, staring dry-eyed at the floor. God, she hated rainstorms . . . and being alone.

The phone rang.

She dove across the bed and grabbed the receiver. "H-Hello?"

"Mom?" Kelly's small, quiet voice slid through the telephone wires.

Lainie swallowed hard. Tears welled in her throat, stung her eyes. It took every ounce of self-control she possessed not to let them fall. "Hi, baby," she breathed, hating the trembling sound of her voice.

"It's raining here in Montana, and I figured it was probably worse at home. I thought . . . you know, I was worried about you."

Lainie squeezed her eyes shut and took a deep breath. *Thank you, God; thank you for giving me this child.* "Nothing to worry about, sweet pea. I'm fine. More importantly, how are you?"

A sigh of relief moved through the phone. "I'm great, Mom. This is a totally cool place. Tomorrow we're heading out. Mr. Hade—he's the trail guide—has provisions tied to trees at certain places. We've got compasses to find the food. Then we set up tents, cook the food, and go to sleep. So I won't be able to call again till we make it back down the trail."

The words caught Lainie off guard. "Oh." She knew it wasn't the right thing to say, knew she should say more, but the words were lodged in her throat, held in place by fear and a parent's desperation.

"Is that okay?" Kelly's voice had gone quiet again, hesitant.

Lainie cursed her own neuroses. "It's fine, baby. Hey, they don't call it survival training for nothing."

Kelly laughed, a high, pure, clear sound that washed through Lainie like an elixir. "Yeah, Mom."

"I . . . I miss you, baby."

"I miss you, too."

"I'll talk to you when you get back. When will that be . . . ten days?"

"Twelve. And, Mom?"

"Yeah, honey?"

"Take care of yourself, okay?"

Lainie thought about the cigarettes, which she never smoked when Kelly was home, and the Jack Daniel's she'd downed a few minutes ago. She winced, feeling the sting of shame and regret. She wanted to say, *I'll try*. It was all she could realistically promise, all she could hope for. But it wasn't enough for a bighearted thirteen-year-old. Kelly didn't deserve to worry about her schizoid mother all the time.

"I will, Kel. Don't you worry about me, okay? You and Jennifer just have fun."

" 'Bye, Mom. I love you."

"I love you, too."

Click. The connection went dead. Lainie listened to

the droning buzz of the empty line for a few minutes, then slowly put the receiver back in its cradle.

She squeezed her eyes shut, felt the familiar sting of tears.

She'd known how it would feel to let Kelly go to camp, of course, known the wrenching sense of loss that would descend, known, too, that she had to say yes.

But knowing that didn't stop the hurt. She reached blindly for the bottle of sleeping pills beside her bed. She needed the oblivion, needed not to think about this for a while. If she thought about it anymore, she was going to start crying. And if she started, she might never stop.

Kelly, I miss you, baby. I miss you so much. . . .

Flipping open the cap, she poured a couple—more than a couple?—capsules into her palm and downed them with the glass of cloudy, tepid water on her bedside table.

She flopped back on the bed, staring up at the midnight blue ceiling dappled with Day-Glo stars. The brilliant golden spots soothed her now, as they always did. She reached across her bed and switched off her lamp, letting the pretend galaxy become her world.

Fleetingly she remembered how ridiculous she had felt when she first decorated her bedroom. It wasn't a grownup's room; it was a child's haven, an escape from the adult world. She'd painted the walls a deep midnight blue that mirrored the night sky. On the ceiling, she'd pressed a thousand glow-in-the-dark stars and painted a fluorescent full moon.

At the time she hadn't known why she'd done it, but when she'd gone to bed that first night, she'd understood. She'd felt like Max in *Where the Wild Things Are*, a child in the middle of a vast, but somehow friendly, unknown. This room lulled her, protected her, bathed her in starlight. Here, even when she couldn't sleep, she was safe.

Outside, the rain raged, pounded against the windows and roof, but gradually Lainie stopped listening to it. After a while, she stopped hearing it altogether. She focused all her thoughts on the monotonous cadence of her breathing, all her sights on the glittering starbursts of her own universe.

She felt the tingling presence of the booze and the pills in her bloodstream, and tried her best to relax, to sink into the softness of the bed and disappear.

It didn't work.

With a disgusted sigh, she jackknifed to a sitting position and yanked her knees to her chest. There would be no sleep for her tonight.

She reached for the crushed pack of Marlboros by her bedside and lit up her last cigarette. Inhaling deeply, she leaned back against the polished mahogany of her headboard and exhaled slowly.

She didn't want to sleep anyway, not really, not the way her sleep was. It was other people's slumber that she craved—quiet, restful, filled with peace. For her, sleeping wasn't like that, never had been. For her, falling asleep was like falling into the bowels of hell itself.

No wonder she was an insomniac. She had been for years upon years. The pills and booze rarely worked, rarely brought the peaceful oblivion she sought. More often than not, she was awake for days, until her body literally gave out. Then she'd fall into a coma-deep sleep that ended only when the horrifying nightmares began.

"Don't think about it," she whispered aloud.

She needed to get her mind on something else, something besides her loneliness and fear.

The book.

The thought came to her like a gift from God. She could switch on her computer and slide into the quiet, comfortable world of her own imagination.

She stumbled into her office and sat down at the computer without bothering to turn on the light. She pushed two buttons and flopped back in her chair. The machine came to life with the familiar *thwop—buzz* and settled into readiness; the droning sound of its mechanical breathing filled the quiet, shadowy room.

The green cursor blinked at her, appearing and disappearing against the blackness of the empty screen.

The large window behind her desk shook with the force of the rain hammering against it. The wooden dividers rattled against the aged glass, made a sound like the chattering of an old man's teeth. Lainie felt a chill of apprehension and hugged herself, trying not to look outside.

But the storm drew her eye, lured her into the writhing, half-lit, tempestuous world. Nature had transformed her ordinarily placid backyard into a pulsing vortex of sound and movement. The swing set, long ago forgotten by Kelly, tossed its empty swings in the wind. Lainie could almost hear the rusty squeak of the old chains. Rain marched across her shake roof and splashed over the leaf-filled gutters, drizzling down the window in sheets of silver.

Lainie swallowed hard and brought her shaking hands to the keyboard, manipulating the keys with the speed of a professional typist, zipping through the menus until she came to the file for her new book, *When Lightning Strikes*.

She smiled at the irony of the title and pulled up chapter sixteen, quickly skimming where she'd left off yesterday.

"You don't have to run anymore, Jessica. Can't you see that? You can stay here, with me. Always ..."

Jessie looked up at him, her eyes drowning in hot tears. "I can't. I wish to God I could."

Joe felt the weight of her fear like a cold hand against his heart. "They'll stop looking for you soon. They'll forget. The West is a place for forgetting, Jess. Hell, most of us don't even use our real names."

Lainie closed her eyes and let out a tired sigh, bowing her head. No wonder she liked the plot of this book so well. There were so many things in her life she wanted to forget, ached to forget. Tiny, niggling memories that besieged her when the sky was dark and the thunder rolled.

The West is a place for forgetting.

If only there were somewhere like that. Someplace where Lainie could start over, could be the parent she wanted to be, the woman she wanted to be. Someplace where _she_ made the rules.

Suddenly a huge, hammering gust of wind ricocheted off her window. Rain clawed at the sweaty pane, thunder roared across the night. Lightning ripped the cloudy sky apart and landed in a white-hot streak in her backyard. A huge madrone tree split down the center in a cloud of blue light and shooting sparks. The eerie light pulsed through the window and smashed into the computer.

Sensations exploded through Lainie. The computer keys heated up, scalded the sensitive flesh of her fingertips. She tried to jerk her hands back, but she couldn't move. Her hands tingled. The acrid odor of burning flesh choked her throat and nose.

Panicked, she blinked at the computer, trying to see clearly. An odd glow emanated from her keyboard, made the keys appear to be floating atop the polished mahogany of her desk. The computer made a quiet *thump*. The words on the screen blipped into nothingness, leaving in their stead a gaping, empty black square wreathed in impossible neon green light.

She tried to scream, but couldn't. A dull, pounding throb started at the base of her skull. Her eyelids slid closed and seemed to stick. She tried vainly to open them. A sandy dryness crept up her throat, made her achingly thirsty.

She tried to remain upright, but it felt as if someone had plucked a string from her insides and was slowly, inexorably unwinding her. She had a crazy, demented vision of what would be left of her when this was over. Nothing but a pile of old, rotted rope.

Sensations swirled like hot mists through her body, seeping, tingling into every drop of her blood. The impossible scent of roses mingled with dust clogged her nostrils, their smells so real and cloying that for a moment she couldn't breathe.

She started to fall forward. It was like a dream fall; slow and spiraling and unstoppable. Her forehead hit the keyboard, and this time the keys were icy cold. She shivered and hunched into a shaking ball.

Slowly, fighting it every step of the way, Lainie fell into the darkness that had come for her.

Chapter Two

Lainie had never felt so relaxed. She sighed deeply, savoring the completely unexpected feeling. She couldn't remember the last time she'd awakened like this, with an almost effervescent sense of peace. She was used to greeting each day with a mixture of dread and distrust.

But not this morning; today she felt great. Refreshed, relaxed. The familiar pain in her hips and lower back had vanished, and for once she felt young at thirty-five instead of irritatingly old.

Then she remembered last night. It hadn't really been like going to sleep. It had been more like . . . falling. . . .

"Weird," she mumbled, hearing a scratchy early morning harshness in the word. She liked it. Anything was better than her regular voice. It was one of the few things she really couldn't stand about herself. Her too wide hips, she accepted; her fleshy thighs, she ignored. But her voice drove her crazy. It had a breathy softness that was completely at odds with her personality.

Reluctantly she cracked one eye open, expecting to see the bumpy, slightly out-of-focus mountain range of computer keys.

She saw dirt. A lot of dirt.

She blinked and tried again, opening her eyes slowly this time.

14

She was sprawled on the main road of a quaint, old-fashioned town. On either side of the street were false-fronted wooden buildings shoved together like wobbly blocks, their entrances connected by a sagging, gray-planked boardwalk.

She frowned. The place looked like every cow town west of the Pecos in the late 1880s.

The detail was flawless. Hell, she half expected Linda Evans and Kenny Rogers to come striding out of the nearest saloon, maybe with Reba singing in the doorway.

She sat back on her heels and put her hands on her thighs. Where was she? And how had she gotten here?

She hadn't been drunk enough to leave her house last night. Had she? Had she somehow boarded a plane headed southwest?

Fear quickened her heartbeat. No . . .

She couldn't have. She *remembered* falling asleep at her computer.

You remember? The word came back at her, ice-cold and cruel. Back in her teenage years, when she'd been doing a lot of drugs, she had often wakened in strange places. And what she remembered usually had only the barest link to reality.

Was that the explanation? Had she been so high—or low—on Jack Daniel's and sleeping pills that she'd slipped into her old routine?

It hadn't happened to her in years. Not since before she got pregnant. Motherhood had saved her, given the tough little girl from the streets a safe haven and a place to belong. Lainie was smarter now, more responsible. She wouldn't have gotten so blind drunk that she'd accidentally board a plane. She no longer had anything to run away from.

Except an empty house . . .

The thought was chilling. She knew she'd drunk too much last night, popped a few too many pills—neither of which she'd done in years. She'd tried so hard to stay on the straight and narrow path recently, but God knew, even though she did her best to be responsible, she failed at almost everything in her personal life. *Anything's possible with you. . . .*

No. She'd come so far since her zone days. She wouldn't have lapsed so easily back into that trap. She couldn't have. And no matter how much sense it made, no matter how precisely it matched her image of herself, she refused to believe it.

"Damn," she cursed, shoving a dirty hand through her cropped hair. Wishing like hell she had a cigarette, she glanced again down the street.

There were people in the street, people and horses and buggies. Everything you'd expect in a scene from *Young Guns* . . . except they weren't moving.

Horses were poised at hitching rails, completely still. In the middle of the street, a wagon was at a dead stop, the horse's hoof frozen an inch above the ground. In the buckboard's seat, two men were looking at each other, faces arrested in masks of anger—eyebrows furrowed, mouths open, eyes narrowed. The boardwalk was dotted with people, everyone motionless and silent.

She brushed her dirty hands on her jeans and got to her feet, cramming her fists in her baggy pockets. Across the street, like a crowned tooth amidst a decaying mouth, sat a brick building—the only one in town, and obviously built to last. It was large and square with perfectly matched windows that flanked twin oak doors. Above the doors, in huge, ornate letters, were the words FORTUNE FLATS BANK.

Relief rushed through Lainie. She should have

known. This wasn't real. None of this was real. She was still asleep at her computer. This was all a dream.

It had to be because this town didn't exist. She'd created Fortune Flats, designed and named the buildings, even imagined the dirty, dusty road. It was the fictional town where her current book was set.

She was looking at chapter one—she could tell by the four horses clustered in front of the bank. The bank was being robbed right now, and Skeeter Johnson—the dim-witted lookout—was standing frozen on the boardwalk, clutching the coil of reins. Waiting, watching.

She grinned. She was dreaming about her book. It was only natural, since she'd gone to sleep working on it.

Suddenly she was excited. She looked up and down the street, trying to soak in as much information as she could. This wasn't exactly as she'd imagined the town; the detail was too perfect. Her subconscious was obviously kicking in, supplying tidbits of information from her extensive research.

What an opportunity! She'd never dreamt in this level of detail before, never actually learned anything from her dreams. But now she saw the possibilities. She could meander through the buildings, see the setting, feel the desert heat, meet the people. It would give her book a verisimilitude unlike any she'd achieved before.

Damn, she hoped she remembered this in the morning.

She headed to the bank first—and why not? It was where the book began.

Killian pointed his Winchester at the teller.

The small, pointy-faced man behind the brass bars blanched. Two nickel-sized spots of color seeped through his pale cheeks. "I-I don't think I oughta give you no money. I-It wunt be right. M-Mr. Harold Springs s-said I w-was responsible for all the funds in this bank."

"Uh-huh."

The teller swallowed so hard, his Adam's apple slid up and down his knobby throat. "I m-mean, *I* wunt mind givin' it to you, but it ain't my money. You u-understand how it is. . . ."

"Shoot him, boss," Mose said in his gravel-stained voice. "We don't got time fer this shit." He spun toward the teller and pointed his pearl-handled pistol at the man's balding head.

"Yeah," Purty chimed from the corner, where three people lay facedown on the floor in front of him.

Killian lifted a gloved hand for silence. "See, Mr. . . ." He glanced at the brass plate along the teller's cage. "Mr. Ernest Lubb, you're trying to be a hero now."

Ernest looked for a moment as if he were going to smile. His pencil-thin lips wobbled uncertainly. The color on his cheeks darkened a shade. "Well, I wouldn't say—"

" 'Cept you got yourself a problem."

The teller choked on the end of his sentence and blinked at Killian. "Wh-What's that?"

"Only one way to become a hero in a bank robbery."

Ernest wet his colorless lips. Sweat broke out along his wrinkled forehead. "H-How's that?"

Killian raised his Winchester a hair, enough so that the gaping hole at the end of the barrel was fixed on Ernest's scrawny chest. "You gotta kill me or die tryin'."

Ernest swallowed hard. "Oh."

"Were you thinkin' on takin' it that far?"

The teller opened his mouth, revealing a set of yellowed teeth. He looked for a moment like he was going to speak, but he didn't. Nothing came out except a high-pitched squeak.

Killian nodded, almost smiled. Old Ernie wasn't going to risk his life for someone else's gold. "Good decision. Now, put all the money in those bags."

Ernest nodded and reached for the big burlap bags Purty had tossed through the bars. With shaking, sweaty hands, he shoved bills and coins into the nearest sack.

Killian lowered the rifle's barrel, but didn't draw his finger off the trigger. His narrowed eyes scanned the bank, taking in every detail, every nuance of sound or movement. Sunlight pulsed through the dusty windows overhead, illuminating the three bodies sprawled, hands behind their heads, on the cold stone floor. Purty stood in the corner, his gun pointed negligently at the people strewn like dolls at his feet. Mose was at the end of the long oak teller's counter, his twin pistols poised and ready.

It was going all right; better than Killian had thought it would. Better than usual, in fact. The break-in had gone without a hitch, and except for Ernie's momentary bout of conscience, everyone had done as they'd been asked. Outside, the town was as quiet as a tomb.

So why did Killian have that nagging, irritating sense that something was wrong?

It could be because of Skeeter. The man didn't have the sense God gave a goat, and he was as likely to shoot Killian as to protect him. But lookout was a damn easy job, after all. Especially in a backwater town with a fat, lazy drunkard of a sheriff. It didn't take any special brains. Just a pair of eyes, and Skeeter had that at least.

Yeah, Killian told himself for the hundredth time since he'd shoved through the bank's oak doors, guns drawn. This job was goin' along fine. Hell, they'd be outta here in less than five minutes.

So why did he *feel* so unsettled? As if it were a goddamn poor day for a bank robbery. As if he were gonna have to kill someone before this thing was over ...

Lainie strolled across the street. When she stepped up onto the boardwalk, it was as if a switch had been flipped. The town burst into bustling, chatting, laughing life. Horse-drawn buggies churned down the road amid a roiling wake of dust and the catchy clip-clop cadence of moving hooves. The boardwalk creaked beneath the weight of a dozen booted feet hurrying from store to store.

The hustle and bustle of the place surprised her. Whenever she imagined an old western town, it was quiet—the crack of old leather as a cowhand climbed down from the saddle, the tinny strains of a poorly played piano through half-open saloon doors. But this was ... more. The town had a pulsing heartbeat of sound and movement, a *life* she'd somehow never expected. All this time she'd thought of the West in vaguely ghost-town-like terms, but it was nothing like that. It was like New Orleans, lively and loud.

She made a mental note, praying she remembered it when she woke up, and reached for the bank's doorknob.

"Stop!" yelled a scratchy male voice.

Lainie paused and turned around. The man holding the horses was staring at her. His face was as pale as the underside of a snake, his rheumy eyes as big as quarters.

"Y-You oughtn't to go in there, miss," he stammered, swallowing hard.

Lainie couldn't help smiling. Skeeter was exactly as she'd created him—a tall, bowlegged cowhand wearing baggy, too short pants and a dirty shirt. Watery, pleasant eyes stared out at her from a dusty, leather-lined face. If she remembered her words correctly, he had the heart of a lion and the brain of a gnat. "You'd best be watching for the sheriff, Skeeter, and don't worry about me."

Skeeter's eyes bulged. He glanced quickly down the road, as if he expected the sheriff to materialize any second. "How'd—"

Lainie slipped inside the bank and shut the door quietly behind her.

"Who the hell are you?" The words boomed across the lobby in a voice so loud, Lainie flinched.

A squat, barrel-chested man pointed two pearl-handled six-shooters at her. She recognized him instantly. Dark, squinty eyes peered out at her from a mass of leathery, wrinkled skin. "I'm talkin' to you," he growled.

Lainie stared at him, surprised in spite of herself at how mean he looked. "Don't mind me, Mose. I'm just watching."

The man in the center of the room spun around. His looming shadow cut across the black and white marble floor, huge and menacing. He was tall, probably six-four, and broad-shouldered, wearing a long, dirty brown duster, black woolen trousers, rough white cotton shirt, and a ragged vest. Scarred chaps hung low on his narrow hips, brushed the dusty leather of his boots. Two pistols hung in the holsters at his sides; their copper bullets studded his wide black gun belt.

A black Stetson was pulled low on his forehead. Beneath the brim, his hair was a wild fringe of silver gray that hung in waves to his shoulder blades. A dusty red mask concealed the lower half of his face, but it didn't matter. Lainie would have recognized him anywhere. His eyes weren't the kind a woman forgot—especially if she'd invented them. They were brown and deep-set, framed by thick, winged black brows, and cold. Colder somehow than she'd expected.

"How did *you* get in here?" he said in a deep, rolling voice that hinted of Scotland.

Lainie shrugged and grinned, as if to say, *Shit happens.* "Skeeter's not the best lookout."

Above the mask, his eyes narrowed. He took a step toward her, the rifle held negligently in his arms. "How do you know about Skeeter?"

She stared, admiring her handiwork. Damn, he was a good-looking man. Handsome, square-jawed, rugged. A thousand dark secrets lurked in his eyes; danger clung to him like a shroud. All he needed now was a Harley-Davidson.

He strode across the lobby, his duster flapping against his legs as he walked. When he reached her, he yanked her toward him. She stumbled against his chest and hit so hard that for a second she couldn't breathe. Her head snapped back. She stared up into his face, seeing all the hard lines and deep furrows that betrayed the harshness of the past she'd invented for him. "Lay down."

She glanced at the cold, dirty floor. "I don't think so."

He stared, unblinking. One eyebrow cocked slowly upward. His hold tightened, almost lifted her off her feet. "This is a bad time to think, lady. Now, get on the goddamn floor."

"Enough is enough." She tried to wrench her arm free, but couldn't. "Look, John—" she said in as reasonable a voice as she could manage.

A muffled sound came through his mask. It sounded like a sharply indrawn breath. He squeezed her arm more tightly and yanked her toward him. "What did you call me?"

Lainie felt a sense of apprehension that was ridiculous. This was just a dream. He couldn't actually *hurt* her. "John. It's your name, isn't it?"

He pulled her close and stared down at her through cold eyes. "How did you know that?"

Lainie remembered suddenly that no one knew Killian's first name. He was a legend among outlaws, a man without a history or a past. He was simply Killian.

She cursed her own stupidity. Whatever happened to dreaming you were gifted and godlike instead of stupid and mouthy?

Lainie's heart beat faster, her breathing quickened. God help her, even though she knew this was a dream, she felt a flicker of fear. She knew Killian, knew him inside and out. She'd created him, fashioned him from the cold darkness in her own soul. He was everything that terrified her in a man. Everything she hated about herself.

She fought the idiotic feeling of fear. This was just a dream, after all, and one that had to follow her plot. She might *feel* danger, but it wasn't real. Any second now she was going to wake up in the safety of her own bedroom. The realization calmed her, gave her immeasurable strength. She didn't have to take any crap from this Neanderthal he-man. Without her, he didn't exist.

Her sense of control returned. She was the creator here, the one with the power. He was nothing more than words on a computer screen. "You don't scare me."

His eyes narrowed. A tiny pulse beat in his taut jaw. "Then you ain't real bright, lady."

"Shoot her, boss," Mose growled. "We don't got all goddamn day."

Killian cocked his head toward the teller. "Get the money, Purty."

Purty dove for the bags of money and clutched them to his scrawny chest, backing out slowly.

Mose cocked both guns and followed Purty, keeping his back to the door.

Killian stood as still as a statue, watching her, his gun still trained on the teller. She could almost *see* the thoughts in his head; he was wondering how she knew so much, how much of a danger she presented.

Suddenly he grabbed her by the back of the neck.

"Ouch," she squeaked, trying to wrench free.

He yanked her backward, his fingers pinching into the tender flesh of her nape.

"Nobody move," he said to the people sprawled on the floor. "We got a lookout waitin' across the street. You can't see him, but he can damn sure see you. He's gonna shoot the first person who comes out of these doors."

Killian curled his arm around her shoulders, pinned her against his massive chest. Lainie tried to wrestle free, but his arm was like a cold steel weight against her flesh as he dragged her out. She kicked at him, clawed at him, struggled to be free. "When I do the rewrite, I'm going to kill you here, Killian. In the middle of the lobby. It's going to be bloody, too. Painful—"

He clamped a hot, gloved hand over her mouth. She sucked in a gasping breath and clawed at his arm.

They burst through the closed door and backed into the hot sunlight. Skeeter hurriedly handed each man a set of reins. Purty and Mose jumped up onto their mounts.

The street was empty, deserted.

Lainie felt a surge of irritation. Where in the hell was Joe Martin? He should be coming around the corner now, guns drawn, silver marshal's star glinting in the sunlight.

She couldn't wait to see him. His appearance in this dream would be a hell of an improvement. A cross between Mel Gibson and Daniel Day-Lewis, he was every woman's ideal hero. A heart-stoppingly handsome man with a needy heart and a sense of humor. Her and Joe in the desert, alone ... Now, *that* would be a dream.

Killian dragged her toward the horses, then tossed her over his shoulder. She hit his back so hard, it drove the air from her lungs. She gasped and slammed her fists into his back. "What are you doing?"

"Shut up, lady."

He flung her onto a saddle and pinned her in place with an unforgiving grip.

Skeeter frowned. "Hey, boss, that's my horse."

"You can have him," Lainie said. "If you'll just tell Tarzan here to let go of me ..."

Skeeter blinked up at her. "Huh?"

Lainie groaned. "I *must* have written better dialogue for you, Skeeter."

"Shut up, lady," Killian snapped. "Skeet, you ride behind Purty. We'll get you a fresh horse at the change."

He shrugged. "Okay."

"Shut up?" Lainie's temper snapped. She *hated* it when a man told her to shut up. "Now, look here, you arrogant bastard—"

Killian silenced her with a thundercloud of a look. "You don't seem to understand your situation, lady. I could shoot you."

"Go ahead if it would make you feel better. Jesus, I can't imagine why I created such a macho pig ... even for a villain."

He grabbed her reins and vaulted into his own saddle. Pulling her horse close, he leaned toward her. "You give me one second's worth of problems, and I'll shoot you."

"Blah, blah, blah."

He looped the reins around his saddle horn and kicked his horse. The stallion lurched forward, dragging

Lainie's horse with him. Lainie snapped backward like a rag doll.

They were off, galloping hard.

"G-Good getaway," she hissed between painful bounces. "I'm sure no one in town noticed."

"Shut up."

Lainie watched through blurry, dust-clogged eyes as the town sped past. Where in the hell was Joe?

"Only me. Only *I* could create a hero who shows up too late." She shook her head, hanging on for dear life. "You'd think I was dating the man."

Chapter Three

They reached the change point in under an hour. Killian glanced backward out of habit, but he knew there wouldn't be a posse today—if you could call a bunch of pansy-assed merchants on fat horses a posse. He'd been robbing banks long enough to read the signs, and today they'd been crystal-clear. The town had been dead quiet, and as soon as the good ol' boys in town heard Killian's name, they'd forget about getting their money back. It was one of the benefits of a bad reputation in the West. Only men with a death wish dared to follow an outlaw to his hideout.

Up ahead, four fresh horses were tethered to a tree. Killian frowned. The moment's relief he'd felt at seeing the quiet expanse of desert behind him vanished.

Just what he goddamn needed ... four horses and five riders.

He jerked on the reins and leaned back in the saddle, bringing his stallion to a skidding halt. The horse he was leading immediately rammed into them.

The woman made a wheezing grunt of a sound at the impact. "God*damn* it," she snapped, straightening enough to glare at him. "Aren't you supposed to signal?"

The other horses slid to a dusty stop alongside them.

Purty and Mose leapt to the ground and started uncinching their saddles.

Skeeter jumped from his seat behind Purty and glanced back toward town. Sweat ran in dirty rivulets down his wrinkled cheeks, darkened the pale blue fabric of his collar. "You think there's a posse followin' us, boss?"

Mose laughed throatily. "Not from that half-assed, backwater nothin' of a town."

"Fortune Flats is *not* a backwater town," the woman said with an uppity snort.

Killian wrenched her off the horse, clamping an arm around her before she could run. Holding her tightly against him, he removed her saddle and dropped it on the dusty ground.

She squealed and kicked out. The tip of her boot slammed into his shin, sending a spark of pain up his leg. "You a—"

He slapped a hand across her mouth and tightened his grip. Her eyes narrowed. Squishing her against his side so tightly she couldn't move, he turned to the men. "We'd best split up, just in case some tinhorn gets a hair up his ass to follow. Skeeter, you take the back way to the ranch; Purty, you and Mose head out toward the canyon. We'll meet up at the ridge in a few days to split the cash."

Mose gazed down at the woman, his eyes slitted and black against his tanned, mustached face. "You want me to kill her, boss?"

"We ain't killers, Mose," Purty said reasonably, tipping his hat back and scratching the dampness from his brow. " 'Sides, we could use a woman up at the hideout."

Mose studied the captive, his speculative gaze moving slowly down her body. "I like my pieces a little skinnier."

She stuck out her arm and flipped up the middle finger of her right hand.

Mose surged toward her. "Why you—"

Killian stopped the other man with a sharp look and pulled her tighter against him. "That an invitation, little lady?"

"Not hardly, asshole."

He spun her around to face him. Her head snapped back. She glared up at him through furious, gray-green eyes. "Get your hands off me, you pig."

Killian felt a smile start. "Most people don't call me a pig to my face, lady." He leaned closer, whispered, "They're afraid I'll kill them."

"You can't kill me, you idiot," she said. "It's *my* dream."

The sheer craziness of the remark caught Killian off guard. He leaned back and studied her, frowning.

Something was wrong with this woman. *Really* wrong. Nothing about her was . . . normal. Not even her clothes. She wore a huge red sweater that hung past her hips. A deep gash of a neckline drooped almost to her waist, showing a band of flesh and a black clingy thing that covered her breasts. The jeans she wore looked to be a hundred years old, bleached to the color of foam and mottled with ratty holes. Even whores wore more.

And clothing wasn't the only strange thing about her. Her hair was cut short, like a man's, only it sort of . . . flared up on top, the stand-up curls defying the laws of gravity. She had a narrow, pale face with sharp cheekbones and full, puffy lips that would have been damned kissable on another woman.

"Yer crazy, lady," Purty said quietly.

Killian loosened his grip on her, and she immediately spiraled away. She made a grunting sound of satisfaction, then folded her arms across her chest and squeezed her eyes shut. "Wake up, wake up, wake up."

He watched her, completely at a loss. "What in the hell are you doing?"

She ignored him. "Wake up, wake up, wake up."

Skeeter turned frightened eyes on Killian. "She's crazy," he murmured. "And she knows my name."

"Mine, too," Mose said in a suspicious voice.

"Wake up, wake up." She sighed audibly. "Goddamn it, wake *up*."

"Jesus H. Christ, boss," Mose growled, saddling his fresh horse. "We been witnessed by an insane woman. I say we shoot her and get the hell outta here."

"You can't shoot 'er for yappin', Mose," Purty said, tying the money bag around his saddle horn and climbing into the saddle. "I say we take 'er back to the ridge. We can figger out how she knows so much up there."

It made sense. And Killian didn't have time to think of a better solution. "Okay, Purty. You take her with you."

Purty laughed, a rich, rumbling sound that seemed to shake the dusty earth. "I done my time with crazies, boss. Sorry."

Skeeter held up his hands before Killian could even speak. "Don't look at me, boss." He cast her a nervous look. "She . . . scares me."

Killian gritted his teeth. *Perfect.* "Fine. She goes with me. You boys go ahead'n take the fresh horses. I'll ride the black for a few more miles. She can ride my roan."

Purty grinned at Killian. "You're gonna need a mite bigger horse, boss. That roan's sorta puny."

The woman's eyes popped open and drilled Purty. "Purty, you make another crack about my weight and

I'll cram those decaying, yellowed teeth down your knobby neck. Got it?"

Purty threw his head back and laughed. The hacking sound reverberated across the silent desert. As the sound faded away, he shook his head and pulled down the brim of his dusty brown hat. "Boss, you got your work cut out for you. See ya back at the ridge."

Mose frowned. It was his usual expression, dour and suspicious. He looked at the woman and slowly shook his head. "I'm tellin' ya, boss. You'd best kill this one. It'd save time in the long run."

Purty slapped him on the back, sending a puff of dust into the air between them. "Mose, you gotta quit bein' so damned generous with women."

Skeeter let out a hoot of laughter and leapt up onto his horse. The three riders barreled backward and spun around, leading their tired horses behind them. When the dust cleared, they were gone; all that remained was the thundering echo of hooves on hard-packed earth.

There was a moment of blessed silence, then the woman spoke.

"I need to ... you know ... have some privacy."

Killian turned to her. She stood there, one hip thrown sideways, her arms slammed across her chest. Frustration was stamped on her delicate features. She wanted to run; he could see it in her eyes, but he also saw that she understood her situation. There was nowhere to go.

He gestured with a hand. "Go ahead."

She tapped her foot for a second, then looked away. "I *said* I'd need some privacy."

He glanced at the landscape around them. It was a huge, brown plain dotted with small, flowering shrubs. He couldn't help smiling. "This is as private as it gets."

She stared at him, gape-mouthed. "You expect me to just cop a squat out here in the middle of all this nothingness? God, there are scorpions out there, and snakes and lizards." She shuddered. "All kinds of grotesque little creatures just waiting for my bare butt to hang their way. Uh-uh. No way."

Killian smiled. "A feminine little thing like you . . . I figured you could piss standing up."

Her gaze narrowed. "Turn around."

"I don't know, lady. I live to see crazy women pee."

She flipped up her favorite finger and spun away from him. As she passed a thin, straggly tree, she yanked off a handful of leaves and marched toward the biggest little shrub she could find.

He grabbed her saddle from the ground and tossed it onto the roan's swayed back, tightening the cinch quickly. He could hear her footsteps fading into the distance, punctuated by unladylike curses.

He turned his back on her. After a few minutes, he heard her come up behind him.

He cocked his head toward the roan. "Get on."

"No way. I'm going to wake up now."

He shook his head. Christ, this was getting old. He sighed and faced her. "Get on."

She stared at him, her fathomless hazel eyes fixed on his. For a second he thought he saw a softening in her gaze, but that was impossible. This woman was as soft as a thorn. "I can't seem to wake up," she said, crossing her arms and looking away.

He reached for his gun, pulled it out, and dangled it negligently along his thigh. "Get on the horse or I'll throw you on."

Her gaze flicked to his weapon, and he could see in the sudden narrowing of her eyes that she received the unspoken threat. She almost smiled, a brief upward tug of the lips that held no humor. "I guess I've got no choice."

"That's right. Now, get on the horse."

"Don't think for a second I'm coming with you because of that gun. You can't kill me. It's my dream." She frowned. "Well, actually it's becoming a nightmare."

He stared down at her, unsure for a moment of how to respond. "Lady," he said softly, "you're crazy."

She gave him a cocky shrug. "You aren't the first to say that."

"I don't imagine I am." Turning, he reached for the rope tied to his saddle.

She swallowed convulsively, her gaze fixed hard on the rope. "Wh-What are you going to do with that?"

"I'm gonna tie your hands." He saw her flinch at his words, noticed the pallor that moved across her cheeks and the slight tremble in her lower lip just before she bit down on it. "Why?"

"Don't." The word was barely above a whisper. "I have a . . . thing about that."

Suddenly she looked young and afraid and infinitely vulnerable. He knew he shouldn't respond, shouldn't let himself respond. He should just press the gun against her breast and repeat his threat. But there was something about her, something compelling and . . . familiar.

Almost against his will, he moved toward her, watching as his shadow engulfed her. "Okay." Even as he said the word, he couldn't believe he was going to be so stupid. This woman was dangerous, possibly deadly, and the last thing he ought to feel for her was compassion. He ought to tie her up, gag her, and set her loose in the desert somewhere to die. *That* would be the smart thing.

You're an idiot, Killian. He backed away from her, away from those damn eyes that held both vulnerability and violence. "I won't tie your hands as long as you keep up. But if you lag for a second, I'm gonna change my mind."

Her breath exhaled in a sharp gust. She laughed. It was a brittle, forced sound. "A second? Not very chivalrous of you."

"And another thing . . ."

"Yeah?"

"If you talk . . . I'm gonna gag you."

"Oh, yeah?" She stared up at him, lifted one thick black eyebrow. The strand of vulnerability in her gaze snapped, left behind a coolness that made Killian wonder if he'd imagined her moment of weakness. "You know, Killian, I just made up my mind about something."

"What's that?"

"I'm going to kill you earlier in the book. You're a real jerk."

He sighed. She was back to being crazy. "Get on the damn horse."

He watched her walk over to the roan and climb into the saddle. Reaching forward, she plucked up the reins and drew them into her lap. Then she turned slightly and looked down at him. "Don't run, okay?" The request came out slowly, reluctantly, as if she hated to ask him for something. "I only rode a few times in Girl Scout camp. I'm no John Wayne."

"Don't run?" He echoed the ridiculous request. "This is a getaway." He strode to his horse and vaulted into the saddle. Leaning sideways, he grabbed hold of her reins and wound them around his saddle horn, drawing her mount close. "Hold on to the saddle horn." Before she could mouth off anymore, he kicked his horse hard and they were off, galloping across the empty, endless desert in a cloud of dust.

He heard her scream, saw her scramble to get situated. Her fingers curled around the leather horn in a death grip, her back hunched forward, her feet flailing in the stirrups.

There was a moment of blessed silence, and then came the curses. She muttered them at first, angry, unladylike words. Gradually she built up steam, until, after ten minutes of riding, she was shouting expletives at the top of her lungs.

He'd been a fool not to gag her.

"Shit," he shouted.

Lainie cast a disgusted look at the man beside her. He was leaning over in his saddle, staring at the ground. His craggy, beard-stubbled face was drawn into an ominous frown, almost frightening in its intensity.

But she wasn't afraid. Hell, no, she wasn't afraid. He might be physically imposing, even threatening, but it didn't matter. He wasn't *real*. His gun wasn't real, his bullets weren't real, his threat wasn't real. In ten minutes she was going to wake up and this whole experience would be transferred to a few pages of honest emotion in her book. It was one good thing about this dream. Before, when she was writing, she'd thought of Killian as a one-dimensional outlaw with a cold heart. A villain whose sole purpose was to make the hero appear stronger, smarter, quicker. Now, she saw Killian in a whole new light.

He was a real asshole.

But he didn't tie her hands.

In that instant she'd seen a spark of compassion that was completely unexpected, a character trait she hadn't given him. She knew there was no understanding in John Killian. There was only violence and selfishness and self-reliance. She ought to know.

And yet, there'd been no mistaking the compassion

she saw in his eyes. For a second—just a heartbeat—
he'd seemed like someone else entirely, someone she
didn't know at all.

"That's impossible," she hissed, bouncing hard on the
leather seat. "He's *exactly* who you created. What else
could he be?"

He reined his horse to a walk. Then he leaned over
again, and stared down at the rust-colored dirt.

Lainie's mount immediately slowed. She clung to the
saddle horn, teeth rattling in her head, as her horse's
gait melted into a bone-jarring trot.

"*Shit*," he said again.

Lainie frowned, making a mental note to work harder
on Killian's dialogue. All he ever said was *shit* and *shut
up*. Neither of which was particularly pleasant—even
for a villain.

She tried to give him a disdainful look, but it was
hard to look disdainful when you were thumping along
in a saddle like a sack of rocks. "I hope you aren't at-
tempting to convey information to me in some limited
prehistoric code."

He glanced over at her, his thick, winged black eyebrows drawn into an imposing frown. "Why the hell
would I want to talk to you?"

"I can't imagine. By all means, keep yelling 'shit' at
the ground."

"The black is limping."

"The black what?"

His gaze raked her. It was a look so full of contempt
that she felt suddenly chilled. "My horse."

"Boy, that was a stretch."

"What?"

"Naming your horse. What'd it take you—ten, twelve
days to come up with that one?"

"Shut up."

She sighed. "I've *got* to work harder on your dialogue. You sound like something out of *Quest for Fire*."

Ignoring her, he brought the black to a halt and dismounted. Bending over, he gently lifted the stallion's foreleg.

Lainie peered down at the hoof. "We've been running for an hour. He's probably just tired."

Killian threw her a disgusted look. He pulled a hoof-pick out of his saddlebag and began picking rocks and dirt from the horse's hoof. "Uh-huh."

Lainie glanced around. They were in the middle of a long stretch of plain flanked by sheer taupe canyon walls. To their right, a muddy, slow-moving river wound in and out of colorful cottonwood stands. A grass of sorts—it looked like the first greening growth of a Chia Pet—dotted the sandy brown soil. Overhead, the sky was an endless robin's-egg blue uncluttered by clouds.

It wasn't at all as she'd envisioned it. The heat was stronger, more invasive, and the land had a raw, tormented beauty she hadn't anticipated. Here beside this ageless tower of stone, she felt very small and insignificant and . . . alone.

The moment's vulnerability pissed her off. She straightened her shoulders and brushed the hair from her eyes. Her expensive salon mousse was starting to wilt. Beside her, Killian removed his saddle from the black's broad back.

"What are you doing?" she demanded.

He gave her another scornful look. "Dancing."

Chalk one up for the he-man. "Let me rephrase that. *Why* are you doing that?"

"He's lame."

Lainie got a sick feeling in her stomach. "You're not going to shoot him, are you?"

This time he didn't even glance her way. "I'd rather shoot you." He threw the saddle behind him. It landed at the base of a short pine tree. Wordlessly he reached for his reins and tied the horse to the same tree.

Then he turned and walked toward her. He moved with a feline, predatory grace, his hips gliding in a thoroughly masculine way. The thudding heat of his footsteps seemed threatening in the desert's quiet.

She realized suddenly what it meant to be larger than life. She'd created this man, invented him from the vast resources of her own imagination, and part of him was what she'd envisioned, but part of him was . . . more.

She watched him, noticing the deep furrows that lined his forehead and the network of lines that pulled at the flesh around his eyes. He seemed older than was possible—he should have been twenty-eight, with a face lined only by hours beneath a hot sun. But the man moving toward her was at least forty, maybe forty-five, with a face that had been ravaged by life's cruelties. There was a restless hunger in him she'd never once imagined, a raw masculinity that somehow frightened her.

She frowned. She hadn't given him all those lines, she was certain of it. She'd given him his size, surely, but not the hard, sinewy leanness that seemed just below the surface. She saw it in his eyes, in the way he moved, in the way he always held his hands near his gun belt.

"Like what you see, lady?"

She bristled at having been caught staring. It was stupid, surely, but a normal human reaction. Everyone knew it was rude to stare . . . even, apparently, fictional characters. "As a matter of fact, I don't. I thought you'd be more . . ."

"More what?"

She frowned, unsure exactly. "I don't know. More evil and less . . . rude."

He reached up and grabbed her by the wrist, pulling hard. She wobbled and fell, sliding down the bumpy leather side of the saddle. The wooden stirrup conked her in the side of her head. "Ouch . . . shit."

"Nice language," he grunted.

"Good elocution," she shot back.

He kept his hold viselike and strode toward a huge tree. She stumbled along beside him, wrenching her hand with every step.

"Damn it, let me go."

At the tree, he came to an abrupt stop and spun her around. The world slid sideways. Lainie literally saw stars before the horizon slowly righted itself. "God*damn* it," she sputtered, bringing her fist up and drawing back to punch him.

He looked at her puny fist and laughed. "Gonna blacken my eye, are you?"

"I just might."

"Believe me, lady, your mouth has already inflicted more damage than your fist ever could."

She pointedly eyed his crotch. "That depends on where I land my punch."

He laughed, and it was a surprisingly rich, compelling sound. "If you touch me there, it won't be to inflict pain."

"Don't flatter yourself. I wouldn't touch you . . . *there* if it were the last *there* on earth."

He reached into his breast pocket and pulled out the dirty, balled-up red bandanna he'd worn in the robbery.

She eyed the scrap of fabric suspiciously. "What are you going to do with that?"

He didn't respond, but she saw the answer in his eyes. She drew in a sharp breath. "You wouldn't da—"

He shoved the rag in her mouth and tied it tightly behind her head.

She glared up at him through narrowed eyes. Fury exploded in her chest. Her heartbeat sped up, her breathing quickened.

He drew back, grinning. "I like you better already."

Lainie punched him, a hard-knuckled jab right in the eye. Then she brought her knee up and rammed it in his crotch.

His breath exhaled in a grunting, cursing rush. He clutched his eye and bent over, gasping.

She felt a blistering sense of vindication. She hoped his eye blackened. And his dick.

That's what you get for comin' after me, pal.

Suddenly he looked at her. His eyes were cold and dark, and filled with a seething power that chilled her to the bone. "So," he hissed softly, "that's the way you want to play this."

Lainie swallowed hard. A teeny weeny spark of fear slipped into her righteous anger. She felt—crazily—as if this wasn't just a dream, and she hadn't just punched a figment of her imagination. She backed up, shaking her head. The gag kept her horribly silent.

He leapt at her, grabbed her wrist, and spun her around, dragging her toward the horses. She kicked, she screamed into the gag, she tried to wrench away. None of it seemed to affect him in the least. He tightened his grip and moved faster.

At the horses, he pinned her to his body and fished a length of rope from his saddlebags. Then he dragged her, still kicking and screaming soundlessly, to a spot beside the pine and shoved her down. Rocks and pebbles bit into her backside. She gave a tiny, muffled yelp of pain and tried to scurry away from him, but he was too fast.

He rammed her wrists together, circling them in an unforgiving band, bruising, pinching. She wiggled and tried to scream. When none of that worked, she glared at him.

"It won't be long. I'm just gonna walk on down to that ranch and see if I can buy another couple of horses."

She screamed into the rag. It came out as a muffled, pathetic little squeak.

He paused, glanced at her. One eyebrow winged upward tauntingly. "Did you say something?"

She glared at him.

In a single, practiced motion, he brought her hands to her ankles and quickly bound her hands and ankles. She squirmed and wiggled to get free, but her balance was tenuous. She tipped slightly and fell, landing sprawled on her side like a bound steer.

He bent over, his upside-down face peering at her. "Was that how you wanted to wait for me?"

Screw you.

He grinned. "Wait, let me guess what you said. Did it start with an *F* . . . end with a *u*?" He waited a second for her answer, then laughed again, a rich, rumbling sound that made her want to rip his eyes out.

"Here you go." Gently he righted her. Then he straightened. "I'll be right back. No more than fifteen minutes. Just—" he smiled broadly—"keep quiet."

Lainie stared, watching him walk away from her. For a few precious heartbeats, she felt an almost violent anger. She thought about all the things she was going to do to him, how she was going to make him pay for treating her this way.

She'd kill him with hot wax in chapter one. She'd draw and quarter him . . . slowly. She'd . . .

She looked up and he was gone.

She was alone.

The towering cinnamon gold walls seemed to close in on her, squeezing the air from her lungs. Heat hit her hard in the face, brought a sheen of sweat to her forehead and throat. Somewhere a hawk cried, its sound a keening, desperate wail in the emptiness.

Her anger collapsed, caved in on itself and left her with nothing. Fear took its place, surging through her body, moving like ice through her trussed arms and legs. A vile, bitter taste invaded her mouth. For a horrifying moment she thought she was going to be ill.

She squeezed her eyes shut, but it was a mistake. Memories came at her hard; disgusting, despicable images pulsed through her mind, spearing through her courage like tiny, poison-tipped arrows until she couldn't breathe. They came at her from all sides; the murmured drone of lowered voices, the shuffling thud of heavy footsteps, the jangling of keys. Hands reached for her, forced her onto a cold vinyl bed. Leather straps closed around her wrists, bit into her tender flesh; a key chinked into place.

She opened her eyes, tried to banish the pictures from her mind, but she didn't have the strength.

She bowed her head. *Please, God, let me wake up now. I don't want this nightmare. Not ... tied up. Please, God ...*

But there was no answer from above, no easing of the burden, no shifting of the images. She closed her eyes again and curled into a small, shaking ball, trying not to care.

After a while, the darkness came for her. She slipped into a place inside herself, an almost catatonic quiet that welcomed her with comforting, familiar arms.

And the dream ceased to matter.

Chapter Four

Killian approached the farmhouse warily, his hands at his gun belt. His every sense was focused on the silence around him.

He was in a small canyon, a place that looked as if it had been scooped into existence by God's own hand. Twisting, upthrust walls of multihued rock curled protectively around the valley, creating a haven safe from the fierce desert winds. Tucked into the corner was a squat, flat-roofed cabin, fenced by sagging strands of barbed wire and gnarled posts. Behind it, eight good-sized horses were clustered together against the coming night.

Killian moved slowly across the sandy yard and opened the slatted-wood gate. Tired hinges squealed at his touch; the sound melted into the melancholy whisper of the wind and disappeared.

He went to the front door and knocked. The aged wood groaned.

Footsteps thudded behind the door. The wooden knob rattled, turned.

Unconsciously Killian straightened. His right hand glided downward slowly; his fingertips brushed the pistol's metal grip.

The door swung open. In the opening stood a short, stoop-shouldered man with a flowing gray beard and eyes like chips of granite. It was the face of a man who'd lived all his life in the harshness of a desert climate, chiseled and creased and darkened by the sun's unforgiving glare. His eyes narrowed suspiciously, raked Killian from head to foot. "Whaddaya want?"

Killian stood still. "I need two horses."

The man spat; a huge, spiraling gob of tobacco hit the dusty earth beside Killian's left boot and immediately disappeared into the moisture-deprived soil. His gaze flicked over Killian's guns, then moved up. "Uh-huh. On the run, are you?"

"That's a question best not asked, old man."

The man smiled, revealing a set of broken, tobacco-stained teeth. "You got my best interests at heart, do ya, stranger?"

"Something like that."

"Uh-huh." The man spat again, then cleared his throat with a phlegmy, hacking sound. "Were you thinkin' on stealin' 'em or buyin' 'em?"

Killian eyed the old man, watching him, weighing him, waiting for a stupid move. "That depends on you."

The man gave a throaty, loose laugh and started coughing again. "You ain't the first outlaw to stop by here. Butch and Elza were by once ... oh, back in eighty-nine. After the Telluride job."

"Yeah?"

"Yeah. I sold Cassidy a horse for sixty bucks." He shook his head and tugged on his beard. "He was a hell of a nice guy, that Cassidy."

"I'm not that nice."

The man looked up sharply, for the first time really looking at Killian's eyes. His rotten-toothed smile slowly faded into a frown.

Killian reached into his pocket and pulled out two

wrinkled twenty-dollar bills. "I'll give you forty bucks for two horses."

"That ain't near enough."

Killian reached for his gun, slid one finger into the cold curl of the trigger. "I think it is."

The man's wide-eyed gaze fixed on the gun. He licked his fleshy lips and glanced behind Killian. His thoughts were obvious; Killian had seen them a thousand times. That first useless, groping reach for help. The realization of what it meant to be faced by a man who lived outside the law.

The old man wet his lips again and swallowed convulsively. His gnarled, liver-spotted fingers convulsed. He shot a nervous glance inside his cabin.

"You want to try to take me?" Killian drawled in a soft, almost seductive voice. "You gonna reach for that rifle you got propped just out of sight?"

"Wh-What rifle?"

Killian almost smiled. His finger twitched against the cool steel of the trigger. "You better be fast."

The old man swallowed hard, made a jerking, gulping sound of fear. "I'm too old to be fast."

Killian let his breath out slowly, his bent arm relaxed a little. He knew then that it was over. "Yeah, I thought you might be."

"I'm a poor man, mister. Them horses is all I got."

Killian eyed the old man, noticing the ragged cuffs of his shirtsleeves and the gaping holes in his jeans. Fleetingly he wondered what the man's life had been like, where it had gone so desperately wrong. No one *tried* to end up like this, alone and defenseless and poor, eking a living from the harshness of the Arizona desert.

Except maybe an old gunfighter who wasn't so quick on the draw anymore . . .

Killian shuddered at the thought and looked away. He

reached into his pocket and pulled out a tattered ten-
dollar bill, shoving it toward the man. "I don't have any
more right now. But I'll bring you another twenty the
next time I come through."

"You askin' me to trust you?"

"I wouldn't say asking."

The man ran his tongue along his teeth. At the movement, his mustached upper lip bulged. "I don't have no
choice, do I?"

"None."

He thought for a minute, then a slow smile pushed
through the leathery wrinkles of his face. He looked up
at Killian. "Funny thing is, I'd trust you anyway. You
got that kind o' face."

The words came at him from out of the blue, catching Killian off guard. He stiffened, felt suddenly cold
inside. "That wouldn't be smart, old man."

The man grinned. "Never said I was a bank teller.
You wanna come in for a cup o' coffee?"

"No."

"Oh." Disappointment etched deeper furrows in the
man's weather-beaten face. Killian felt a stab of sorrow
for the man—no doubt he was lonely as hell. "Well,
come on, then. I got a couple of real good horses. Captain and The Bitch."

Killian almost smiled in spite of himself. "Captain
and The Bitch, huh?"

He had no doubt which horse he'd give to the
woman.

He found her curled up in a little ball where he'd left
her. The vast desert fanned away from her in all direc-
tions, melting in the distance into a bumpy ridge of
blue-gray hills. A quivering, threadbare pine tree stood

guard beside her, its drooping green limbs a slash of color against the endless golden earth.

Killian frowned. Even from this distance, he could see that something was wrong. She was motionless; it looked from here as if she wasn't even breathing. She lay huddled at the base of the ponderosa pine, her chin tucked against her chest, her eyes squeezed shut. The two horses stood pressed together against the wind that whistled down from the hills, their heads drooped low. Leaves danced and writhed above the dirt, tumbling across the sandy ground.

He kicked the big Appaloosa gelding into a trot. "Lady?" he called out.

She didn't move. Didn't even swear at him.

He reined Captain to a halt and dismounted. Tossing the reins around a sagging pine branch, he squatted down beside the woman.

She lay as still as death, but at the base of her throat a pulse beat, a bluish red throbbing against the creamy hollow of her skin. Her hands were clasped together, the fingers pale and limp. The colorless oval of her cheek was damp and streaked with dust and sand. Strands of dark hair clung to the moist skin at her temples. The dirty scrap of bandanna was like a bloody slash against her skin.

He looked away for a long moment, then slowly closed his eyes. A sour feeling, dangerously close to shame, stung his gut. When had he learned to do *this* to a woman, simply to keep her quiet?

He reached out, traced the pale, blue-white curve of her cheek. Then he untied the gag and pulled it from her mouth. "Lady, wake up."

She shuddered. The dark fringe of her eyelashes fluttered.

Slowly she opened her eyes and looked up at him.

Her eyes were darker than before, a rich mossy green against the pallor of her skin. A single, curly lock of black hair fell forlornly across her forehead. She looked up at him, and in her gaze he saw bleakness and something more, something he understood all too well. A sadness that was too old to be in such young eyes.

He spoke without thinking, his voice quiet and low. "I'm sorry." The admission surprised him. It came from long ago, from a place in his soul that used to feel emotions like sorrow and regret and shame.

A shadow of a smile ghosted her lips, so fleeting and unexpected that he wondered if he'd imagined it, maybe even willed it. "I . . . can't wake up."

He frowned, confused. He would have understood fear or anger or hatred, even tears. But not this, not this quiet admission that meant nothing.

"You are awake."

She shook her head, loosing another flopping lock of curly black hair. "No, I'm not. I'm dreaming."

Killian sat back on his heels. He couldn't make sense of her, not anything about her. One minute she was a spitting hellion, the next a vulnerable innocent, the next a raving lunatic.

"We've got to get going."

"Yeah," she said softly, almost dreamily. "The posse can't be far behind."

He frowned. "What do you mean . . . posse?"

"Joe Martin—"

A cold feeling moved through him at the name. "The sheriff from River Rock Falls?"

She nodded. "Uh-huh. Harold Springs hired him to hunt you down and kill you."

Killian felt as if he'd been punched hard in the jaw. He reeled backward, staring down at her, hoping to hell she was crazy. Because if she wasn't, he was in deep shit. "How do you know that?"

"Well, he was supposed to attempt to thwart the robbery and fail. It takes him four hours to get a posse together to track you down." She frowned thoughtfully. "I'm sure he'd still get the men together—even though he never showed up at the bank."

He let his breath out slowly, trying not to lose his temper. "I asked how you know this."

"I wrote it."

"Oh, for Christ's sake—"

Her eyes pleaded with him to believe her. "It's true."

He stared down at her, hard. "Martin's following me?"

"Yes."

"Why are you telling me this?"

"Leave me here," she pleaded softly. "I can't take any more of this dream. Leave me here to meet Joe— he's my hero."

Another completely ridiculous statement. Killian stared down at her, measuring her words, trying to draw a bead on her. It didn't make any sense that she would know these things—but then again, she'd known his name. And Skeeter's. And Mose's.

"You can't know these things," he said softly, not taking his eyes off her. She blinked up at him. Her mouth trembled and she bit down on her lower lip, but she didn't look away. It was the most honest face he'd ever seen. He frowned. "But you do."

She squeezed her eyes shut for a heartbeat and sighed. "Yeah, I do."

He couldn't reject her information. It was too damned reasonable.

Joe had always hated him. The lawman held Killian responsible for killing an elderly couple on their way

home from the Silver Springs bank. It didn't matter to
Joe that Killian had been in Texas that month, or that
Killian wasn't a murderer. At least, not an intentional
one.

To Joe, all that mattered was revenge. Killian had
been one step ahead of Martin for years. If the ranger
was in Arizona, he was after Killian.

"Will you leave me here?" she asked quietly.

He saw the desperation in her eyes, and he refused to
be moved by it. If there was even a possibility that Joe
was behind him—and God help him, he believed her—
Killian needed every advantage to stay alive. "No."

Moisture brightened her eyes, gave them a sad lumi-
nescence that made his chest ache. She looked away, as
if ashamed of her own emotion. "Why?"

"You might be my ace in the hole if things go bad.
Joe'd let me go to save your life."

He untied her hands and feet and drew the ragged
rope away, cramming it in his big duster pocket. Then
he started to stand.

She reached out and grabbed his arm, her fingers
curling tightly around the dusty canvas of his coat
sleeve. "Please," she whispered, looking up at him
through frightened, glassy eyes. "Please let me go. I
need to wake up now."

He looked down at her, feeling sorrier than he wanted
to. But that fleeting emotion didn't change anything; he
wouldn't allow it to. He'd spent years surviving on gut
instinct, and right now, crazy or not, he believed her.
Joe Martin was shadowing him. He could almost feel
the threat of death, hovering, waiting. He'd lived with
that feeling a long time now, almost embraced it. It kept
him from thinking about anything except staying alive.
And there were a lot of things in his life he didn't want
to think about.

"I'm sorry, lady," he said again, and this time he put a steely coldness in his voice. "But that really isn't my problem."

Lainie clung to the saddle horn with aching hands. The leather was sticky and damp, and the overpowering odors of horse and sweat and dust were killing her. She almost wished she had the gag back. She'd give anything to keep the dirt and grit out of her mouth and nose.

She squeezed her eyes shut, feeling a moment's relief at the soothing darkness. If only she could curl up somewhere, in some forgotten corner of her own mind, and go to sleep. Maybe then she could finally wake up. . . .

Only it wasn't that easy. The dream was so . . . strange.

Why couldn't she wake up?

Maybe there was something different about this sleep. Maybe it was . . . unnatural.

A cold finger of fear moved through her. It was horrifyingly possible. Maybe she'd drunk too much booze and popped too many pills. Maybe she wasn't merely asleep—maybe she was in a coma.

"Oh, Jesus." The words slipped from her mouth, through her chattering teeth. Was it possible? Was this what life was like for the thousands of coma victims who seemed to lie in deathlike sleep? Had poor Karen Ann Quinlan been trapped like this in the terrifying landscape of her own subconscious mind, chained to an endless, unstoppable dream from which there was no relief?

It made such terrifying sense. Maybe she was still at her computer, slumped in unnatural slumber atop her keyboard. . . .

Her fear accelerated. She took a deep breath and forced herself to calm down. She refused to let it beat her, refused to let herself become a victim of her own emotions.

If it *was* true, this dream would run its course. She would wake up when—and only when—the pills and booze had worked their toxic way from her system. Not one moment before. Like so many other frightening times in her life, she wasn't in control. She couldn't make herself wake up, or force the dream to stop. She could only hang on and be strong.

Be strong.

The words calmed her immensely, gave her a goal, something to hang on to when she found fear creeping up from the darkness. She'd survived worse things in her life; she'd survived drugs, violence, poverty, parental abandonment . . . even life on the cold, hard streets of Seattle.

It would take a hell of a lot more than some stupid dream to beat her.

She straightened her chin and stared out at the landscape. The flat, arid land spilled out in front of her. Against all odds, there was life here, grafted onto the waterless plain in swabs of flowering green. Trees, gnarled and bent and twisted, clung to the parched yellow dirt.

It seemed impossible that life could exist where water was so scarce. And yet, the plants not only existed; they adapted and thrived, and threw their hopeful bits of color across the sandy ground.

That's what she would do. Adapt and thrive. This dream wouldn't last much longer—it couldn't. Soon, any minute, in fact, she was going to wake up with a pounding headache and a mouth that felt like the inside of an old boot. But until then, she was going to do what she did best. She was going to survive.

She glanced at the man beside her. He sat tall and straight in the saddle, riding with a lithe grace and ease that came from years of experience. At the sight of him, shame curled in her stomach, sharp and bitter.

This morning, when he left her bound and gagged in the middle of the endless desert, she'd retreated to a place inside herself, someplace dark and safe. It was a place she hadn't used in years, a haven, and it welcomed her back with unexpected ease.

Something inside her had collapsed at that moment, crushed in on itself. God help her, she'd almost given up. Like before. So long ago . . .

But she knew better, damn it, and it wasn't a mistake she'd repeat.

No more shit-taking from macho man, no more tears, no more whimpering. From now on, she was Alaina Costanza again, and she didn't take crap from anyone.

Especially not figments of her own imagination.

They rode side by side in utter silence for hours. The sun gradually gave up its hold on the sky, sinking slowly toward the ridge of mountains to the east. The two unsaddled horses galloped freely alongside them.

"They're behind us."

Lainie was in so much pain, it took her soggy brain a minute to process the information that he-man had spoken. Dully she glanced at Killian.

He slowed his horse to a trot.

The Bitch followed suit, her gliding gait melting into a bone-rattling trot. Agony ripped through Lainie's insides at the change of pace. She made a tiny, gasping sound of pain and clung to the saddle horn with sweaty, aching fingers, bouncing hard in the unpadded leather seat.

Jesus, it felt as if someone were hammering her internal organs with a mallet. She prayed she could hold on just a minute longer. Her vision blurred, turned the darkening desert into a smeary wash of towering black rock formations and gunmetal gray sky.

Killian stopped suddenly and raised his hand. "I hear something."

Lainie bounced right past him.

He surged ahead in a sudden lope and yanked her reins, drawing her to a jarring stop. "I said stop."

Lainie sighed; it was an expression of relief that seemed to well up from the bottom of her soul. Her butt was planted. She eased her right leg out of the stirrup and started to dismount.

He grabbed her upper arm, hard. "Stay."

Irritation gave her a spark of personality back. She may be down, but she wasn't out, and jerk-wad here couldn't give her dog commands. "Now, look here, I—"

He threw her an exasperated glance. "*Please* shut up."

Lainie was too tired to argue. Sounds of the coming night pressed in on her, noises that only seconds ago she hadn't heard. The whirring thump of bird wings, the symphonic chatter of the wind through the trees, the heaving, wheezing breath of the tired horses.

She crossed her arms and stared out at the lonely land. The evening sky seemed endless, a dome of lavender silk dotted by charcoal black strafers and thousands of twinkling stars. Here and there, spires of twisted rock jutted up from the earth like towers to Heaven. The whole place had an eerie melancholy to it, and yet there was a magic here, too, an almost primeval spirituality that whispered of people long gone and a time forgotten.

"Hear that?" he whispered, slowly pulling the hat off his head and running splayed fingers through his damp hair.

Lainie strained for a noise worthy of "that." It took a long time, but gradually she became aware of the low, thudding heartbeat that came from far away.

"What is it?"

"Horses. Ten or twelve of them, I'd say."

Lainie's pulse picked up. "Joe Martin," she breathed, feeling a tingling sense of anticipation.

Killian cursed harshly and plunged the dusty hat back on his head. "Let's go."

"Are they far behind us?"

He glanced backward, his eyes narrowed. "One mile, maybe less."

"I'm tired," she said. "Maybe we should make camp."

He laughed. It was a sharp, unexpected sound that echoed through the stillness. "Nice try, lady."

Lainie saw him turn toward her, and her stomach dropped to somewhere around her knees. "No, please—"

He smiled. "Hang on."

She surged forward and clutched the saddle horn just as he smacked her horse on the butt.

Chapter Five

Killian slumped in his saddle. Exhaustion pulled at him, rounded his shoulders, but still he kept moving. Captain plodded onward, his huge hooves plunking and sloshing through the slow-moving stream that had long ago gouged this canyon from the mesa above.

He closed his eyes, listening to the sounds of the night. *Plunk, splash, plunk, splash.* He tried to hear the faraway vibrations of a dozen running horses, but couldn't.

Maybe they'd lost the posse. Only the finest Indian tracker could follow hoofprints in moving water, and they'd been winding their way through this jet black canyon for hours.

But he didn't believe they'd lost them. Not if Joe Martin was in the lead. For a long time Killian had lived on instinct, and he'd learned to trust his gut feeling. And right now his gut was telling him to keep going.

"It's impossible," the woman muttered behind him.

He knew he shouldn't ask. God knew he didn't give a shit what she thought about anything, but somehow, with them out here all alone, he felt compelled to respond. "What's impossible?"

"I'm tired."

"That's not impossible. I'm exhausted."

"But I'm asleep."

"Yeah, sure you are."

"Hey!" Her voice held a sudden sharpness, as if she'd just thought of something. "Maybe if I *dreamed* I went to sleep, I could actually wake up."

Killian couldn't think of a response, so he kept his mouth shut.

"What do you think? Could we go to bed—" She coughed. "I mean, could we go to sleep?"

"No."

There was a long pause, then she said, "The posse slept at Entrada Pass tonight."

Killian drew back on the reins and turned around, trying to see her in the jet blackness behind him. All he saw was the silhouette of her body against the amethyst canyon opening behind them. "How do—"

The Bitch rammed into Captain's butt. The gelding snorted and crowhopped to the right, slamming Killian's leg into the sandstone wall.

"I *asked* you to signal before you stopped," she snapped.

"How do you know where the posse slept ... uh ... will sleep?"

"I wrote it."

He sighed and turned around, staring unseeingly through the gray, moonlit slit at the end of the canyon.

"Does it matter?" she asked in a soft voice. "I *know*."

He couldn't deny it. She'd known so many impossible things, what was one more? And this one ... Hell, he wanted to believe her. "Entrada Pass, huh?"

"Yeah. There's a small stream and a grove of cottonwoods—"

"I know what it looks like. Okay, we'll go as far as the caves tonight and make camp."

"Thank you, God," she breathed in a voice that sounded as tired as he felt.

He almost smiled. "You're welcome."

In spite of herself, Lainie laughed. No doubt it was lack of food and water. Her brain was eroding; it had to be if she thought Mr. Macho was funny.

She stared straight ahead, trying to make him out. He was a tall, broad-shouldered silhouette, a black horseman against the lavender slash of sky that lay beyond the entrance to the canyon.

They rode in silence for another hour, through one winding, stream-lined canyon after another. And even though she was exhausted, she couldn't close her eyes.

This place was incredible. At one moment, jet black and freezing cold; a second later, moonlit and magical. It was so much more than she'd expected. She'd read about the rock formations that filled the American Southwest, from Monument Valley to Arches to Canyon de Chelly. She'd studied them all when she created this landscape, her fictional "The Ridge" hideout.

She'd seen photographs, literally thousands of them at all times of day and night. She'd seen the colors, the curves, the canyons . . . but never had she seen the *majesty*. Everything about this place was more than she'd expected, bigger, taller, redder, hotter, colder. The sky went on forever, the canyon walls rose into heaven itself. It was a place worthy of the greatest writer, a place that had to be seen.

They emerged at last from the series of canyons and entered a huge, sweeping mesa. Lainie gazed around and drew in a sharp breath. The land was unlike anything she'd seen before. The earth stretched out before her, an endless, moon-drenched plain dotted with black shrubs and twisting towers of smoke-colored stone.

"My God," she murmured, feeling suddenly cold.

"The Ancient Ones called this place the Valle de Muerte," Killian said quietly.

"Lovely. You've picked the Valley of Death as our campsite."

Killian dismounted, then turned around and reached a hand up for her.

She looked down at him, surprised by the gesture. He stood there, silently, staring up at her, his face half-shadowed by the night, half-touched by the moonlight. She crossed her reins over the horse's mane. Then, uncertainly, she reached out and placed her cold, aching hand in his gloved palm. The coarse, warm leather folded around her fingers, gave her an anchor in the darkness.

She lifted out of the saddle and swung her right leg over the horse's huge, red-speckled hindquarters. At the motion, her left leg wobbled in the stirrup and gave way, unable to support her full weight. With a shriek of horror, she fell to the dirt in a bone-crushing thud.

He had the gall to laugh.

She glared up at him and staggered to her feet, wiping the dirt off her jeans. "That wasn't funny."

He grinned. "Yes it was."

Lainie thought about it, tried to imagine what she'd looked like, shrieking and flailing and falling. She had to admit it was a little funny. She might have smiled if she hadn't been dead tired. Slowly, clutching her lower back in fingers that had gone numb ten miles ago, she hobbled away from the horse. In some distant, hazy part of her brain, she thought that she should tie the horse up first—she'd always have a character do that. But frankly, she didn't give a shit. If the horse ran from here to Texas, she'd wave good-bye.

She staggered forward. Her foot landed in a hole,

twisted her ankle hard. She gasped as pain shot up her shin.

"Christ," he cursed. She heard the utter disgust in his voice, but she didn't care much about that either.

He moved toward her, his footsteps crunching quickly through the pebbly dirt. Suddenly he touched her, swung her around, and swept her up in a movement so fast, it left her dizzy and breathless.

God help her, she wilted at his touch. An exhausted sigh escaped her lips. She knew she should kick and scream and rip his eyes out—it's what all those feisty heroines did at a high-handed macho move like this. But she couldn't. Didn't even want to.

All the energy she'd fabricated evaporated. Without it, she felt suddenly as weak as a newborn kitten. She brought her arms around Killian's neck and let her head loll against his chest. Her eyes fluttered shut.

The even in-and-out rhythm of his chest rocked her gently. She frowned sleepily. There was something almost sadly familiar about this moment, as if once—long ago—she'd been carried by him. Everything about him was familiar: the sweat and dust smell of his clothing, the threadlike softness of his hair as it touched her cheek, the loose-hipped rhythm of his walk.

They'd done this before, the two of them. . . .

She realized her own foolishness and forced a weary, tired little laugh. She was hallucinating again. Of course there was something familiar about Killian. She'd created him, for God's sake. *Everything* about him was well-known to her.

He set her down on a rock beside the stream. The gurgling rush of the water was a thread of normalcy in the shifting strangeness of the desert. Here, at last, was something she recognized.

"Can you make a fire?" he asked.

She looked up at him. He was a looming, faceless shadow against the moon-bright sky. "If you've got a Bic lighter or a blowtorch."

She felt his gaze on her face and she knew, even in the utter darkness of shadow, that he was frowning. As usual, he didn't know what to make of her. Finally he looked away and then let it go. He searched through his baggy duster pockets and pulled out something, tossing it at her feet. A metal box hit the ground with a tiny clang.

She stared down at the little tin box, feeling a ridiculously overblown sense of relief. She recognized it from the 1895 Montgomery Ward catalog. It was a pocket match safe.

"How about that?" he said in a barely controlled voice. "Can you make a fire with matches?"

She reached out and grabbed the box, curling her blistered fingers around the cool metal, then she tried to stand up.

It felt as if someone had kicked her in the crotch. She made a gasping, wheezing sound of pain and started to fall.

Killian was beside her in an instant, his arm curled around her shoulders to help her stand. "Are you okay?" he asked, his voice rich and disembodied in the darkness.

"Did I give birth a few minutes ago?"

There was a long pause. "No."

"Then I'm definitely not okay. I feel like shit."

"You're not used to riding?"

"Give the man a teddy bear. No, Killian, I am not used to riding."

He leaned closer, tightened his hold. "It hurts in the beginning," he whispered in a rough, Scottish-tinged growl that caused a surprising spark of response in Lainie's blood.

When she was steady, he drew away from her, leaving her colder and lonelier than she'd been a second before. "You make the fire. I'll get us something to eat."

She watched his shadow glide through the grayness of the night as he set about the chores of preparing the horses for the evening.

Lainie limped around the clearing, gathering sticks and roots. Then she piled them in a perfect Girl Scout heap and set it afire. Within moments, a hardy puff of smoke spiraled into the night. She felt as if she'd just won the Pulitzer.

"I did it!"

He glanced over at her, and even in the darkness, she could see the surprise on his face.

"Okay, okay," she said, feeling like an idiot, "so it's not brain surgery, but for a woman from the city, it's pretty good. After all, I haven't used anything but Presto logs in years."

There was a long silence, then, "I think it's best if we don't talk." He tossed his bedroll down by the fire. It landed with a dusty smack and rolled sideways.

Lainie felt a sharp sting of longing. She stared at the sleeping bag, imagining its warmth around her aching body. She thought about stretching out, going to sleep, waking up. . . .

Then reality hit. She realized what she was looking at—and what she was not looking at. "There's only one."

He shrugged. "That's all I ever need."

One sleeping bag: two bodies. Perfect. She shook her head. "Just my luck. This dream turns hot and sexy when I feel as if I've been run over by a Mack truck."

"Nothing's getting hot and sexy, lady."

Lainie laughed bitterly at his response. It was a new low; even men in her dreams found her unappealing. "Don't sound so scared, Killian. I'm not going to rape you."

"I didn't think you were."

"A gentleman would offer his bedroll to a lady."

This time it was he who laughed.

"It's not funny," she snapped.

"We can share it."

"Yeah, we could. . . ." The words tasted bitter on her tongue. Lainie frowned. She didn't want to bed down with Mr. Macho. She wanted to stretch out and fall into a deep, dreamless sleep—a sleep from which she could wake up.

He untied the bedroll and flipped it out along the cold, bumpy ground.

Lainie winced. She had trouble going to sleep on her Serta. This was going to be impossible. "That's it?" she said with an irritated sigh. "Just a sleeping bag on the dirt? Where's your tent?"

"I only bother with a tent when it rains. Now . . ." He patted the bag. "You want the top or the bottom?"

She ignored his ill attempt at humor and glanced again at the makeshift bed. Her choices were limited. It was either kill him or share his bedroll.

She wondered how she could kill him.

She couldn't sleep with him. She couldn't sleep with anyone; she never had been able to. It was one of the by-products of a lifetime of being alone. Oh, she'd had sex with men—more than a few, and for most of them, *men* was a ridiculous compliment. But she hadn't slept with them.

The thought of sharing a bedroll with Killian made her feel queasy and unsettled. She chewed on her lower lip, looking away from the thin bag and the large man.

"I won't be there long. . . ." she said, trying to make the idea palatable and failing miserably.

He set a pan on the fire and dumped a can of beans into the blackened inside. "What do you mean?"

She frowned, still thinking. "Once I go to sleep, I'll wake up."

"Uh-huh."

She warmed to the idea. It felt right. Once she went to sleep, she'd eventually wake up. And this nightmare would be over. "Then I'll be back in my bed on Bainbridge." She looked at him. "No offense, but I'm getting tired of you. I want to go home."

He stared at her, his eyes narrowed and assessing, his mouth drawn into a frown. "You're not going anywhere until we talk, lady."

"Lainie," she said.

"Huh?"

"My name is Alaina Costanza. People call me Lainie."

He snorted. "Whatever. The point is, you've got some talking to do, but I'm too damn tired and hungry to bother with you tonight."

"It's just as well," she answered. "You wouldn't believe me anyway."

He gave her a hard look. "You better hope I do."

Lainie felt a shiver of apprehension slide down her back. She crossed her arms and glanced away from him, unable to keep staring into the threatening darkness of his eyes. He was exactly the man she'd created—hard, uncompromising, selfish, and cruel.

She stared out at the dusky, inhospitable valley and suddenly felt small and frightened and alone.

Jesus, she hoped the dream ended before his questioning began.

* * *

God, it was dark out here. Really dark.

Lainie stood at the edge of the now-slumbering fire. The small hump of sticks had burned down to a glowing, throbbing coil of red-gold embers. Remnant scents of supper—baked beans and coffee—clung to the cool night air, lending an impossible homeyness to the desolation of the desert.

"You gonna stand there all night?"

Lainie didn't look at him. He'd asked her the same question five minutes ago. She hadn't answered then, either. She couldn't say precisely what was wrong, but something was. She felt . . . disconnected and vaguely afraid. As if something were hovering out there, in the endless darkness, waiting for her to close her eyes.

"That's crazy," she murmured, trying to sound strong and resilient. Even to her own ears, she failed. Out here in the great alone, all she sounded was weak.

"*You're* crazy, lady," he said, slowly kneeling beside the fire.

She was careful not to make eye contact. She didn't want to look at him right now, didn't want to see her obvious neuroses reflected in his brown eyes. She just wanted to be left alone. She wanted to wander to some lonely place with a queen-sized bed and tumble into a dreamless sleep.

The kind of peaceful, restless sleep she'd never experienced in her life.

She needed that now. Needed it with an intensity that frightened her. She crossed her arms tightly and spun away from the fire, pacing.

All she had to do was crawl into the bag and go to sleep. It sounded simple enough. Hell, it couldn't be any simpler.

But it didn't *feel* simple.

She shook her head. "Stupid, stupid, stupid."

"No one would argue that point with you."

Lainie ignored him and kept pacing. His attitude was really starting to irritate her. When she woke up, she was going to seriously revise his character.

The sharp, familiar scent of cigarette smoke wafted on the breeze. For a bittersweet moment, she thought she was home again, waiting for Kelly. . . .

But that was the cruelest dream of all.

Slowly she turned around. Killian was sitting cross-legged beside the fire, his hat tossed casually aside. Moonlight caught in his long, unkempt hair and turned it to brilliant strands of sterling silver. The night shadowed his face, re-formed it into a plane of sharp angles and sunken hollows. A cigarette dangled from his mouth, a disembodied, hovering red dot in the darkness.

A cigarette. Thank God. She moved toward him, close enough to feel the fire's heat against her shins. "C-Can I have one of those?"

He looked up sharply, surprise stamped on his features. One black brow arched mockingly upward. "A lady doesn't smoke."

She tried to smile. "I've never been much of a lady. And I started smoking when I was eleven."

"Eleven?" There was a softness in his voice that surprised her. "That's young."

She laughed, a bitter, snorting sound. "Yeah, it can be."

"Your folks didn't mind?"

"They never said." The acid words, neither true nor false, stung. She forced a smile and looked away.

He reached into his pocket and pulled out his tobacco and papers. Slowly, still looking up at her, he rolled her one and handed it to her across the fire.

She took the cigarette in trembling fingers and lit up, inhaling deeply. Without a filter, the smoke scorched her throat and hit her lungs hard, reminded her of how rarely she actually smoked. It should have tasted searing and awful, but for once, it tasted good.

He watched her intently and took another drag. Smoke swirled across his face, masking it for a moment. "You're a strange one, lady."

She kneeled down beside the fire, welcoming the waves of warmth against her body. "So I've been told."

"Tomorrow we'll make the ridge." He brought one knee up and dangled his arm across it. "Then we'll talk."

"I won't be here tomorrow."

"Uh-huh." He took a last drag and flicked the wasted cigarette into the fire. Then he slid into his bedroll and looked at her. "Come to bed."

Coughing, she tossed the remainder of her cigarette into the fire and tried to make herself stand up. Her legs felt like pudding and her heart was thumping so fast, she couldn't hear anything else.

What in the world was wrong with her?

Everything she wanted and needed was lying over there, waiting for her. All she had to do was crawl into that sleeping bag and go to sleep and this nightmare would finally end.

She forced herself to a stiff-legged stand and walked beside the fire. At the bedroll, she stopped and looked down at him.

Arms crossed behind his head, hair a tangled silver mess, he lay there, looking unconscionably handsome. Arrogantly male.

He grinned. "Ready for bed?"

She winced, feeling another sharp stab of fear. It wasn't that she was afraid of him. *That*, she could almost understand. It was something else; something she couldn't put her finger on, something just out of reach.

"Move over."

He sidled an infinitesimal amount to the right.

She crossed her arms, tapped her foot impatiently. "Very funny."

He shrugged. "That's all the room there is."

Lainie peeled out of her boots—and knew instantly that she wouldn't get her swollen feet back into them without a crowbar. Forcing a smile, she crawled down alongside him and wiggled into the narrow, sheepskin-lined bag.

They lay there, side by side, without moving. She could feel his presence beside her, warming her. His breathing, slow and regular, filled and emptied the air between them, a heartthrob of sound in the desolation.

She stared up at the diamond-strewn velvet sky. It seemed so huge, this endless night sky. And suddenly she felt very small, very alone, even though she was pressed closely to Killian. The sky seemed to push down on her, the night to close around her. She squeezed her eyes shut.

Take me back, God. Please, let me get back....

The wind laughed at her feeble prayer.

And the truth came at her like a blow to the heart. She knew then what she'd been afraid of, what formless terror had caused the quickening of her heart.

She never slept well, and never on command. She'd been an insomniac since childhood. She worked and worked and worked until, finally, depleted, she fell into an almost coma-deep sleep. Otherwise, the nightmares came, preyed upon her sleeping mind and drew her into a terrifying world of thunder and shadows and evil.

She wouldn't be able to sleep tonight. She knew it suddenly with a bone-chilling certainty. It would be like all the other restless nights in her life; nights when she lay awake in her bed, her eyes wide and gritty and aching, her thoughts drawn into a quagmire of hopelessness and despair.

She wouldn't be able to sleep. There would be no escape from the dream.

And she needed it, needed both the respite from the dream and the oblivion of sleep. Sweet Jesus, she needed it. . . .

She pulled the sleeping bag up to her chin and thumped her head back onto the cold ground. She stared up at the blanket of stars and thought of her bedroom at home, so cozy and welcoming and warm.

For the first time since the ordeal began, she cried.

Chapter Six

Killian woke with a start.

He tensed, concentrated on the sounds of the desert. Behind him, the little creek gurgled a quiet, sloshing melody as it moved over the rocks and branches in its path. A breeze, cool and sharp and crisp, whistled through the cottonwood trees, jostling their leaves. From far away came the keening cry of a hawk; its shadow glided against a sheer, rust and brown cliff. Everything was as it should be here, quiet and peaceful.

Then he remembered the woman. He could feel her beside him, feel the warm heat of her leg pressed against his, the bony knob of her shoulder wedged alongside his forearm.

A memory filtered through his mind, as soft as a sigh, a whisper. He frowned. Crying. He'd heard it last night as she'd lain beside him, her slim shoulders jerking with each shuddering, indrawn breath. She cried unlike any woman he'd ever heard. No sobbing theatrics, no hiccuping coughs, just soundless tears, somehow all the more heartbreaking for the silence of them. For an incredible moment, he'd found himself almost responding to her, almost turning on his side to say something.

The memory irritated him. A heavy frown ribbed his forehead.

Beside him, she lay as still as stone, but her breathing was quick and uneven. It was not the sound of sleep.

Reluctantly he glanced sideways at her.

He didn't know exactly what he expected to see, but it wasn't this. She lay stiff as a board, her arms crossed across her body, corpselike and cold. Her eyes were lifeless and dull, an almost muddy green against the pallor of her skin. She looked as if she hadn't slept in a lifetime.

"You didn't sleep," he said, wondering how he'd known that, and why he'd bothered to say it.

"No." There was a wealth of pain in the simple word.

Killian didn't know what to say. She looked so . . . vulnerable right now, beaten.

She turned slightly and met his gaze.

The pain and hopelessness in her eyes hit him like a physical blow. It came to him suddenly—crazily—that she'd looked at him like this before. He felt . . . disjointed . . . confused. Something about this moment was impossibly familiar.

She bit down on her lower lip, but it was too late. He'd seen the tremble in her mouth. "I'm in a coma," she murmured. "That's the only explanation. I've had hours to think about it, and it's the only answer that makes sense. I'm in a hospital bed somewhere, with needles sticking out of my arms. Maybe on Demerol." She glanced up at him, her face drawn into an earnest frown. "I want to wake up now."

He almost asked her who Demerol was, but he stopped himself just in time.

It didn't matter. Demerol could be her husband and it didn't matter. None of this craziness mattered. All that mattered was getting her back to the ridge and finding out how the hell she knew so much about him and his men.

"You're not listening to me," she said, her soft voice becoming a bit more strident. "I *said* I need to wake up now."

"You are awake," he said.

"Ha. Naturally you would think so. This is the only world you know."

Another meaningless statement to which there was no rational response. Thank God. The more she talked, the less he cared about the vulnerability he'd seen in her eyes.

He pushed the sleeping bag back and reached for his boots, checking them quickly for snakes. Plunging his stockinged feet in the worn, broken-in leather, he got to his feet. "Grab a few more sticks for the fire. I'll get the coffee started."

She sat up and gave him a wry, forced smile. "I suppose a double tall latte with skim milk is out."

"Huh?"

She sighed, shook her head. "I've *got* to work harder on your dialogue."

His eyes narrowed. "Is that an insult?"

"It depends on your point of view." She sighed. "Aw, hell, I don't feel up to fighting with my own imagination. Coffee's great. What are we having with it?"

"Beans."

"One of my favorite breakfast foods." She peeled the sleeping bag back from her legs and crawled out, then she turned and started rolling up the bag.

Killian watched her. She was crouched low, her once stiff and now wavy hair flopping against her cheek. The earrings she wore—and there were at least three in each ear—glinted in the early morning sunlight. Her profile was sharp and defined, her skin creamy and pale. There was a sadness to her mouth, a downturn to the edges that made him wonder what kind of life she'd had. She was damned young to look so sad.

He pulled his gaze away from her and stared at the rock wall behind them. He was losing his mind. What the hell did he care why she looked sad? She meant nothing to him.

She finished tying the sleeping bag and sat back on her heels, running a hand through her hair. The short black curls bounced immediately back in place, covering one eye. "I need some mousse."

He ignored her. At least he tried to. "Uh-huh."

"And an Excedrin. This Demerol is giving me a headache." She stared at him, obviously waiting for him to respond—as if he had a moose standing by—and when he didn't, she sighed dramatically.

He shook his head, completely at a loss. "Where in the *Christ* are you from, lady?"

She gave a hollow laugh and didn't look at him. "The posse left way before dawn. They wanted to get the jump on you."

He stared at her for a second, feeling the blood drain from his face. What in the hell had he been thinking, for Christ's sake?

He made a growling, angry sound of disgust. That was the problem. He *hadn't* been thinking. He'd been staring into her goddamn eyes and wondering why she was so sad, wondering who would let a child smoke at eleven.

He cursed his own stupidity. It didn't occur to him to wonder how she knew about the posse. He accepted it as truth. Somehow he knew she was right, and the knowledge made him even angrier. He'd been so caught up by the sorrow in her eyes that he hadn't even bothered to question her.

But as soon as they got back to the hideout, he'd

remedy his negligence. He'd back her against the wall and tie her up if he had to. Somehow, he'd figure out who in the hell she was and why she'd been at the bank.

"Get up," he growled.

"Don't blame me," she snapped. "It's not my fault they're following you."

He spun on her. "It is," he said tightly, and as he spoke the words, he knew they were true. "Somehow, it is."

She shrugged and tossed him the sleeping bag. "Arguably, of course, you're right. Everything in this dream is my fault. But *you're* the outlaw."

He stomped on the fire, making sure it was completely out, then saddled up their horses. He gave her exactly two minutes of privacy behind a bush, then he grabbed her around the waist and dragged her toward her mount.

Naturally, she kicked and screamed. "Let go of me, damn it. I need a toothbrush."

He flung her onto the horse and glared up at her. "Do I need to tie your hands?"

"No." She spat the word.

"Does the posse catch me today?" he asked.

She smiled, a sickeningly sweet display that made him want to punch her. "Believe me now?"

He gripped her forearm hard. "Does the goddamn posse catch up with me today?"

"Yes. At Bloody Gorge."

He frowned, feeling a brush of cold fear at her smile. Bloody Gorge was a deadly box canyon—the perfect place to corner an outlaw and kill him like a rabid dog. He started to turn away, then he noticed her expression. "Why are you grinning?"

"You're going to die there. Slowly, horribly, with

blood spurting out of several attractive orifices." She shook her head, made a *tsk*ing sound. "It's one of the better action scenes I've written."

"Lady," he said, "if I die, you're comin' with me."

"Oh, I don't think so. It's my dream, you see, and I'm going to be rescued by Joe Martin." She smiled at the thought. "And he's a hunk of burning love, believe me."

He turned his back on her in disgust and strode to his horse. Vaulting into the saddle, he smacked Captain and The Bitch on the butts. Both unsaddled horses trotted alongside the black.

The woman's face twisted into a grimace. She clutched her reins and clung to the saddle horn. "Oh, hell . . ."

He felt a moment's satisfaction, then he kicked the black hard. The stallion surged into a gallop. The woman's roan leapt alongside, keeping up as Captain and The Bitch followed close beside them. They sped across the bumpy, uneven ground, raced up and down hills, and wound through canyons.

But even as they ran, Killian could feel the posse behind him, closing in for the kill. He glanced back time and again, searching for a sign, but all he saw was endless golden desert.

Joe Martin was back there, shadowing Killian's every move, waiting and watching, closing in.

For the first time in fifteen years, Killian felt an honest-to-God sense of fear. Somehow—he didn't know how he knew, but somehow he did—this woman was going to get him killed.

They were on a narrow trail carved from the sheer face of a treeless mountain. A blistering hot sun beat down on them, battered Lainie's face. She sighed tiredly; it was an oddly disembodied sound.

"Damn!" Killian cursed and yanked back on his reins. The black slid to a bouncing, clattering stop on the edge of a sheared rock slope. Thousands of tiny pebbles rattled and rained down the crevasse beside them. The two riderless horses behind him slowed, then halted.

Lainie yanked back on her reins to keep from ramming into Captain's huge, spotted butt. Her horse stopped dead, sending Lainie crashing into the saddle horn. The leather horn drove into the tender flesh of her stomach. She gasped hard, tried to find a breath.

"We'll have to go back. *Shit.*"

Dully Lainie lifted her head and followed his gaze. Ahead of them was a narrow, high-walled canyon that seemed to have magically appeared between two immense, twisted rock spires. She'd been staring straight ahead and hadn't seen the opening. The space between the two stalagmitelike towers was invisible until you were directly in front of it.

She could see that ordinarily it would be a hell of a getaway door. But not today; now there was a huge, triangular rock wedged into the opening.

"I take it that rock is a new addition to the entrance," Lainie said tiredly, retrieving the canteen from her saddle and opening it. She took a drink, letting the sun-warmed, metallic-tasting water soothe her aching, dust-clogged throat.

He grabbed his own canteen and took a long drink. "Yeah," he growled, wiping his mouth with his sleeve. "It's new."

"So, what now?" She glanced around. They were on a slick sandstone ledge. The trail was one horse wide, a skinny path of level dirt gouged along the side of a textured stone mountain. A gaping maw of red earth slid down to their right, slumping into a valley of shale and fallen rock. Far below, a thread of brown water pushed through a band of dying green.

He didn't even bother to look at her. He twisted in his saddle and gazed back at the thin, inhospitable path through which they'd just come. "We'll have to backtrack and make a run for it."

"Backtrack? A run for it?" That didn't sound good. In fact, it sounded really, really bad. "We haven't exactly been walking." She peeked down at the crevasse and shuddered. "And it's no place to run."

He pulled back on his reins. The black dipped his head and hunkered down, picking his way backward.

Lainie watched in horror as the riderless horses followed suit. She saw their big, muscled backsides moving toward her. She gripped her reins and shook her head. "I don't think so. Uh-uh. I am not backing out of this canyon."

Her horse dropped his head.

"No," she whispered. "Please, no . . ."

The four horses backed up; their slow, clomping steps rang through the air. Lainie clung to the saddle horn, her eyes squeezed shut. The rapid-fire thumping of her heart drowned out the horses' plodding steps.

"Lainie!"

Killian's shout roused her. She opened her eyes and stared at him, breathing hard.

"You have to turn."

Lainie looked down to her right. The world dropped away from her, slid in a red-rock wash one thousand feet below. "Oh, my God . . ."

"Don't panic—"

She gasped. "Don't panic? I'm on the edge of the frigging world and you're telling me not to panic—"

"Calm down. Here's what you do. Very gently, press your right foot against the roan's side, then gently pull back on the reins."

Lainie let out a trembling breath. She wanted to do as he asked, even tried to, but she couldn't move. She couldn't breathe. "I . . . can't."

"Yes, you can. Try."

She bit down on her lower lip and looked at him. She felt foolish and stupid, but she couldn't move, couldn't do as he asked. *Some heroine,* she thought with disgust.

He looked at her, and the gentle understanding in his eyes surprised her. There was no censure in his gaze, no disgust or impatience; there was only concern and something else, something that made her heartbeat speed up and her throat go dry. He knew what it meant to be afraid, really truly afraid. And he knew how hard it was to conquer that fear, how impossible it was sometimes to find the strength to go on.

"You can do it," he said softly.

Amazingly, he made her feel as if maybe she could. She started to look to her right.

"Don't look."

She snapped her head back around. "That's good advice," she said, wetting her dry lips. "Good advice." Slowly, afraid even to breathe, she curled her aching fingers around the reins. Her eyes sought his. Their gazes locked, and somewhere deep inside *him*, she found the strength she needed.

"Use your foot first."

She nodded and swallowed hard. Then, with infinite care, she pressed her heel into the roan's heaving side. The horse sidled away from the drop-off.

Lainie's breath exhaled in a trilling little laugh. She pressed her foot against him again, and the horse responded by moving closer to the safety of the sandstone wall.

"Good job," Killian murmured. "Now, draw back on your reins again."

Lainie nodded and followed his direction. The roan dropped his head and backed up. Lainie's left foot scraped along the rock wall, wrenching sideways at the motion, but she didn't care. They finally came to a small, oval clearing where the trail zagged in the other direction.

"Stop there," Killian said sharply.

Lainie reined her horse tight against the wall.

Killian backed up and pivoted fast, coming to a stop beside her. He looked down, and she saw in his eyes the same cold terror that sat in the pit of her stomach. "You okay?"

The quietness of his voice surprised her, made her feel strangely afraid all over again. She brushed the damp hair from her eyes with a trembling hand. "Yeah, sure."

He smiled. "You did good."

She gazed up at him, unable to look away. For a heart-stopping moment, she thought he was going to reach over and touch her. Her skin tingled in anticipation, her pulse raced. All she could manage was a breathy little, "Thanks."

But he didn't touch her, he just stared down at her. All at once he frowned, and the look in his eyes changed completely. Gone was the compassion, the understanding of fear, the caring. Suddenly his gaze was intense and assessing. Once again, they were strangers.

She felt the loss of that moment, that connection between them, as keenly as a slap. She told herself it was stupid to feel hurt; she'd imagined the moment anyway. But she couldn't make herself believe it. For a second—no more than a heartbeat—she'd seen something in him, something real and important. Something she'd sought all her life inside herself and never found. And she had no idea what it was, and no idea if he'd felt it, too.

Finally he looked away from her and whistled. It was a low, commanding sound that echoed off the sheer rock walls. The horses started moving again, picking their way one by one through the twisting, zigzagging path.

Once again, Lainie was bringing up the rear.

It took them the better part of two hours to make it back to the trailhead. They emerged onto the flat mesa top just as the sun was beginning its slow downward arc. Sunlight and shadows intertwined across the level copper-hued earth, writhing and dancing amid the sagebrush.

Killian reined the black to a halt and sat back in his saddle. Tilting his hat, he sopped the sweat from his brow with his sleeve. Jesus, it was hot. He reached back and untied his canteen, taking a long, satisfying gulp.

The woman brought her horse up alongside his. He glanced at her and was just about to say something— when he realized what she was wearing ... and what she wasn't. She was slumped in her saddle, her shoulders rounded, her chest caved in on itself. That ridiculous sweater was gone now, its sleeves tied around her waist. She was wearing only those old, faded jeans and that skintight black thing around her breasts. The skin above and below the black fabric was an angry red.

"You're in deep shit, lady."

She snorted and reached for her own canteen. "No kidding. I've been saying that since this stupid dream started."

"That burn's gonna hurt like hell in the morning."

She glanced down at her arms and wrinkled her nose, then shrugged. "Cancer alert, cancer alert."

He stared at her, unable to think of a response. She was always doing that to him, throwing him off guard with her outrageous responses. "You should cover yourself back up."

"I was sweating like a pig."

He shook his head. "*Jesus*, lady, you talk like a cowboy."

She grinned and ran a hand through her sweaty hair. "You should have heard my mom. She could curse a blue streak."

"I'm sure she was a lovely woman. Now, put that sweater back on."

"There's been a mistake, obviously."

What the hell was she talking about now? "What mistake?"

"Two, actually. First, you apparently believe I give a crap what you think, and secondly, you are under the delusion that my skin can actually burn." She gave him a condescending smile. "Trust me, I can't burn . . . not drunk as a skunk and passed out in my house on Bainbridge."

His eyes narrowed. He reached for his gun and let his fingers curl lightly around its cold steel grip. He was just about to say something when a memory flashed through his mind. Unbidden, he saw her as she'd been this afternoon, terrified and vulnerable. As they'd stood on that ledge, facing each other, with the world dropped off away from them, he'd looked in her eyes and seen something that scared the hell out of him.

He refused—flat refused—to feel it again. And the best way to keep her at bay was to keep his mouth shut and his gun pointed at her. "I'm not gonna take care of you when you pass out from sunstroke, lady. So put that sweater back on."

She stared at him for a long time. Their gazes clashed hard. Her small, pointed chin edged upward. "I'll have you know this sports bra is perfectly acceptable where I come from. I wear it for aerobics."

"Uh-huh." He tightened his hold on the grip, edged the pistol from its holster. "A bra, huh?"

"Who the hell do you think you are . . . Blackwell?"

He didn't say anything. It was better that way.

She stared at him for another few seconds, then heaved a sigh of obvious disgust. "Fine, I'll put the damn sweater back on, but it's going to be uncomfortable and you're going to hear about it."

"Now, why doesn't that surprise me?"

She untied the baggy sweater and flung it over her head. The bulky red material settled in folds on her thighs and gaped across that bra thing. She gave a false, sugary smile and retied her canteen onto the saddle. "Feel better, he-man?"

He started to respond, then stopped. A sound caught his ear. He frowned and turned toward it, his every sense focused on the noise, far away and indistinct, yet unmistakable. A chill slid down his back, mingled with the hot moisture of his sweat, and caused a shudder.

"The posse," he murmured.

"No shit, Sherlock. They're closer than ever. I was going to point it out before you had a cow about my shirt."

He stared at her for a second, slack-jawed. *Had a cow?*

She gave him a cocky smirk. "Were you going to speak?"

He wrenched his gaze away and stared into the distance. He could just make out the first tendrils of dust blurring the horizon. It was a sight he knew well, too well.

"Horses," he said tightly. "About ten."

"Twelve, actually. Shall I give you names?"

He didn't glance at her. He was afraid that if he did, he'd punch her. "No."

"Joe Martin is the leader."

"So you've said." He pulled his hat back low on his brow. "We're gonna have to race for El Diablo."

"Since I never invented a place called El Diablo, I assume you're speaking metaphorically. But you're wrong. The shootout takes place at Bloody Gorge." She misinterpreted his look as interest and went on. "It's a little melodramatic, I know. *Bloody Gorge.* But I was getting close to deadline. Anyway, it worked fine. You died at Bloody Gorge . . . in a spectacularly painful way, I might add."

"I think it's safest if you don't talk."

She gave him a wry smile. "Funny . . . men often say that to me."

He didn't bother to state the obvious. "It's gonna be a hard run for the next few hours. El Diablo's a good fifteen miles from here."

"We're not going to El Diablo."

For the first time in a long time, he felt a genuine smile start. "Yeah, we are. And when we get there, I'm gonna put you in front."

The first hint of concern tugged at her full, dusty lips. She frowned at him. "Why?"

His gaze slid from her face to the huge, baggy sweater. "That red sweater'll make a nice big target."

Her frown twisted into a grimace. "Is that a crack about my weight? Because if it is—"

He let out a whoop and kicked the black hard. The stallion snorted and took off. The ground rumbled and shook as the horses surged into a gallop.

Behind him, he heard the woman scream. The sudden movement of her horse obviously knocked the wind from her lungs, because for a moment—a blessed second—it was quiet.

Then the cursing began again.

Chapter Seven

"I have to stop. Goddamn it, I have to stop!" Lainie tried to scream the words at the top of her lungs, but all that made it past her parched, sunburned lips was a feeble, throaty croak. She leaned back and sawed mercilessly on the reins. Her horse snorted and tossed its head, slowing for a few steps, then surging forward again.

Lainie landed back in her seat so hard that for a moment she couldn't breathe. She opened her mouth and sucked in a lungful of dry, searingly hot air.

Killian stopped suddenly. The other three horses dropped down to a trot and then halted, snorting and wheezing from the long run.

Lainie reached back for her canteen and tried to untie the leather straps, but her fingers were so sore, she couldn't will them to function.

"It's too quiet." Killian glanced around.

Lainie noticed it, too. She looked around. In the distance, the sun was just inches above the horizon, a huge, brilliant orange ball suspended in a violet sky. Miles of copper red earth and faded sagebrush fanned out to their left; to their right was a steep, tree-strewn hill. Behind lay the winding, twisting canyon that led nowhere. In front of them was a three-hundred-foot stone cliff, its face striated with layers of gold and red and gray. Shadows of the coming night slashed across it.

It *was* quiet out here. Creepy ...

Lainie shivered and hugged herself. All day there had been noise in the desert: the echoing heartbeat of hooves, the clatter of small stones as they tumbled down hillsides, the cant of the animals' breath.

Now there was nothing.

Suddenly a sound cracked through the quiet, splitting it, echoing off the canyon. A bullet whizzed past her head, so close she felt a whisper through her hair. The sharp scent of gunpowder filtered through the air.

"*Christ!* They're closer than I thought. Hold on."

The black took off at a gallop.

Lainie threw herself forward and clutched the saddle horn just as her horse lurched. The four horses raced across the sandy desert and crashed into the trees.

She saw in horror that Killian was leading them up the mountain. She wanted to scream, but she couldn't do anything except hold on as her horse strained to make it up the slick, rocky face.

Sticks and branches clawed at her, yanked on her clothing, and tried to pull her out of the saddle. Lainie gritted her teeth and hung on, her eyes squeezed tight against the dust churned up by the horses' hooves. Her mount wheezed and snorted, surging up the slick face.

More shots rang out, cracked into trunks, and split branches. A bullet blasted through Lainie's sleeve. There was the wrenching hiss of torn fabric.

"Killian!" a male voice boomed up at them.

Relief poured through Lainie. Finally this horror was

over. She'd imagined that voice a million times. *Joe.* Any minute now she'd be rescued. . . .

But it didn't happen. They clambered up the sheer hillside, horses straining, for what felt like hours. Then, suddenly, they stopped. It took Lainie a moment to realize that her saddle was no longer pitched at a ninety-degree angle. The horses were on level ground again. She drew back slowly, shaking, and opened her eyes.

They were on the crest of the hill, clustered together on a narrow ridge.

She looked around, searching for the towering rock walls and stone spires. "Where's the gorge?"

He grabbed her by the waist and pulled her sideways, carrying her to a small lip of a clearing along the path, where he stopped abruptly and dropped her.

Before she could even grunt in pain, he was gone again, racing back to her horse.

"What are you doing?" she asked, watching as he wrenched the saddle off her horse and threw it aside.

From far below, Lainie could hear the muffled sound of raised voices, men arguing. The merchants and farmers who made up the posse didn't want to risk actually getting hurt. They didn't want to get too close to Killian. In the end, they would turn around and go home to their families, to safety.

All except Joe. Any minute, he was going to follow them. And he'd do it alone.

Killian grabbed a rope from his saddlebags and cracked a huge, splayed limb from a pine tree. Dragging the limb, he tied a knot around its branches, then tied the other end of the rope around the horse's tail.

He whooped and smacked the horse on the butt.

The roan took off like a shot, sliding down the loose-rocked hill in a dusty cloud. The branch crashed along behind him, breaking off trees and starting a thousand tiny avalanches. It sounded as if a dozen horses were careening down the mountain out of control. Gunfire exploded through the air in panicked bursts.

Killian bolted back to the saddle and flung it over his shoulder, then threw it on The Bitch, tightening the girth-strap in a matter of seconds. "That'll buy us some time. Get on."

Lainie groaned. "No ... please ... leave me here."

He lurched toward her and scooped her into his arms. She fought to be free, clawing, scratching, slapping at him. "Let me go. Damn it, let me go! I want to wait for Joe."

He threw her into the saddle and tossed her the reins, then leapt onto the black. He made a quiet clucking sound with his tongue and urged his mount off the narrow path. The huge stallion stood at the rim for a second, snorting and pawing at the loose earth.

"Come on, boy," Killian said quietly, glancing back down the hill.

Below, there was silence. The gunfire and the voices had died.

Suddenly the black lurched forward and disappeared.

Lainie gasped. A cold sweat slid down her back. She felt the animal beneath her bunch up, quiver. "Oh, no."

She just had time to fall onto the saddle horn when her horse followed the stallion over the edge.

The horses crashed and slid down the sandy, tree-strewn slope, their hooves flailing for purchase. Dust engulfed them, stung Lainie's eyes, and clogged her nose and mouth. She gagged and gasped and tried to hang on.

Then, as quickly as it had begun, it was over. They'd reached the level ground on the other side of the hill.

Killian stopped and turned around in his saddle, staring back up the slope. The air around them was quiet, dusty.

Lainie slumped in her saddle, feeling the miles they'd ridden as sharp, stabbing pains in every muscle of her body. Her eyes slid shut, her breath expelled in a shuddering sigh.

She felt a moment's utter, debilitating defeat. It took everything from her, twisted her insides with despair, left her feeling broken and afraid and alone.

But she wasn't alone.

Joe will follow. Forever.

The words moved through Lainie like a balm, returning to her a spark of hope and courage. Joe would rescue her; she was sure of it. All she had to do was wait.

And stay.

She straightened. She'd ridden all day, eaten enough dust for ten lifetimes, and been shot at. *Shot at*, for God's sake.

Enough was damn well enough. She wasn't going to let the dream keep manipulating her. It was time for her to take control, time for her to call Mr. Macho's bluff. Time for Alaina Costanza to make her stand.

She was waiting for Joe. Right here, right now. He'd done his part; he was here. Now it was time for Lainie to stop playing the victim.

She wrapped her reins around the saddle horn and slid to the ground. The minute her feet hit, shards of pain shot up her legs and radiated outward.

"What the hell are you doing?"

"Staying."

"Get on that goddamn horse right now."

She flipped him off. "It's over, Killian. I'm taking my dream back."

"Don't start with that again. Not now."

"You better hurry. Joe's probably on his way up the hill now. When he gets to the top . . ."

Killian cursed and vaulted out of the saddle, striding toward Lainie. Yanking the gun from his holster, he pointed it at her. "Get up and get on that horse."

She moved toward him. As she closed the distance between them, surprise widened his eyes. She kept moving, inching toward him until the cold steel of his gun touched her breast.

From far away came the first cracking sound of a horse moving up the hillside. The sound gave her strength, renewed her spirit. Joe was coming.

She smiled coldly. "Go ahead, shoot me."

A muscle in his jaw tensed. "You're willing to die for him?"

She leaned into the gun, daring him to pull the trigger. "You couldn't shoot a woman, Killian. It's not in your character. Not after what happened to Emily."

The color drained from his face. The gun in his hand trembled against her flesh. "How do you know about Emily?"

"I wrote it."

They stared at each other in silence, both breathing hard. She waited for him to say something. Behind them, the sounds of Joe's horse struggling up the hill intensified, filled the clearing with grunting, pounding noise.

Slowly he withdrew the gun from her chest and eased it back into the holster.

Lainie grinned. "See, I told—"

He reached out and grabbed her sweater, yanking her toward him. She stumbled forward and slammed into his chest. Her head snapped back.

She blinked up at him in surprise, felt the ragged strains of his breath against her lips. His face lowered toward hers.

An icicle of fear slid down her back. She tried to shrink away from him. He held her fast.

For one terrifying, debilitating moment, she thought he was going to kiss her. Memories surged up from her past, filled her with icy terror. *Oh, God, oh, Jesus . . . no . . .*

But he didn't. He brought her close, so close she could see herself in the dark pools of his eyes. "Maybe I won't kill you." He said the words softly, but they seemed to reverberate through forever. "But it doesn't mean I won't hurt you. It doesn't mean I won't let someone else hurt you. Now, get on that horse or I'll throw you over the saddle like a sack of salt and tie you down."

Lainie gasped, tried to draw back. "Y-You wouldn't."

"Get on the goddamn horse, lady. *Now.*"

He loosened his hold and she stumbled backward, clutching the sweater to her breasts. Breathing hard, she staggered back to her horse and climbed into the saddle. When Killian was mounted he turned back to her. "If you lag behind, I swear to God, I'll strip every piece of clothing from your body and let you ride into the hideout stark naked."

Her eyes rounded. "But the men—"

"Yeah . . . the men."

She swallowed again, wet her parched lips. "I'll keep up."

For the first time in hours, he smiled. "I bet you will."

Killian turned back in his saddle and spurred the black. All three horses moved at once, surging into a thundering gallop across the purple- and pink-stained desert.

Lainie squeezed her eyes shut and clung to the saddle horn. She told herself it didn't matter that she'd given in, that she'd been afraid—just for a second—of being tied up again. Joe would still find her, still rescue her.

Besides, it was just a dream, just a stupid pointless dream.

But it didn't *feel* like a dream.

She concentrated on breathing evenly, listening to the gentle ebb and flow of sound, blocking out everything until she was calmed. The strength she needed was there, inside her, as it always was, as it always had been. She reached for it, clung to it, let it warm the cold places in her heart. This was just a dream, and sooner or later it would end. He couldn't hurt her.

She could survive it, as she'd survived so many other things. She'd given up her courage once, long ago, and she'd never do that again. Never.

Long into the night, they raced on. After about an hour, darkness cloaked the valley, spilling at first over the canyon walls, then puddling, thick and invincible, on the desert floor. They galloped on, heedless of the darkness, hooves pounding on the hard-packed dirt. Lainie clung to the saddle horn with sore, shaking fingers, her eyes squeezed shut, her heart slamming in her chest.

Behind them, faint but unmistakable, was the distant thunder of a single horse. That sound was Lainie's lifeline, the only thing keeping her going. With every sound, every footfall in the night, she was able to let herself believe that this nightmare would end.

Joe. Joe. Joe. The single word became a prayer that matched her heartbeat, punctuated her every breath. He was back there, alone but undaunted, following her and Killian into this boundless darkness.

Soon—please God, soon—he would catch up and rescue her, and this devastating nightmare would end.

Suddenly a gunshot rang out.

Joe.

Lainie felt a wave of hope. She forced herself to unfurl, to straighten in the saddle. She blinked, trying to see something in the black tomb that had become her world.

She twisted in the saddle and peered behind her. There was nothing; the void behind them was impenetrable, empty save for the thundering beat of hooves.

From somewhere came another gunshot.

She realized that the sound had come from above them, not behind. Disappointment brought a sharp, stabbing pain to her stomach. Dully she turned back around and glanced up.

The gun fired again, a blink of yellow-bright light amidst the darkness. It came from high above them, on what had to be a mesa shrouded by nightfall.

An answering shot bit through the night behind them. There was a moment's hesitation, then gunfire exploded from the invisible ledge above. A dozen shots rang out simultaneously. Sunburst explosions lit the ridge.

"Whoa, boy." Killian brought his horse to a halt and dismounted.

Silence fell into the valley again. And this time it was quieter, more oppressive.

It took Lainie a moment to realize what had happened. There was no longer a distant thunder of hooves gobbling up the ground behind them.

Joe had stopped.

She wanted to scream but didn't have the energy.

Killian materialized beside her. "Martin won't follow past here," he said softly. "He knows it would be suicide."

Lainie glanced up, trying to see the men who stood there. "Those are your men." Her voice felt as if it came from another person.

"Guards." He straightened. "We've got a few more hours and we'll be in camp. Then, lady, it's you and me . . . without your precious Joe to worry about."

Lainie squeezed her eyes shut and slumped again, feeling beaten and tired and lonely. The dream was veering away from her plot, taking her somewhere she couldn't begin to understand. Joe was supposed to have rescued her by now, and Killian was supposed to be dead.

Joe, only Joe, had kept her going these last few hours. Knowing that he was behind her, doggedly trailing her every move, had given her strength. Without it, without him, she felt more alone than she would have thought possible for a dream.

Killian's footsteps crunched through the darkness for a moment, then stopped. Leather creaked tiredly as he swung into the saddle. He made a soft clucking sound and urged his mount forward.

She let out her breath in a trembling, exhausted sigh. Her hard-won courage slipped a notch; she fought to reel it back in, wind it around her.

She needed to wake up, needed to wake up *now*. But she had no idea how to do it. No idea at all how to end this dream. Frustration clawed at her, made her want to scream and cry and pound her fists.

Opening her tired, gritty eyes, she stared into the nothingness of the night and kept going.

It was the only choice she had.

Chapter Eight

Sounds drifted toward Lainie, taunted the ragged edges of her consciousness. She lifted her head and blinked tiredly.

The world was still inky black. They were in a seemingly endless tunnel, full of twists and turns and switchbacks. Sheer stone walls curled around them, forced them to ride single file. For hours, no sounds or light had infiltrated the darkness; nothing except the steady clip-clop of hooves on slick rock.

Now, suddenly, she heard something.

She pried a hand free of the saddle horn and rubbed her aching eyes. She swallowed thickly, unable to form enough saliva to wet her parched throat.

"Whoa, boy." Killian's gravelly voice floated back to her. It was the first time he'd spoken in ages. In his words, she heard the same bone-deep exhaustion she felt.

Lainie drew back on her reins. She started to speak, but gave up when she heard the feeble, scratchy sound of her voice.

From somewhere came the rumble of throaty laughter, the whispery buzz of raised voices. Killian turned sharply to the left and went a few feet, then turned to the right.

Her booted feet grazed the sheer stone walls. Sand

rained down at the touch, pattered softly on the slick rock floor. Outside, the sounds became louder.

They kept moving, silently plodding forward. After a long while—Lainie had long since discarded any hope of measuring time—she noticed an eerie gray light at the end of the tunnel. Killian turned in to it and disappeared.

Lainie's heartbeat sped up. Anxiety rejuvenated her. Afraid to be left alone, she kicked her horse to a trot and followed him.

Lainie burst from the tunnel's darkness and found herself in the midst of a laughing, talking crowd.

At her appearance, every voice died. Dozens of dirty male faces peered up at her, their countenances distorted and frightening in the bluish moonlight.

There was a slight pause before one of the men chuckled. It was a throaty, slurred sound that burst through the silence like gunfire. "You brung us a woman."

"I get her first," another man yelled. "Henry was first last time."

For an instant, Lainie couldn't breathe. Killian's threat flooded back to her. *It doesn't mean I won't let someone else hurt you. . . . If you lag behind, I'll strip every piece of clothing from your body and let you ride into the hideout stark naked. . . .*

She fought for strength, or at least the appearance of it. Killian—even Killian—wouldn't do this to her, wouldn't throw her to this crowd.

Would he?

God help her, she wasn't sure.

The men moved forward, pressing in on her. She heard their breathing, the throaty, coughing sounds of their laughter, the whispered words of encouragement to one another.

Damp fingers curled around her ankle. She tried to kick out, but her captor laughed and pulled hard.

She flew sideways, landed in a dozen outstretched arms. Hands pawed at her, tangled in her hair, touched her face, her lips. The earthy odor of unwashed bodies and sour breath slammed into her nostrils, gagged her.

Panic pulsed through her blood, making her feel sick and queasy. She opened her mouth to yell for Killian, to curse him or beg for help—she didn't even know what—but nothing came out except a shrill, hysterical scream.

The crowd's laughter grew louder.

A sob caught in her throat. She tried to tell herself it was just a dream, nothing to worry about, but she couldn't calm herself with the familiar words. Fear sucked her in, made her fight like a wildcat. Gasping for air, she twisted and tried to wrench free.

Then she saw him. Killian sat on his horse, his hat drawn low on his forehead, his reins looped around his saddle horn. He was staring at the moon, his face dispassionate. Suddenly she remembered the moment on the cliff today, and the understanding she'd seen in his eyes.

"Killian." She screamed his name again and again until he looked at her.

Slowly he turned, and in the half-darkness, their gazes locked. She clenched her jaw and held back tears by sheer force of will. She wanted to speak, to shame him into stopping this.

Instead she just looked at him. *Don't let them do this to me,* she thought. *Think of Emily. . . .*

He blanched suddenly, as if she'd spoken. She thought he was going to reach for his gun, but he didn't. His eyes narrowed, his gloved hands curled into tense, dangerous fists. He looked away, stared for a long time at the cliffs in the distance, then, slowly, reluctantly, he turned back to her.

When their gazes met, she felt an electrical jolt that struck her at the core of her being. Something passed between them in that look, something dark and dangerous ... and familiar. In that instant, that heartbeat of time, she saw something in him that couldn't possibly exist, something she hadn't written.

He slid down from the black and dropped to the ground. He strode toward her, his footsteps silent, his eyes fixed on hers.

The crowd parted. Hands peeled away from Lainie's body, leaving warm, sweaty imprints on her flesh. She staggered to a stand and hugged herself, battling the sudden chill of the night.

Killian stopped beside her. He touched the tender flesh beneath her chin and forced her gaze upward. The frayed, roughened leather of his glove was damp and unforgiving. Reluctantly she looked at him.

He was so close, she could smell the masculine leather and woodsmoke and dust scent of his clothing, feel his breathing against the damp flesh of her forehead.

She felt his gaze, narrow and probing, on her face, stabbing deep beneath the veneer of calm. In the darkness of his eyes, she saw a hint of her own reflection, and knew somehow that he saw more than she wanted to reveal.

"Ask me for help," he said softly, running a finger up her throat.

Lainie swallowed hard, hating him in that instant more than she'd ever hated another human being. "Please ..." A sickening sense of shame curdled in her stomach. She couldn't believe she was letting him do this to her. "Please don't let them hurt me."

"Who's boss in this place?"

Hating him, loathing him. "You are."

He looked away from her, staring out at the crowd. The moment seemed to stretch into forever, a pregnant, poignant silence. The bastard knew that every breath, every second, was interminable for her.

"Okay, boys," he said at last, his rumbling, tobacco-graveled voice serrating the quiet. "Nobody fucks her but me."

"Nobody *what*?" Lainie said. The fear vanished as quickly as it had come, swept aside by a rising tide of fury so raw and elemental, she staggered at the force of it.

Killian looked down at her, frowning. "Nobody fu—"

She slapped him across the face, hard. "Don't you dare repeat it." She realized a half second too late what she'd done. The crowd drew in a collective gasp. Utter silence crashed into the clearing.

Killian grabbed her by the shoulders and yanked her to him. She blinked up, trying to force her trembling lips to form a smile. "I didn't mean it. . . ."

Killian raised a hand to her. Instinct told her to flinch, to shrink back, but years of experience kept her motionless. If anything, the familiarity of his movement gave her strength, returned her equilibrium. She'd faced this moment a hundred times in her life, maybe more.

She straightened, met his gaze head-on.

His hand froze in midair. A heavy frown folded across his forehead. Slowly his hand lowered.

"Goddamn it," he hissed, grabbing her arm.

Wordlessly he yanked her toward him and pushed through the crowd, dragging her along beside him. There was a mumble of dissension as she left, a grumbling of malcontent.

She stumbled along beside Killian, trying to believe

that this was all a dream—nothing more—but something was wrong.

It didn't *feel* like a dream. Even though it was weird and inexplicable and everything a dream should be, it felt ... real. Suddenly all she could think about were the discrepancies, the things that didn't fit. Like no Bloody Gorge, no rescue, no sheriff interrupting the robbery.

She pushed the thoughts away with a shiver.

It was a dream, damn it. What else could it possibly be?

All of a sudden, it was gone. The adrenaline and fear that had sustained Lainie for the last few minutes evaporated, leaving in its stead a bone-deep weariness. She couldn't remember when she'd been so completely depleted, so utterly exhausted. And she'd had a lifetime of tired with which to compare it.

"You're lagging," Killian said, yanking her forward.

She stumbled along to keep up with him, her small legs trying to match his punishing stride.

Moonlight drizzled through the layer of haze overhead, punching through the clouds in spears of blue-white light, illuminating the outlaw's hideout.

They were in a narrow, twisting valley not more than a half mile across. Sheer rock cliffs ringed the hideout, loomed in the darkness like the folded wings of some giant bird of prey. Meager moonlight lent the valley an illusory, dreamlike softness. The sharp odor of sulfur hung in the air.

Lainie tried to look around, tried to care where she was and what the hideout looked like, but it was impossible. Her eyes were gritty with fatigue; opening them burned and brought tears.

Finally Killian stopped at a small one-room cabin

built of split logs. He yanked on the leather thong that held the door closed, and the planked slab swung open with an echoing creak.

"Wait here." He went inside, disappearing almost immediately into the smelly gloom of the cabin. She heard his footsteps clumping across the planked floor, then the sharp scratch of a match being struck. A tenuous yellow light appeared in the darkness, gaining strength as Killian touched the lighted match to a lantern wick.

He set the lantern down on a table. "Come in."

"What? You aren't going to carry me across the threshold?" She felt her way through the open doorway.

The first thing she noticed was the smell—old food and must—the second was the bed.

Singular. *The* bed.

She thought briefly about throwing a fit. But frankly, she was too tired. She'd sleep with Hannibal Lecter if she had to. Anyone, anywhere. All she wanted to do was close her eyes and forget about this horrific nightmare. She leaned against the splintery doorjamb and closed her eyes. The even rise and fall of her own breathing calmed her. She felt as if she were floating, her fingertips tingled.

She was close—really close—to falling asleep. She knew the signs, the sensations that told her the end was near. *Finally.*

There was a creak of tired leather and the thump of chair legs hitting the wooden floor. "Okay, who the hell are you?"

She forced her eyelids open, and winced at the pain of the action. Fatigue blurred her vision, turned the man seated at the table into a shadowy, black-hatted blur. "Not tonight. I'm really tired."

"Oh, and I give a shit about that."

Lainie felt a grudging smile start. The tingling in her

fingertips moved outward, splayed across her hands, and shot up her arms. Dizziness came at her hard, sending a spray of stars across her hazy field of vision. She swayed. "You're going to have to."

"Why's that?"

She gave him a tired, watery smile and fell forward. The dirty black floor smacked her hard in the nose. A small, thankful sigh escaped her chapped lips.

"Christ!" Killian jerked out of his seat and lurched toward her, dropping to his knees at her shoulder. She lay sprawled on the cold, dirty floor, her face pressed against the wood, her arms motionless at her sides.

She was out cold.

He sighed and sat back on his heels. Tossing his hat onto the bed, he shoved a hand through his dirty hair.

What in the hell was he supposed to do with her?

Everything about the woman mystified him. She was unlike any female he'd ever met: sharp-tongued, opinionated, even crude. She didn't seem to care about anyone or anything—not even herself.

It was a detachment he understood all too well. He'd lived like that for years.

He surged to his feet and backed away from the woman lying on his floor. He didn't want to understand anything about her. All he wanted were answers, then he could send her on her way.

Spinning on his heel, he crossed the tiny cabin and yanked a bottle of whiskey from the overturned soup crate that held his provisions. He took the cork in his teeth and pulled it out, spitting it into the darkness of the corner, then took a long, satisfying drink. The booze burned a trail down his throat and warmed his insides.

Reluctantly he looked at the woman. Alaina, she'd called herself. Alaina Costanza.

He wiped his mouth with his sleeve and reached for

the lantern, curling his fingers around its cold metal handle. Lifting it, he brought the light to the woman and kneeled once again beside her.

Even in sleep, there was a sadness to her features. Her eyes were closed, her lashes sealed in a jet black half-moon against her skin, but he could visualize their gray-green depths. They held a dozen secrets, those eyes, each of them dark and disturbing. In her eyes was a look he knew all too well—the look of someone who'd seen the underbelly of life and walked away, but never escaped.

A strange tingle traced his fingertips, and he realized that he wanted to touch her. He clenched his hand into a fist, surprised by his response to her. He hadn't wanted a woman in years.

And yet, he was drawn to her in some indefinable way. He wanted to feel the soft arch of her throat, trace the full lips that even in sleep held a downward curve of sorrow. He felt—insanely—that the sadness didn't belong there, that he'd seen her once without it.

"Who are you, Alaina Costanza?" he whispered, hearing the tired harshness in his voice.

At the sound of his voice, she moved slightly, let out a sigh that somehow stirred his heart. It was a quiet, squeaking sound that started an ache of loneliness in Killian's exhausted soul.

It didn't make a lick of sense.

He eased away from her, shaking his head. Hell, he didn't want it to make any sense. He didn't want to have a reaction to her at all.

He slid his arms underneath her body and scooped her up, carrying her to the bed. She curled immediately in a self-protective ball on the gunmetal gray woolen blanket. The sagging, half-empty pillow looked harsh and dirty against her pale skin.

A tiny smile pulled at her lips. "John . . ." she whispered, his name tangled in a sleepy sigh.

Killian stood rooted to the spot, more afraid at that moment than he'd ever been in his life.

This woman would kill him. He knew it suddenly, in the way of a gunman who is facing a better shot. She would kill him.

And there wasn't a damn thing he could do to stop it.

Chapter Nine

Killian sat on the edge of the bed. The sagging leather thongs beneath the mattress creaked at his weight. He eased off his boots and tossed them into the darkened corner, where they landed with a *thwack*. His hat and shirt were the next to go. He unbuttoned the rough cotton shirt and tossed it toward his boots. It sailed through the air like a dirty surrender flag and landed in a heap atop his boots. Then he took off his jeans.

Slowly, reluctantly, he stood. Cold seeped through the floorboards and invaded his woolen stockings. He shivered as the night air caressed his bare chest.

Behind him, the woman made a quiet sound.

He crawled into bed beside her. As he drew his legs onto the bed, she made another sound and rolled onto her stomach.

He looked down, knowing immediately that it was a mistake. She lay with her face to him, her left hand so close to his body that he felt warmth from her fingertips. Black hairs fanned out roosterlike from her forehead, brushed the nape of her neck. The silver hoops in her ears glinted in the lamplight. She looked innocent in sleep, peaceful in a way he hadn't seen before, her sharp features softened by the dirty white blur of the pillow beneath her head. Her puffy lips, as soft and smooth as the pinkened underside of a shell, drew his gaze and held it.

He reached out, almost touched her before he stopped himself. His hand hovered above her back. Warmth seeped up from her body, traced the sensitive flesh of his palm. He moved his hand slowly, an inch above her back, down the length of her spine. When he finished, his fingers were trembling and his mouth was dry. He fisted his hand and brought it back to his side.

He leaned sideways and extinguished the lantern, then slid down in the bed and lay still, drawing the blanket up to his chin. The gentle ebb and flow of her breathing filled the room, echoed in the darkness, and felt painfully familiar.

It's not her. It has nothing to do with her.

A tightness squeezed his chest until it hurt to breathe. He sighed, hearing in the silence the tired harshness of the sound. It had been so long—a lifetime—since the loneliness had gnawed at him, left his insides ragged and drained.

But now, with her lying still and vulnerable beside him, he realized the burden of his isolation; it crushed against his lungs, squeezed his throat. He hadn't lain in bed with a sleeping woman since Emily.

Emily.

Those days came back to him, oozing up from the darkness of his past. He had taken it for granted then, that he could crawl into bed with his wife and hold her tight. He had drawn her close, held her thoughtlessly against him, never once realizing the impermanence of it all, never thinking that in the blink of an eye it could be ripped from him.

It hadn't been until it was gone, until he crawled night after night into his cold, empty bed, that he'd realized what it meant to sleep with another person. Just sleep. It represented to Killian everything that he'd had with Emily, every sweet, pure emotion he'd felt and lost and expected never to recover. Didn't even want to recover.

Beside him, the woman whimpered quietly.

He tried to ignore the sound, soft and somehow filled with sorrow. It was just a sleep noise, an involuntary release of breath.

He squeezed his eyes shut, banishing the weak glow of the moonlight through his window, plunging himself into the solitude of complete darkness. But he couldn't ignore her, couldn't pretend he was in bed alone. Couldn't even pretend, not here alone in the darkness, that it was only memories of Emily that roused him right now.

It was Lainie herself. Something about her ... intrigued him.

The sound of her breathing mesmerized him, curled around him like gossamer strands. He could feel the warmth of her body alongside his, smell the sunshine and dust scent of her hair and the leftover hint of perfume that clung to her clothing. And for the first time in forever, he remembered what it had felt like to want a woman.

Shadows. Darkness, shifting in on itself, moving. The magpie chatter of young men's laughter.

"Here, chicky, chicky, chicky. Don't make us come after you." More laughter, piercing through the night.

Lainie thrashed from side to side, trying to get away from the voices and the darkness that swirled around her, weighting her arms and legs and dragging her downward, downward. She couldn't move, couldn't free herself. Her body wouldn't respond to her brain. Terror washed through her in an icy wave. Her teeth started to chatter.

Another sound penetrated the inky veil. The scratchy snap of a rope being drawn taut, the whispery rustle of hemp on hemp.

A scream built inside her, filled her lungs with pounding, pulsing life. She opened her mouth to scream. Thick, fetid air rushed in. Only it wasn't air, it was viscous and slimy and mudlike. The slime curled around her throat, coated her tongue. She coughed and gagged and tried to spit. The sharp, metallic taste of bile backed up in her throat. Nothing made it past her mouth except a feeble, terrified whimper.

"Don't . . . please . . ."

Hands pulled at her clothing, clamped over her mouth. She tasted the salty moisture of sweat, smelled its humid odor.

They laughed again; the high, cackling sound exploded in the darkness, gaining strength until the air vibrated with it.

Tears stung her eyes, burned deeply, and slid down the sides of her face. Sobbing, she flailed to be free.

"Alaina."

The voice echoed in the dark horror around her, roused her. The sound of it was a lifeline. She bolted upright and reached out, her fingers and hands searching blindly for something solid.

"Lainie, wake up."

I'm dreaming. The words rushed through her like a balm, soothing her instantly. She blinked, still tasting the acrid taste of terror on her tongue.

The nightmare receded slowly, as it always did, moved back into the distance of memory. It was one she hadn't had in years, but she should have expected it tonight. After what she dreamed had happened with the men at the hideout . . . She shivered. Of course, the old nightmare would come back.

Thank God, it was all over now.

She sniffled and reached blindly toward her bedside table for a Kleenex.

"Are you all right?"

The voice hit her like a slap. She stiffened, tried to see through the impenetrable darkness, searching for the Day-Glo stars on her ceiling. "No way," she muttered. "No goddamn way."

"No way what?"

Lainie felt as if she were doing a freefall. Any moment the earth would rush up and smack her in the face. She knew what she had to ask, the name she had to utter, but at the thought of it, her stomach tightened. "Killian?"

The bed squeaked. A match flared in the darkness, then moved as if by magic into a smoky lantern. Light blossomed in the glass globe and radiated outward, illuminating the man sprawled in the bed beside her. He was sitting up, his massive chest wreathed in shadow. A gray blanket hugged low on his hips, just below a red cotton drawstring waistband. Thick coils of black hair formed a vee of darkness against the copper smoothness of his skin.

She buried her face in her cold hands. "Oh, my God. Oh, my *God* . . ."

"Alaina, what is it?"

She lifted her heavy head and looked at him. He sat there, half-naked, looking so goddamn *normal* that she wanted to cry.

"How can you still be here?" She meant to scream the question at him, but the words came out softly, mangled and somehow broken. For the first time in years, she felt utterly defeated.

"I live here."

"It's real," she said softly, feeling the hot moisture of tears. "This is all real. *You're* real."

"You really thought it was a dream?"

She laughed. It was a sharp-edged sound, steeped in bitterness. "I didn't think it could be anything else."

"Are you crazy?"

Hysterical laughter welled up in her, squeezed her chest, and exploded in a high-pitched cackle. She threw her head back, giving vent to the laughter until, suddenly, she was crying. The salty taste of the tears burrowed into her mouth, flooded her tongue. As quickly as it came, the hysteria vanished, leaving in its place a yawning sense of despair. She hung her head, stared through her tears at the hands clasped in her lap. "Am I crazy?" she said.

The moment she whispered the words, she wished she hadn't. They called forth a battalion of dark memories, moments in her life when she *had* been crazy, days and nights she'd spent huddled in a cold room with metal bars on the windows, telling strangers the story of her life. She shook her head, trying to banish the images, to quell the rising tide of nausea that wrenched her insides. "Yeah, I've always been crazy. But this . . ." She looked up at him suddenly, and in the shadowy darkness of the cabin, their eyes met. She looked at him, knowing her gaze revealed her pain and confusion, and unable to hide it. Later, she knew, she would feel a drenching regret for having looked at him so openly, for having set her vulnerability on the blanket between them, but now . . . now she had no choice. She needed him to believe her, to believe *in* her. She needed someone to tell her this wasn't happening.

"This is . . . different," she whispered brokenly. "I'm not this crazy."

"You still think I'm a dream." He said it matter-of-factly, but she could see in his eyes that he thought she was loony-tunes. That look, that instant, almost broke her heart. She felt a saturating sense of isolation.

"Tell me something about yourself," she pleaded. "Something I don't know." *Anything to prove I didn't create you.*

He sighed. "Lady, you don't know shit about me."

She squeezed her eyes shut and tried to smile. It was a dismal, trembling failure. "I knew you'd say that."

He reached for her, grabbed her wrist. "Who are you?"

She tried to wrench free, but his grip wouldn't let her. She felt his fingers, burning into her skin, bruising her. "It *is* a dream," she whispered, trying to believe her own words.

He jerked her chin up, forcing her to look into his eyes. "I can give you a nightmare, if that's what you want."

Lainie wrenched backward so forcefully, she fell off the bed. She hit the cold floor with a thud and crawled quickly to her feet. She stood there, breathing hard, staring at him. She was letting fear eat at her, swallow her strength, and right now she needed her strength, every ounce of it. She drew in a big, shuddering breath and straightened. At her sides, her hands curled into fists. "I won't believe this. You're not real. You can't be. . . ."

"I'm real."

The words, spoken quietly and with a confidence she'd kill for, infuriated her. "I'm the author, goddamn it, I *invented* you."

"Lainie—"

"Don't talk to me," she screamed, wincing at the

high-pitched desperation in her voice. "You don't know me. . . . I know you."

She backed away from him, trying to control her breathing.

Calm down, Lainie. Don't go off the deep end. She couldn't afford to get hysterical right now. She needed to be calm, to go somewhere by herself and figure out what in the hell was happening to her. There had to be a reasonable explanation.

She ran for the door and yanked it open. Before he could follow, she shot outside, letting the door bang shut behind her.

This wasn't real, she told herself over and over again, clinging to the words like a mantra as her bare feet pattered on the icy dirt.

It couldn't be real.

Lainie raced blindly down the narrow trail that bisected the outlaw ranch.

At the end of the encampment, she veered down toward the stream and raced along a grooved cattle trail that edged the water. To the left, a hillside beckoned, offering a quiet place.

She splashed through the stream and clambered up the slick bank on the other side. Rocks slid down the slope and hit the grassy canyon floor just below.

Her breathing came in great, wheezing gasps that seemed to fill her lungs with fire, but still she kept scrambling upward, ignoring the cuts and scrapes that stung her fingertips and the searing heat of dirt in her eyes.

On the crest of the hill, she collapsed, shaking and cold, to the ground. It took her about five minutes to regain her breath. For a few heartbreakingly perfect moments, she closed her eyes and almost forgot where she was. Where she thought she was.

Then a bird cried, and it all came back with a vengeance, staggering in its intensity. She lifted her head, blinked dully at the sleeping hideout. The cabins—about ten of them—were spaced along the dirt road, stumplike blocks of black against the steel gray stone walls. Another ten or twelve tents, their canvas roofs a paler shade of gray, were interspersed among the cabins, making them look sturdy and permanent by comparison.

In the distance, a wolf howled. The lonely, vibrating sound rode on the chilly predawn air like the last lingering notes of a sad song before it disappeared.

Lainie brought her knees up and hugged herself. She felt inexpressibly cold, as if she might never really be warm again.

"It can't be real." She said the words softly, wishing she could put a spine into her voice.

She took a deep breath and forced herself to calm down. There was no point in going off the deep end. She just had to be rational. That was not something she was usually good at—remaining calm and logical. She was more used to swinging her fist first and asking questions later. But this time it was important. She had to look at her situation squarely, without fear or panic, and try to understand. *Okay, it can't be real. Why?*

"It can't be real," she said slowly, "because it's fiction." Yes. That was it. The facts comforted her, gave her an anchor in the shifting bleakness of her world. Fortune Flats, and "The Ridge" hideout, and Killian were all figments of her own imagination. None of it could possibly really exist.

She wasn't crazy. After all, if it was just Arizona in 1896, she might have to face the possibility of time travel. But time travel couldn't be possible to a fictional place. It couldn't.

She sighed, relieved. "So where the hell am I?" She glanced around, taking in the towering stone walls that came full circle around a large oval plain. A single crack marred the smoothness of the sandstone cliffs, and that was the entrance to the tunnel. It was a perfect hideout. Two men could hike out to the ridge above the entrance and keep a posse of one hundred men at bay. If a rider couldn't get into the tunnel, he couldn't get to the hideout.

It was exactly as she'd envisioned it. As she'd created it. It wasn't that this hideout couldn't exist; it was simply that it didn't. She'd done a ton of research on the old West, and there were three primary outlaw hideouts. Brown's Hole, Robber's Roost, and Hole in the Wall. This one, The Ridge, was a combination of all of them. And Lainie had created it.

So that left the question: Where was she, really, since she couldn't in fact be here?

Drugs. She was on life support back home, hooked up to a morphine IV that was a bit too strong.

The minute she thought it, she discarded the idea. She'd taken morphine—more than once. It made her feel . . . tingly, sluggish, lighter than air. Not delusional.

Dead. She was dead somewhere, lying in a coffin in an empty church, awaiting rebirth.

She shivered at the thought and hugged herself more tightly. *That* was too grisly to contemplate.

"Okay, so I'm sleeping at home. It's an ordinary dream."

The words were wimpy-sounding, wistful. She knew the moment they left her lips that she couldn't believe in them anymore. Too many things didn't fit.

Like the proportion. It was a simple thing; nothing

much, really. But how often did you have dreams in which the proportion was perfect? In which doorways never bled to the side and turned into fishhooks, and clouds never merged into an immense ice cream cone?

Everything here was perfect, fixed, immobile. The wolf's cry had sounded real, the wind touched her face in soft, realistic feather-strokes. Nothing at any point in this dream had been bizarre, impossible, fantastic. The horses never changed into goats or flew over cliffs.

And pain. How often did you dream you were in pain?

She eased her sweater down her shoulder to reveal the angry red of her sunburn.

Who in the hell dreamt they got sunburned?

Shot, maybe. Stabbed, strangled, run over, certainly. But sunburned?

Gingerly she touched the burnt skin, felt the familiar sting of it through her shoulder. She winced and drew her hand back. It *felt* real. So did the rock-bites on her bare feet and the scrapes on her hands. And the blisters on her backside were too ugly to consider.

She sighed and closed her eyes, not wanting to think about it anymore and yet unable to think of anything else.

Warmth caressed her face.

She opened her eyes and watched, spellbound, as dawn crept over the rim of the canyon, tossing a gauzy, purplish pink net across the smooth rock walls. Light slid down the steep, naked cliffs, turned the stone to burnished gold. The cottonwood trees along the stream seemed to turn toward the light with a glossy green shiver.

And in that instant, as she smelled the dirt and dryness in the air and felt the familiar touch of the sun on her face, she knew. She just knew. It was no dream.

Somehow, it was real.

Her mind fumbled for something—some philosophy or point of reference to cling to—anything that would make this moment possible. Time travel, magic, and death all came to her as possible explanations, but she discarded them promptly. She'd dug through a fair amount of metaphysical research for a ghost book she'd once done. None of it had touched her, or made much sense. In the end, she'd decided most of it was a bunch of bunk. But even so, nothing she'd ever heard or read about made travel to a fictional world possible.

Despair pulled her into a dark pit from which she couldn't seem to emerge. She felt tired suddenly, inexpressibly tired. For the first time in years, she wanted to crawl in a hole somewhere, in the dark, and simply cease to exist. Maybe then she could finally wake up and all of this would have been a nightmare. She and Kelly would—

She gasped and threw her head up, looking around again. Her heart started pounding in her chest, so loud and thudding, she couldn't hear anything else. Panic sluiced through her body, left her shaking and icy cold.

Kelly.

Soon Kelly would come home, laughing, excited, filled with stories of camp. She'd knock on the door, or pick up the telephone ... something, anything to get hold of her mother. But there'd be no answer, no door flung open in greeting, no answering shriek of welcome, no "I missed you." The house would be cold and empty.

Lainie had seen that empty house before, had come home to it when she was eleven years old. At the memory, she felt sick.

She squeezed her eyes shut, battling the wave of horrifying images and memories that crept at the edges of her mind, taunting her, reminding her. She remembered it all: the glare of fluorescent lighting, the clicking hum of a rattling old radiator in a state-run building, the smell of a hundred new beds with sheets that never belonged to her first. *We don't know where your parents are, honey. You'll have to come with us. . . . The Georges are such nice people. . . . The Yannicks are such nice people. . . . The Holdens will take you for a while, but no more acting up. . . . The Grays will take you, but . . . The Rivers . . . The Smiths . . . The Kents . . .*

Oh, yeah. Lainie knew what happened to children who came home to empty houses.

But it wouldn't happen to Kelly.

Lainie wouldn't let it.

She scrambled to her feet, ready to run, to scream, *something*. But what? For a breathless moment, she couldn't move, couldn't think about anything except her baby. Her precious, beautiful little girl.

A scream built in her throat. Reflexively she clamped a hand over her mouth to still it.

"Oh, God." The terrified, formless prayer slipped through her fingers.

Fortune Flats. The words came to her like a gift from God, giving her something to cling to, something to hang on to.

However she'd gotten here, it had been through Fortune Flats. That had to be the doorway. If there was a way home, it was through Fortune Flats.

She had to go back.

Chapter Ten

Lainie could barely breathe by the time she reached Killian's cabin. The stitch in her side was a great, stabbing pain that intensified with each inhalation. She skidded to a stop and grabbed for the latchstring.

But before she even touched it, doubt crashed in on her.

He won't help you. No one will help you.

A tiny, yelping sound of panic escaped her.

She took a deep breath and held it until she felt dizzy, then slowly she exhaled. "Calm down, Lainie," she said firmly. "Calm down."

Unexpectedly she remembered the ledge. Killian had been different then, not the hard-bitten outlaw with a gun, nor the ruthless villain she'd created. He'd talked her through her fear, and in his eyes she'd seen an understanding that surprised her. Maybe if she could find that in him again, draw it out of him, he'd help her.

It wasn't much hope, but it was something, and she'd worked with less.

She let out one final breath and shoved the door. It swung open with a whining creak and cracked against the wall. Dirt rained down from the open rafters. The chicory aroma of coffee hung in the small room, thick and tantalizing.

Killian sat on the bed, fully dressed, a tin cup of coffee in one hand. The blankets lay bunched up beside him, a tangle of grayed linen sheeting and charcoal wool.

Lainie swallowed hard, tried to appear rational and calm, even though her heart was slamming against her rib cage and her knees were rattling together.

She looked at him, knowing her lower lip was trembling but unable to stop it. "I-I need to leave now."

He cocked one great, winged eyebrow and took a sip of coffee. "Really?"

She heard the sarcasm in his voice, saw it in the glittering depths of his brown eyes, and surprisingly, it hurt. She told herself it didn't matter. He was nothing to her; less than nothing. One way or another, with him or without him, she was getting back to Fortune Flats. "Really."

"Want some coffee?"

"No, I do *not* want some coffee. I want to get out of here, now."

He set his cup down on the crate beside the bed. Swiveling to the side, he got up and walked slowly toward her. "You aren't going anywhere until we talk."

"There's no point in us talking. It won't get me back to . . ." At the thought of Kelly, something inside her seemed to give way. The meager hope she'd fabricated dissolved, left her empty inside. Suddenly and for the first time in her life, she didn't care about her pride or looking good or appearing strong. She was desperate and frightened and she didn't care if he knew it.

He saw her second of vulnerability and pounced on it like a hunting cat. "Back to what . . . to who? Your precious Joe?"

She wanted to have the inner strength to meet his penetrating gaze, but she didn't. "Home." Her voice caught on the word, trembled. "I just want to go home."

"You're not going anywhere, lady. Not until I get some answers about you."

"Answers?" She hurled the word back at him, hearing the rising edge of hysteria in her voice. "I don't have any goddamn answers for you, Killian."

He took a step closer. "You'd better have."

She spun away from him and backed up, putting as much distance as possible between them. Control was a thin, wavering strand that edged further and further from her grasp. She swallowed convulsively and tried to compose herself, but it was impossible. Her hands were shaking, her heart was pounding. All she could think about was Kelly, her precious Kelly, and getting home.

"Come here, Lainie," he said in a deceptively soft voice.

She glanced wildly around, looking for a way out. She had no answers to give him, none that he would believe anyway. Her fear accelerated, her breathing sped up.

Then, out of the corner of her eye, she saw a glint of silver. A second later, it registered.

A gun. Power.

Without thinking, she surged for the pistol and grabbed it. Spinning around, she pointed it at Killian.

He stopped dead. "Jesus, lady—"

What now? She needed something to make him vulnerable—just long enough so that she could get the hell out of here. Only one thing came to mind—and she wished it were something else. "T-Take off your clothes."

He didn't know what he'd expected her to say, but that sure as hell wasn't it. He couldn't help himself. He laughed. *"What?"*

"Take off your clothes and throw them to me."

A smile quirked one corner of his mouth. "You don't need a gun to see me naked, Lainie."

"I do *not* want to see you naked."

"Now, that's a little hard to believe, given the circumstances."

"Shut up and strip."

He started unbuttoning his shirt.

She stared at his chest as the fabric gaped open. Then she swallowed hard and glanced away.

"I won't do it unless you look."

She stiffened. For a second that was her only reaction, and then slowly she looked at him. His fingers returned to the buttons on his flannel shirt, undoing them slowly, one by one. Still staring at her, he eased the shirt off his shoulders and let it dangle from one finger. "Over there?"

She nodded stiffly. He thought for a second that she was going to speak, but she didn't. Her lips tightened into a disapproving line as he started undoing the copper buttons at his fly.

Every scrap of color slid out of her cheeks and puddled at the base of her neck in splotches of red. The flesh at the corners of her eyes flinched, and he could tell that she wanted to look away.

He unhooked the last rivet and slid his pants down his long legs. When they puddled around his ankles, he stepped aside and kicked the fallen jeans into the pile.

He stood there, wearing only a pair of old linen drawers, and scratched his naked chest. "Far enough . . . or do you want to see more?"

She sighed impatiently. "Don't you understand that I've got a gun on you? I could kill you, for God's sake, and you're acting as if I'm seducing you."

"I've heard of women who liked the power of a gun. Why, once—"

"Shut up!" She took a deep breath. He could see the effort it took for her to speak calmly. "Take off your underwear, please."

Slowly, making every movement count, he leaned over and started peeling off the wrinkled linen drawers. Naked, he kicked the underwear and straightened.

The look on Lainie's face almost made him bust out laughing.

She was standing as stiff as a switch, her white-knuckled hands fused on the pistol's grip. Her face was pale, her eyes bulged. A nervous swallow slid down her throat. "Get over there. In the corner."

"The bed's more comfortable. . . ."

"Move."

He meandered in the direction of the corner, loosing a quiet whistle as he walked.

"Stop that. This is serious."

He backed into the corner and crossed his arms. Legs spread, naked, he grinned at her. "It doesn't feel serious."

"It will if I fire at you." She kept the gun trained on him while she gathered up all his clothing and threw it out the window.

He surged toward her. "Hey—"

"Back off."

Suddenly it wasn't funny anymore. It wasn't a seduction, and it wasn't a game. Not to her anyway.

His cocky grin fizzled. He studied her, looking for a tremble in the barrel of the gun, or a sheen of sweat on her brow. But she stood curiously calm, legs spread, both hands locked on the gun's grip.

All at once he understood what was happening, and it started a slow, burning anger inside him. "You *are* Joe Martin's spy."

She laughed bitterly and put on her boots. "Hardly."

"Joe's not out there anymore, you know. He left right after we got here. Ask the lookout if you don't believe me."

"Then I'll find my way back alone." Keeping the gun pointed at him, she grabbed his half-full canteen and bedroll.

He frowned. "You saw it out there, Lainie. You'll die."

"Maybe." She backed to the door and opened it behind her. Slipping through, she banged it shut.

Then, as quickly as she'd appeared in his life, she was out of it.

Lainie hurtled down the road, trying to look inconspicuous and failing miserably. Men were everywhere. They slipped out of their tents and cabins and milled about, watching.

She came to the mouth of the tunnel and skidded to a stop. A shudder of fear and revulsion moved through her, made it hard to take another step. She stared into the blackness, smelling the dank odor, remembering the twisting labyrinth that lay beyond. Her heart was pounding so hard, she couldn't think or hear. She could barely breathe as she took her first step into the darkness.

Behind her, a gun clicked. Lainie froze. Cursing beneath her breath, she slowly turned around.

A bearded man stood about ten feet away. His gun was drawn. Men curled around him in a dirty, menacing horseshoe. "Hello, little lady," he said in a scratchy voice.

She swallowed hard. "You're the lookout, I suppose."

He used his gun to tip the hat back on his head. "I am. And you ain't—"

Raucous voices cut him off. All the men started talking at once. Booming, hacking laughter spiked the air, echoed off the mesa walls.

Suddenly Killian shoved through the crowd of men. Stark naked, he strode toward her.

Lainie's knees went weak. "Oh, no . . ."

He gave her a cold, predatory grin. "Never count on an outlaw's modesty."

Before she could answer, he slung her over his shoulder. Her face smacked into the hard curl of his butt. A firm globe of pale flesh filled her vision.

Male voices clamored to be heard above the laughing din.

"Hey, boss, poke her one for me!"

"Reckon that's one piece you oughta tie to the bed!"

Lainie slammed her eyes shut and clenched her teeth together.

Killian shoved through the crowd and marched back to his cabin. Lainie bounced against his back with every punishing step. He didn't stop at the door, just kicked it open and pushed through, slamming it shut behind him.

Before she'd even realized he'd stopped, he flipped her over his shoulder again. She stumbled backward and hit the cabin wall, wincing as pain bit through her shoulder blades. She closed her eyes, blocking out the sight of him.

But even blinded, she felt his presence, was achingly aware of every step he took, every creaking snap of the floorboards. Heat brushed against her face, the air rustled, carrying with it the now familiar scent of dust and smoke and man.

"Open your eyes, Lainie," he whispered, and he was so close, she could feel the movement of his breath against her lips.

She cracked one eye open and immediately wished she hadn't.

He was a hairsbreadth in front of her, his naked body so close, she could feel the heat of him against her clothing. Arms framed her head, fists pressed against the wall on either side of it. His face was tilted down to hers, filled her field of vision so completely that the cabin faded to nothingness behind him.

"You don't learn very quickly. Where were you going?"

She forced herself to meet his gaze. "I asked you for help," she said. "You said no, so I was going alone."

He drew back from her, just enough so that he could look into her eyes. "Alone." The word was a curse. "You don't get it, do you? There is no alone for you, Lainie. You belong to me."

"Dream on."

Softer. Closer. "You belong to me, Lainie. I could do anything to you in here and no one would stop me." His lips almost touched hers. "Anything . . ."

"There's nothing that can make me belong to you, Killian. Believe me, I know. I can survive *anything*. No matter what you do, I'll escape. You can't watch me every minute of every day."

"Oh, really? I could tie you to the bed."

Fear spilled through Lainie in an ice-cold wash. She stiffened, tried to pretend the threat meant nothing, that it didn't frighten her. She looked up at him suddenly, caught his gaze, and saw in the narrowing of his eyes that she'd failed, that he saw her fear.

He pulled back, frowning. "You can't leave here, Lainie."

Can't leave. The two words scared her more than she would have thought possible. She thought of Kelly coming home to an empty house, and she started to shake. With great effort, she lifted her heavy chin and stared up at him. Her eyes glazed with tears. "I want to go home. Is that so impossible for you to believe?"

He stared down at her, and she thought for one insane moment that he was going to touch her. But he didn't, he remained still and stiff. Then he grabbed her arm and led her toward the bed, shoving her down on the lumpy mattress.

"Please," she said again. The word came out throaty and harsh.

He flinched and grabbed a pair of pants. Stabbing his legs into them, he buttoned the fly and sat across from her. The mattress sagged and the bed creaked beneath his weight. "Who are you?"

She stared down at her hands, unable to meet his gaze. "I'm no threat to you or the men. If you take me back to the Flats, I'll never say a word about this place."

He leaned back against the skinned log bedpost and studied her. When he finally spoke, his voice was soft. "Everyone knows where this place is. Our safety is not in the secrecy, but in the defendability."

"Oh." It was all she could manage.

"Look at me."

Reluctantly she looked up into his face. He was staring down at her, his eyes narrowed and dark. There was an intensity in his look that pulled the breath from her body and left her feeling strangely exposed.

His hold on her eased slightly. He drew back, watching her closely. "If you've got a story to tell, lady, you'd better tell it now."

"You wouldn't believe me," she said softly, depressed by the truth of her words.

"Are you so sure?"

She gave a sharp, bitter laugh. "Believe me, I'm sure. *I* don't believe me."

He let her go and walked to the table. Pulling out a chair, he sat down and crossed his arms. Then he looked at her, and this time there was no compassion in his gaze, no softness or caring or concern. There was only a searing coldness that seemed to cut through the distance between them. He looked every inch the outlaw, the man used to getting what he wanted with a loaded gun.

"Tell me," he said, and Lainie knew in that second that she would lose. Whatever battle she waged with this man, she would lose. Her only hope lay in telling him the truth, and hoping that the man she'd seen on the ledge really existed. That deep inside the outlaw was the remnant of the lawman he'd once been.

She swiped at her tears, hoping he hadn't noticed, but of course, he had. He noticed everything. "It started two days ago. In 1994."

Chapter Eleven

"What?"

She gave him a weary look. "Sit back down. It gets worse."

Killian stared at her. She sat on the bed, hunched over, her hands clasped in her lap. The ridiculous sweater hung off one shoulder, revealing a curl of pale skin. There was no trace of laughter in her bright eyes, no hint that she was toying with him. The look she gave him was pathetic and earnest.

Slowly he lowered himself back into the chair. "Go on."

"My name is Alaina Costanza." She held up a hand before he could interrupt. "I know you know that, but I wanted to start at the beginning. I'm Alaina, and I was born . . . in 1958."

He stared at her, blank for a second. When he realized what she was saying, he started to laugh, but the sound died in his throat when he looked at her stricken face. "Jesus Christ, you expect me to believe that?"

She sighed quietly, a sorrow-filled sound that somehow touched his tired heart. "I don't expect anything. I'm just telling you my story." She attempted a smile. "It gets weirder, in fact."

"Go on."

"I've tried to sort through it, make some sense of it,

but I can't. All I know is, two days ago I was sitting in front of my computer, writing this book, and now I'm here in 1896." She wet her lower lip, then bit it hard.

He shook his head, completely at a loss. He wanted to laugh and throw her out of his life, but something about the way she looked right now, the vulnerability and pain in her eyes, made him hesitate. He felt a spark of compassion for her, and it pissed him off. "Jesus, Lainie—"

She was on her feet and kneeled in front of him in a heartbeat. "Look at me, Killian. I'm wearing ratty old Levi's, a sweater that can't possibly be in style, a bra that won't be invented for one hundred years, and my ears are triple-pierced. How often do you meet women like me?"

Never. The answer came out of the blue, surprising him. He stiffened and drew back. The look in her eyes, so needy and vulnerable, set off a chain reaction of memories. He winced and gritted his teeth, forcibly looking away from her.

"Look at me, Killian. Please . . ."

He didn't have the strength to ignore her, but sweet Christ, he wanted to. The soft, tremulous way she said *please*, as if he—*he*—could help her, sucked him into a cold, frightening darkness.

"Killian . . ."

He made a sharp sound, half desperate groan, half angry growl, and forced himself to look at her. For the first time, her bizarre clothing suggested something else, something impossible.

He rolled his eyes. Jesus, she was making him lose what little mind he had. He had to get some perspective here. "Viloula wears pants, and if you called her a man, she'd smack you one."

"And my hair?"

"Your barber shouldn't have been given scissors, let alone been allowed to cut your hair, but it hardly means you're from the future. Hell, Arizona's hair looks like a rabbit's been gnawing at it—he isn't from 1994."

Her voice dropped to a whisper. "And my clothes?"

He shrugged. "Women disguise themselves as men in the West. It's safer sometimes."

She held up her hands and gave a weary sigh. "Okay, okay, I get your point. How can I prove it to you?"

He laughed, but it was a hollow, empty sound. "Tell me my future."

She gave him a disarmingly honest look. "How could I? I could tell you who the next president will be, what year we first send someone to the moon, anything—but how could you check it? Why would you believe it?"

"I wouldn't."

"If I'm not from the future, how did I get here? How do I know so much about you and your men?"

"You're a spy for Joe Martin. He sent you here to get evidence against me so that you could help him lock me up. Joe's been looking for a witness against me for years. Only he didn't count on me kidnapping you."

"And who told him when you were going to rob the bank?"

"An information leak from my side." He shook his head. "I don't like the idea, I'll admit. But it's a damn sight easier to believe than time travel."

"I'm not Joe Martin's spy, Killian. I swear it." She looked up at him. "I know it sounds crazy, but I've got to get back to Fortune Flats. Nothing else matters. If you could just take me there . . . please . . ."

Suddenly, and for the first time, he was scared of her. Scared shitless. What he wanted to do was shove her away and run, run far and fast and put as much as he could between him and her pathetic eyes.

His jaw tightened at the quavering desperation in her voice. It flung him back in time, made him remember what he hadn't remembered in years. Maybe he had been the kind of man to help people, but that was ages ago, a lifetime. And there was no going back.

Since then, he'd made a choice with his life; he wanted to be alone, without responsibility for anyone except himself. That's why he was here, in The Ridge, living with ruthless outlaws and fools. No one expected anything of him here, and he never let them down. He never wanted to be responsible for someone else's life again. He wasn't any good at it, wasn't any good, period. People—women—who entrusted their lives to him ended up dead.

He stared at the walls, barely breathing, using everything he had inside to dredge up a dull, disinterested voice. "What's in Fortune Flats?"

It took her so long to answer that reluctantly he looked down at her. He knew instantly that it was the wrong thing to do.

She gave a tiny shake of the head. At the movement, a single tear fell down her cheek, and he had an absurd impulse to wipe it away. "I don't know, but it's where I landed. I thought maybe it would be the way out."

He blew an angry sigh. "Why are you telling me this shit?"

"I need your help."

Anger brought him to his feet. She stumbled back and fell on her butt. He grabbed her by the shoulders, his fingers digging into the soft flesh of her upper arms, and yanked her to her feet.

Her head snapped back. Tears glazed her eyes, made them look fathomless and dark. The expression in them, the sadness, hit him like a punch to the gut.

"What in the Christ do you want from me?"

"I need a guide back to Fortune Flats. That's not asking so much."

He shook her, hard, then drew her close. The words *Fortune Flats* flitted through his mind, but he barely heard them. All he heard were the pounding, impossible words *I need*. Fear and anger exploded in his chest. "It's too goddamn much from me," he growled, shoving her back. "And quit looking at me like that."

She stumbled back but didn't look away. Another tear slid down her cheeks, splashed on her throat. "There's no one else to help me."

"Too bad."

The look she gave him was hot, as vital as a touch, and it made his throat constrict. "Jesus Christ," he hissed, stumbling back from her, trying to put some distance between them. "Don't you understand? I can't help you."

"You mean won't," she said in a frayed voice that made him feel like shit.

And suddenly, as quickly as it had come, the anger was gone. Instead, he was filled with a cold, aching regret. Memories hurled themselves at him in rapid-fire succession, made him almost lift his hands to ward them off. "No," he said in a hoarse voice. "I can't."

She moved toward him. He heard each footstep, felt it like a blow to the heart. Right in front of him, she stopped. He stiffened, stared past her, seeing only the blankness of the walls, and the darkness of his memories.

"You were a hero once."

He drew in a sharp breath, backed away from her. "What do you mean?"

"Back when you were a ranger." She stared steadily up at him, her gaze unflinching in its honesty. "Some of that must still be inside of you."

Time slowed to a crawl. The cabin spilled away, left them standing toe to toe in a darkness where nothing existed except the two of them. He heard the slow, even strains of her breathing and the thudding of his own heart. Her words settled on his chest, cold and heavy and suffocating. "How do you know that about me?"

"I wrote it."

He grabbed her again, pulled her close. "Don't get glib with me, damn it. What else do you know about me?"

"Everything."

Slowly he let her go, surprised to find that his fingers were shaking. He stepped back and tried to get a handle on his emotions. It had been so long since someone had mentioned his past. With suddenly cold fingers, he rolled a cigarette and lit up. A hazy film of smoke obscured her for a second, veiled that wrenching sadness in her eyes. He turned and walked across the cabin, putting as much distance between them as he could. Then he sat down. The whining creak of old wood exploded in the too quiet room.

He let out an even breath and forced himself to calm down. She couldn't know everything about him. If she did, she wouldn't ask him for help. No woman who knew about his past would make that mistake. "So what do you know about me?"

Lainie flinched at the question. It felt as if a grenade had just landed in her lap, without the pin. She dragged her tongue along her cracked, dry lower lip and looked at him, suddenly afraid. The seconds crawled by, ticked, ticked.

"Now!" he barked.

She flinched and sank back on her heels beside the bed. The hard wood of the floor bit into her knees, but she barely noticed. He sat across the room from her, smoking, leaning forward on the chair. There was an intensity in his eyes that scared her, a coiled power in his body that reminded her of a hunting cat. She cleared her throat and met his angry gaze. "You are John MacArthur Killian, born 1866 in Scotland. You arrived in America in 1880 with ten bucks in your pocket. You became a Texas Ranger, and were a good one, until . . ."

He stilled, seemed almost to stop breathing. The smoke drifted across his eyes. "Go on."

Lainie had to force the words up her dry throat. "Until . . . Emily . . . died."

"How did she die?" he asked quietly.

"There was an outlaw—I don't think I named him—"

"Rem Clide," he answered steadily.

She frowned. "Really? I don't think I named him. . . ."

"Go on."

"Anyway, the outlaw and his gang, they . . ." She winced, remembering the violence of the scene. She dropped her head, unable to look at him. It had been therapy for her, something she'd known that someday she'd have to write, but still it had sickened her. "They raped and killed her. . . ."

The chair creaked. He let out his breath in a long sigh, and she heard the pain in the sound, felt it as if it were her own. Slowly she brought her gaze up from her own hands and looked at him.

Sorrow and regret deepened the harsh lines in his face, made him look older, harder. "You're close," he said at last, and this time his voice sounded raw and forced.

"Close? I'm exactly right."

He looked at her then, and in his eyes she saw a bleak despair that was all too familiar. She'd felt it a million times in her life. "No."

She frowned. How could she be wrong about anything? It wasn't possible. She'd created him. That shifting, suffocating sense of weirdness descended on her again, left her feeling unsure and off balance. "Where am I wrong?"

He shrugged, as if the discrepancies didn't matter. "I was born in 1853."

She shook her head, calculating his age. That birthdate would make him forty-three. He looked forty-three; hell, he looked older than that. But still, it wasn't possible. She'd created him, devised all the vital statistics of his life. He was twenty-eight years old. "No . . ."

"Yeah, and Emily . . ." He looked away. When he finally spoke, his rich voice was strained. "Emily wasn't murdered."

"What?"

"You heard me."

"But . . . but I wrote that scene. It wasn't just part of your character biography, not just background information. I wrote the scene, word for word. I *know* what happened."

"You're wrong."

Lainie was so stunned that for a moment she couldn't speak. "But . . ." Her voice was barely a whisper. "How . . . then?"

He gave a quick, almost undetectable shake of his head.

Silence fell between them. She knew she couldn't breach it, and that he wouldn't. They would sit this way forever, both feeling battered and alone, staring at each other, but seeing something else entirely.

She saw all her notes on Killian, strewn out across her desk. She'd charted and examined and written down every moment of his life, every aspect of his personality. She knew him—she thought—inside and out. But she was wrong. Somehow, she was wrong.

She looked at him. He was sitting stiffly, his face obscured behind a curtain of gray smoke. He was staring at her, but his eyes had a glassy, faraway look. Her words had opened a doorway to the past, and he'd fallen in.

With a start, she realized that she had no idea what he was thinking about, what he was remembering. Here was a man she'd created, invented, and now, impossibly, she had no idea what he was thinking. Or who he was.

What was happening here?

Suddenly he surged to his feet and kicked the chair away from him. It skidded across the floor and crashed into the wall. "Enough," he hissed, yanking open the door and throwing his half-smoked cigarette outside.

She scrambled to her feet. "Killian, please, all I need is—"

"I don't give a shit what you need." He scowled at her. "Don't say anything else. You got it?"

At the anger in his voice her last tenuous thread of hope snapped. He wouldn't help her. There was none of the hero left in this villain she'd created. He was as hard and mean and bitter as the past she'd given him. She'd been a fool to think otherwise, to think, even for a second, that he would help her.

She fought the urge to sag to her knees again. Instead, forcibly, she lifted her head and stared at him. "I asked for your help, but I don't need it. I can leave here on my own."

"You haven't been paying attention, Lainie. I'm God here."

She laughed bitterly. "One of the benefits of surrounding yourself with fools and losers."

"I picked *you* up, didn't I?"

She pushed past him and strode to the door, reaching for the latchstring.

"They'll shoot you in the back if I give the order," he said softly.

She froze midstep. Her hand fell away from the raw-hide strap. Slowly she turned around. "You wouldn't give that order."

"I already have."

She paled. "D-Don't do this. I have to get back to . . ."

His eyes narrowed. "To who?"

To her utter humiliation, she felt the tears again, stinging and hot. "Kelly," she whispered.

He frowned. "Who's Kelly?"

"My daughter."

"You're a *mother*?"

She nodded without looking at him. "Yeah. I . . . I don't want my baby to come home to an empty house." She lifted her gaze and implored him one last time with her eyes. "You know what that's like . . . coming home to an empty house . . . don't you, Killian?"

He paled, drew in a sharp breath. "Enough," he said through clenched teeth. "You want help, I'll get you help. Come on."

"Really?"

But he was already gone. He walked through the doorway and disappeared outside. Lainie lurched forward and sprinted after him, trying to match his punishing stride.

He walked and she ran down the dirt road that bisected the camp. At the last little cabin, he stopped and pounded on the door. From inside came a muffled, hoarse voice. "Come in."

Killian shoved the door open, then turned around and grabbed Lainie by the arm, dragging her into the dark interior. "Here, Viloula, I got a crazy woman for you. Keep her the hell away from me."

Chapter Twelve

The house was small and cluttered, with newspaper-covered walls and dusty wood floors. No candles were burning at this hour, no lamps were lit. The place smelled of smoke and dirty laundry, with just a hint of something sweet and cloying.

Incense.

Pale sunlight seeped through threadbare burlap curtains, catching the steel surface of a cookstove and the iron curve of a bedpost, but no more. Stacks and heaps of leather-bound books were shadows within shadows along the far wall, disjointed spires that rose alongside canned goods and bags of sugar and flour. Socks and trousers and shirts hung from the laundry line that sagged between the bedpost and a nail alongside the window.

An old, withered black woman sat motionlessly at a rickety wooden table. A half smile curved her dark lips. Her fuzzy gray hair was drawn back from her face, giving her a shrunken appearance. Swags of ebony skin folded across her cheeks, sagged at her small, pointed chin. Broken, askew spectacles hung at the very tip of her fleshy nose and magnified two intensely alert black eyes. Absently she touched the breathtakingly beautiful necklace around her throat. It was wrought gold with a huge lavender stone that caught the light in the room and tossed it back in a thousand glittering shards.

Killian dragged Lainie alongside him.

The woman pushed the spectacles higher on her nose and peered at Lainie. There was something . . . unnatural about the old woman's gaze, as if she saw things that no one else saw.

"She doan look crazy to me, Killian," she said at last in a singsongy voice that was surprisingly youthful. "She look scared."

He snorted. "What she looks like is trouble."

"So what you want wit' Viloula?"

"Find out who the hell she is and why she's here. She's got some ridiculous story about time travel."

Viloula drew in a sharp breath and looked at Lainie. "Dat true, child?"

Lainie bit her lip nervously. "It's true."

Viloula looked as if she were going to smile, but she didn't. She sat perfectly still, her face expressionless save for the piercing darkness of her eyes. "Dis make for a very interesting day. Sit down."

Lainie edged away from Killian and sat stiffly on the wooden chair across from Viloula. Her fingers dug into the splintery edge of the seat.

Killian made a snorting sound of disgust and reached for the door. "Good luck, Vi."

Viloula gave him a look that would curdle milk. "*Both* of you, sit down."

He glanced back. "I'm not listening to her horseshit, Viloula."

She crossed her skinny old arms and stuck her pointy chin out. "Den I woan neit'er."

Killian rolled his eyes and strode to the chair beside Lainie. Wrenching it backward, he sat down hard and crossed his arms, glaring at Viloula. "Happy?"

She didn't answer. Instead, she reached up to the beautiful amethyst necklace at her throat and curled her scrawny fingers around the heavy stone. "So, young Alaina. What have you to say?"

Lainie blanched. "I didn't tell you my name."

"Didn't you?" She waved a hand carelessly. "No matter. All dat matters is de traveling t'rough time. It is true?"

Lainie took a deep breath and met Viloula's potent gaze. "Either that, or I'm completely crazy. Or else this is romance writer hell—you fall into a bad plot and can't get out."

"It is not hell, child. It is Arizona. How long have you been here?"

"Two days." She cast an arch glance at Killian. "Nimrod here won't believe me."

Viloula turned to him. "Why not?"

His answer was a disgusted snort.

Lainie shook her head, ran a hand through her wild hair. "I don't blame him. It doesn't make sense. . . ."

Viloula was on her like a pouncing cat. "Under whose rules, in whose eyes?"

Lainie made a tiny shaking motion with her head. "The world has certain rules, scientific facts. People don't just . . ."

"What, Alaina? People doan just what?"

She caught Viloula's gaze, held it. The more she looked into the old woman's intense black eyes, the more she was afraid of something. She fought the fear, pushed it back. "I made this up," she whispered. "I *created* it."

Viloula laughed; it was a soft, quiet sound without malice. "So you are a god."

"No, of course not. I'm a writer."

"Ah," Viloula breathed, obviously fighting a smile. "A writer."

"I'm glad you find this so frigging funny." Lainie slammed back in her chair and crossed her arms. "I'm telling you the truth. I created this place. It's the setting for my new book."

"Lean closer, child. Put your hands out on the table."

Lainie swallowed thickly. Stretching forward, she placed her hands on the table. Viloula took hold of them, wrapped her thin, sandpapery fingers around Lainie's.

The old woman closed her eyes and began to hum softly. After a few moments, she started to sway slowly from side to side. Gradually the humming increased, grew louder, melted into some sort of dark incantation in another language. For a split second, Lainie felt an honest-to-God spark of hope.

Then, as quickly as it had begun, the music stopped, leaving behind a suffocating silence.

Viloula clasped Lainie's hands more tightly in her old, gnarled fingers. Her gaze was piercing and seemed to see into Lainie's very soul. "You t'ink you created dis place, and Killian."

Lainie nodded, saying nothing.

"And you believe dis . . . creation was pure invention."

She shrugged. "It was based on some research, of course. You know, about the time period and outlaws, the Southwest. Things like that. But the characters, I invented."

"Or t'ink you did."

Lainie gave a disgusted sigh. "Quit with the oblique references. If you have something to say, please say it. I'm aging."

"I will need to do some work, t'row de cards before I'm sure about everyt'ing, but . . ."

"But what?"

Viloula's gaze was steady, honest. "You are meant to be here. Dere's a reason."

Lainie's breath caught. Hope brought her forward in her chair. "What reason?"

"Killian," Viloula said on a sigh, a frown pulling at the heavy folds of her forehead.

"What?" Killian answered tersely.

Viloula touched her necklace, stroked it lovingly, her eyes glassy for a second. Then, sharply, she looked at Lainie. "I have questions."

"Okay. Shoot."

"Don't tempt me," Killian muttered.

"What were you doing just before you . . ."

Lainie snorted. "Fell off the face of the frigging planet? I was writing."

"Writing what?"

"This book. It's a historical romance about a woman who gets kidnapped by a villain and saved by the hero."

"Complex plot," Killian said under his breath.

Viloula ignored him. "And . . ."

Lainie looked away, staring hard at the wall. Memories besieged her, brought a sickening sense of shame and guilt. "I was drinking heavily . . . and I popped a few sleeping pills. I don't do that often, but I was . . ." She laughed bitterly. "I was . . . upset. I've thought about it and thought about it. At first I thought I was in a coma at home, and this was all a dream. But it doesn't feel like a dream. I wish to God it did."

"It is not liquor dat brought you here, Alaina. Or pills," Viloula answered softly. "*Why* were you upset?"

"Kelly." It was all she said, just the quietly spoken name. She stared down at the table, noticing the splinters and scratches in the planked wood. "She left . . . and I missed her."

"Ah ..." Viloula said softly, almost more to herself than to Lainie. "Who else left you, Alaina?"

Lainie gasped. Her head snapped up. She tried desperately to dredge up a cocky smile. "Wh-What do you mean?"

"Someone abandoned you. . . ."

Lainie wanted to respond with a laugh, but she couldn't manage it. Her throat felt thick and tight. "My parents," she said softly, feeling a familiar queasiness at the admission. Even now, after all these years, it still hurt to say it aloud.

Viloula stared at her, then slowly shook her head. "Dat was not de first time."

Lainie frowned. "I don't understand."

"History repeats itself, child, but it starts somewhere. For you, it began here in 1896 ... with Killian."

Lainie frowned. "Killian? What can he have to do with this? He's a *character*, for God's sake. What I need is a way back home."

Viloula touched the amethyst medallion at her throat, closed her eyes. The stone sparkled with a brilliant, magical lavender light. "You and Killian are joined. Your souls are connected. I see dis clearly."

"Then you'd better open your eyes, Vi," Killian said.

Lainie crammed an open hand through her ragged hair. "Could we please stay focused here?" She jerked forward, slammed her elbows down on the table, and stared hard at Viloula. "I *created* Killian. I made him up."

"No."

Lainie stiffened, felt a hairline frisson of fear against her spine. "What do you mean?"

"You created Killian, but not until after you'd met him. You re-created him."

Lainie rocked back in her chair. *"What?"*

She and Killian said the word together. It bounced off the cabin's wooden walls and vibrated for a second before it was lost.

"You'd better talk fast, Vi," Killian said in a low, gravelly voice that reeked of danger.

Viloula frowned, as if searching for the right words. "De soul is life and spirit . . . everyt'ing dat we are. It remembers all our lives."

Killian rolled his eyes. "Oh, for God's sake—"

"Dere are many ways to get in touch wit' a past life, many ways to call up de memories." She turned to Lainie, gave her a steady, honest look. "You have done it t'rough your writing, doan you see?"

Lainie shook her head. Cold fear radiated out from her spine. Suddenly she didn't want to hear what the old lady had to say. All she wanted was a guide home, a way back. "No, I don't *see*."

Viloula leaned forward. "When you write, you t'ink you are imagining. But maybe for writers it is not so simple. Maybe you are remembering instead."

"Viloula—" she pleaded, not knowing what else to say.

"It is not hard to understand. In anot'er time, you loved Killian, but somet'ing went de wrong way. It ended bad, maybe he abandon you, but in your soul— where de memories of love doan die—you remember dis man. And you write about him."

Killian frowned. "Come on, Vi. You're piling the mumbo-jumbo on pretty thick. I don't know this woman from squat."

Viloula didn't even look at Killian, she just kept staring at Lainie through those intense, unreadable black eyes. "T'ink about it. It explains why you know dis place, and Killian. You have been here, *lived* here, before."

Lainie squeezed her eyes shut. "I won't believe it."

Viloula leaned forward, whispered, "You see te trut' of it, doan you? You see dat t'ings here are different dan you t'ought. In little ways, maybe, but it is not de world you created. Not exactly. You wrote Killian as you remembered him, maybe as you wanted him to be. Part of dat will be de trut', part of it will be wrong, and some will be de imagination."

A long silence fell between them.

"This is un-goddamn-believable," Killian growled. "I brought her here to prove that she's a liar, and you back up her insane story."

"You are her soul mate, Killian," Viloula said un-flinchingly. "Dis is de knowledge you sought from me."

He lurched to his feet. "What in the *Christ* is a soul mate? No! Don't answer that. I don't want to know."

"Look at her, you old fool," Viloula hissed, her voice rising suddenly, taking on a new power. "*Look*. Den tell me dere is no familiarity, no sense dat you have known her before."

He turned, stared into Lainie's eyes. She felt a shiver move through her at the intensity of his gaze. She tried to look away, but couldn't. She had a sudden, unex-pected reaction to the sight of him. Unaccountably, she remembered the ledge and the other times when she'd looked at him and seen more than the character she'd created. A glimmer of *maybe* flitted through her head, brought with it a crushing sense of fear.

"See?" Viloula's voice was hushed and seductive, and Lainie felt it draw her into the fantasy. Even as the thought of a soul mate terrified her, it romanced her. What would it mean? she wondered fleetingly. What would it feel like to be treasured, loved, cared for?

"I know you as well as anyone does, Killian," the old woman said in her hypnotic voice. "I understand dis world, your world. It is a place of guns and death. Now, for de first time, you must see wit' your heart."

He seemed for a second to have stopped breathing, he went so still. An unfathomable emotion darkened his eyes to black. "What makes you think it'd be the first time?"

Spinning away from them, he strode for the door, reached for the latchstring.

"Killian?" Viloula called out.

He stopped, but didn't turn around. "Yeah?"

"I am sorry."

There was a long pause before he answered. "Don't be. You couldn't have known." Then he pushed through the door and disappeared.

Lainie stared at the closed door for a long time, trying to gather her thoughts. They were swirling around her, sucking her into a rising sense of panic. Soul mates . . . lost loves . . . second chances. What did it all mean?

It overwhelmed her. Suddenly she had nothing to believe in, nothing to hang on to. All she'd ever had, since the agony of her childhood, was her own courage and her daughter's goodness. That was all. It had always been enough, but now it was woefully inadequate. She needed something more. She needed . . . faith, and it was the one thing she'd never had.

She sighed, feeling old and inexpressibly tired. As always, she'd have to go on without it. Somehow, she had to find a way back to Kelly, and it didn't matter what she believed in or didn't believe in.

Kelly. As always, the name was enough to calm her. She took a deep breath and thought for a second about her daughter, the love of her life.

Kelly was what mattered, only Kelly.

It was time to cut through the shit. Who cared about soul mates and life choices and chances to solve old problems? She had something a lot more pressing to handle right now.

She gave Viloula a steely look, feeling stronger. "So you're saying that Killian is my soul mate, but I don't recognize him or feel anything for him."

"I t'ink you should feel *somet'ing* for him. . . ."

Lainie nodded curtly. "Yeah, right. The point is, I don't care. I just want to get home."

Viloula frowned. The heavy flesh of her brow pleated. "But you need to be here. Somet'ing happened in de past dat made your future impossible. You have to stay here and solve it to—"

"Solve it?" Lainie threw herself backward in her chair and crossed her arms. "Look, Viloula, I don't need some mumbo-jumbo about realigning my karma or changing the past to help me in the future. I need to get back."

"Back? But you're here. Dere's no going back."

The words drove through Lainie like a knife. She got to her feet and stumbled backward, slamming against the wall. "Don't say that."

Viloula pushed heavily to her feet and moved toward Lainie. She wore a thick flannel shirt and ratty wool pants, hitched tight around her small waist by a fist-wide man's belt. Frowning, she moved toward Lainie. "What is it?"

"I have to go back," Lainie whispered. "It's Kelly."

"What about dis Kelly?"

"She's my daughter."

Viloula stopped dead. "A child?"

Tears gathered in Lainie's eyes again. It was too much for her suddenly, more than she could handle. "My baby," she murmured, hugging herself. "I have to get back to my baby."

Viloula buried her face in her hands. A quiet moan

escaped her. "Sweet Jesus. Sweet Jesus, a child. A *child*. None of de books say anyt'ing about getting back to a child."

He was in deep shit.

Killian stood in the doorway of his half-assed excuse for a home and stared out at the encampment. Sunlight glanced off the naked, textured surface of the sandstone cliffs, turned the rock from gray to gold. Everything was still and quiet. Frost clung stubbornly to the rooftops and tents, sparkling like glitter-dust in the sunlight.

The air in the hideout seemed thick this morning, almost stagnant. No birds swooped and dove yet, or chattered in early morning call. No wind whistled through the cottonwood leaves. It was preternaturally quiet.

Killian let out a steady breath and eased forward, leaning against the doorjamb, watching Viloula's cabin. A confusing mix of emotions left him feeling uneasy and vaguely restless. He didn't for a second believe that crap of Vi's about him and Lainie being soul mates, but he had to admit—at least now, in the solitude of his own cabin—that there was something between them. Something strange and unexpected and frightening.

You know what that's like, Killian, coming home to an empty house. . . .

The words slammed through him again, made him wince.

A grim, bitter smile curved his lips but didn't light his eyes. That's why he'd taken her to Viloula's. It had had nothing to do with using the old woman's obeah magic. He'd just wanted to get away from Lainie, away from the wrenching sadness in her eyes and the quiver of desperation in her voice. And the impossible connection he felt when he looked at her.

She knew him; knew the dark, ugly secrets of that

empty house on the prairie. Knew the secrets that haunted him and the realities that had driven him from civilization fifteen years ago and turned him into the ruthless, selfish outlaw he'd become. Somehow . . . she knew.

"Jesus," he cursed. Reaching back into the cabin, he yanked his flannel work shirt out of the corner, where he'd thrown it some weeks back. It smelled of woodsmoke and dust and decay. He reached into the breast pocket and pulled out an old bag of tobacco. Rolling a cigarette, he lit it and took a long, thoughtful drag. Smoke wreathed his face, blurred his vision for a second, and stung his eyes. The sharp, familiar scent filled his nostrils.

He leaned against the doorjamb and took another drag. He could see her silhouette through the dirty window. She stood stiff and erect. He wondered fleetingly if she still looked so sad, still looked as if she'd never had a friend in her life and never really been one.

All she'd asked him for was a little help.

Help. Need. The words drove through him, sliced through the defenses he'd set up so long ago. It was surprising how badly they hurt; even worse, even more painful, was the realization that he couldn't help her. He'd known it, of course, known for years that he was a worthless excuse for a man. But somewhere, in the back of his mind, he'd always thought that maybe someday he could go back, become once again the young man filled with dreams and fueled by honor.

He smiled bitterly. Now he knew the truth; he'd known it the second she asked him for help. There was no honor left in him, if in fact it had ever really been there. It was one of the things he'd left behind so long ago, one of the many things that died in that little house on the windy prairie. He couldn't help her. Hell, he couldn't help anyone.

People who counted on John Killian died alone.

He flinched at the thought of Emily. He still couldn't believe he'd mentioned her to Lainie.

Why? Why had he mentioned his wife?

The question drew the strength from him for a moment. He hadn't said his wife's name aloud in ten years, maybe more. And yet, with Lainie, it had come naturally.

Why? The question was cold and stark. It jabbed him, pierced the armor he'd spent a lifetime creating.

He told himself it had been because he'd wanted to prove to her that she was wrong, and he wanted to believe it. He wanted it more than he'd wanted anything in years.

But he couldn't quite manage it. He was many things—a cheat, a loser, an outlaw—but he wasn't a liar, especially not to himself. He'd always looked life square in the eyes and taken the heat head-on.

He'd told Lainie because, somehow, he'd needed to tell her. And that wasn't even the most frightening realization. He'd told her the truth because she'd needed to hear it, part of it anyway.

She'd needed it; he'd known that somehow, and it had moved him to respond.

He cursed harshly and threw his cigarette to the ground. It lay there, rocking, its red and gray tip smoldering against the cold, hard dirt. A pathetic wisp of smoke trailed upward, melting away in the air.

He glanced down at Viloula's place again, drawn in spite of himself to look for her. She was still standing in front of the window. Instinctively he knew that she was afraid. He *felt* her fear, tasted it on his tongue, smelled it in the freshness of the morning air. It was as if it were his fear, too.

"Christ," he cursed softly, and rubbed his tired eyes, shaking his head. He was losing his mind. Pretty soon he was going to start believing that bullshit about time travel and soul mates and love that lasts forever.

He backed into his cabin and shut the door. Shadows rushed in and cut off the weak heat of the morning sunlight. Dust filtered down onto his head from the timbered rafters.

He had to stay away from her. He knew it, believed it with every bit of rationality in his mind. If he was smart, he'd throw her on the back of a horse and take her to Fortune Flats, then put her on a train bound for anywhere.

Vaya con Dios, crazy lady.

She could tell Joe Martin whatever she wanted about Killian's Ridge. The law knew everything there was to know about it anyway. She couldn't hurt him with her words.

But she could kill him with her eyes. There was a darkness inside her, a pain that mirrored his own.

It was that understanding, that empathetic knowledge, that scared the hell out of him. He'd never felt it for another human being except Emily, and that had taken years to develop. Yet he'd felt it for Lainie from the moment he'd seen her lying on the desert floor, bound, gagged, and vulnerable.

No doubt about it. He ought to stay the hell away from her.

But he wouldn't. He knew that. Because today when she'd looked up at him through those teary, frightened eyes and asked for help, he'd felt something. Something he hadn't felt in years. For a second, he'd almost wanted to say yes.

And with that thought, that realization, he was plunged back into the cold darkness of a hell he thought he'd walked away from years ago.

Chapter Thirteen

"Come here, Alaina. I will make you a cup of tea."

Lainie barely heard the words. She stood at the window, her arms wrapped tightly around herself, her eyes aching with tears that wouldn't fall. Sunlight had long since erupted over the mesa top, gilding the ridge. Heat pushed through the dirty glass and traced her cheeks, but still she was cold inside. So cold.

Viloula took ahold of her elbow and maneuvered her to a chair. Lainie let herself be led, too tired to fight it. The strong, humid scent of boiling water filled the tiny cabin, gave it a homey feel.

Viloula went to the stove, then returned with a cup of steaming hot tea and a piece of cold corn bread smothered in butter. "Eat dis."

Viloula sat down at the table across from Lainie, scooting close. "You look so unhappy, child," she said in a tired voice.

"Wouldn't you be?"

Viloula closed her eyes and nodded slowly. "You must love her very much."

Lainie squeezed her eyes shut, battling tears.

"Maybe dat's what dis is all about," Viloula said quietly. "Just somet'ing simple. Like love."

Lainie opened her eyes. "I don't think I'm up to talking about this craziness anymore, Vi. Just give me a second, okay?"

Viloula took a sip of her tea, then set her cup down with a clink. She eased the spectacles down her nose and peered at Lainie above the bent metal rim. A gentle smile curved her thin lips.

Lainie felt a jolt of hot emotion at the look. She'd never seen one like it before, though she'd waited all her life for it and long ago given up. It was the loving glance of a mother to a daughter, a caring concern that warmed a place inside of Lainie, a place that had been cold and dark and lonely for years.

"I saw you looking at my necklace before," Viloula said quietly. "You like it?"

Too shaken to do anything else, Lainie lowered her gaze to the stunning jewel at Viloula's throat. The lavender stone glimmered with hidden light. "It's beautiful."

"It is much more dan dat." She leaned forward. "It is a *magic* necklace."

"Oh," Lainie said, for lack of anything better.

"Ever since you got to camp, de stone has been hot on my skin. And I have . . . known t'ings."

"Like what?"

"Like . . . you were coming."

Lainie sighed. "But not going."

"Who knows what will happen, Alaina? God is mysterious in His ways."

"That's for sure. He slings my butt back in time one hundred years, and for what? Because I have a soul mate who is pining away for me? Whose undying love called me back through time?" She snorted. "Yeah, right."

Viloula didn't flinch at the derision in Lainie's voice. "T'ink of it, Alaina. *Imagine* it. A love dat not'ing, not even death or time, can kill."

Lainie shook her head. "I'm too old to believe in fairy tales, Viloula. I just want to get back to Kelly."

"You are never too old to believe in love, Alaina. Look at me. I have only been in love once in my whole life—and wit' a bear of a man who lost his arm and t'ought I couldn't love him anymore. Dere was never anyone else for me. But I keep believing dere will be."

"Sounds like Alzheimer's to me," Lainie muttered, but even as she spoke the bitter words, she felt something strange happen inside her. It was as if the words she tried so hard to discount had landed, taken root in that cold, forgotten corner of her heart.

What if.

To Lainie, they'd always been magical words, a writer's lifeblood. The beginning of every story. *What if . . .*

"What if is right," Viloula whispered. "What if Killian once loved you so much dat you remembered it one hundred years later, t'rough another woman's heart? What if you loved him so much, you came back t'rough time to find him again?"

Lainie squeezed her eyes shut tighter, refusing to let herself be drawn into another useless, pointless fantasy. She'd engaged in this kind of wishful thinking a million times in her life. It didn't work. "And I thought I was the romance writer."

"Just t'ink about it. Dat's all I'm saying."

"I don't want to think about it." Despite her best efforts, her voice sounded weak and unsure, a throwback to the frightened, lonely child she'd once been.

"Yes, you do. Dat's why you are here. Your heart remembers. . . . Somewhere inside you, your heart remembers."

Lainie sighed tiredly, fighting the allure of the old woman's words. It was just a theory, a wish and a prayer by a woman who believed in both to a woman who believed in neither. It didn't matter that once, years ago—a lifetime—Lainie had believed intensely in white knights and soul mates and everlasting love, that she'd spent night upon night waiting to be rescued by someone who loved her, someone who cared. She'd come a long way since then. She wasn't the little girl at the barred window anymore, waiting for someone to change her life. Now she was a woman full grown who made her own way.

"I don't remember Killian, Viloula. I don't know him and I don't love him and we aren't soul mates, and even if we are, I don't care."

There was a long pause before Viloula answered, and in the silence, Lainie felt a tightening in her spine, a growing sense of apprehension. *Don't say any more*, she thought desperately. *Don't make me want to believe again. . . .*

"Kelly," Viloula said at last. "She is your daughter, right? De only person you have ever loved?"

Lainie frowned, confused by the sudden change in topic, but she breathed a sigh of relief nonetheless. Anything was better than talking about soul mates. "Yeah."

Viloula gave her a sharp, knowing look. "De name is very close to Killian."

The implication was so powerful, so unexpected, that for a second, Lainie couldn't breathe. She sat perfectly still, her mouth parted on a quiet gasp. "Oh, my God . . ."

Viloula nodded slowly, her expression earnest. "De heart remembers what de mind cannot."

Lainie sputtered. "E-Even if that were true, you can't love someone again just because you loved him in another life. We're different people, with different experiences; it can't—"

"God can make anyt'ing happen."

"But it doesn't make sense."

Viloula gave her a sad nod. "I doan t'ink it is supposed to."

Lainie started to sink more deeply into her chair. Again she wanted to give up, to disappear. The realization angered her, reminded her that she couldn't afford the luxury of depression. She pushed back in the chair and pitched to her feet. "That's enough. I just want to know one thing: Can you get me out of this time, Viloula? Can you tell me where to go or what to try?"

Viloula's face creased with worry. "Killian is de answer."

"What do you mean?"

"If Killian is de reason you're here, den you have some problem to solve with him or some lesson to learn."

"Uh-huh."

"De lesson is de doorway. You cannot escape from dis time; you can only leave." She nodded and whispered, "Destiny."

"Then I'm leaving tomorrow. I've got a child to think about. Enough sermonizing about lost loves and misaligned karma. Tomorrow—unless you come up with a better idea—I'm heading for Fortune Flats alone."

"Killian won't let you go."

Lainie didn't flinch. "Then I'll kill him."

Viloula started to say something else, but Lainie wasn't listening. She turned and reached for the door.

"Wait."

She glanced behind her. Viloula stood against the wall, her hands clasped at her waist. "I did not say I could not help. I jus said dat Killian is de answer. Dere is much I can do to help you. Dere's de cards, de palms . . . ot'er t'ings to help me understand your destiny."

Lainie's breath caught. She hadn't really expected to be helped in this journey; she'd expected to do it as she did everything. Alone.

She moved quickly back to the table and sat down, more than half afraid that Viloula would suddenly change her mind, laugh, and say it was all a joke. That there really was no way home.

Viloula reached for a small wooden box from beside her bed and drew it to her chest. Pale light spilled through the window and wreathed her. The dark folds of her skin looked velvet-soft in the glow, her eyes glittered with secrets.

Lainie paused. "Should I be afraid of what we're going to do here?"

"Afraid?" Viloula frowned, apparently thinking. Then, finally, she nodded. "Yes," she said quietly. "I t'ink dere is much to fear."

Viloula shuffled the cards slowly, her gnarled fingers working in a jerky, disjointed fashion. The sandpapery whirring of the falling cards was the only noise in the quiet cabin.

Lainie sat stiffly at the table, knees and ankles pressed firmly together. She stared at the multicolored fan of the cards and felt another stirring of fear.

She tried to make light of her uncertainty, but her voice cracked and gave her away. "Y-You're sure those tarot cards aren't the devil's work, now? I've got enough problems without facing an exorcism."

Unsmiling, Viloula laid out seven cards in the fanlike shape of a human hand. "Dis card . . ." She pointed to the card at the heel of the hand. "Dis is what knowledge you have from de past. Touch it wit' de heel of your hand and turn it over."

Lainie did as she was told.

"Lovers," Viloula said softly, and smiled. "Now, turn over de ring finger. It is de karmic lesson you must learn."

Lainie touched the card with her ring finger and turned it over.

Viloula frowned. "De tower. It mean great destruction . . . a battle wit' de dark side of yourself. You must make a great change. Hmmm . . ."

"Lovely."

"Now, de little finger."

Lainie felt an unexpected twinge of nerves. Irritated by it, she touched the card with her pinky and flipped it over. A chill passed through her at the sight of the card. *Death.*

Viloula hissed quietly.

Lainie lurched back from the table and smacked the cards away. They piled together; a few fluttered to the floor. "I don't want to do this anymore. I want to read books." She gestured to the hundreds of books stacked along the wall.

Viloula looked up at her. "I learned somet'ing from dat."

"Yeah? What?"

She gave Lainie a knowing look. "Dere is a great darkness inside of you. You must face it to learn your lesson."

"Unfortunately I'll die in the process. Thanks a bunch."

"Sit down, Alaina." When she complied, Viloula went on. "Dat card can mean many t'ings beside death—change, loss, good-bye."

Lainie forced a smile, though she didn't feel like it. "Well, that's a relief. So where do we go from here?"

Viloula seemed to hesitate. Her gaze darted to a small

glass jar in the windowsill. "Dere are other t'ings we can try. Runes, palm reading . . ."

"Well, let's get started. Kelly will be home soon."

Viloula pulled her gaze away from the little bottle and frowned at Lainie. "What makes you t'ink time passes in the same way here as it does in the future?"

Lainie felt a cold rush of fear. She'd never thought otherwise, never allowed herself to think that maybe Kelly was already home, maybe all this was already over. "Oh, God, Vi . . . I just assumed . . ."

"When did you leave?"

"I left on August twelfth."

Viloula glanced at the yellowed calendar nailed to the wall behind her stove. "It is de fourteenth of August now."

Lainie let out her breath in a relieved sigh. "Thank God."

"You've got time on your side."

Lainie laughed. It was a harsh, bitter sound. "Hardly."

Silence fell between them, thick and strained for a minute, then Lainie forced a smile. "Come on, Vi," she said softly, "let's get to work. My *soul mate* could decide to shoot me any minute."

Killian sat back in his chair, trying to concentrate on the cards in his hand. He saw them in a blur of red; Queen, ten, seven, four, and three of hearts.

"You in or out, Kill?" Hambone Davis asked in a thick, alcohol-slurred voice.

It was the best hand Killian had all evening and he couldn't care enough to answer. All he could think about was the woman, Lainie, and the way she'd made him feel.

"Killian? For Chrissakes—"

"I'm in," he said softly, slapping a couple of gold pieces down on the table. "Call."

Arizona Ted coughed and reached for the whiskey bottle, taking a long, dribbling swallow. With a loud burp, he wiped his sleeve across his mouth. "I fold."

Hambone flicked his coins onto the pile. "Pair o' Jakes, ten high."

Killian tossed his cards on the table, barely noticing that he'd won until Hambone started sputtering and Arizona chuckled.

"You shore got somethin' on your mind today, Kill. I ain't seen you so distracted at cards since that time you was shot."

"He wasn't distracted then, Zona. He was just plain pissed. I was scared shitless every time I beat him."

Arizona laughed, reaching for the bottle again. "You mean scared shitless that *one* hand you won."

"Was it only one?" Hambone grabbed his own bottle and took a gulping drink. "Felt like more." He grinned. "Course, like I said, I was scared shitless."

Both men seemed to think that was hilarious. They burst out laughing; their booming voices filled the small, dank cabin and let loose the sharp stench of whiskey.

Drunks, Killian thought with a sigh. They thought anything was funny. He was just about to rake in his winnings when the door behind him smacked open.

"Well, if it ain't our supreme leader and his lap-dogs," came Purty's drawling, Texas-fed voice from the darkness.

Hambone's face spurted color. He surged to his feet. "Who you callin' a lapdog, you rotten-toothed son of a bitch?"

Purty grinned and strode into the small cabin, spurs

jangling on the hardwood floor. "Down, boy. We got the split money."

Every trace of animosity vanished from Hambone's face, replaced by a sudden feral greed. Slowly he sank back into his chair. "How much?"

"I ain't counted it all, but we reckon about eleven thousand altogether."

Arizona let out a low, appreciative whistle. "Hell, that's a lot o' money. We ain't split that kinda pot since the payload robbery. That was ... what? Ten thousand ..." He frowned, thinking.

"Yes, Zona, this is more," Purty drawled.

Mose pushed through the door behind Purty, blocking the pale light of twilight. "Skeeter back yet?"

Killian nodded absently and retrieved his winnings, stuffing the coins and bills in his duster pocket. Then, slowly, he rose.

"Where is she, boss?" Mose said from the darkness behind him.

Killian turned around. Even in the darkness, he could see the hard edge in Mose's gaze, see the angry tilt to his chin. Killian knew immediately what had happened. Mose had wanted to kill Lainie from the beginning, and he'd had three days to twist that instinct into an obsession.

"Who's that, Mose?" he said casually.

Mose frowned. "You know who I'm talkin' about, boss."

After that, no one said anything. Thick, strained silence filled the room. Purty and Mose exchanged frowning looks.

"You talkin' about that spitfire of a woman he brung into camp?" Arizona said, eager to know something that Purty didn't, for once.

Purty nodded, spat. "That'd be the one, Zona." He turned to Killian. "You find out who she is?"

Killian shrugged. The story she'd given him wouldn't wash with Mose. Not by a long shot. "Not really."

"Then I will," Mose said.

Killian noticed immediately the change in Mose's tone of voice. It was belligerent, questioning. And for the first time in ages, Mose hadn't called Killian "boss." It was a backdoor challenge to Killian's authority.

He walked toward Mose, taking slow, easy steps. He moved in close, so close that the other man frowned and backed up. Then Killian straightened, used every inch of his tall frame to tower over Mose. His shadow slid across Mose's fleshy face. "Will you, now?"

Anger slitted Mose's eyes, but he gritted his teeth and stayed silent. The only evidence of his fury was the dull red creeping up his rough-shaven throat.

"Jee-sus Christ, boss," Purty whistled into the silence. "You'd think he was talkin' about your ladylove. We just want to know who the hell the whore is and how she knows so damn much."

"He's ballin' her," Arizona said matter-of-factly.

"Oh." Purty's leathery face split into a yellow-toothed grin. "She didn't happen to mention how she knew our names, did she? You know, in between a few 'Oh Gods' and 'Harder, harder.'"

The men laughed.

Killian stepped back from Mose, saying nothing. It was vaguely irritating to hear the boys talking about her that way, and the realization that he cared angered him.

The laughter died away. "Seriously, boss," Purty persisted. "She say how she knew our names?"

"Nope."

Mose didn't crack a smile. "We're gonna ask her a few questions, boss."

They had every right, Killian knew. As their leader, he should know the answers, but since he didn't, he sure as hell couldn't stand in their way. The boys deserved to know if she was a threat.

"Yeah, sure," he said evenly. "Question her. But any decision about what to do with her is mine."

Purty looked faintly surprised. A frown pulled at his wrinkled brow and bunched the mustache beneath his hooked nose. "Of course it is, boss."

Killian wished he could take back the revealing sentence. Instead, he straightened and strode to the door. "Let's get this over with."

Chapter Fourteen

Viloula let out a weary sigh and eased the spectacles from her nose, setting them down on the open book in front of her.

Lainie thumped her book shut and rubbed her bloodshot eyes. Her head felt full, spiked by a dull throbbing at the base of her neck. With two fingertips, she massaged her temples. Panic was a heartbeat away; she kept it in check by sheer force of will. But it was there, increasing with every second that passed, tearing at her self-control. The more desperate and frightened she became, the angrier she felt.

"I t'ought dere'd be more . . . guidance," Viloula said, cradling her wrinkled face in her hand.

Lainie gave a short, sharp laugh. "That would be asking too much of religious texts, surely."

Viloula frowned, looked up. "Dat's twice you have been blasphemous."

"Blasphemous?" Lainie shot the word back. "You're joking, right?"

"Of course not. It is God dat rules our universe, shapes our lives. Certainly you believe in Him?"

"No."

Viloula studied her. "Oh, I t'ink you do . . . even t'ough you wish you didn't."

"Fascinating as this theological discussion is, I'd like

to get back to the business at hand. Did you find out anything that would help me get home?"

Viloula shrugged, reaching for her now lukewarm cup of tea. "More of de same."

Lainie shoved a hand through her messy hair. "I've read religious and pseudoreligious dogma from voodoo to Catholic to Muslim—even a bunch of half-baked cults I'd never heard about. None of them even *mention* the possibility of my situation. Only the Eastern religions seem to have any answers. And they're all the same, spouting the same ridiculous platitudes about karma, rebirth, second chances, and life lessons."

"At leas' we know dat you and Killian are lovers from de past and dere will be a great change."

Lainie rested her elbow on the chair's arm and rubbed her eyes again. "Oh, yes. At least we know that. This is some grand, cosmic classroom in which I'm to learn the lesson that God—a man—believes I need to learn."

"I'm not sure God is male or female. I t'ink—"

"Yeah, I care. The point is, we've found all we're going to find here."

In a jerking, angry motion, Lainie downed the dregs of her tea and wiped her mouth with the back of her hand. She was on her own, as usual.

Viloula made a soft, clucking sound with her tongue. "You are not alone, Alaina."

Alaina paled and stared at Vi for a second, then she slammed her tin cup down. "Don't read my mind, Vi. It's irritating."

"We will get you home, child."

Lainie laughed derisively. "Yeah? How? You got a crib sheet there that outlines my failed lesson in this life?"

"In trut', I have one last idea. I t'ought—"

"Get out here, girl!" A man's voice rang through the camp.

Viloula glanced at the closed door, frowning. "Dat's Mose's voice."

Lainie skidded back and got to her feet so fast, the wobbly chair crashed to the floor beside her. "Mose?"

Vi looked at her sharply. "You know him?"

"He wanted to kill me . . . to save time in the long run."

"Dat is Mose, all right."

A thundering knock rattled the thin door. The little cabin shuddered and groaned at the onslaught. Dust showered down from the rough-hewn rafters.

Viloula got to her feet and moved protectively beside Lainie.

The door swung open and Mose strode inside, then backed against the corner. Hat drawn low on his forehead, he stared at Lainie through narrowed, suspicious eyes, his small, mean mouth obscured by a huge handlebar mustache.

Purty sauntered in behind his friend, arms hanging relaxed at his sides. A good-natured grin curved his lips and sparkled in his rheumy eyes. "Evenin', Miss Viloula." He turned to Lainie, his grin broadening. "Miss."

Killian brought up the rear, moving silently in beside Purty. Lainie instantly noticed the hardness in his gaze and the way his right hand hovered at his gun belt. He kept the wall at his back. He was looking for trouble, that much was obvious. The question was, would he stop it or start it?

Mose cleared his throat. "We want some answers, lady."

Lainie drew herself upright and stared hard at Mose,

not giving an inch, masking her fear behind a cocky, defiant stance.

Purty hooked a thumb through the waistband of his jeans and moved forward. "The gal's gotta answer a few questions."

"Like, how'd you know our names?" Mose boomed out.

Viloula shot a worried glance at Lainie.

Lainie smiled and gave her a meaningful look. *I'm a writer,* her look said. *Trust me.*

Viloula nodded slowly, as if she understood. "Go . . . go ahead, Alaina. . . . Tell him the trut'."

"No, tell us a goddamn lie," Mose snapped, surging forward. Purty stopped him with a quick hand movement.

Inspiration struck. Lainie grinned. "You want the truth, do you? All right then, the truth is . . . I'm Viloula's granddaughter."

Silence crashed into the cabin. Viloula's mouth dropped open at the blatancy of the lie.

"She thinks we're stupid," Mose hissed, his eyes narrowing.

Lainie struggled to hold back a smile. "Why, Mose, I would never think *that.*"

"You're white," he said, taking a threatening step toward her.

"Am I?" One dark black brow winged upward in silent question.

Mose stopped.

Purty studied her, his smile flattened now. "I knowed a whore once in Abilene. Her daddy was black as night, and she was pale as you or me, Mose."

Mose turned slowly to Viloula. "You're one of us, Viloula. You backin' her story?"

"Yes," was all Viloula said, but it was enough. Lainie

knew that the men couldn't question the old woman. As Mose had said, she was one of them.

"You told her about us?" Purty asked.

Viloula nodded. "She left Seattle just two weeks ago. I meant to meet her in de Flats—but she ran into you boys instead."

Lainie looped her thumbs through her belt loops and grinned. "It was quite a piece of luck."

Viloula shot her an irritated look.

The frown on Mose's face was so deep and dark, it looked as if he were standing in shadows. He watched Lainie's every move, studied her, but he didn't say a word.

"Can I get you boys a cup of coffee?" Viloula said, gesturing toward the stove.

"Naw," Purty said, "we got to divide up the loot from the robbery."

Lainie gave him a broad smile. "An outlaw's work is never done."

Purty shook his head. "Lordy, you shore got a mouth on you, lady."

Viloula elbowed her, hard. "She get her mout' from her papa. He was a slick-talking shoe salesman from Detroit."

Purty grabbed Mose by the arm and maneuvered the bigger man out of the cabin. Killian waited, watched them go, then he turned back to the women.

"That was a hell of a performance," he said in a soft voice. He leaned against the doorjamb, one leg crossed over the other. To all outward appearances, he was relaxed, calm. But Lainie wasn't fooled. There was a tenseness in his body, a dangerousness in his eyes. He reminded her of a coiled snake, all sleek, contained power, waiting to strike.

"Maybe it's not a performance." She gave him a superior sniff. "It's genetically possible, you know. In fact—"

He grabbed her by the shoulders and pulled her toward him, lifting her off her feet. "Don't make that mistake, Lainie."

She tried to sound cocky. "Wh-What mistake?"

"I'm not stupid."

Their gazes locked. Lainie felt a strange sensation move through her body, not quite fear, and yet close to it. Whatever it was, she'd never felt it before. It made her heart pump harder, made her breathing speed up. Slowly, still staring down at her with a look so hot, she felt singed, he let her go. Casting a disgusted look at the tarot cards heaped on the table, he turned away from her. At the door, he stopped. "I'll expect you back in my cabin in fifteen minutes for supper."

"Yes, master."

Without another word, he left.

Lainie stood there, unblinking, staring at the closed door, wondering what it was he'd made her feel for that second, why her body had reacted so sharply. After a long while, she felt Viloula's gaze on her back, pointed and intense. She turned toward the old woman, and immediately wished she hadn't. There was a small, knowing smile on her puckered lips.

She said a single phrase. "Soul mates."

"Soul mate schmole mate," Lainie said for at least the third time since leaving Vi's cabin. Sure, he seemed a little ... familiar. So what?

The last thing she needed was a soul mate. She stood outside Killian's closed door, staring at the wooden planks bound together by weather-blackened leather. The latchstring hung limply alongside the door, its edges frayed by years of heavy-handed use.

Somewhere a bird chirped, and it was an absurdly normal sound. She inhaled deeply, smelling the sharp, coppery scent of dust and the lingering remnant of woodsmoke.

He's your soul mate, she told herself for the hundredth time since leaving Vi's.

Yeah, and I'm Julia Roberts.

She knew she should believe in what Viloula had told her. In for a penny, in for a pound. If she could believe that she'd turned on her computer and zapped back in time one hundred years, certainly she could stomach the thought that someone back here had called to her, maybe even loved her.

Not.

She shook her head, smiling sadly at the irony. A romance author who didn't believe in love. Judith would be appalled.

Maybe once, a long time ago, she'd believed in that kind of emotion. Maybe once she'd even believed that if love existed, it would find its way to her. But those days, those naive days, were long gone and couldn't be resurrected. Now the only love she believed in was a mother's love. That was something tangible, something immutable and powerful and unconditional. She loved Kelly, and Kelly loved her.

It was enough for Lainie; it had been from the moment she'd conceived Kelly. She didn't need a soul mate. Didn't even want one. Besides, with her luck, he'd go out for a pack of smokes and she'd see him next on "America's Most Wanted."

The thought made her smile. Whatever Mr. Macho was to her, soul mate or fiction or somewhere in between, she didn't care. She had all the emotion she could handle in her life right now. She didn't need a soul mate.

Feeling stronger, she yanked on the latchstring and shoved the door open. The first thing she noticed was the mouthwatering scent of simmering meat. Her empty stomach rumbled loudly as she went inside.

A single lantern sat on the rickety table, creating a pocket of light in the dingy interior. The bed was a shadow in the corner, noticeable only by the paleness of the sheeting in the meager light.

"You're back."

Lainie started and spun around. Killian was standing to her left, behind the arc of the door and against the wall. He stood in front of a tall, narrow bookshelf, one hand poised against the books, as if he'd been just about to withdraw one.

She gave him a snide look. "Just about to read *Crime and Punishment*?"

"Why? You want to borrow it?"

Lainie couldn't help herself. She smiled. And it felt good, damn it. After all the doom and gloom and grief and fear, it was nice to find something to smile about. "What are you doing here?" she said, moving toward him. "Aren't there banks that need robbing?"

He backed away from her, and she sensed fear in him. He didn't want her to get too close.

Now she was sure they were soul mates.

She looked at him, really studied him in a way she hadn't before. Before, all she'd seen was the man she created in her book; anything more or less than that, she'd discounted. Now she really tried to see the man himself.

He stood against the bookcase, one booted foot resting on the lowest shelf. One hand, lean and long-fingered, lay splayed against the hard curve of his thigh. The cotton shirt, once white and now a battered, over-washed shade of gray, hung limply on his broad shoulders, the collar gaped to reveal a plunging vee of black chest hair and tanned skin. Dusty black wool pants hugged his legs and dragged in frayed edges across the top of his boots.

He filled the corner of the cabin, and not only by sheer physical size. He was a presence somehow, a man one would have noticed in any setting. A man's man; a woman's fantasy. Long, unkempt hair the color of old steel brushed well past his collar, curled in a silver fringe at his shoulders. His face was tanned and lined by years beneath a hot sun; it was a face with character. But even with all that, it was his eyes that moved her most profoundly. Everything else about him, she expected—still more than half believed she created. But not those eyes. There was something in his gaze she wouldn't have put there, wouldn't have imagined, and she didn't know what it was.

She couldn't deny that right now, looking at him, she felt something. She didn't think for a second that it was a leftover cosmic love or anything, but it was definitely something.

Frowning, confused, she moved toward him. She came to within inches of him and stopped, staring deeply into his eyes, wondering if it would be like that scene from *Heaven Can Wait* when Julie Christie saw the soul in Warren Beatty's eyes.

Their gazes met, held. Deep in his brown eyes, she saw her own reflection; beyond that, she saw a spark of barely contained fear. He flinched.

For a second, maybe more, she forgot to breathe. She gazed up into his life-lined face and felt—absurdly—as if she'd finally come home.

"What are you looking at?" he asked.

You. She wanted to say the word casually, toss it to

him as if it meant nothing, but she couldn't. Her throat felt thick and her breath was coming too fast.

Suddenly everything Viloula said made a horrible, frightening sense. He *did* seem familiar to her, and more than that, he felt important. Her mind seized on a dozen moments, snippets of time that drew them together. They were little things, barely grasped and quickly lost, but they meant something to her; the way he'd looked at her when he'd untied her hands, the strength he'd given to her on the ledge, the sadness in his eyes when he spoke of Emily.

She opened her mouth to say something, but nothing came out. She didn't know what to say, or how to say it.

"Don't look at me that way."

She heard the scratchy, gravelly sound of his voice and knew that he'd felt it, too, that unbelievable spark of possibility.

Fear slid down her back. She wrapped her arms around herself and backed away from him. Suddenly she didn't want to be this close to him, didn't want to feel anything for him.

All this crap about soul mates would only screw her up and mess with her mind. She had to remember, *always*, that Kelly was her sole priority. She could have loved Killian since Cleopatra rode the Nile and it didn't mean squat. All that mattered was getting home. And he was either with her or against her. Period. And now was the time to find out which it was.

"Viloula told you I was telling the truth," she said.

"So what? The woman believes in gnomes and fairies and trolls."

Lainie didn't laugh. "I need you to help me get to Fortune Flats."

He flinched. His eyes narrowed, but not before she

saw a glimpse of some dark inner torment. "I don't care what the hell you need."

She frowned. He looked . . . scared. But that was ridiculous. What did he have to be frightened of? Slowly, watching him, she moved closer. "Are you going to take me to Fortune Flats?"

"No!" His sudden roar echoed in the small, dark cabin, seemed absurdly out of place. Almost as if she'd struck a nerve with her quiet request.

She knew she should let it go, but she had a little strength right now, and a lot of desperation. He was the only way out of this hellhole; without him, she might never see Kelly again.

She looked up, saw again the raw pain in his eyes, and it moved her, made her feel as if she understood him just a little. That dizzying sense of déjà vu came back, harder, stronger, as if they'd stood like this before, squared off and hurting, neither one able to reach out.

He grabbed her, yanked her toward him, and gave her a hard shake. "Quit looking at me like that." His voice was low and gravelly. "I can't help you."

"Killian—"

He pushed her away from him and spun away, pacing the small cabin. His every footstep was a pounding hammer of sound that rattled the floorboards.

She watched him, not knowing what to say. A sinking, panicked feeling clutched her insides. She wanted to reach out, to say just the right thing that would make him change his mind, but she couldn't think of anything except *why*? Why are you so unwilling to help me?

"Sit down," he said abruptly. "Supper's ready."

Lainie noticed the settings on the table for the first time. She walked over to the rickety wooden table and sat down, staring down at the bent, dented tin fork and scratched blue metal plate.

A strange, almost nostalgic emotion moved through her at the sight of the table. It was so damned ordinary. And yet . . . so different. It was a stupid thing to realize right now, and had no bearing whatsoever on her situation, but no man had ever cooked for her before.

She scooted closer to the table, pressing her hands into her lap. She wasn't sure what to do right now— was she supposed to offer to help, or sit here like a bump on a log? What?

He appeared beside her, as if drawn by her thoughts. He plopped four steaming potato wedges on her plate, then forked a thick steak beside it. The aromas combined, threw her back in time for an instant, reminded her of a dozen ordinary, everyday moments she'd spent huddled with Kelly in their quiet kitchen.

Killian clanged the pot on the side of the table and settled across from her.

They sat there, neither looking up, neither speaking. Silence threw its thick, awkward net across them, drew them close and yet kept them strangely distant. The scratching whine of tin tines on metal plates underscored the quiet, gave it a melancholy edge.

Lainie slowly cut her steak, focusing on the ordinariness of the task. Taking a bite, she stared down at her plate, chewing as quietly as she could.

"You really have a daughter?"

She was so surprised by the question that she dropped her fork and jerked her head up. "Yeah."

He smiled, but it looked forced and stiff. "That's pretty hard to believe. You don't seem too . . . motherly."

The statement hurt. She gave him an equally stiff smile. "You don't need anything special to be a mother, Killian, trust me. Rabbits eat their young."

He stared at her, an unreadable emotion in his eyes. "I guess not . . . if someone would let a kid smoke at eleven."

She froze, stunned by the intimacy of the insight. Her hand shook a little and she clenched it. She tried to glance away from him, but she couldn't. He was looking at her with a sadness, an understanding that shouldn't exist. It was a look that said he knew, that he'd somehow seen more of her than she'd wanted to reveal. "Yeah, well," she mumbled. "I'm not that kind of mother."

She watched him, waiting for him to say more, but he didn't speak again. He looked down and started eating once more. She did the same. After a while, the heaviness in the air started to seep away, melt into an almost companionable silence. She felt—crazily—as if they'd done this before. . . .

When she was finished, she pushed back in her chair and got to her feet. Across the table, he did the same. Without looking at each other, they started to clear the dishes away.

They both reached for the pan at the same time. Their fingers brushed. Lainie felt the heat of his skin against hers. She stiffened and drew in a sharp breath. Her head snapped up, their eyes locked.

For a split second she looked into his eyes and felt as if she'd known him all her life. She knew she should let go of the pan, fling her body backward, and get away from him. But she couldn't move. "Help me," she murmured in a quiet, trembling voice. "Take me home. . . ."

Her jerked away from her. The pan clattered to the table between them, splashing cloudy water across the splintery wood. Staring at her, his eyes darkened by some pain she couldn't begin to understand, he backed away.

"Wait," she whispered. "Please . . ."

Suddenly a gunshot blasted through the night.

Killian squeezed his eyes shut. "Thank God." His voice was scratchy and raw and tired-sounding.

She glanced at the window where a bustling stream of shadows scudded past. "What is it?"

"The party's starting." He reached for a whiskey bottle from the supply crate. "Whenever we bring back a haul from a job, we get drunk."

She felt the moment's connection with him fade away, as if he were moving farther and farther away from her, though he hadn't taken a step. The loss of that second, that feeling, was sharper and more painful than she would have thought possible.

Get a grip on yourself, Lainie. She straightened her shoulders and tilted her chin, wiping the sadness from her face with an ease born of practice. She'd let him see too much, had given him too much power.

But now it was over. She'd thrown away her pride and asked him for help . . . begged him . . . and it hadn't worked. She had her answer. An unequivocal no.

A sinking sense of regret settled against her heart, made her chest ache. Why had she expected anything else?

He set the bottle down on the table with a sloshing clank and turned away from her. "Come on. Let's go."

She stood her ground. "I am not going to a party where drunk men carry loaded weapons."

He turned slightly. His shadow engulfed her, cut off the meager warmth of the lantern light. "I'm not going to leave you here alone."

"Then stay with me."

He flinched at her softly spoken words. "I could tie you to the bed."

The gaze she gave him was steady. "Yeah, you could."

He leaned toward her, close enough to touch. She smelled the smoky scent of his shirt, felt a whisper of his hair against her temple. "If I leave you alone, will you try to escape?"

"What's it to you if I do?"

He drew in a sharp breath. His eyes narrowed. "You're not going anywhere." Spinning on his heel, he stalked to the door and swung it open, yelling Skeeter's name.

Within seconds, the scrawny cowhand skidded up to the door, an empty whiskey bottle dangling from one fist. "Yessir, boss." He gave a wobbly salute.

"This lady's my . . . guest for the evening. Stand outside the door and guard her."

Skeeter frowned. "But the party, boss. Mose and Purty 'n the boys are shootin' up the drinkin' tent and chasin' after some o' them whores we brung up from Carson City."

"Sounds lovely," Lainie said loudly, craning around to see Skeeter better. He stared at her like a stuck pig. Then, slowly, he frowned.

"All right, boss. I'll stand here."

Killian started to head for the door, then stopped. Slowly, almost as if he didn't want to, he turned and looked back at her. Then, with a bitten-off curse, he grabbed his hat and pushed through the door. It slammed shut behind him, leaving her alone once more.

She sighed and slumped on the bed, burying her face in her hands. Emotions mingled with facts and swirled around in her head until she was dizzy for thinking about all of it.

She thought about Kelly, about time and the nature of its passing, about soul mates and second chances and karma. Impossible information warred with undeniable feelings and became a dull headache at the base of her neck. But underneath it all was the question, burning and insistent. A question she couldn't dispel no matter how hard she tried, no matter how hard she concentrated.

Is he the one?

She didn't know. God help her, she didn't know. But she knew one thing, and it filled her with sadness.

If he was the one—her soul mate—it was too late.

Chapter Fifteen

Viloula stood in the center of her cabin, alone. The sounds of the night filtered to her ears. Next door the party was just starting. From somewhere far away, some darkened edge of the canyon, came the hooting, lonely cry of an owl. Chilly night air closed around Viloula, pressed icy fingers around her bare throat.

She wished fleetingly, and not for the first time, that her mama were still alive. Genvieve would know how to interpret Viloula's strange, fitful visions, would understand her apprehension.

Something terrible was going to happen; she was certain of it. The moment she'd looked into Alaina's eyes, she'd seen the terrifying truth, heard the whispered words.

There would be a death. . . .

She didn't question her knowledge, though she knew that others would. She had been taught since childhood to trust in her feelings, in the innate knowledge that remained hidden in the furthest reaches of her mind, seeping forward into the cold, hard daylight only when it must.

For generations, men—who had lesser access to these memories—had scoffed at such knowledge, labeling it women's intuition and discarding it as worthless.

But Viloula knew better, as had Genvieve before her,

and innumerable generations of women before her. Intuition was knowledge, as certain as anything learned from any book and infinitely more powerful.

They had known each other before, she and Alaina and Killian, and now they were moving toward a danger, all three of them. A danger that couldn't be avoided.

There would be a death....

Goose bumps crawled across Viloula's flesh. The time had come for Viloula to look into a place she'd studiously avoided all her life. A place that terrified her with its darkness, its uncertainty. A place where the past and the present and the future coexisted, a tangled web of lives over and lives yet to be.

She glanced at the small glass vial on her windowsill. Soon, when the camp fell once again into quiet, she would reach for it. And having once taken hold of the glass, there would be no turning back.

"Please, God," she whispered, her voice broken and throaty in the darkness, "let me have the strength to help her."

The strength to help us all ...

Everything was ready. It was time.

Lainie let out a heavy breath and glanced at the supplies at her feet. A ragged sack lay on the floor, its dirty sides bulging with supplies she'd gathered from the cabin, its mouth tied tight with a fraying scrap of rope. The canteen hung at her right hip; the wide leather strap pulled taut between her breasts and bit into the tender flesh at her throat.

Lainie went to the window and pushed aside the rough burlap curtain. The camp was empty, quiet except for the hum of raised voices and laughter coming from the drinking tent. Light seeped through the tent, silhouetted the crush of people moving inside. The tinny whine of a fiddle floated on the air.

Killian was in there.

She leaned forward a little, touched the tip of her nose to the cold glass. Her breath fogged the pane, turned the world into a hazy surreal smear. She wondered what he was doing, what he was thinking.

Yet, somehow, she knew. He was distant, untouched by the crowd of humanity swirling around him. Like her, he was always alone, no matter who was around him. It should have surprised her, the innate knowledge of a man she couldn't possibly understand, but it didn't. Viloula's words came back to her, filled her with a terrible longing. *What if . . . soul mates . . . a love that won't ever die . . .*

For a second, it hurt to breathe. She could admit to herself, alone and in the dark, that she wished Viloula were right. She'd always wanted to believe in a fairy-tale love, wanted to believe it was possible. Long ago, before life crushed her spirit so completely, she'd believed in a million moments like this, in the hot magic of possibility.

Amazingly, she was beginning to believe in it again. And—naturally—it was too late. Sadness pulled at her lips, turned them down at the corners. Regret was a hard knot in the pit of her stomach.

She wished it weren't too late, wished she could have taken the time to see Killian one last time, look in his eyes. Maybe she would have seen the past, maybe she would have seen the future. And maybe she would have seen nothing but a dark reflection of her own confusing needs and wants.

She didn't know. Would never know.

Frowning, she stepped back from the window and let the curtain shudder back in place.

Unfortunately, it was time to go. She had no choice. Viloula hadn't come up with a way out of here, and Killian obviously wasn't going to help her.

As usual, everything was up to Lainie. And she wouldn't let Kelly down. Straightening, she went to the door, grabbed the latchstring, and pulled the door open.

"Pssst. Skeeter," she hissed through the barely open door. "Psst."

The scrawny cowhand scratched his butt and looked around. "Huh?"

Lainie cracked the door open a little wider, enough so that he could see her. She pasted a sugary smile on her face. For this plan to work, she had to be what she'd rarely been in her life. Feminine and helpless.

"Oh!" he said, his voice spiking up an octave. "It's you."

"Skeeter, I seem to have misplaced my compass." She said it airily, as if she were a lady who'd just dropped a handkerchief. "Would you mind getting me another?"

"Whaddaya need a compass for?"

"I'm practicing for the Olympics."

His face creased slowly into a frown. She brightened her smile and tried to look as vague as possible. "Surely you know what the Olympics are. . . ."

He puffed up, threw his narrow chest out. "Course I do."

She nodded. "Then you'll get me the compass?"

He dug into his baggy pants pocket. "Actually, I got one right here. You c'n borrow it iffen you want."

She reached out, closed her fingers around the compass, and snaked her find back. "Thank you, Skeeter. You're a real gentleman." She started to close the door, then stopped. "You know, Skeeter . . ." She batted her eyelashes and brought a fluttery hand to her throat. "I'm sorely parched."

He brightened. "You, too? Hell, I'm thirsty as a dead dog on a summer day."

"The problem is, Killian took the only bottle of whiskey. Maybe you could run on down to your place and get us something. . . ."

He cast a furtive glance sideways. "I dunno. The boss tole me to stand here."

"You could come right back. I wouldn't tell him you left. I swear I wouldn't."

He glanced down the deserted street. "It ain't far to my place. I could be back in a second."

"Who'd notice an itty bitty slip of time like that?"

He looked down at the drinking tent at the end of the road, then at his own tent half as far away. "Okay," he whispered, leaning close. "I'll get us a bottle and be right back."

She licked her lips and smiled. "I can taste it already."

Skeeter dragged his hat lower on his head and started for his own tent, moving cautiously, jumping at every shadow.

Lainie spun into high gear. She grabbed the knapsack she'd packed and the full canteen and slung them over her shoulder.

She poked her head out the door. The coast was clear.

With a sharp, indrawn breath, she ran for the tunnel. The supplies on her back clanked with each pounding step, her heartbeat hammered in her chest.

She plunged into the tunnel and skidded to a heaving stop. Darkness curled around her, black and suffocating.

She reached into her canvas bag and pulled out a candle, lighting it. The candle cast weary gold light along the sandstone walls, but even with it, she couldn't see more than a foot in front of her face. In her shaking hand, the light danced and writhed in snakelike patterns on the damp stone.

Slowly she crept down the black pathway. The dank smell of a place unseen by the sun clogged her nostrils. She dragged her fingers along the rough sandstone wall and kept moving forward.

She didn't care how scared she was, how lonely she felt. This was the only way out, the only way back to Kelly.

She'd find her way back or die trying.

Good-bye, Viloula. She focused her thoughts on the words, tried to send them through time and space to the old woman. It was all she could do, and she wished it were more.

Good-bye.

Killian stood at the rear of the tent, his hat drawn low over his eyes. A half-empty bottle of whiskey sat on the floor in easy reach. Something about him—his eyes, his stance, something—must have warned people to stay away from him, because not a single person came near him.

Raucous laughter and hoarse voices exploded in the small tent; the pungent smell of unwashed bodies was almost overpowering. People were a blur of movement all around him, dashing, shoving, jostling their way to a makeshift dance floor. In the corner, Purty played the fiddle—poorly. The whining screech of the bow on loose strings vibrated above the din.

Killian watched the action without seeing it. He stood stiff and unmoving, his body held rigidly in check. At his sides, his hands were balled in tight fists, ready.

He wanted to punch something, someone, anything.

Anything to release the anger that seethed beneath the surface, made him feel restless and uneasy and tense.

He didn't know what to do, how to exorcise the emotions that swirled through his mind like a hot, red mist. He wasn't used to feeling this way. Hell, he wasn't used to feeling at all anymore. For years he'd been cold and calm. Always calm.

Now he was anything but calm. It felt as if there were a bomb inside him, sitting heavily in his gut. Tension radiated beneath his skin, tightened his muscles until they ached.

He leaned back against the sagging canvas wall and forced out a steady breath, trying to bring his raging temper under control. But no matter how hard he tried, or how much he drank, he couldn't forget.

Help me, please . . .

Her soft-spoken plea came back to him, hitting with the force of a hammerblow. He winced, felt a sharp pain in his chest. He yanked up the whiskey bottle and took another long, dribbling drink. He wanted—needed—to get rip-roaring drunk. Anything to make him forget what she'd asked of him, and how he'd felt when she asked it. But he couldn't forget; that was the hell of it, that was the reason he stood here, alone in the middle of a crowd of people, his emotions a turbulent, seething boil in his head. For a second, when he'd looked down into her watery, desperate eyes, he'd wanted to help her.

As if he could. *Christ.*

He told himself it meant nothing, that stupid, useless desire to help her. Hell, he would have said—or thought—anything right then, anything to make her stop looking at him like he was a goddamn hero.

But deep down, he knew the truth, and it scared the hell out of him. He'd wanted to reach out to her, to offer a side of himself he'd thought he'd discarded a life-

time ago. Something about her brought out a renegade
remnant of the man he'd once been, once thought he'd
be forever. The man who believed in love and honor
and commitment; the idealistic lawman who was going
to save the world and make it a safe place for innocent
people.

It had ruined him, that idealism. When he lost it—
buried it in a lonely grave in a nothing little town—he'd
been left with only a searing emptiness, a dark-edged
regret. He'd spent years running from everything and
everyone, trying to escape from the hatred eating inside
his heart like a cancer. But there'd been no escape, not
from himself.

Now those days were a hazy blur for him. He could
barely remember what it felt like to actually want something, to care about something.

Until he looked at Lainie. Then he remembered it all
in blinding, aching clarity. He remembered the pride
he'd once taken in wearing the badge of a Texas
Ranger, remembered the dreams he'd once held so
close.

At the thought, he felt another surge of anger. He
grabbed the bottle of whiskey and took a long drink.
The alcohol seared his throat and filled his stomach
with fire. He winced, wiped his mouth with his sleeve.

Didn't she know? She knew so goddamn much about
him, about his life and his past. She had to know what
a failure he was as a man, what a loser.

So why would she ask him for help?

And why would he want to try? He knew better. Jesus, he knew better. He didn't know which scared him
more—the desire to help her or the realization that he
couldn't.

Every time he'd ever tried to help someone, he'd
failed. Utterly, miserably. He wasn't any good at it.

People who counted on him died. It was as simple—as horrifying—as that.

Help me, please . . .

With a bitten-off curse, he shoved away from the wall and surged into the crowd. He had to do something to get his mind off her. If he didn't, he was going to explode.

"Killian!" A trilling female voice punched through his thoughts, brought him up short.

He glanced to the left. A woman pushed through the crowd toward him, her mammoth breasts leading the way like a pair of bowsprits. Loose swells of sweaty cleavage jostled with every step. Right in front of him, she stopped, cocked her head, and gave him a seductive smile. "Ye're mighty unsociable-like tonight, Killian. Like always."

A bitter smile curved his mouth. This is what he needed. Fast, furious, impersonal sex. A good romp that would keep his body so busy, his mind would shut down.

He grabbed the whore and drew her close. With a throaty laugh, she stumbled toward him and tilted her face for a kiss. "Ooee! The girls ain't gonna believe *this*," she purred, smearing herself against him.

He made the fatal mistake of looking at her. Heavily made-up blue eyes blinked up at him sleepily, but he didn't even see them.

He saw Lainie's sad, hazel eyes instead. The image of them, desperate and sheened with tears, was like a blow to the heart. Stark, ice-cold fear rushed through him. Jesus, she was inside him. He couldn't get away from her sad eyes and pitiful request.

He stumbled back from the whore without mumbling a word. Clutching the whiskey bottle, he took a long, burning draw and slipped through the crowd.

The canvas door beckoned. He ducked his head and ran for it. He got halfway across the tent before he realized what he was doing, where he was going.

He'd been going to Lainie.

The thought slammed through the alcohol-induced haze and brought him to a dead stop. He stood in the center of the crowd like a fool, reeling and drunk, his mind unable to release its grip on Lainie and her sad, sad eyes.

He groaned quietly and bowed his head. Jesus, there wasn't enough alcohol in the world to make his problems go away. Not this time. He could drink from now until Sunday and he'd still be thinking of her.

You know what that's like, Killian, coming home to an empty house. . . .

He winced at the memory of her observation, so damned intimate. When he'd looked down at her then, he'd felt as if he were falling into the dark pool of her eyes. And there he'd found a warmth, an understanding he couldn't imagine. He'd thought—fleetingly and with longing—that she knew what it felt like to be kicked in the teeth and still go on. Knew what hell it was sometimes, how much willpower it took, just to keep living.

He walked slowly to the door and went outside, heading for the barn. There, he leaned against the wall and slid slowly to his butt, drawing his legs close. The black, black night curled around him, stars flickering overhead. Music and noise and laughter drifted on the slight breeze, muffled and low. The party was right there, not more than fifty feet away, and for the first time in years, he felt achingly alone.

He banged his head back against the wooden wall and let out a harsh sigh. He had to get away from her and stay away from her. Otherwise . . .

He shuddered at the thought of *otherwise*.

If he didn't get away from her, she'd keep asking him for help, keep whittling away at the shell he'd worked so hard to create. Surprisingly, she'd found a weakness; one he hadn't even expected. Somewhere, deep inside him, was a remnant of the lawman he'd once been.

It was the most terrifying realization he could imagine. Because he might want to help her, might even try, but in the end, when the chips were down, he wouldn't be there for her.

And he couldn't survive failing someone again. Not again.

"Oh, no." Skeeter poked his head through the half-open door to Killian's cabin and dropped the whiskey bottle. It hit the hard-packed dirt at his feet with a thud. The sharp, pungent smell of alcohol wafted upward. "I'm a dead man."

She was gone.

His knees started knocking together. He swallowed convulsively, licking his paper-dry lips. Killian wasn't going to be happy. Not happy at all.

Skeeter bent down and retrieved the fallen bottle. It was still more than half-full. He eyed the sloshing amber liquid, smelled its familiar sweetness. And suddenly he was desperately thirsty.

He wiped the glass mouth and took a long, gulping swallow. Then another, and another.

Finally he pulled back and looked at the bottle. He could go get Killian now, or he could get drunk first. Either way, he was in a world of hurt.

There was no contest. Skeeter leaned against the cabin door and folded downward. His butt plunked on the cold dirt, his knobby knees came up like twin mountain peaks.

Drunk was better.

He drank the remainder of the bottle in fiery swallows, then staggered to his feet. A slippery laugh escaped him. He clamped a bony hand over his mouth and tossed the bottle away.

He pushed off from the cabin and stumbled down the street. Halfway to the drinking tent, he started to sing. A laughing, nothing little ditty about whores and drawers. He burst into the drinking tent with a flourish.

"Hey, Skeet," said a barrel-chested woman who looked like his father. "Where ya been?"

He gave a yelp and skedaddled sideways, muttering something about Killian.

Killian. Suddenly he remembered, and a cold wash of fear almost sobered him. He staggered through the crowd, clearing his way by pushing aside people even drunker than he was.

"Skeeter." His name was said quietly, with a steel edge of danger that brought him to a dead stop. His knees started shaking again.

"B-Boss?" he said, casting a reluctant look to his left.

Killian stood against the yellowed canvas wall, his hat pulled low on his head, his arms crossed. His mouth was wreathed in shadows, but even so, Skeeter could tell that the man wasn't smiling.

Lord, he wished he had a drink. Plunging his shaking hands in his pockets, he pitched toward Killian, stumbling to a halt beside him. "I . . . I reckon you're wonderin' what I'm doing here."

"Where's Lainie?" Killian said.

Skeeter gave his boss a blank stare. "Who?"

Killian's jaw clenched. "The woman."

"Oh. Her." Skeeter's chin dropped. He had a sudden, almost overwhelming urge to piss his pants. "She . . . left."

Killian stiffened, pulled away from the wall. "Where to?"

Skeeter swallowed again. "I don't know, but she asked for my compass."

Killian's jaw tightened. "Tell me you didn't give it to her."

"Okay, I didn't."

Killian tossed his hat back and glared down at Skeeter through ice-cold eyes. "Did you give her your compass?"

He nodded, unable to push a single syllable up his parched throat.

Killian let out a long breath. "Then she's gone."

Skeeter nodded. He waited a heartbeat for Killian to shoot him. When he didn't, Skeeter relaxed. "If it helps, Mose never liked her anyway."

"No." The word was spoken softly, but with a razor-sharpness that clutched Skeeter's bowels. "That doesn't help much." Without another word, Killian shoved past Skeeter and barreled through the crowd, disappearing through the open canvas flap.

Skeeter breathed a sigh of relief. He'd lived through it. Thank God. "Hey!" he yelled out. "I ain't been laid yet."

A whore came runnin'.

Killian strode down the road toward his cabin. It took everything inside him, every scrap of self-control he possessed, not to break into a run.

Shoving the door open, he burst into the small, darkened room. Shadows lay heaped along the walls and floor. Moonlight sliced through the dirty windows, writhed on the wrinkled sheets, and gave the bed an eerie blue glow.

A scrap of paper caught his eye. It was on the table,

stuck in place by the sharp point of a hunting knife. He grabbed the cold leather handle and yanked the knife out of the wood. Picking up the scrap of paper, he moved to the circle of lamplight to read it.

You should have helped me.

Fear backhanded him. His heart started beating so fast, he could barely think. Sweat broke out on his forehead, a cold, itchy trail.

She'll die out there.

The thought churned through his mind, brought a sick, sinking feeling to his stomach.

He tried not to care, tried to tell himself it was all for the best. What did he care if she died out there? What was she to him?

He shuddered. Now, *there* was a question he didn't want to answer. Didn't dare answer.

He crushed the note in his hand and threw it at the wall. It hit with a scratchy whisper and floated to the floor.

He fisted his hands and looked at the closed door.

Let her go, you fool.

But he couldn't. God help him, he couldn't let her go into the desert all alone. Out there, with no weapon and no guide, she wouldn't last two days.

"Christ," he hissed, already moving toward the door. It wasn't the smart thing to do, but he couldn't help himself. He had to go after her.

Amazingly, there was something of the hero left in him after all.

He grabbed the lantern off the table and barreled out of his cabin, running for the tunnel. He plunged into the darkness and stopped, his breathing coming in great, heaving gasps.

"Lainie?" he called out. The name vibrated through the stone wall and mocked him.

No one answered.

Fear clutched his heart in a cold grip. He ran into the tunnel, splashing light along the walls and floor as he went. Up and down the twisting corridors, he ran calling out her name until his voice was hoarse.

Finally he broke stride and stumbled to a tired halt. He'd searched every passageway, every turn, and still he hadn't found her. He sagged against the damp stone wall, breathing heavily.

"Lainie," he wheezed, and bowed his head, fighting the pain of a sudden, blinding headache. He squeezed his eyes shut and rubbed his temples, concentrating on the simple task. Anything to keep the image of her out of his mind, but of course, it didn't work. Everywhere he turned, he saw her. In the shadows along the wall, in the splash of light along the floor. And her words, so soft and musical, pounded through his mind like some rhythmic metronome, thudding through his heart with every footstep. *I need your help ... your help ... your help. ...*

Why in the Christ had he turned his back on her?

His fear seemed such a small thing now, so inconsequential compared to her desperation. So what if he couldn't help her? He could get her back to Fortune Flats.

I'll get her back, God, he thought desperately. *I'll send Skeeter with her. ... Just let her be all right.*

Slowly he lifted his head. His eyes were gritty and tired and turned the world into a smeary blur of shadows within shadows. His headache intensified. He blinked to clear his vision.

"Ah, Lainie ..." His tired voice cracked on her name. He shook his head.

"Killian?"

It was just a whisper of sound, so soft he thought

he'd imagined it, conjured her voice from the shifting of the air.

Still, his breath caught. Hope hammered in his chest. "Lainie?"

"Over here."

He swung to the right. Light fanned out, touched a small, dark heap along the far wall. He took a hesitant, disbelieving step, then ran for her.

She lay curled in a ball, her knees drawn tight to her chest, her cheek pressed to the cold earth.

He dropped to his knees, almost afraid to believe she was really here. He set down the lantern and touched her cheek. Her skin was gritty and icy cold.

She turned slightly and looked up at him. Lantern light illuminated half her face, gave it the glow of warm gold.

"Lainie," he whispered, touching her cheek in a feather-stroke. "I'm sorry. . . ." His voice was thick and hoarse.

"I'm freezing," she whispered. As if to punctuate her sentence, she shivered hard.

He swept her into his arms and grabbed the lantern. Carrying her, he raced back to the camp and got her into his cabin, tucking her into the warm bed.

He sat down beside her as gently as he could. She lay on her back, her spiky hair a halo around her pale face. The grayed pillow mounded on either side of her face, made her look shrunken and incredibly fragile.

Fragile. He frowned slightly. That wasn't a word he'd ever considered in relation to Lainie. She was vulnerable, yes. But mostly she was hard and tough and determined. Hell, he'd never known anyone with a stronger will.

But now, seeing her in his bed, looking as lost as a child, he saw that she was fragile, too. Maybe more fragile than anyone he'd ever known. Behind all that bluster and defiance and cockiness, she was just as scared and lonely and alone as he was.

And she wanted *his* help.

The words hurt, caused a sharp ache in his chest. It was such a little thing she was asking. A normal man could do it with ease. But not him. Killian had been down that road before. He was a miserable failure at any kind of commitment—even one this small. He refused to let her count on him, refused to let her down.

She opened her eyes and looked up at him, her breathing shallow. "Thanks." The word was hoarse and ended in a cough.

He stared at her, trying to understand what it was about her that moved him so much, that scared him so deeply. She didn't look all that different from a hundred women he had known; she was no prettier, no smarter, no softer. But there was something . . .

He thought of her as he'd found her, balled up and alone and crying in the dark. And suddenly he was furious with her, furious that she would risk her life in so careless a way. "You shouldn't have gone out there alone."

One thick black eyebrow arched. "Really? It's not like I had a choice."

He sat very still. That tension was back inside him, tightening his muscles. His jaw clenched, his hands fisted. He felt the anger rising through his blood like a quick-moving tide. "People always have a choice."

She struggled to sit up. Without thinking, he reached out to help her. The simple touch was electric; he felt a jolt of awareness sizzle through his blood. He yanked his hand back.

She must have felt it, too. She made a small, gasping

sound and tilted her face up, staring at him through wide, unblinking eyes.

She angled back from him a little, as if the intimacy of their nearness was frightening. "Next time, I'll take a horse."

"Next time?" He sprang up from the bed and spun away from her, pacing the small cabin. Back and forth. Anger choked him, made it difficult to breathe. It took all his self-control not to pick her up and shake her until her teeth rattled.

"Yeah, Killian, next time," she said evenly. "I have a child to get back to."

He surged forward and grabbed her by the shoulders, lifting her off the bed. "You idiot! Don't you know that you could have *died* out there? If I hadn't come along ..." His throat thickened suddenly, made it impossible to force the words out.

He let go of her and stumbled back. She crumpled onto the bed, but didn't look away. Those dark eyes lifted to his, asked for a million heart-wrenching choices.

He jerked around and strode to the stove, grabbing a coffeepot. The pots clanged and clanked as he fumbled through the dry goods with shaking hands.

She'll do it again. And maybe next time, he wouldn't be there to save her. Maybe next time, she'd make it farther and he'd never find her again. The thought scared the shit out of him.

Lainie watched him trying to make coffee. He was burrowing through the pots and pans like a madman.

He was angry ... and scared.

She frowned, sitting up straighter. "Killian? Come here."

He froze. He sat there crouched in front of the supplies, his long, silver hair a tangled curtain that swung below his collar. Then, slowly, he got to his feet and turned around.

She slipped out of bed and walked toward him. They came together near the warmth of the stove. He looked down at her and she could see the anger in his eyes, and the fear, too.

"What are you so afraid of, Killian?"

He took forever to answer, then almost too softly to hear, he said, "You."

Warmth moved through her at the simple word. She shivered slightly and almost smiled. He glanced away for a moment. She could see the barely banked anger in his face, in the tightness of his jaw and the taut skin around his eyes. Finally, almost reluctantly, he looked back down at her.

Their gazes met, held. For a dizzying second, Lainie couldn't breathe. They were alike, somehow. Both lonely and lost, both afraid of connecting with other people.

And suddenly she understood. He'd let Emily down. John MacArthur Killian, the legendary Texas Ranger, had let down his own wife. He hadn't been there when she needed him and—somehow—she'd died. He blamed himself.

Lainie knew how that felt. She'd spent years—a lifetime—blaming herself for her parents' irresponsibility. She'd taken it all onto her slim shoulders; they'd left because she was selfish and unlovable. Somehow, it was her fault that they didn't love her.

Killian had done the same thing. He'd taken Emily's weakness as his failing. That's why he was here, an outlaw living among social outcasts.

Lainie had asked the one thing of him he couldn't give. Or didn't believe he could give. Help. Because to give it, to help her, he'd have to believe he was a good man.

She wanted to reach out to him then, to trail her fingertips along his beard-stubbled cheek. But she didn't. A lifetime's worth of fear held her immobile, wanting what she knew she couldn't have. "I'm not like Emily," she said quietly.

The color drained from his cheeks, left him pale and drawn. His voice fell to a strained, throaty whisper. "What do you mean?"

She swallowed hard. "I've already . . . survived what Emily went through."

Silence crashed into the cabin.

"Oh, my God," he said in a rush of breath. "That's what your nightmares are about . . . why you don't sleep. . . ."

She shook her head slightly. "That's . . . part of it." She looked up at him, trying to tell him so many things with her eyes that she couldn't put into words. "It was really . . . ugly and it took me a while to get over it, but I did get over it. I *survived*."

"Alaina . . ."

The way he said her name almost broke her heart. Before she knew it, she was moving toward him, her face tilted up to his, her gaze steady. She saw the compassion in his gaze, the pain, and it drew her.

He barely touched her at first. She leaned infinitesimally toward him and closed her eyes. Suddenly, violently, his arms closed around her, held her so tightly, she couldn't breathe. She felt the slow, even thudding of his heart against her body, heard the soft whisper of his breath at her forehead.

She'd been waiting all her life for this moment, this touch, this simple understanding of her pain. Blinking back tears, she pressed her face against his shirt, breathing in the masculine, familiar scent of him. And suddenly it seemed possible that they were soul mates.

She reached up to touch him. "Killian—"

Lowering his head, he whispered harshly in her ear, "Jesus, Lainie, what are you doing to me?" Then he pushed her away and spun around, raising his hands. "Enough," he growled. "Enough."

She blinked, confused by the sudden change. "Enough, what?"

He turned to her, gave her a look so bleak, she felt its impact like a slap. "I can't do this. Tomorrow I'm sending you to Fortune Flats with Skeeter. That's the help I'll give you."

She moved toward him, strangely disappointed. It should be a victory for her, a triumph. He'd said he'd get her back. But all she felt was abandoned. "But—"

"But nothing." He backed up, keeping the distance between them. "Stay the hell away from me, Lainie." His voice was harsh, raw.

Before she could answer, someone knocked on the door.

"Come in," Killian said sharply.

The door swung open and Viloula stood in the doorway. In her hands she carried a small jar. There was a glassy, faraway look in her eyes and her hands were shaking. She looked at Lainie. "I have one last t'ing to try."

Lainie took a step toward the old woman. "What is it, Viloula? You look worried."

Viloula gave her a weak, lackluster smile. "I been up all night reading . . . and t'inking. Den I t'ought about dis." She held up the vial. The contents glittered like gold dust, caught the light, and seemed curiously alive. "Dis might tell me how to get you back home."

Lainie drew in a sharp breath. Hope exploded in her

heart, but she quickly suppressed it, unwilling to let herself believe. "How?"

Viloula looked from Lainie to Killian. "Follow me."

"Now?" Killian asked, frowning.

Viloula gave him a look so stark in its fear that Lainie was stunned. "If I doan do it now, I might not find de strengt' to do it."

"But, Viloula—"

"Now," she said sharply. Then she turned and left the cabin.

Chapter Sixteen

They walked together in a heavy, awkward silence, no one knowing what to say. Finally, after what felt like hours, they came to the place Viloula had chosen. On a lip of land just above the camp lay a flat plain, circled by towering walls of jet black rock. Overhead, the sky was a midnight blue veil studded with bright lights. As they watched, a star shot across the heavens, leaving a glittering white shower in its wake.

A sign, Viloula thought with a relieved sigh. She had chosen the right place.

"Killian, build us a fire," she said, spreading her coat out on the ground. "Lainie, you sit here."

Watching Viloula carefully, saying nothing, Lainie stepped over a pile of rocks and sat down on the coat. Within moments, Killian had a fire going, and he and Lainie were seated beside it.

Viloula placed the jar on a flat rock and stood back, studying it. Firelight caught the glass and spun through it in a kaleidoscope of color, turning the contents into a glittering pile that resembled crushed copper.

All Viloula's life, she'd prepared for a moment like this, waited for it. She'd believed—always believed—in the infinite possibilities of the universe. Her mama, the great obeah healer, Genvieve, had whispered in Viloula's tiny ears of the impossible and the improb-

able. She had grown up knowing that someday she
would be touched by the impossible, would taste its
sweetness, be touched by its hot magic.

The moment was here; she could feel it in every
quickened beat of her heart. And she was afraid.

She stared down at the bottle. Years ago, she'd gotten
it from an old Indian, a blind man named Pa-lo-wah-ti
who'd told her that someday she would need it. In it, he
said, she would find the visionary answer to a great
question.

She reached for the bottle, not surprised to find that
her hands were shaking. Curling her fingers around the
cold glass, she wrenched off the cork top and swallowed the drug, washing it down quickly with water
from her canteen.

"Viloula!" Alaina called out. "What are you doing?"

The reaction was immediate. Viloula's knees melted,
her shoulders rounded. Slowly, feeling every motion,
she crumpled to her knees.

"Vi?"

She heard Alaina's high-pitched, frightened voice,
but it seemed to come at her from a million miles away.
She tried to smile, but her lips were heavy, uncontrolla-
ble, and her mouth was so dry, she couldn't speak. Her
arms were deadweights pinned to her side. She felt the
powdery brush of dirt beneath her fingertips.

How long ago had she taken the drug? She couldn't
be sure; time seemed to be spiraling away from her. She
glanced down, and the ground seemed alternately to be
too close, then too far away to focus on. Below, glistening with firelight, lay the discarded bottle. It looked
fragile and unimportant without the inner magic of the
narcotic. A hollow vessel of clear glass.

Tiny rocks bit into her knees. She felt each individual
pebble, each twig, as a spear of fire through her joints

and up into her thighs. Beside her, the fire danced and writhed, sent rainbow streamers into the dark sky. She tilted her chin to watch the dazzling display. Color exploded across the sky, gushed up from the trees, encompassed her, overwhelmed her. A shooting star sped across the heavens in a flow of showering sparks. It was close, so close she could touch it, ride it. . . .

Back, back, back, she leaned, until she lay sprawled in the dirt, arms spread.

A face appeared above her, a pale blob of color against the dark sky. "Vi?" The word—was it her name?—was deep and vibrating, drawn out to an impossible length.

Alaina.

Viloula blinked, tried to wet her lips enough to speak. She wanted to reach out, to touch Alaina's face, but before she could move, the ground vanished, and suddenly she was falling, spilling through an endless, lightless void. It was a magical, dizzying sensation that left her laughing and breathless. Stars sped past her like fireflies, caressing her face with light and warmth.

Then she was floating, her body riding an invisible wave of air. Back and forth, back and forth. She closed her eyes, released a heavy breath, and felt as if she were dissolving, melting into the air itself, as if she were a feather, or less, nothing at all. . . .

The vision hit her like a crack to the jaw, wrenching the breath from her lungs. She gasped, tried to reach out, but she had no hands, no arms. It was just a sound at first, a booming, thunderous echo of gunfire.

Killian. The name exploded in her mind, sent panic spiraling through her blood. She was suddenly hot, suffocatingly hot. She felt the prickle of sweat on her brow. Her heart beat so fast, she couldn't catch her breath.

Run! Run! She tried to scream the warning, but her throat was so dry, she couldn't, or she had no throat, or no memory of how to speak. She didn't know, couldn't be sure. Everything was shifting in on itself, moving. The world was a kaleidoscope of blasting color and deafening sounds.

She thrashed from side to side, not wanting to see any more. A harsh, desperate whimper pushed past her lips.

Blood. It splashed across her eyes, dripped down her cheeks. She felt its slimy downward movement on her skin, tasted its metallic bitterness.

She clawed at her face, screaming, trying to get rid of it, but the more she touched her face, the bloodier her hands grew. Wildly she looked down at her body, trying to see her wound. She got a fleeting glimpse of blue fabric darkened by blood.

Killian was beside her, and for the first time his face was crystal-clear in her mind. She was afraid for him, desperately frightened, though she didn't know why.

Killiannnn . . .

He dissolved into the night and the blood vanished.

Gasping, fighting for air, she sat up. In the distance, shimmering and uncertain, she saw two bodies intertwined. Sounds came at her hard. She heard a woman's crying, the roaring echo of thunder, hammering rain, gunfire. The noises fused into one throbbing din and battered her ears, deafened her.

She clamped her hands over her ears and suddenly there was silence, utter, breathless silence. Her vision zoomed across the desert, focused on the people in the distance. Lightning electrified the sky, illuminated their faces and the jagged, broken rock behind them. A huge, fiery red sun hung inches above a black plain of earth. An ornate silver cross hung suspended in the air, its shadow cast across a huge rock wall. Then the cross shimmered, moved, tumbled end over end across the sky, and disappeared in a puff of purple smoke.

Alaina. Killian. Blood. Tears. Sunset.

The lightning struck again. And Alaina was gone.

Shuddering, Viloula squeezed her eyes shut. "More," she cried out, her voice scratchy and weak. It couldn't be over. Whose blood had she seen? Whose death? "More . . ."

But the images began to slide into one another. They blurred, started to fade. Panic squeezed her throat, made her gasp for breath and claw for answers. *Oh, God. Oh, Jesus, no . . .* It couldn't end yet, not yet. She didn't know enough. Whose blood had she seen, whose tears? What was happening?

Weak, dizzy, she fell backward, into a darkness so deep and black and thick, there was no escape. It closed around her, seeped into her nose and mouth until she couldn't breathe, clogged her ears until she couldn't hear, and weighted her arms and legs.

With a last, shuddering breath, she melted into the nothingness.

Lainie paced from one end of Vi's little cabin to the other, gnawing hard on her thumbnail.

"Will you please stop that? You're giving me a headache." Killian leaned forward in his chair and covered his face in his hands. A deep, heavy sigh slipped through his fingers. "She's been asleep too long."

Lainie started chewing on her thumbnail again. Panic was close, clawing at her. She fought it, tried to concentrate on remaining calm, but couldn't. She felt so damned helpless and afraid. She and Killian had been in this room for hours, waiting for Viloula to wake up. Whatever sparks had connected them before were gone now, lay frayed and forgotten in the silence between them.

He turned to her, and in the dim lamplight, she saw the network of lines that pulled at his mouth and eyes. He looked drained and exhausted . . . and afraid.

Lainie brought her cold hands together, twisted her fingers into a tense ball. "She shouldn't have taken it. Not even to help me get home."

Home. The word and all that it meant slammed into her. How many days did she have to get home? How long before Kelly returned to an empty house and the government stepped in to "help out"?

Don't think about it. Not now, not yet.

She released her breath slowly, concentrating on regaining her composure, or at least the illusion of it.

"Oh, God . . . I have to get home."

Killian threw her a dark, accusatory look.

She went to perch on the chair beside his. Leaning toward him, she tried to make him understand. "I know you think all of this is nothing, but it's not. It's life or death, and Viloula knew it."

"Yeah. Only it's your life and her death. Did she know that?"

Lainie felt as if he'd hit her. With a trembling breath, she sagged back in the chair. Bowing her head, she stared at the hands folded in her lap until tears turned them into a pale smear against her red sweater.

"Hey." Killian's voice was soft, husky. "I shouldn't have said that. It's not your fault. Viloula knew what she was risking. It's not your fault."

Lainie didn't look at him. She couldn't. Instead, she nodded.

He started to reach for her, then drew back.

She lifted her moist gaze to his face.

"I just care about her," he said quietly.

"Yeah. Me, too."

They stared at each other, and in his gaze, Lainie saw the same helplessness that threatened to overtake her. She thought she should say something to him, but she had no idea what. The memory of his violent hug was so close, she could almost feel his arms around her again, warming her.

"Are . . ." She tried not to finish the sentence, but she couldn't help herself. "Are you really going to let Skeeter take me to Fortune Flats?"

He nodded.

"Why Skeeter and not you?"

He didn't look at her. "Don't look a gift horse in the mouth, Lainie. Just accept it."

She gave a soft, hollow laugh. "I've never been good at just accepting things."

Slowly, reluctantly, he met her gaze. There was a bleakness in his eyes that took her breath away, made her feel—again—as if she knew him. As if his pains were hers, somehow. "I can't help you, Lainie."

"You mean you won't."

Without answering, he turned back to the sleeping woman. "Here, Viloula," he murmured, reaching into the water basin beside him. Pulling up the towel, he twisted it. Water streamed through his fingers and splashed into the bowl. Gently he pressed the wet rag to her fevered forehead.

The simple gesture threw Lainie back in time for an instant. Suddenly she was a young mother again, nursing her baby daughter through chicken pox. She remembered keenly how alone she had felt when Kelly's fever spiked, how incompetent she'd felt.

She would have given anything to have someone beside her, someone to help her.

She cast a sideways glance at Killian. He sat hunched

over Viloula's bed, his big, suntanned hand covering one of hers. His hair was dirty and limp, hanging in a ratty silver tangle over his collar. A day's growth of black beard shadowed his cheeks, made his face look bruised in the pale light.

He'd never looked more handsome. She remembered how she'd felt when he had rescued her in the cave. In that instant, everything Viloula said seemed more than possible. Killian wasn't just a character in her book, wasn't simply a physical embodiment of her imagination.

Suddenly it hurt to look at him. She closed her eyes, but in the enforced darkness it was worse; she imagined his touch on her forehead, heard his softly spoken words: "You'll be all right, Viloula. You'll be all right."

A shiver traced her spine. She opened her mouth and stared at him, feeling unaccountably dizzy.

She'd spent a lifetime wondering what it must feel like to be cared for, looked after. She'd sought that welcoming, comforting touch in a hundred men's hands, until, at last, she'd stopped waiting for it. She'd even thought that she'd stopped wanting it.

But now, watching Killian minister to Viloula, she saw the naked, painful truth. She'd never stopped; it had lain dormant inside her beneath an avalanche of enforced coldness. She felt it now, an aching, hurtful need to be held and touched and cared for.

As if drawn by her thoughts, he looked at her. "Are you okay?"

She swallowed hard. "Fine."

He stared at her for a long time, as if seeking something in her eyes. "Go to sleep," he said at last. "I'll watch her."

Sleep. The word filled her with a sinking sense of despair. He made it sound so easy; go to sleep. He might as well have suggested she try brain surgery. "I'm not tired."

He frowned. "I can see it in your eyes."

His eyes saw more than she wanted to reveal. The silence between them thickened, became laced with undercurrents.

Unable to stand it, she spun away from him and went to the stove. "You want a cup of coffee?"

"Yeah," he said as she reached for the tin pot. "Coffee would be great."

She pulled a speckled blue cup from the shelving behind the stove, poured him a cup of strong, black coffee, and crossed back to the bed.

Without meeting his gaze, she handed it to him.

He took it, set it down on the bedside table. "Thanks."

"No problem."

After that, the silence fell again, thick and heavy and strained.

Killian threw the damp washrag down on the bedside table and leaned back in his chair, letting out a harsh sigh. God, he was tired. He raked his fingers through his tangled, dirty hair and came forward, resting his elbows on his knees and covering his face with his hands.

He listened to the slow, steady sounds of Viloula's breathing. The old woman was sounding better, and her fever had finally broken about a half hour ago.

Tiredly he lifted his head and glanced sideways.

Lainie sat sprawled in a chair in the corner, her legs pushed out in front of her and crossed at the ankles. Her head was cocked to one side, her mouth parted slightly. Her arms hung limp at her sides.

As he watched her, she frowned in her sleep, made a soft, breathy sound that might have been the word *no*.

She moved restlessly, her head snapped suddenly to the left. Then she quieted again, fell silent.

She looked painfully vulnerable right now, and the need to go to her, to wake her from her fitful sleep, was powerful. So powerful . . .

He frowned and forced his gaze away from her. He'd made a decision, he'd given her what she said she wanted: a way out of this hellhole. As soon as Viloula wakened, Killian was going to send Skeeter and Lainie to Fortune Flats with his blessing.

There, he thought, *that ought to do it.* He was acting like a goddamn hero, doing what she asked of him. So why did it make him feel empty and lost? As if he wasn't doing the right thing at all.

Why Skeeter and not you?

"She's asking too much," he said softly, wincing at the desperate tenor of his voice, wondering bitterly who he was trying to convince.

"Alaina?" Viloula's cracked, reedy voice cut through his thoughts.

Relief rushed through him, banished the fear and apprehension for a heartbeat. "Thank God. Viloula?" He turned to Lainie, raised his voice. "She's trying to say something."

Killian's voice, ragged and hoarse, roused Lainie from her stupor. She blinked hard, sat upright in her chair. "What?"

"She's trying to say something."

Lainie stumbled to Viloula's side and skidded into the chair, clutching the seat edge. She scooted closer to the bed, leaning over Viloula. The old woman lay motionless, looking frail and withered against the linen sheeting. Purple shadows puddled beneath her eyes; her lips were colorless and dry.

Lainie swallowed hard. "I'm right here, Vi. Right beside you."

"Lainie? Killian?" Viloula's voice was raspy, spiked by shallow, painful breaths.

Lainie shook her head, blinded by hot tears. "Don't talk, Vi. Don't try—"

Viloula smiled. It was weak and trembling, and the most beautiful smile Lainie had ever seen. "I'm starving," she grumbled.

Lainie let out a relieved laugh, then clamped down on her lower lip and covered her mouth with her hand. "Viloula?" she ventured. "Are you all right?"

The old lady nodded. "I had a vision."

Lainie drew in a sharp breath. Hope pounded in her chest, made it hard to hear anything but her own heartbeat. "Do I get home?"

Vi looked at her. "You leave here."

Lainie felt as if a ten-thousand-pound boulder had just been lifted from her chest. "Where?"

Viloula let out a hacking, rattling cough. "I saw de place clearly. It is a rock. . . . De Navajos call it de rock dat lightning struck." She looked at Killian. "You know dis place?"

He nodded. "Yeah. It's fifty, sixty miles due east."

"When do I need to be there?" Lainie asked anxiously.

Viloula frowned, thinking. "I saw a cross. . . . I t'ink dat mean de Sabbat'."

"Okay, Sunday. What time?"

"A storm, very bad. And de sun was setting." Her frown deepened. "De storm is de key. You must be at de rock when de lightning strike again. If you miss it . . . dere will be no more chances."

Lainie felt a flutter of fear. She pushed it away, refused to give in to it. "I'll be there."

Viloula rolled her head slightly, stared up at Killian. "You were wit' her."

He gave a hollow laugh. "Those are some drugs, Vi."

Viloula reached for the amethyst at her throat. Unhooking the golden clasp, she eased the heavy stone necklace off her throat and pushed it toward Lainie. "You will need dis, child. To find your destiny."

"No, I couldn't—"

"Dis necklace has de magic to fulfill your destiny." A smile lit her black eyes. "It will come back to me."

Lainie took the necklace, felt its cold, impersonal weight in her palm. Slowly she put it around her neck and clasped the catch. The weighty stone settled in the hollow at the base of her throat and warmed the skin. A small, rhythmic pulse seemed to emanate from the amethyst.

Viloula looked at her hard. "Use it wisely."

"How?"

"I doan know."

"I don't understand. . . . I didn't need the necklace to get here."

"But you will need it to get back, I t'ink."

Lainie's voice was tight with emotion. "Thanks, Viloula. I pray to God you'll get it back."

"I will." She turned slightly to face Killian again. "It is a dangerous journey," she whispered. A tiny frown pulled at her mouth.

Lainie knew instantly that Viloula was withholding something. "What are you hiding from us, Vi?"

Viloula flinched at the question, drew in a fluttery breath. Her eyes took on a glassy, faraway look, and Lainie was somehow certain that the old woman was reliving the vision. "Dere will be a deat'," she said finally in a dull, quiet voice.

Lainie shivered. *There will be a death.* "Whose?"

"I doan know."

"Perfect," Killian said, leaning back in his chair.

Viloula ignored him and looked at Lainie. "It is all up to you, Alaina. You need to believe. . . ."

"Believe in what?"

Viloula closed her eyes and sank back into the bed. "I doan know dat, eit'er. Maybe in destiny . . . maybe in love . . . maybe in yourself."

For a long time, neither Killian nor Lainie spoke. Then, finally, he pushed to his feet. "I'm exhausted, Lainie. I'm going back to the cabin to get some sleep. Are you coming?"

"I think I'll stay here a second longer."

After Killian left the cabin, Viloula's eyes cracked open. "Is he gone?"

Lainie nodded. "Yeah."

Viloula released a weary sigh. "You and Killian must leave in de morning."

Lainie shook her head. "He's sending Skeeter as my guide. Killian's not going anywhere."

Viloula frowned harshly, her gray lips puckering. "Wit'out Killian, maybe dere is no destiny, no doorway." She wagged a gnarled finger at Lainie. "You doan go nowhere wit' Skeeter, child. It is Killian dat must take you."

"Jesus," Lainie sighed. "It just gets worse and worse. I can't *make* Killian take me anywhere."

Viloula reached out, curled her bony fingers around Lainie's hand, squeezing. "Dat boy want to take you, Alaina. Trust an old woman to see what de young ones cannot. He want to take you, he just afraid. You know what dat is like."

"Yeah," she said softly. "I know what it's like to be afraid."

Viloula squeezed her hands again, drew her close.

"Remember what I tole you. Your lesson . . . dat is de doorway to de future, not some rock."

Lainie tried to smile, but couldn't manage it. "I hope I figure out my cosmic failing before I get there."

"You know de lesson, Lainie. In your heart, you know it."

Lainie leaned forward. "Come with me, Vi."

Viloula shook her head. "It is no journey for an old woman."

Lainie swallowed hard, feeling the embarrassing sting of tears. "I . . . I'll miss you, Vi."

She smiled, though her eyes were misty, too. "Didn't you learn anyt'ing from all dat reading, child? Dere ain't no good-bye in dis life. You and Killian and I . . . we always be together, somehow." She pressed a thin, cool hand to Lainie's cheek. "You are stronger dan you t'ink you are, Alaina. You will make it home."

Lainie stepped back reluctantly, put distance between herself and the first friend she'd made in years. She knew this moment, recognized its poignant sharpness all too well. Viloula could say whatever she wanted, but Lainie wasn't fooled. If there was one thing she *did* believe in in this life, it was this moment, this word. She'd said it too many times. Too many . . .

"Good-bye, Viloula." Fighting tears, she turned and ran for the door.

"Believe, Alaina," Viloula whispered.

Then the door slammed shut behind her, and Lainie was alone. She leaned back against the cold, splintery wood and closed her eyes. Unconsciously she reached for the medallion at her throat. Curling her fingers around the stone, she felt its comforting weight. A strange calm seeped through her. She let out a long breath and sagged against the door.

"So," hissed a masculine voice in her ear. "You stole the old woman's necklace."

Lainie's eyes popped open.

Mose was standing beside her, a rifle cradled negligently against his chest. Black, beady eyes drilled her.

Stay calm. Lainie knew about men like Mose; they fed off fear. It gave them an edge that they wielded like a sharp sword. She gave him a slow, deliberate smile. "Why, hello, Mose. I was just saying good night to my grandmother."

"If you're Viloula's grandkid, I'm Grover Cleveland."

She forced a cocky smile. "Hello, Mr. President."

His dark, swarthy face pulled into a heavy frown. "Don't get smart with me, lady. I'm just itchin' to kill you."

She wanted to draw back, but stood her ground. The overpowering stench of bad breath laced with whiskey slammed into her nostrils. "Then you'll have to kill Killian, too."

A deadly smile curved his mouth. "You think I wouldn't?"

Lainie swallowed hard. "I know you would, Mose."

"You got twenty-four hours."

"To do what?"

He pressed closer, rubbed himself against her leg, and brought his face into the crook of her neck. She stiffened, feeling the shooting heat of his moist breath along her skin. The wet tip of his tongue flicked up her neck.

She gasped and squeezed her eyes shut for a moment, barely breathing.

He pulled back just enough to stare into her eyes. His gaze was cold and dead and dangerous. "Tomorrow I'm gonna take over this camp, and when I'm leader . . ."

He licked his thick lips, left a trail of spittle behind. "You're mine."

"Yeah, right," she said throatily.

He leaned close, shoved his hand between her legs, and squeezed. "You must be good—Killian ain't had a woman up here in years."

Lainie wrenched away. Shoving past him, she ran for the cabin. His throaty laughter nipped at her heels, spurred her to run faster. When she reached Killian's cabin, she was breathing hard, and fear was a cold, throbbing coil in her stomach.

At the door, she stumbled to a stop and glanced back.

Mose used his rifle to tip his hat back. Then, still laughing, he turned and walked away, disappearing into the drinking tent.

Lainie let out a sigh of relief. She stood there a long time, staring at the door, until her breathing was normalized. Then, slowly, she went inside.

Chapter Seventeen

Killian lay sleeping, his jet black lashes sealed against his sun-darkened skin. His mouth was parted just enough to see a hint of the strong white teeth beneath. The blue chambray of his shirt was stretched taut across the broadness of his back. Grayed linen humped in a wrinkled mass across his buttocks and covered his long legs.

Lainie gazed down at him. She got a sudden, fleeting image of him sprawled on rumpled sheets, cropped black hair in sharp contrast to the stark white pillow beneath. He looked young and boyish and breathtakingly handsome.

She backed away from him, frowning. He didn't look anything like the man she'd just imagined. Nothing. It was as if she was seeing Killian as she'd seen him before, somewhere. . . .

Soul mates. The words filled her with longing, then regret. She backed away from the bed, as frightened as she'd been a second ago with Mose.

But she wouldn't let fear stop her. Not then, with Mose, and not now with Killian.

If Viloula was right—and Lainie prayed to God that she was—Lainie had to make Killian take her to the rock.

At the thought, longing moved through her. God,

she'd give anything to be able to walk up to Killian, smile up at him, and say, "Take me to the rock." If she could believe in him, trust him, maybe there wouldn't be this painful ache in her chest. She wanted—needed—to trust him.

Yet she couldn't. Getting to the rock was too important. Maybe in a perfect world, she'd spend more time with Killian and find out what invisible strands bound them together, discover why anger and fear were so close to the surface in him and why he was so afraid to help her.

But God knew, this wasn't a perfect world, and she didn't have the time to do that. She had to be at the rock by sunset on Sunday, and she had to be there with Killian.

She went to the bedpost, where his gun belt hung limply over a knot in the wood. Taking the gun out, she eased the gun belt off the post and set it on the floor. Then she retrieved the canvas sack she'd filled earlier. Adding a double supply of everything and a change of clothes for him, she swung it toward the door. It hit the floor with a muffled *thwop*.

She went to the bed and stared down at Killian.

A moment's hesitation paralyzed her, made her hand shake slightly. The gun wobbled.

Stop. She gripped the handle more tightly.

For this to work, she had to be as strong as steel, as determined as ever in her life. She had to be ready to shoot him, otherwise the gun was more of a liability than a tool.

Could she shoot him? Her heart clutched at the thought. If only she could trust him, she thought again. God, it would be so wonderful. . . .

Dreams. She forced herself to think of Kelly and the

empty house. Memories hurled themselves at her, sickened her.

Yeah, she thought. She could kill anyone to keep Kelly safe.

"Killian. Wake up."

The words came at him through a hazy cloud of sleep. "Lainie," he murmured, smiling. A surprising warmth seeped through him. It had been so long since he'd wakened to the sound of a woman's voice.

"Get up."

He frowned. Her voice was cold, angry. The momentary warmth vanished, left in its place a cold chill. He tried to push all thoughts of her from his mind, tried to remind himself that he felt nothing for her. Nothing.

Blinking hard, he rolled onto his back and sat up. The dark cabin curled around him. It took his bleary eyes a minute to focus. When he did, he saw the gun.

The sight of her standing in the center of the room like she was Wyatt Earp made him laugh. He thanked God for it; the ridiculousness of the moment made his fear seem insubstantial and irrelevant. "You're going to shoot me, Lainie?"

"Not if you take me out of here."

She was serious. Jesus. He frowned and ran a hand through his hair, eyeing her warily. "I gave that job to Skeeter. Shoot him."

"I don't want Skeeter," she said quietly. "I want you."

The words hit him so hard, he reeled backward. "Get out of here, Lainie," he said in a hoarse voice.

She flicked the gun a little. "Get out of bed. We're packed and the horse is ready. Let's go."

He stared at her, trying to think of what to do. She stood as still as a rail, arms chest-high, chin up. Her skin was so pale, it looked translucent against the dark intensity of her eyes. Her lips were a tense, colorless slash. "You wouldn't really kill me, Lainie."

Pain glazed her eyes for a heartbeat, then vanished. "I don't want to."

Everything about this moment was crazy. He felt . . . disconnected, confused. But he knew one thing for sure: He wasn't taking Lainie out of this camp. He'd already decided that. He wasn't going to play the hero for her, and he wasn't going to lose himself in the needy vulnerability of her eyes.

Not him. Slowly he got out of bed and walked toward her. She backed up. "Stop. I mean it. Stop."

A grim, humorless smile curved his mouth. He was in his element now, had slipped into the role he knew so well. The outlaw; he used the persona as he'd used it for years, as a shield to hide the weak and selfish man within. "A gun's only as good as the man—or woman— holding it. How good are you?" He kept moving, his hands loose and swinging at his sides, his eyes fixed on her.

She flicked her wrist to the left and pulled the trigger. There was a cracking explosion and a spray of yellow-bright light. The pungent, acrid scent of sulfur filled the room. He felt the whiz of a bullet pass his ear and the shattering crack of glass. Behind him, a jar exploded. Nails burst outward, clattered on the floor.

He stopped dead, staring in shock at the gaping hole in the wall behind him and the drifts of flour on the floor. Slowly he turned back to Lainie.

She pointed the gun at his heart and drew back the hammer. Steel hit steel in a deafening *click.* "I need to be at the rock by sunset Sunday. After that, you can walk away."

For a blinding, terrifying moment, he didn't even

want to argue. He wanted to give in, gracelessly and with a measure of hope he hadn't known in years. Christ help him, for a second, he wanted to change. The thought scared the shit out of him. He was forty-three years old. Too goddamn old and banged up and disillusioned to turn into someone's white knight.

He moved toward her, lifted his palms in helpless despair. "You're asking the wrong man, Lainie. I'm no goddamn hero."

She didn't blink. "Let's go."

He stopped. His hands fell to his sides. A cold, crushing sense of inevitability descended on him, pushed at his shoulders until they rounded with defeat. He saw suddenly and with a rising desperation that they'd been heading toward this moment from the second they met. And nothing he could say or do would change it.

She expected a hero, demanded one. Unfortunately, what she got was a broken-down outlaw with a soul full of regrets. They were both screwed.

He felt as if he were being drawn into some great blackness from which there was no escape. "I won't be there when you need me," he said softly, so softly that he wasn't sure she heard. But he heard, and the ringing truth of the sentence made him sick. Bowing his head, he moved toward her. "Let's go."

She moved in beside him, tucking her smaller body close to his. Together they walked out of the cabin and headed down the street. Lainie kept the gun close to his ribs. On either side of them, lightless cabins sat quietly against the jet black mesa. The only sound in the night was the rhythmic thump of their footsteps and the clatter of their supplies. Captain plodded slowly along behind them, his head hung low.

"Is that Skeeter up there?" Lainie whispered, seeing the lookout.

"It is."

"Put your arm around me."

He froze, felt another flash of fear. Christ, the last thing he wanted to do was touch her. He forced a laugh, tried to sound nonchalant. "You don't need a gun to seduce me, Lainie. Your charming personality is more than enough."

"Put your arm around me."

"Whatever you say. You're the one with the gun." He curved one long arm around her shoulders. He meant to keep his touch cold and impersonal, but at the feel of her body, so warm and soft, something inside him gave way. He drew her close. A little too close. His hand slid down the hard curve of her shoulder and settled at her upper arm. The sunshine and dust scent of her clothing filled his nostrils.

"Hey, boss, that you?" Skeeter called out, drawing his rifle.

"It's me, Skeet. Me and the woman."

Skeeter lowered his rifle. A frown wrinkled his forehead. "Where'd ya find her?"

"She was . . . out taking a piss."

Lainie rammed the gun against his ribs so hard, he jumped to the left, dragging her with him for a step.

"You goin' out?"

Killian nodded. "Purty's in charge till I get back."

"Where ya goin'?"

"I'm taking the woman to the rock that lightning struck. I'll be back in a few days."

Skeeter stepped aside. "See ya, boss."

They walked past the lookout and came to the end of the street.

"Mount up," Lainie said under her breath. When he didn't move, she poked him in the ribs again. "Now."

He stabbed his boot in the stirrup and climbed into

the saddle, trying to shake a heavy sense of impending doom. "Why are we only taking one horse? Two would—"

"I'm in charge here." Keeping the gun pointed at him, she clambered into position behind him. Settling comfortably, she pressed the gun into his side. "That's why there's one horse, and you knew it. Now, let's go."

Killian spurred Captain forward. "You're the boss."

But not for long. He clenched his jaw and stared straight ahead. She might have a gun on him now, but she wouldn't be able to keep it up. Sooner or later—and it better be sooner—she'd accidentally give him a heartbeat's worth of time. That's all he'd need with someone like her, just an instant. Then he could get the gun away from her and take control back.

And get the hell away from the naked vulnerability in her eyes . . . and the sickening need in his own.

Lainie's arm ached with exhaustion. They'd been riding for hours upon hours, and neither of them had spoken a single word. In the darkness of the cave, Lainie had been ramrod-stiff, her body angled away from his so that there would be no accidental contact. But in the long, wearying hours since, she'd softened a little. Every now and then she'd find herself falling slightly forward, find her arm resting against his thigh.

It was irritating, and when she realized what she was doing, she drew back sharply and cleared her throat, jabbing the gun against his ribs for good measure.

It was because of the heat, she knew, and the endless, glaring light of the sun. She brought a sweaty hand to her brow and shoved a lock of damp, sticky hair from her eyes. Lord, she was tired. And hungry. And weak.

She stared at the broad back in front of her, and before she knew it, she was thinking about how solid it looked, how strong. How comfortable it would be if she could lean forward just a little and press her cheek against his back and go to sleep . . .

A quiet sigh escaped her parched lips. The horse rocked beneath her, swaying in a gentle, seesawing motion that made her sleepy. Her eyelids fluttered shut. The sudden darkness enfolded her, wrapped her in familiar warmth and took her to a different place, a world of towering fir trees and incessant rain, of cloud-thick gray skies and whispering wind. It felt so real that for a heartbreakingly perfect moment, she tasted the cool moisture of Seattle air, smelled a wisp of cedar.

Home. She was on her way home. It was that thought that had sustained her since leaving the hideout. When the weight of the gun became unbearable, when her fingers hurt from so many hours in the same position, she took strength from the quiet plodding of the horse's hooves, from the slow, steady movement east. Every step they took brought them closer to the Rock, closer to the daughter she'd unwillingly left behind.

"Kelly." The word slipped from her mouth, hovering in the silent air for a second before it disappeared.

At the thought of her daughter, Lainie felt a stunning sense of hopefulness, of relief. She'd done it, just as she'd promised herself. She'd handled the problem and figured out a way to get back. She was on her way home.

In her mind's eye, she saw Kelly fling open the door and hurtle into the kitchen, her long black ringlets bouncing against her back. Her face would be sunburnt from the weeks in Montana, her cheeks pinkened and peeling. She'd be smiling, her crooked teeth framed by the silver track of new braces.

Mom, I'm home.

He reined Captain to a stop. "This is probably a good place to make camp."

She pulled back, blinked. "Camp? The sun just set. I want to ride as far as possible tonight."

"You have. Now, get off."

She pressed the gun more tightly against his ribs. "You've obviously forgotten that I have a gun on you."

"Sure, Lainie. Outlaws forget shit like that all the time."

"Then—"

"Then nothing. This is the last water for twelve miles. It's the end of the line for tonight."

"I'm not thirsty."

"The horse is. Now, get off before I swing my arm back and knock you off."

Lainie stared at his back again, and this time there were no thoughts about resting her head against him, no daydreams drifting through her mind. This was the moment she'd dreaded all day. It was so safe with him in front of her on the horse, the gun pressed to his side. It placed her in a position of power. But when they were both on the ground . . .

"Put your hands behind your back," she said.

"Why?"

"Just do it."

He wrapped the reins around the saddle horn and did as she asked. She untied a length of rope from the saddle's skirt and twisted it around Killian's wrists, binding them as tightly as she could.

She looked away quickly, but not before the image of bound wrists had registered in her mind. A shudder moved through her, settled as a tightness in her chest. She couldn't help feeling a twinge of regret at doing this to him. It was so demoralizing, so . . . She shook the thought off, trying not to care.

"Is that too tight?"

"It'll make dancing difficult."

Lainie edged backward, off the skirt and onto the hairy hump of Captain's butt. "Get down."

Killian brought one booted foot over the saddle horn and twisted in his seat, sliding downward. He hit the ground with a dusty thump and turned to her. He stood directly beside her, his face tilted up to hers. The black hat cast his face in shadow, so she couldn't see anything except the jarring whiteness of his teeth.

"Move back. I want to dismount."

He didn't move. "I wouldn't want you to fall," he said in a quiet, seductive voice that filled her with longing.

Her throat felt tight. "I'm not going to fall. Now, back up."

"No."

She stared down at the shadowy lower half of his face, knowing—as he did—that if she slid off the other side, the horse would be between them. She couldn't shoot him, and if she didn't have a clear shot at him at all times, she wasn't in control.

And she shuddered to think what would happen out here if she ever lost control.

"Are you going to stay up there all night?"

Slowly she brought her left foot over the saddle's seat and shifted to face him. Dangling both feet directly in front of Killian, she looked down at him. The memory of his embrace came at her without warning, stunning her in the intensity of her reaction. For a split second she imagined herself slipping downward, letting herself be enfolded in his powerful arms, letting herself be comforted.

Fool. She pushed the images away. Clutching the cantle's leather rim in tired, sweaty fingers, she slid downward. The toes of her boots touched his legs, rustled the warm denim of his pants, before her feet hit the ground.

His body loomed in front of her, pinned her between him and Captain's damp flank. The humid scent of the animal's sweat filled the air between them. Killian stood as still as a statue, his legs spread slightly, his arms behind his back. She felt the heat of his body against her, felt the warmth of his gaze on her face.

She wet her lips nervously and aimed the gun at his chest, thankful that his hands were tied. That had been a good decision. "Back up."

He waited a full minute, then did as she asked. When they were about ten feet apart, he smiled. "I can't be much help with my hands tied."

"That's true, you can't." She flicked the gun to the side an inch. "Sit there. I'll make us a fire."

He stared at her, saying nothing, not moving. Lainie straightened, forced herself to meet his probing gaze head-on. *You're in control here,* she reminded herself a dozen times in the split second the silence lasted. *Only you.*

Slowly he backed up and sat down on a fallen tree. "I guess I can watch a woman work."

"Of course you can. It's how the West was won." Without another word, Lainie gathered up a few branches and twigs, and threw them onto a pile alongside the river. Reaching into the saddlebags, she pulled out the matchbox and lit the fire. Soon wispy trails of smoke spilled upward, followed by crackling, licking flames.

"I have to take a piss."

She gave him a tired wave. "Thank you for that urinary tract update. So go."

There was a silence that seemed to last forever, until finally he laughed. It was a rich, rumbling sound that drew Lainie's gaze. He was staring at her, and through the shadows on his face, she could just make out his eyes. They were crinkled in the corners, drawn in what would have been a smile on any other man.

She frowned suspiciously. "What?"

He got to his feet and walked toward her. She flinched at every step and wanted to turn away. But she stood her ground, tried to look disinterested. He came to within inches of her and stopped. Leaning close, he whispered in her ear, "My hands are tied."

It took Lainie a split second to get it. Then she drew in a sharp breath, her eyes widened. "I'm not untying your hands."

"Then you'll have to unbutton my trousers and take my—"

"Enough!"

He laughed again, and she wanted to slap his face. "Fine," she spat, shoving him away from her. "Turn around."

Still laughing, he stumbled backward and spun around, wiggling his fingers.

She advanced warily, keeping the gun prominently in front of her. With one hand, she untied the sagging knot and unwound the rope. "You have two minutes."

Without looking back, he strolled away from her, fading into the darkness just beyond the fire's glow.

Lainie backed up slowly and found her own place for privacy. When she was finished, she set the gun down on the dirt and stretched her fingers, hearing the snapping creak of tired bones. Standing, she let out a long sigh and pushed the damp tendrils of hair from her eyes. The endless darkness of the desert spilled out before her, a wavering palette of gray and black shadows that melted into a starless, lightless night sky.

"Lainie?"

His voice came at her from the darkness, a curious mixture of anger and worry. The control she'd fought for slipped a notch. She hugged herself, trying to make the feelings go away. Slowly she turned toward him.

In the campfire's throbbing circlet of light, he stood tall and straight, his black duster flapping softly in the wind. There was no sardonic smile on his face this time, no taunting curve of a thick eyebrow. His face was drawn into an intense frown. Deep lines etched his mouth and eyes.

"Lainie?" He took a single step forward, then paused, his eyes searching the darkness for her.

She saw an impossible caring in his gaze. She felt suddenly as if she were falling, tumbling into the warm heat of his brown eyes. Her heartbeat picked up, sweat itched across her forehead.

What would it feel like if Vi were right? she wondered again. What would it feel like to have a man like that to protect you, to care about you? To keep you safe . . .

Safe.

The word slipped through her, brought with it an aching sense of longing and loss. She tried to push the foolish thought aside. There was no *safe* in life; that was a lesson she'd learned a long time ago, and if there was, it wouldn't be with a man like Killian. But the thought wouldn't go so easily this time. It resisted, beckoned.

Safe.

She forced a harsh laugh, disgusted with herself. It was almost impossible to believe, but after all the therapy and work and pain, she still had something of the dreamer inside her.

No, not the dreamer, she thought bitterly. *The coward.* She had to admit—to herself at least—that deep down, she was afraid. Everything about this journey scared her, from the endless desert to the doorway at the end.

She was used to being afraid, of course. She'd spent more than half her life in constant fear, but this was different somehow. Out here, she felt so desperate sometimes, so frighteningly alone. No wonder she had the unfamiliar hope that Killian would protect her.

But it was only a dream; she had to always remember that. He wouldn't protect her and he wouldn't voluntarily get her back to Kelly.

With an exhausted sigh, she reached down and picked up the gun. The weapon felt cold and hard and reassuring in her grip. She straightened, strode toward the fire. "I'm right here, Killian."

She stepped into the golden cloud of light, the gun held stiffly in front of her.

He sighed. "I thought you'd set off on your own."

She heard the worry in his voice, and it filled her with a sad regret. In another time, another place, they might have meant something to one another. But not here, not now. She tightened her grip on the gun. "Not me, Killian."

He stared at her for a long time, then turned and started to walk away.

She hefted the gun up a bit, aimed it at his back. "Don't move."

He spun on her. "For Chrissakes, Lainie, it's the middle of the night. Where do you think I'm going to go? I'm just gonna make us something to eat."

She kept the gun aimed at his chest and moved warily forward. "Okay. Go to the saddlebags and get some food."

He strode across the small campsite to Captain, who stood calmly alongside the fallen tree, his head drooped forward. Burrowing noisily through the saddlebags,

Killian pulled out some beef jerky and canned beans, then untied the mess kit and hauled it back, dropping it at the fire. It hit the ground with a jarring clank. A tin coffeepot bumped over a few stones and rolled to Lainie's feet.

She glanced down at it.

That split second was all he needed. Lainie heard a whirring *thwop*, and looked up.

A huge circle of rope slithered through the air and fell in a hoop over her head. She gasped as the rope snapped tight around her body, pinned her arms to her sides. Hemp bit through her sweater and abraded her flesh.

The gun fell from her limp fingers and clattered to the ground, useless. She stumbled forward and almost fell, righting herself at the last possible second.

He pulled her toward him, almost wrenching her off her feet. Her legs shot out in front of her, bootheels skidding through the dirt as he reeled her in.

She stumbled and pitched forward; her knees hit the dirt hard.

He walked slowly toward her.

Fear and fury exploded in her chest. She surged to her feet and hurled herself at him, trying to wrench her arms free so she could scratch his eyes out. "Goddamn you," she hissed.

He grabbed her and shook her hard. "Lainie. Stop it."

She twisted and fought and threw herself backward.

"Damn it, Lainie," he yelled, throwing his arms around her until she couldn't move, couldn't breathe.

She felt his arms around her, clamping and hard and unforgiving. Nothing like the embrace of before. This was the truth, she thought desperately. *That* moment of caring had been the lie. . . .

And suddenly it overwhelmed her. She thought of Kelly—her beautiful baby girl—and she was lost.

It was over. She had failed, and God knew she wouldn't get another chance. Not by sunset on Sunday.

She should have felt betrayed and furious. But she didn't; she felt hollow and beaten. Everything seeped out of her, melted into the dusty ground at her feet. The fear she'd been holding at bay surged up and swamped her, moved through her blood in a dizzying wave. She went limp in his arms.

He seemed to feel the change. His hold loosened.

She sagged downward, crumpled at his feet. Her head bowed forward. She didn't have the strength anymore to hold it up.

There was no courage left inside her, no well of strength to draw from. Not this time.

She was too tired to do anything, too defeated and drained and beaten to beg or plead. Tears swelled in her chest, a hot, pounding ache that wouldn't release itself. She was too broken for tears. Her sorrow was too deep.

She had failed.

Chapter Eighteen

She sat slumped forward, the rope pulled taut around her upper arms, digging into the rough yarn of her sweater. Her head was bowed, her hair dusty and dampened by perspiration. She'd drawn her hands into her lap, where they lay limply atop her thighs. Behind her, the gun lay where it had fallen, the silver barrel cocked against a gray rock.

She looked frightened and vulnerable and beaten.

The anger drained out of Killian, left him with nothing, not even fear. He stood there like a statue, stiff and immobile, staring down at her. He remembered suddenly what she'd told him about her past. He felt mean and low ... so goddamn low....

Was this how Emily had looked the night they came for her? A vulnerable, frightened woman, on her knees, praying for mercy from men who had none to give....

He winced at the image. Shame settled in the pit of his stomach, mingled with a sinking, sickening sensation of regret. When had he become the kind of man he'd always despised? Had he really sunk so low that he would hurt a woman easily, that he'd bind her and wrench her through the night because it suited his own purposes? And when he knew some hint of what she'd been through in the past ...

"Jesus," he whispered, knowing the answer, hating it

with every fiber in his being. Wishing he could make it untrue.

He dropped to his knees in front of her.

"Lainie." He said her name softly, not knowing what else to say, not expecting her to respond.

She lifted her head, met his gaze with eyes that were liquid and shimmering with tears. She looked utterly, devastatingly defeated. "Please . . ." she said, then fell silent again, as if she didn't know what to ask for, or wouldn't ask it of him.

Jesus, it hurt just to look at her.

He reached out and loosened the rope, eased it away from her shoulders. The scratchy fibers caught on her sweater for a second, then released, slid down her body, and landed across her thighs in a whisper of sound. But it wasn't good enough, just taking the rope off her. He wanted never to have thrown it at all. His shame intensified, became a stabbing pain in his gut.

And suddenly he couldn't fight her anymore. Didn't even want to. He was tired, so damn tired of keeping her at arm's length.

He'd take her to the Rock. The decision lifted a weight off his shoulders, made it possible for him to breathe again.

Maybe then he wouldn't look into her sad eyes and feel like such a failure.

"I'll take you where you need to go, Lainie."

She drew in a sharp breath, but didn't move, didn't look at him. "Why?"

It was a question he didn't want to examine too closely. He shrugged. "Does it matter?"

This time she looked at him, and her eyes were glazed with tears. "You'll help me get home?"

The way she said the word, *home*, was the way he'd once whispered Emily's name. It resonated with emotion, with a longing that bespoke more than just a place to sleep, but a corner of the heart, a resting place for a weary soul. It saddened him somehow, made him wish—for the first time in years—that he belonged somewhere, that he had a place called home.

"Yeah, I'll take you. But ..." He paused, stared down at her. "But you should know, when the chips are down, I probably won't be there for you. I'm not too dependable."

"I'll take my chances," she said softly.

"Uh-huh." Somehow, he'd known she would say that. "Where's home?"

"Bainbridge Island, Washington ... 1994." She tensed, her moist gaze fixed on his face, and he knew that she was waiting for him to laugh.

Strangely, he didn't feel like laughing. "You believe it's real, don't you?"

Squeezing her eyes shut, she nodded.

"I'll try to get you home, Lainie. Wherever home is."

She stared past him, gazing out across the shadowy desert, her shoulders rounding downward. "I want to trust you. . . ."

The quietly spoken words touched him more than he would have thought possible. He understood what it felt like not to trust anyone. How alone it sometimes made you feel. He forced a laugh, hoping she didn't notice its hollow ring. "You're like me, Lainie. We don't trust too many people."

She shook her head. "No."

"Then I guess it'll mean something when you do trust me." The minute the words left his mouth, he winced, wondering what in the hell had made him say that. He was the most untrustworthy person he knew. Trusting him would get her killed.

She didn't smile, just looked at him with those heart-breakingly sad eyes. "It would mean everything."

Lainie sat on a boulder near the fire, her legs stretched out in front of her and crossed at the ankles. A half-empty whiskey bottle was beside her. The crackling red-gold heat licked at the soles of her boots, but for the first time in her life, she felt warmed from the inside.

And it scared her to death. At the thought, she took another drink, thankful that Killian had left the supplies next to her when he went to wash the dishes. If there was ever a time she needed bottled courage, this was it. She wanted to get so drunk, she couldn't think. Couldn't feel. Couldn't hope.

Almost against her will, she glanced across the campsite. Killian was a shadow among shadows, a dark shape squatted in front of a tarnished ribbon of river water. The rhythmic sounds of his labor filled the night, the gritty scraping of sand on tin, then the plunging splash of rinsing the dishes. He'd been washing dishes so long, she knew that he was avoiding her as well.

Why had he agreed to take her to the Rock? The question jabbed back at her time and again. She hefted the bottle and lifted it to her lips, taking another long, desperate gulp. The fiery liquid burned a path to her stomach and set it aflame.

It brought with it the memory of that second, that unbelievable moment in time, when he'd said he'd take her to the Rock. She'd thought for one terrifying second that she would embarrass herself by bursting into tears.

She wanted to believe it. Sweet Jesus, she wanted to believe it more than she'd ever wanted anything in her life. And when she looked at him, when she felt the whisper-soft touch of his finger at her chin, she'd almost let herself.

But if she did, if she let herself believe in him, trust him, she could lose everything.

Why would he help her? That was the key question, the starting point for all of it. And there was no good reason, nothing that made sense. There was nothing in it for him.

No, he had to be stringing her along, he had to be. He was waiting for her to break down, to trust him completely, and then he'd pull the rug out from underneath her, leaving her breathless at the turnaround.

She could almost hear his laughter in the rustling of the wind on the water. *You didn't really believe I'd take you to the Rock, did you? You didn't really believe . . .*

She couldn't afford to believe in him. She had to bide her time and play along, find out what his angle was. She'd play along with his little game as long as they remained heading east.

She wouldn't trust him.

A shiver of longing moved through her. But, God, she wished that she could.

She was blind. Either that, or it was exceedingly dark out.

Lainie loosed a throaty giggle. It sounded a little hysterical, a little ragged around the edges, but that wasn't surprising. She was dead drunk and dead tired. A deadly combination, she thought with another laugh.

She made a lunging stab at getting to her feet.

"Having a little balance problem?" Killian's growly voice came from nowhere.

Blinking hard, she looked around for him. At the sudden movement, her legs wobbled, turned watery. She sank to her knees on the cold ground.

His gaze flicked from her to the fallen, empty whiskey bottle. One eyebrow lifted slowly, mockingly.

She winced. Embarrassment moved through her in a hot wave, brought a flush to her cheeks that irritated the hell out of her. She lifted her heavy head and tried to focus on Killian. He was a blur of flesh and cloth and silver hair. "Jesus, Lainie, what are you doing?"

"Genuflecting. I thought it was required."

He laughed unexpectedly. It was a rich, rumbling sound that filled her with a vague sense of loss and longing. "Only on Sundays. You may rise."

Easy for you to say. She staggered to her feet, trying to look casual, even though she felt as if she were climbing the face of K2.

"So," he said with a sigh. "You're drunk."

"Nooo." She giggled and immediately clamped a hand over her mouth. It had sounded strained, that laugh, and the very tenor of it depressed her. It reminded her harshly that she was running from something—just like Vi had said—running hard and fast and getting nowhere.

"I can't say I'm surprised."

She frowned. Unable to see him clearly, she stumbled forward until his face came into focus. "Whaddaya mean by that?"

"You're afraid to believe I'll get you to the Rock," he said quietly. "I know a little something about fear."

"Ha!" It was a harsh, grating sound that wanted to be a laugh and wasn't.

"Really? Then why get blind drunk the second I turn my back?"

She gave him a crooked, soggy grin. "Shows how much you know. I _always_ get blind drunk. It has nothing to do with you."

He stared at her a long time. She shifted uneasily beneath his perusal, and knew that she wasn't drunk enough to be with him, that she might never be drunk enough. His eyes seemed to pierce her armor, to see the frightened, vulnerable girl she'd never been able to completely eradicate. "Let's go to bed, Lainie."

"So thass it," she said in a rush. "Thass what this 'trust me' is all about. You want to get me into bed."

He sighed. "No. I meant, let's go to sleep. You'll feel better in the morning."

"I feel good now. And sleeping is . . ." She started to say, *meant* to say, *the last thing I need;* she even opened her mouth to say it, but what came out was different. "Hard for me."

Lainie couldn't believe she'd said it, couldn't believe she'd thrown her vulnerability out there for him to see. She glanced wildly around for another bottle of whiskey. She wasn't drunk enough; Jesus, she wasn't drunk enough.

"I know how that goes."

She paused. It seemed to take an hour for her to turn to look at him, and when she did, she wished to hell she hadn't. He was looking at her with an understanding that unaccountably made her want to cry. She sniffed and raised her eyebrows, trying to look sober and casual. "I want another drink."

"You've had enough."

She clicked her heels together and shot her right hand forward. "*Heil* Hitler."

He ignored her and sat on the fallen log near the fire. Beside him, two sleeping bags lay side by side. He pulled off his boots and set them aside, then crawled into one of the sleeping bags, patting the one beside him. "Come to bed. You need the sleep."

You need the sleep. The words washed through her,

leaving her ragged and shaken. "I . . . don't sleep well. You go ahead."

"Come here, Alaina." His voice was soft and rich. It seemed she'd waited a lifetime for that voice, that quiet request. Before she knew it, she'd taken a step toward him.

When she realized what she'd done, she jerked to a stop.

"Don't be afraid," he breathed.

She stiffened. "I'm not afraid."

"Prove it. Lay by me."

That had been a stupid thing to say. She hadn't walked into his trap; she'd hurtled into it. And now there was nothing left to do but back up her words with action. Slowly she crossed the campsite, only stumbling over her feet twice, and dropped onto the edge of the bedroll.

He reached down, took her boot in his hands. Startled, she glanced at him before she could stop herself. Their gazes met. She saw in his eyes a gentleness that stole her breath.

He leaned over and pulled the boot off, tossing it aside. Then he reached for the other foot.

"I can get that," she said in an irritatingly weak voice.

He was angled toward her, so that he had to turn his head to look at her, and when he did, they were almost close enough to kiss. "I know you can. Let me."

The words sent a shiver through her. She dredged up an ineffective smile and wished she had another drink. She wasn't drunk enough to be in bed with this man. Not by a long shot. "Whatever."

He withdrew the boot and threw it beside the other one, then eased back, leaning against the makeshift pillow he'd propped on a fallen log. Once again, he patted the bag beside him. "Come on, Lainie. Get in."

Warily she crawled into the bag and yanked the sheepskin-lined duck fabric up to her breasts.

For a long time they sat there, both silent and staring. Lainie felt his presence beside her, warm and strong and waiting. She knew that he wanted something from her, but she didn't know what, couldn't imagine what.

Her heartbeat sped up. Fear blossomed in the pit of her stomach, making her swallow convulsively. It had always frightened her to feel out of control, and right now it felt as if she were spinning, as if everything she knew, or thought she knew, were being slowly, inexorably drawn away from her and concealed in some impenetrable darkness. She wanted to reach for it, to say or hear something normal, something expected. Wanted desperately to feel something besides this vague, blurry sense of isolation and loss.

"There were years when I didn't sleep at all," he said at last.

The words surprised her so much that for a moment she forgot her fear. She turned to him. She wanted to say something, but she couldn't think of a thing. So she just stared at him, waiting.

"And then there was that year I spent in the opium dens in San Francisco." He turned and gave her a crooked grin. "Of course, it could have been two weeks."

She almost smiled. A strange sensation moved through her, loosened her tensed muscles and made her relax. Tentatively she wiggled backward and sat beside him, her lower back pressed against the creaking log. Suddenly she felt the whiskey, felt it as a liberating heat in her blood. "I know that feeling," she said with a hiccuping snort.

"But it doesn't matter. Some things you can't forget," he whispered, and there was a sorrow in his voice, a pain that touched something deep inside her, something that hadn't been touched in years.

She looked at him, unable to help herself. He sat slumped, his head bowed. He was staring at his own hands, curled on the green fabric of the bag. She knew instinctively that he was seeing something else entirely, something that hurt.

She wanted to touch him, to brush the silver strands of hair from his face. The reaction scared her, made her pull back.

But he turned to her, held her close with the honesty in his eyes.

"Wh-What do you want from me?" she said, unable to make her voice anything but a whisper.

"Nothing," he said quickly, too quickly. Then he gave her a brittle smile. "I guess right now I want you to sleep."

Confusing emotions hurtled through her. She tried to focus on them, tried to figure out what she felt right now and what she was afraid of. But the more she tried to understand, the sleepier she felt.

A small, fluttering sigh escaped her lips; her body melted into the warm sleeping bag. The whiskey was a soothing warmth in her blood, a slight buzzing in her ears.

He leaned down toward her, so close she could feel the soft flannel of his shirtsleeve against her cheek. She thought for a terrifying moment that he was going to touch her. She flinched and tried to twist away, but she couldn't move. Or maybe she didn't really want to. Her heart started pounding in her chest.

"Good night, Lainie," he said quietly, then rolled onto his back.

She lay tense and unmoving, staring up at the night sky, battling an irritating sense of disappointment. "Good night, Killian."

They lay there, side by side, without touching. It was a long, long time before either one of them slept.

Chapter Nineteen

Someone screamed.

Killian jerked awake, instinctively reaching for the gun beside him. His fingers dug through the dirt, found the metal grip, and closed around it as he snapped to a sit.

Disoriented, he blinked and looked around, searching for the source of the danger. Darkness pressed in on him, a million stars glittered in the night sky. It was quiet now; no hint of the scream lingered in the cold, breezeless air.

He frowned. Had he imagined it? He let out his breath in a slow, steady stream and slumped forward. Setting the gun down, he closed his eyes and massaged his temples. The beginning strains of a headache pulsed behind his eyes.

A sound drifted to his ears, soft at first, like the whining whimper of a newborn kitten.

Lainie. Of course.

Turning, he glanced down at her. She lay on her back, asleep. Her face was twisted into a grimace, her eyes were squeezed too tightly shut. Her hands were pale, fingers clutched talonlike around the green fabric of the sleeping bag. She writhed from side to side, emitting a low, throaty moan with every motion. "No . . . no . . ."

He leaned down toward her. "Lainie, you're dreaming."

"Get away from me." She hissed the words and tried to say something else, but all she managed was a hoarse cry and then a broken, sobbing sound.

"Lainie ... you're dreaming. Wake up."

Suddenly she screamed and sat up so fast, she knocked him off balance. Wild-eyed, she looked around, blinking, and he didn't know if she was awake or still gripped by the horrors of sleep.

"Lainie?"

She spun to look at him. He winced at the sight of her, so deathly pale and terrified. She screamed again and shoved her way out of the sleeping bag. With a desperate, hacking breath, she stumbled away and ran to the almost cold campfire. There she stopped dead.

He could hear her breathing, ragged in the silence. Her shoulders rounded, then she hugged herself and straightened.

He didn't know what to do, what to say. She looked so alone out there, so frightened and lonely and disconnected from the world.

He peeled out of the sleeping bag and got to his feet, padding silently toward her in stockinged feet. He reignited the fire and set the now cold coffeepot on the flames. He plucked two tin cups from the pile of used dishes and waited for her to say something.

The seconds spilled into minutes and passed in silence. The fire crackled and popped, the coffee began a slow, roiling splash against the metal pot. And still neither one of them spoke.

He watched her, saw the stiff tenseness of her body, and knew that she hadn't shaken the fear yet. It hovered around her like a dense fog, pulled the color from her cheeks and left her lips pale.

She was such an odd mixture of strength and vulnerability. So often she made him think of Emily, though there was only the most fragile of similarities between the women. Emily had been all feminine softness with a quiet weakness running throughout. She hadn't been able to deal with life's cruelties. She'd depended on him for everything—and that had ruined both of them.

Lainie was so different, so hard and angry, but the strength she showed seemed to come more from fear than resolve, as if she'd spent a whole life fighting and didn't know any other way. And yet, down deep, she was perhaps more fragile than Emily, more easily hurt.

Maybe Lainie was what Emily would have become if she'd had the strength to keep living. If she'd learned how to fight for life. Strangely, it was Lainie's vulnerability that drew him to her, but it was her strength that he admired. Lainie might ask him for help, might depend on him, but she'd never rely on him like Emily had.

He pushed to his feet and moved cautiously toward Lainie. Pouring a cup of coffee, he offered it to her.

She reached out, curled her fingers around the handle, and drew the cup close, letting the steam pelt her chin. "Thanks." Her voice was hoarse still, a little soft.

"Sit down, Lainie," he said, gesturing to a nearby rock. Then he sat down on a log across from her.

She was careful not to look at him. Nodding briefly, she lowered herself slowly to the rock and lifted the cup to her lips. "Thanks for the coffee."

He knew he shouldn't say anything now, should just keep silent and sit beside her. But he couldn't do it. He felt compelled to let her know that he understood. "I had nightmares for years afterward," he said softly.

Slowly, almost against her will, she looked up at him. Her face was still pale and drawn, her eyes still shadowed and steeped in pain. "How do you do that?"

"What?"

She waited so long to answer that he thought she wasn't going to. Then, quietly, she said, "Know what I need to hear?"

He didn't know what to say. The moment seemed fragile suddenly, easily broken by the wrong word. But it felt as if she'd opened the door to him, just a little, given him the first honest glimpse into her soul that he'd ever had, and it was a dark, lonely place just like his own. "What are you so afraid of?"

She looked away, shrugged. "I'm afraid I won't get to the Rock in time."

He knew as she said it that it was a half-truth, a partial answer. There was so much more in her eyes. "No. You've been scared a long time, Lainie."

She stared out at the desert, unmoving, so still that she seemed to have stopped breathing, then slowly she turned to him. He could tell that she was trying desperately hard to be casual. "All my life," she said softly.

"Because of the . . ." His words melted into an awkward silence.

"You can say it. Rape. But no, that wasn't what started it. It took me a long time to sort through the pain of that night, but after a while it started to dim. The body heals a hell of a lot faster than the mind."

He knew he shouldn't ask, but he couldn't help himself. "So what started it?"

She shrugged. "A lot of people have tried to answer that question. They all had opinions about my mind, about how it works." She gave a brittle laugh. "Or didn't work. Doctors, psychiatrists, social workers, foster parents. Everyone's taken a crack at figuring me out."

He frowned, trying to sort through the confusing jumble of her words. But he knew it wasn't the words that mattered. It was the answer. "Any of them ever do it?"

"Maybe one. Dr. Gray . . ." She said the name softly, as if it meant something. "She seemed to think I needed to be safe."

You could be safe with me. The thought came at him from nowhere, blindsiding him. He tried to push it away, tried not to believe in it, but it was too late.

"You're safe now," he said quietly.

She turned to him quickly, her eyes wide. Their gazes met for a second, and he saw a flaring of hope, then a crushing bleakness. She laughed; it was a forced, harsh sound. "Yeah, I've heard that one before. There is no safety in life."

He looked at her a long time, wondering what to say. Somehow, his thoughts bled into words and slipped from his mouth. "You scare me, Lainie."

She frowned. "How?"

He shook his head. He'd spoken without thinking, and now he felt slightly disoriented. Putting emotions into words had never been easy for him, but he knew that he had to try. He didn't want this moment to pass into nothingness, into the murky realm of what-might-have-beens. "I . . . lost my heart once to a woman very much like you. But she didn't have your strength."

"What does that have to do with me?"

"I'm not sure."

For a breathless second, she didn't respond, just sat there, motionless, staring at him. Then suddenly she jerked to her feet. "What a weird conversation. Let's get going, Killian. It's almost first light."

The connection between them was gone, severed cleanly. He watched her walk away, her body held stiff and rigid, her chin high. She strode to the camp kit and started burrowing through the supplies for bacon and beans.

As he watched her, listening to the rattle and clank of her nervous hands riffling through the goods, he knew what his broken heart had to do with her.

He wanted her to know he was capable of that kind of emotion.

"Christ," he cursed softly. He knew without a shadow of a doubt that caring about Lainie would be the biggest mistake of his life.

And somehow, without even knowing when, he'd already made it.

Killian squatted by the small stream, staring unseeingly at his own reflection. He held the last breakfast plate, half-washed and forgotten. With a sigh, he eased back to a sit and let the plate clatter onto the rock beside him.

He stacked the bent tin dishes and carried them back to the campfire, repacking them before he turned to Lainie.

She sat huddled in a ball by the fire, looking at her feet, her arms drawn taut around her shins. She was terrified but trying to be brave, like a pathetically trapped animal, waiting, wondering if it should gnaw its foot off to be free.

He winced at the thought, feeling sick inside and knowing it was his fault. He'd bound, tied, and gagged her, humiliated and beaten her. No wonder she was afraid of him.

He'd hurt her; that, he knew. But lots of people had hurt her. He could see it in her sometimes, that residual haunting in the eyes that told him more about her than he wanted to know.

What he saw in her eyes broke his heart.

Suddenly everything he'd tried to be for the last fifteen years started slipping away, dissolving in the dirt at his feet. He couldn't cling to the shell he'd built around his soul anymore. It hadn't protected him anyway. All his hard, cold detachment hadn't saved him from this moment. From this woman.

He moved toward her, kneeled in the dirt beside her. "Lainie?"

She turned to him slowly, gave him an agonizingly frightened look. "You've changed your mind," she said dully. "We're going back to the hideout."

He wished he could blame her for not trusting him. "No," he said quietly. "I haven't changed my mind. Lainie, I'll do everything in my power to get you home."

She frowned at him. "Why?"

It was the second time she'd asked him that, and this time he saw the pathetic pain in the question. It told him so much about her life—a life startlingly like his own. Hollow and empty. "Because I need to." And with that realization, he found a thread of the man he used to be. He clutched it, holding fast. It felt good to be honest, for once. Damn good.

She didn't answer, just looked at him.

He knew he shouldn't say anything, that he should simply back up and walk away. But he felt so drawn to her right now, so connected, that he didn't want to let this moment go. It was the first time in fifteen years he'd wanted to be with someone, wanted genuinely to know someone, and he didn't want to go back to being alone so quickly.

He wanted to touch her, to reach out and stroke her hair and tell her that it was all right, but he was afraid of how she would react. So he sat there, staring at her, wanting to touch her, waiting to see how close she wanted to be.

A dozen words filled his head, but none of them made it up his dry throat. Their gazes met.

He felt a crushing sense of inevitability; it swept him up in the hot magic of possibility. He stared at her, speechless, wondering if she felt it, too. The heady sense of beginning something new.

"Well," she said finally, "I guess we should get going."

"Yeah," he said, but he couldn't help smiling. He felt suddenly as if he'd been given a second chance in life, a chance to redeem his lost soul by saving her. "Let's go."

Lainie sat as stiffly as she possibly could on the moving horse, her body angled away from Killian's. She was terrified to actually touch him. She wasn't sure why she was so scared; common sense told her it was a ridiculous, baseless fear, but still she felt it, as real as any fear she'd ever known. As crazy and impossible as it sounded, she felt as if there was almost nothing separating them, a barrier as clear and breakable as a piece of glass, and that if she reached out, moved beyond that invisible wall, there would be no going back.

For the past few hours, they'd ridden in silence, through the crisp, predawn darkness and into a blisteringly hot summer day. And even though they hadn't spoken, the air felt heavy with unvoiced conversations and hidden emotions, like a full gray raincloud ready to burst.

She didn't want to talk to him; more important, she didn't want to listen. At first when she'd landed in this time period, Killian had been exactly what she'd expected, the man she'd created from a blue screen and a keyboard. But now he was more . . . so much more.

You're safe now.

The words kept coming back to her, irritatingly resilient, terrifyingly seductive. It was a promise no one had ever made to her before, and try as she might, she couldn't make it sound hollow or untruthful. He'd said it so quietly, so simply. She'd waited a lifetime to hear those words, and it seemed horribly unfair and twisted to hear them now, from a possibly fictional man who died one hundred years before she was born. And only days before she would leave him forever.

She tried earnestly not to believe in him or his promise, but she couldn't help herself. The simple words were the most provocative she could imagine, the most compelling thing a man could have said to her.

She stared at his back, broad and solid in front of her. The foamy blue fabric of his shirt was stretched taut across his shoulders, the seams tired and frayed. Sunlight caught in his long hair, turned the wavy strands to a curtain of steel that brushed his collar.

What would it feel like, she wondered, to simply lean forward and rest against his back, to let his silent strength be her shield? To just once, and perhaps to no one but herself, admit that she was scared and didn't want to be alone. To let herself be weak.

Without meaning to, she scooted a little forward. Her crotch slid up onto the thick leather skirt, her thighs came into contact with his legs.

She froze, barely breathing, waiting for him to make some humiliating comment.

She sat that way a long time, stiff and unmoving. The desert fanned out from them on all sides, an endless, searingly hot plain dotted with ocher spires and striated mesas. In the distance a hawk soared, its shadow a gliding feather against the bloodred rock wall. A filmy cloud crept past the sun, throwing a cool blanket across the heat for a split second, and then moving on.

He didn't say anything, didn't laugh or taunt or touch her. The heat from his legs created a curious sense of intimacy. Their booted feet dangled alongside each other's, like lovers' feet at the edge of a sun-warmed lake. She tried to ignore it, tried not to care how good it felt to be this close to him.

A shiver of longing moved through her. It was such a simple thing, a nothing little intimacy that most people took for granted as a normal part of life. But not Lainie. Intimacy had never been simple or expected or received. It was the carrot before the horse's nose that had directed so much of her life. The search for someone to care about, who would care about her in return. She'd sought it with an increasing despair until Kelly's birth. Then, thankfully, she'd found a love she'd never dreamed of, and so much of the cold darkness in her soul had been forgotten.

Or she'd thought it had been forgotten. Now, feeling his body against hers, knowing that she longed to rest her cheek against his back and slip her arms around his waist, she saw the bitter, frightening truth. It had never been forgotten; her little-girl dreams hadn't been completely buried. They'd simply lain dormant, waiting, waiting. . . .

"You can lean on me, Lainie." Killian's deep voice brought her crashing out of her own thoughts.

She fought to regain her composure. "Wh-What?"

"You must be tired. Lean on me and go to sleep."

The longing came back, wrenched through her body so hard, she had to close her eyes against it. She wanted to lean on him. God help her, she wanted it.

"Lean on me, Lainie," he said again, softer this time. "Go ahead."

Her resistance crumbled. Slowly, biting her lip, she leaned forward and pressed her cheek to his back. His shirt was soft against her skin and smelled of sunshine and dust and sweat. She exhaled evenly.

After a few moments, she felt herself begin to relax. The swaying, rocking-chair motion of the horse lulled her. The back of Killian's hat shaded her face, cast it in a cooling darkness that soothed her weary body.

She sat that way, pressed against him, for miles, until it was no longer enough. Suddenly she needed more. Gingerly, almost hoping he wouldn't notice, she curled her arms around his body and clasped her hands at his waist.

She tensed for a second, waiting for his response.

His big gloved hand settled atop hers. The sun-warmed leather of his glove coiled around her fingers and gave a gentle, reassuring squeeze.

It was the most tender touch she'd ever known.

Night fell across the desert slowly, turned their small campsite into a warm and welcoming enclave of flickering light. A heavy mist hung in the dark air, heralding a coming rain.

Cottonwood trees curled protectively around the little site and kept the moist breezes at bay. Beyond the trees lay a thin stream that fed into a glassy, starlit pond. The moon was the barest of crescents, no more than a blue-white parenthesis against the jet black sky.

Lainie sat huddled alongside the fire, her legs drawn tight to her chest, her chin resting on one bent knee. The leftover scents of coffee, bacon, and biscuits lingered in the cool night air. Across the fire, Killian sat alongside the tent he'd erected a few moments ago.

Firelight leapt and danced across his face and slid down the concave surface of the tent.

They hadn't spoken in more than an hour. They sat apart, in their own solitary worlds, gazing at the fire. It had been awkward at dinner. The quiet, repetitive scraping of tin forks on tin plates grated on Lainie's nerves, left her somehow hoping he would look up, would say something. But he hadn't.

His silence tore at her, even frightened her. She had this strange, inexplicable sensation that he was waiting for *her* to say something, for *her* to reach out to him.

It was ridiculous.

And yet, not so ridiculous.

Today as she'd pressed against him on the back of the horse, she'd felt a confusing jumble of emotions. At first she'd been tense and wary, waiting for him to ridicule or humiliate her. When he'd remained silent, and given her that incredibly gentle touch, she'd begun to relax. The pent-up breath released from her lungs, her eyes fluttered shut, and she'd felt the most unexpected, most exhilarating sense of peace she'd ever known. For a few precious hours, she'd felt safe.

The moment she realized it, the fear set in. She'd drawn back sharply, pulled her hands into her own lap, and stiffened.

"You okay?" he'd asked.

She'd heard so much in his voice, and it frightened her even more. It was as if, impossibly, he understood why she'd drawn back. As if it had hurt his feelings.

"Fine," was all she said, but there was a brittleness to her voice that betrayed every emotion he aroused in her. In that instant, sitting behind him, completely hidden from his penetrating gaze, she felt naked and totally exposed. And it scared her to death.

She couldn't imagine what he wanted from her. Time

and again, she tried to convince herself that his gentleness was all an act, a pretense to get her guard down so that he could take advantage of her.

But, God help her, she couldn't make herself believe it anymore. The more often she tried, the more thoroughly she failed.

She felt safe in his arms.

She squeezed her eyes shut at the terrifying realization. It washed through her like ice water, left her chilled and in need of warmth. It was all an illusion.

Or was it?

Remember Kelly, she told herself for the thousandth time, but even those words didn't warm her anymore, didn't give her the armor she needed to protect herself from Killian and the gentleness of his touch.

She stared at him across the fire. He was stretched out, with one leg bent, one arm dangling across his knee. His eyes were fixed on her, only her, and she felt suddenly as if he saw everything she tried so hard to hide: the shadowed secrets in her eyes, the fear and uncertainty and confusion in her heart. Of course he'd seen her shiver. A nothing, lightning-fast shudder, but he'd seen it . . .

You're safe now.

The words seduced her again, stripped away her courage and left her weak and vulnerable. She stared into his eyes and tried to tell herself that he was lying, that he hadn't meant it, but she couldn't find a lie in his gaze. All she saw was caring and concern, and it made her remember his words again.

And that touch. It was nothing, she told herself. Just a meaningless press of one hand to another. But it had sparked so many unexpected responses in her, had made her snuggle close to him and feel the warmth of his body against her breasts.

Heat sprang into her cheeks at the remembrance, her heartbeat sped up. The truth came at her hard, reminding her with humiliating clarity why she was suddenly so afraid of him. For an instant there, when she'd been holding him close, she'd felt a flash of honest-to-God desire. Not the ordinary willingness to have sex that she'd felt in the past, but something . . . more.

She looked away quickly, unwilling to meet his gaze. The glistening surface of the pond caught her eye, reflected the starlight through the shadowy line of the trees. Brilliant, blue-white moonlight gave the area an ethereal, otherworldly glow. *Water.*

That's what she needed, she realized suddenly. The nineteenth-century equivalent of a cold shower. She needed to get away from him, submerge herself in cold water and cleanse the weakness from her soul. She lurched to her feet. "I'm going for a swim."

Before he could say a word, she raced across the campsite and through the trees. At the edge of the pond, she stopped and glanced back.

He was a shadow alongside the fire, his cigarette a bright red glow suspended in the darkness.

He hadn't followed her.

Lainie let out her breath in a relieved sigh and looked down at the pond. It was a pool-sized piece of glass studded with starlight. Moonlight edged it, curled around and above it, sliced through the shadowy canopy of trees.

She stripped quickly down to her panties and bra and touched her big toe to the water. It felt cool and welcoming after the heat of the day. Smiling, she walked into the water.

The pond was shallow, no more than six feet deep. She ducked under the surface and swam to the other side, where a ring of huge stones bordered the edge.

Stretching her arms out along the rocks, she floated on the water, eyes closed.

Cool breezes skidded across her moist face and caressed her nipples. The water lapped gently against her thighs, tickled her toes. Overhead, the leaves chattered softly among themselves.

She focused on the pure physical pleasure of the moment, letting the fear seep from her mind.

Five days, she thought sleepily. Just five more days and she'd be at the Rock . . . and home.

She shouldn't have let Killian get to her. It was stupid. She merely had to remain strong for five days, and then this nightmare would be over.

"Over." She whispered the word, taking strength from it. She could survive five days with Killian. So what if he aroused some surprising emotions in her? She could fight that as long as she stayed alert, stayed away from him.

As long as she didn't touch him or let him touch her.

And how hard could that be? She had spent a lifetime not touching people. Certainly she could keep her distance from Killian for less than a week.

A small, satisfied smile curved her lips. She could do it. Sure, she could. All she had to do was stay away from him.

"I thought you might like some soap."

Killian's voice cut through the silence, brought her jerking upright. She immediately plunged beneath the surface and stared at him. "G-Get out of here."

He moved toward her. He was a tall, broad-shouldered shadow, backlit by the bluish light of the moon. His footsteps crunched toward her, slow and steady. At the edge of the water, he crouched down. She heard the cracking snap of his knees.

"Do you want some soap or not?"

"Sure," she said, trying not to sound nervous, and failing miserably. "Leave it there."

"Give me your hand." The rich burr of his voice warmed her in spite of the coolness of the water.

Reluctantly she reached out. He took her hand, curled his warm, strong fingers around her slick, cold ones. At the contact, so unexpectedly hot against her wet flesh, she shivered and tried to draw back. He held her tightly. When she stopped fighting, he said, "Open your fingers."

She let her fingers relax. Her damp palm lay open in his.

She felt his gaze on her body, hot and pointed, slipping through the glassy shield of the water. Beneath the cold water, her body felt trembly and hot, her insides knotted.

He pressed a small, well-worn bar of soap in her hand. The unexpected scent of sandalwood lifted to her nostrils.

She immediately closed her fingers around the soap and yanked her arm back. It splashed in the water. "Th-Thanks," she managed, hating the breathy softness of her voice.

His knees creaked again as he got to his feet. Wordlessly he walked away from her. She heard each snapping crunch of his bootheels on the sandy dirt, and with each step he took, she felt a slowing of her heartbeat.

Then suddenly he stopped, and her heart lurched into her throat. She stared directly across the pond, trying to pierce the darkness. She could see his broad smile. "What are you doing?" she asked.

He wrenched off one boot. Then the other. "Taking a bath."

She gasped. "Oh, no, you're not."

He laughed, a rich, rumbling sound that slipped

across the water and touched her as he started unbuttoning his jeans.

Lainie squeezed her eyes shut. *Oh, God, oh, Jesus. This is it. . . .*

He slipped into the water; she felt his entry as a gentle rippling of water against her skin.

She sat crouched in the water, tense and waiting, her heartbeat a thudding hammer in her chest. He said something. Her heart was beating so fast, she couldn't make out his words.

"What?"

She heard a rippling splash, and then nothing.

"Killian?"

He came up beside her, flipping his wet head back. Droplets sprayed her face. His naked chest, glistening with water, filled her gaze. She froze, her mouth gaped.

She edged away from him, her arms pinned across her breasts. "Wh-What are you doing?"

He glided toward her and took hold of her shoulders, gently turning her around. "I'm going to wash your hair."

"N-No, thanks."

He pulled the soap from her fingers and dipped it under the water. Letting go of her, he scrubbed the soap to create a foam, then started washing her hair.

At the touch, she stiffened. She wanted to pull away, knew it was the smart thing to do, but suddenly she couldn't move. She was paralyzed by the jumble of emotions his touch sparked.

She stood there, motionless, breathing hard, afraid to stay, unwilling to pull away. Foamy peaks of soap slid down the sides of her face and puddled on the surface of the water. His fingertips moved through her hair, caressed her scalp, and kneaded the knots from the back of her neck.

"I wish I could see your face right now," he said quietly.

A shudder of longing moved through Lainie at his words. No one had ever said anything like that to her before; it implied something she wasn't used to. As if *she* were the woman he wanted to be with right now, not simply a body in darkness.

Before she could fight against the words, they seeped past her armor and lodged in an area dangerously close to her heart. Water lapped against her breasts like feather-strokes, brought her nipples to a tender hardness. The first tingling throb of response pulsed between her legs.

God help her, she wanted to turn around and kiss him. She wanted to curl her arms around his neck and draw him close, to press up onto her toes and rub her body against his, feel the curling softness of his hair against her breasts.

It was just lust, she told herself. Just garden-variety lust.

He rinsed her hair and gently turned her around. She looked up at him, and suddenly she was thinking about kissing him, wondering what it would be like.

Just lust, she told herself again. *Ordinary lust. It doesn't mean a thing.* Her hormones were out of whack; that was all.

She cleared her throat and tried to sound casual. "Th-Thanks. How 'bout if I make us some coffee now?"

"I think I have a taste for something else." His gravelly, rough-edged voice made her think of a thousand forbidden things. Hot, secret touches and sexy whispers.

She wanted to look away, but couldn't. "What?" The word cracked.

"I think you know."

The look he gave her was so hot, so smoldering, she felt herself blush.

Almost what you'd expect of a soul mate.

She tried to shake off the ridiculous thought, but once it landed in her mind, it stuck firm.

Lean on me, Lainie. Go ahead.

You're safe now.

Every kindness he'd ever showed her came back now with stunning force, took on a new, impossible meaning. She shivered.

Was it possible? she wondered. Had they loved each other before, in a time and place that neither could recall? Was it possible that the faces and names had changed, but the souls had remained constant? Could hearts remember what minds could not?

The question caught fire and consumed her. She tried to fight it, tried to tell herself it was all a lot of mumbo-jumbo and didn't mean a thing, but the idea was seductive. She felt its power move through her, crumbling any resistance in its path.

It's just lust, she told herself yet again, desperate this time to believe it. She didn't want to be soul mates, didn't want to believe in some everlasting love that existed in 1896.

He moved closer in a ripple of water, his gaze fixed and measuring on her face.

"It's just lust," she muttered softly, tilting her chin. And there was one certain way to prove it.

Chapter Twenty

She was going to kiss him.

She didn't want to kiss him; Killian could see the reluctance in her eyes. He could see, too, the cold glint of determination in her gaze. She was going to kiss him to prove something.

He couldn't wait to see what it was and how far she'd go to prove it. He backed up a little and sat down on the edge of the pond, scooting back to dangle his legs in the water. All of a sudden he wished he was naked, instead of clad in wet, clinging drawers. At his movement, she paused for a second, frowning. Then she tilted her chin again and muttered something about lust.

"Stand up," she said in a throaty voice.

"You sit down."

She hesitated for a moment, then slowly moved closer to him. Through the cool water, he felt the heat of her leg. In a quick movement, he grabbed her around the waist and pulled her on top of him.

She gasped and started to pull away.

"Don't," he whispered.

She froze.

He sat perfectly still, waiting, smiling.

She didn't move, just sat there, straddling him, her knees in the dirt, water streaming down the sides of her face, breathing quickly. Then, slowly, she glanced down at him.

The look in her eyes almost stopped his heart. She was leaning slightly backward, a curly lock of black hair blocking one eye. The other was fixed on him, and he could have lost himself in the dazzling gold and green and gray lights of her eyes. He saw more in that instant than he'd seen altogether before this moment. He saw the dark, rich lashes that ringed her eyes and the tiny network of lines that bespoke long, lonely years in one so young. He saw pain and something else, something he hadn't seen in her eyes before and never expected to see.

It was almost desire.

Before this instant he wouldn't have recognized *almost* desire; it seemed a contradiction somehow, an impossibility. But now, looking up into Lainie's eyes, he saw exactly that. It was a look he hadn't seen in years—since the night he'd first taken Emily. The look of a woman who didn't know exactly what she wanted, but wanted it nonetheless.

The look of a virgin.

Sweet Jesus ...

She leaned toward him slowly, and as she came close enough to feel his breath against her face, the desire faded from her eyes, turned almost to fear. Her breathing sped up. Her fingers tightened around his. She shifted her weight, and the movement of her nearly naked body against his sent a thousand shards of sensation shooting to his groin. He felt himself swell, strain against the soaked, twisted fabric of his drawers.

When she was but a hair from him, she puckered her lips and closed her eyes.

The kiss was quick and chaste and over almost before it had begun.

She pulled back quickly and let out a shaky, laughing breath. "Nothing," she said with a broadening smile. "No fireworks or shooting stars. Nothing. I didn't feel anything at all. I guess it wasn't lust after all. Phew."

She grinned suddenly, then bit down on her lower lip, as if she were uncomfortable with the smile but unable to control it. The gesture made her look impossibly young and breathtakingly beautiful.

She shifted her weight, settling more heavily atop him. He could feel the hard, rounded curves of her bottom pressing into his lap, rousing him.

He groaned. She seemed completely oblivious to the havoc she was wreaking in his body.

She smiled down at him, eyes sparkling, teeth clamped down on her lower lip like a schoolgirl. Then she started talking, babbling about something.

He stared up at her, mesmerized. The water had softened her hair. Damp, glistening curls lay across her forehead and above her ears. Silver beads of water streaked down the sides of her face. Her hazel eyes were bright, unshadowed by the angry darkness that so often touched them, crinkled in the corners by her smile. Everything about her seemed suddenly softer.

It was the first time he'd seen her smile, he realized, and he was stunned by the transformation. She looked heartbreakingly young and innocent and lovely. And she had no idea how woefully inadequate that kiss had been.

He leaned toward her.

The steady stream of her dialogue dwindled into silence. A frown tugged at her thick eyebrows. She drew slightly backward. "What are you looking at?"

"You." He reached out; his fingers curled around her upper arms, squeezing gently, kneading the tender flesh.

"Wh-What are you doing?"

"Touching you."

The last remnant of her smile faded. She was left staring down at him through huge, unblinking eyes, her front teeth clamped nervously against her full lower lip. "I don't want you to touch me."

He gave her a slow, mocking smile. "You should have thought of that before you started this."

"Maybe I didn't think it through well enough." She pulled back, tried to get away.

"I wouldn't do that if I were you."

"Do what?"

He let his gaze slide slowly from her face, down the soft swell of her barely-covered breasts to the vee between her legs. "Wiggle."

She froze. Her naked thighs tensed atop his. "Let me go," she whispered.

"I don't think so." He looked up. "You kissed me. I think I deserve the same opportunity."

His hands slid down the slick, wet softness of her arms. The necklace glowed with an eerie lavender light against her flesh, accentuated the paleness of her skin. He touched it, wondering at its magic, then brushed one finger across the tiny blue-tinged hollow at the base of her throat.

Her nervousness was a living, breathing force between them, a tangible presence as real as the water and sandalwood scent of her skin or the heat of her legs against his.

He kept his gaze fastened on her face, her eyes. His fingers, roughened by years in the saddle, trailed a teasing pattern atop hers. He felt the silky-soft flesh, the puffy, raised lines of her veins.

She shivered, made a quiet, gasping sound at his touch, but didn't draw away.

Finally he released her gaze. Glancing down, he

plucked up her left hand, turned it over, and rested it in his, studying it. Her pale, pliant fingers lay open to him like the petals of a single, perfect rose. He trailed a fingertip along one of the creased lines in the soft center of her palm. Her flesh twitched beneath his touch, her fingers instinctively curled inward; he felt their velvet pads against his little finger.

"Are you finished looking at my hand?"

He glanced up, saw the anger in her eyes, and felt a smile start. "Your hand? Yeah, I guess I'm through."

She yanked her hand from his and shoved it behind her back, then tried to scoot off him.

He tightened his hold and held her in place. "You started this," he said in a quiet voice. "I'm going to finish it."

"I didn't start *this*."

He caught her gaze and held it. One eyebrow arched slowly upward. "Are you that innocent?"

She sighed. "I was never innocent. What do you want from me, Killian?"

"A kiss."

She gave him a skeptical look. "That's it? Just one kiss?"

"One *real* kiss. Not that half-ass nun's peck you gave me last time."

"I don't want to kiss you."

He smiled up at her, moving his hands slowly up her arms. She blinked, swallowed convulsively.

"One kiss . . ." he promised.

"So what. Fine." She stiffened. Her lips folded together in a colorless line.

Gently he pulled her toward him. Their lips touched, briefly at first, no more than a caress. He felt her sharply indrawn breath, felt the shiver that moved through her body.

"Lainie ..." He whispered her name, only that and nothing more, and then his mouth slanted over hers, claimed her. His tongue slid along her taut lips, urging them to open, to allow him entry.

She made a tiny whimpering sound and tried to draw back.

He forced himself to slow down, to be gentle. Squeezing his eyes shut, he eased the pressure of his kiss. The move surprised her. Her lips parted slightly, softened. A relieved breath slipped from her mouth to his.

This time he kissed her with gentleness, almost lovingly, in a way he hadn't kissed a woman in years. Maybe in a lifetime. His lips covered hers. The tip of his tongue caressed her lips, then eased between them and tasted the sweet moistness of her mouth.

Her tongue touched his, whether by accident or design, he didn't know, didn't care. At the cool, moist contact, desire pulsed through his body, swelled and ached. The intensity of his response caught him off guard. He hadn't felt anything like it in years, hadn't known true desire in ages. He'd forgotten how consuming it was, how hot. He moved uncomfortably on the hard ground, feeling the firm, round pressure of her bottom on the hardness between his legs.

Shaking, he drew back.

She sat as stiff as a nail, angled forward for the kiss, her eyes squeezed shut as if to block the reality of what had just happened. Tiny droplets of water clung stubbornly to the tips of her lashes. "Open your eyes, Lainie."

A heartbeat passed, then two, and then slowly she opened her eyes. Their gazes met, held, and for an instant Killian's world shifted. He felt as if he were falling into the warm, hazel pool of her eyes. He found himself thinking about things, wanting things he hadn't wanted in years, maybe forever.

Then he saw the sadness in her eyes, and he felt as if he'd been punched. His sudden optimism started to dissolve, slip through his rough, old man's fingers. Desperately he tried to reach for it, tried to hold on to something so ephemeral and fleeting, he couldn't begin to give it a name. "One more," he asked quietly, hearing the sharp edge of panic in his voice and not caring at all. For the first time in years, he felt an honest-to-God emotion in his soul, something that wasn't bitter or angry. He felt the desire, almost a need, to connect with this woman, to make her feel some portion of what she'd made him feel. And it scared the shit out of him to think that he would fail.

"See me this time," he said, gently brushing a lock of hair from her eyes. "One more kiss . . ."

She stared down at him, unblinking. Her lips were parted slightly, still moist from his kiss. The breath that squeezed past them was rapid, shallow.

Her face filled his vision, became his world. The soft, pliant feel of her bare skin beneath his fingertips taunted him with excruciating images of other parts of her body, equally soft, equally pliant.

"One more . . ." She said the words softly, as if she were pondering them. Her eyes fixed on him, the dark gray-green pools huge and glassy against the heated flush of her cheeks.

He couldn't speak for wanting her. His lips tingled with the memory of her touch. Anticipation tightened every nerve until it was all he could do to sit still and wait. But he knew that this time it had to be her decision, or whatever this moment could mean would disappear.

Slowly, as if it were somehow against her will, she leaned toward him. Their gazes held, unwavering, until her face blurred before him, became a smear of pale skin and dark hair and green eyes.

Her lips touched his, a butterfly-fast landing, and then drew back. A low, frustrated groan wedged in his throat, burned for the release he wouldn't allow. His fingers splayed out, pressed against her back.

He angled toward her. She met him this time, kissed him back, tentatively at first, then with the first taste of passion. Her mouth formed to his, her tongue touched his in a lick of fire.

He clutched her to him, needing her suddenly, feeling and stroking and touching her. The kiss deepened, turned hot and wanting. It consumed him, overpowered him until he couldn't breathe, couldn't feel or hear anything except the exquisite pressure of her body against his and the pounding of his own heart. She made a soft, mewling sound of need.

The thought of it, of her wanting him, aroused him like nothing ever had before. One hand slid around her body, moved up to the cottony edge of her undergarment. He felt her flinch, felt the puckering formation of goose bumps on her stomach. Still kissing her, he moved his hand upward, cupped one small breast.

She stiffened but didn't draw away.

His thumb breezed across her nipple, brought it instantly to hardness. At the feel of it, pebbly and straining, he groaned. His other arm slid down from her back, moved around to her chest.

Suddenly she slid off of him and scrambled backward, splashing into the water.

He frowned at her, confused. "Lainie—"

"We can't do this," she said breathlessly, lurching to her feet. "It's not right."

He was breathing too hard to speak for a moment, but when he looked up at her and saw the blatant fear in her eyes, the need drained out of him. Without its heat, he felt cold, empty. He sighed. "It felt right. You know it did."

She paled. Swallowing hard, she clambered out of the water and grabbed her clothes, clutching them to her chest.

"That's the problem, isn't it?" he said softly.

Without another word, she spun away from him and disappeared into the night's darkness.

He closed his eyes, bowing his head. A deep, weary sigh escaped him, hung limp in the night air. He could hear her, running again, hard and fast and thoughtlessly.

"Don't go," he whispered, knowing she couldn't hear him, knowing she wouldn't listen if she had.

For the first time in years, he felt lonely.

Lonely.

She'd made him feel something, something he'd thought impossible for a man like him.

And she had felt something, damn it. He was sure that she had. But he was afraid that it wouldn't matter to her, that she'd never give either one of them the chance to feel it again.

And God help him, he wanted to feel it again, wanted to take her in his arms and hold her tightly, to give her a safe place in the world.

The realization stunned him.

He frowned. Jesus, he was a forty-three-year-old out-law with nothing to offer a woman except a lifetime full of regrets and lost chances, and yet . . . unbelievably, he wanted to change. For Lainie, because of her. He wanted to change.

If only she'd give him the chance.

Chapter Twenty-one

She would never kiss him again. No matter what. She didn't care if they were soul mates or blind dates or dying of hypothermia. She would never kiss that man again.

She swiped at her mouth, but it didn't help; she couldn't wipe her lips enough to erase the memory of him. She felt him beside her, around her, inside her, felt the lingering memory of his touch; the scent of him clung to her clothing and haunted her.

Stop it, stop it, stop it.

It shouldn't have meant anything, that kiss. She'd kissed a thousand men in her lifetime, maybe more. She knew what a kiss was—and what it wasn't.

For years she'd kissed any man who looked at her twice, who wanted to kiss her. She'd thought that something magical would—could—happen with one of the men, just one. That one night, one special, never-to-be-forgotten night, she'd kiss the right man and she'd feel something. She'd feel ... connected, a part of something besides herself, maybe even normal.

But it had never happened. Kisses had always been like sex for her—cold, wet couplings that went on in dark, forgotten places with men whose names she could never recall. None—not one man—had ever really aroused her, had ever made her feel anything except a vague, queasy sense of selling herself short, of giving her soul to the lowest bidder and walking away with less than nothing.

Dead ends. Dark alleys. Utter and debilitating loneliness. That's what kisses had always been, been for so long that she'd forgotten until this moment that she'd ever wished for anything more. Suddenly she remembered what she'd tried so hard to forget. She remembered sitting in that horrible room, so stark and white and cold and smelling of antiseptic and Pine Sol, staring through the iron bars, wishing—Oh, Jesus, *wishing* she'd had even one good memory to counteract the horror, to make her believe again in white knights and happy endings. . . .

And now, finally, here it was.

When he'd kissed her, she'd felt as if she'd finally come home, as if all the frightened searching of her life, of her heart, had been for this, for the feel of his hands on her body and his lips on hers.

Jesus, it was frightening.

"Idiot." She spat the word. Her lips trembled, her eyes ached, and the need to cry swelled in her chest like a hot, smoldering stone.

Soul mates. Lovers. The words came at her hard, knocking the breath from her lungs with their poignant intimacy.

What if, what if, what if . . .

She stared back at the pond, at the man sitting hunched beside its moonlit glow. She tried to tell herself that none of it mattered. What she felt, what he felt, what they might or might not have once been to each other; none of it mattered. Nothing mattered but Kelly and getting home.

But deep down, she couldn't make herself believe it this time. Deep down, she knew that that kiss mattered. Perhaps more than any other single moment in her life.

* * *

"Lainie?" Killian's voice floated through the darkness, reaching out to her.

"I can hear you."

"It's dangerous out there. Come on in."

She glanced back, saw him standing alongside the fire. One side of his body was splashed with golden light, the other half was sheathed in shadow. At the sight of him, so tall and broad-shouldered and strong, she felt an almost overwhelming sense of loss. She wanted to run to him and throw her arms around him and let him kiss her again.

"I think it's more dangerous with you," she said softly.

He took a step toward her. A twig snapped beneath his heel. "I won't try to kiss you again."

His quiet promise should have surprised her. She wished that it had. But instead, she'd expected it, known somehow that he didn't want to hurt her.

If only he knew how easy it was . . .

She pushed tiredly to her feet. There was no point in hiding out here in the darkness. She had to face him sooner or later, had to figure out a way to wrench some honest strength from her too weak soul. They still had five days—and nights—together. She couldn't avoid him forever.

Turning, she walked back to the campsite. When she stepped into the light, Killian made a sharp sound of relief.

She glanced at him, and immediately wished that she hadn't. Nerves tightened her stomach, set off a flurry of butterflies.

"Come sit by the fire," he said, not moving toward her. "We could . . . talk."

The suggestion caught her off guard. "About what?"

He frowned, and at the movement, the shadows on his face shifted. "Does it have to be about something? Jesus, Lainie, haven't you ever just shot the shit with a man?"

"No." The single word hurt, revealed so much more than she wanted to reveal.

"Come on." He stepped backward, sat cross-legged on the ground.

She moved slowly toward him, dreading each step. The fire's heat washed through her in a shudder. About five feet from him, she sat down and drew her legs against her chest.

For an eternity, neither of them spoke. Lainie stared hard at the fire, trying not to feel warmed by it. "You shouldn't have done that," she said without thinking, and she honestly didn't know if she was talking to him or herself. The moment the words escaped, she wished she could take them back.

"Done what?" he asked, but he knew. She knew he knew.

Reluctantly she looked up. "Kissed me."

"You kissed me first."

"Yeah, but my kiss was nothing. Yours . . ." Across the fire, their gazes locked, and her words dwindled into silence. She tried to think of a way to finish the sentence that would make a joke out of it. Nothing came to mind. Her words hung there in the quiet, limp and pathetic.

"I felt it, too, Lainie."

Her heart tugged hard. She bit down on her lower lip and wished she could look away, but his gaze held her in a velvet grip that seemed to promise everything. "I didn't say I felt anything."

"No, you didn't. I did."

Suddenly she believed everything she saw in his

eyes, and it scared her to death. She lurched to her feet. "This is about sex, isn't it?"

He frowned up at her. "What?"

She surged toward him, yanking her sweater off and flinging it toward the tent. "This . . . seduction of yours. It's about sex. You want to have sex with me."

He rose slowly, his gaze fixed on her face. "Lainie, don't—"

"You don't have to screw with my mind, Killian. If you want sex, just ask for it." She laughed, a harsh, hollow sound that brought tears to her eyes. She fumbled desperately with the buttons on her pants. Her fingers felt swollen and useless. "Anyone can have sex with me."

He grabbed her by the shoulders and drew her to him. She tilted her face to say something—anything. But the look in his eyes stole her voice. He looked sad and infinitely tired.

"Lainie," he whispered hoarsely, drawing her close for a hug. His strong arms curled around her and held fast.

With that touch, so gentle and reassuring and safe, she felt all the fight go out of her. She sagged against him.

Finally he drew back, but didn't let go.

Not wanting to, but unable to stop herself, she looked up at him. "I don't know what you want from me, Killian." Her voice was harsh and barely audible. Shame filled her chest, made it difficult to breathe. "But whatever it is, I don't have it to give."

"Maybe you do."

She stilled, almost forgot to breathe. Her heart beat so rapidly, it sounded like thunder in her ears. It was a provocative thought, romantic. Maybe . . .

She had a second's worth of fairy tale, then reality

hit, crushing her newborn hope. She'd had these thoughts a million times in the past, and a million times she'd been forced to admit the humiliating truth. There was something in her, something dark and ugly, that made men push her away. And she was too old now to think that she could change.

"I don't have anything to give you, Killian."

"You couldn't be more wrong, Lainie." At the quiet, gentle way he said her name, she looked up. He touched her cheek, a feather-stroke that brought a shiver of response.

"I'm not wrong, Killian. Trust me."

"No," he said softly. "You trust me."

The words, so close to Viloula's advice, made Lainie's heart beat faster. "What do you mean?"

"Lainie, it's been fifteen years since I wanted a woman." He paused, seemed to steel himself. "And that was Emily. I loved her."

Lainie swallowed. "I know."

"Since Emily's death, I haven't cared about anyone." He sighed. "No one ... until now."

"Don't—"

He silenced her with a look. "I don't pretend to know what it means, or where it's going with us, Lainie. But I know this: You can give me what I want. Because all I want is you."

She shook her head. "You don't know me, Killian. If you did—"

"Then let me."

She frowned. "Let you what?"

"Let me know you."

She gasped at the quietly spoken words and stumbled away from him. When there was some distance between them, she stopped.

"I-I can't," she said.

"Lainie . . ."

The way he said her name made her want to cry. She wished suddenly that things were different, that *she* were different. She wanted to take her words back, say she'd try. But she couldn't manage it. Years' worth of false hopes and bitter disappointments kept her silent.

She stood stiffly, stared up at him, unable to say anything.

A gentle rain started to fall. She felt the cool splash of droplets on her upturned face, smelled the fresh scent of the water mingling with the aroma of soap that clung to her skin.

The shower blurred her vision, turned him into a tall, silver-haired smear before her eyes, until she couldn't read the expression on his face anymore, couldn't tell if he was smiling or frowning.

She stepped back and swiped at her eyes. It was gone; the moment of intimacy, of possibility, melted into the rain and was washed away.

Tears, she thought tiredly. It was as if God were up there, crying softly for what she'd become.

Chapter Twenty-two

Killian and Lainie lay side by side in the little tent, listening to the rain patter the dark fabric, watching the squiggly lines slide down the sloping sides. Outside, the fire was a dim, inconstant glow.

Lainie lay with her eyes wide open, the sleeping bag drawn taut across her chin.

Let me know you.

It was amazing how romantic those words were. She felt as if she'd waited a lifetime to hear them, to believe them. But now that the moment was at hand, she was terrified to open up. She couldn't imagine why he cared about her, and she couldn't help feeling that it was an illusion. Maybe even something out of her book that had no basis in fact, that didn't really exist.

"What are you thinking about?" he asked.

Her thoughts were far too jumbled and depressing to reveal. She shrugged. "I don't know . . . just listening to the rain, I guess."

They lapsed into silence again, amid the thumping splatter of the rain.

"Tell me something about yourself, Lainie," he said after a while.

She tensed. "Like what?"

"I don't know. Anything. What's your favorite color?

What's your birthday? What food do you like? Where'd you grow up? ... Anything."

She answered slowly. "Black. December thirteenth. Anything someone else cooks."

He laughed. "You forgot where you grew up."

She had hoped he wouldn't notice her omission. "That answer's not so easy. There's a long version and a short one. Most people prefer the short."

He turned on his side. Bending one arm, he rested his face in his palm and stared down at her. "Then I guess I want the long version."

She was thrown back in time for an instant, to the years she spent alone, huddled in doorways or locked behind the hospital's iron bars. She squeezed her eyes shut, ignoring the terrifying images that leapt to mind. "It's boring."

She felt his gaze on her face, probing and intense. Part of her wanted to roll away from his scrutiny. But another part of her, the part that had recently come to life, wanted to know what he saw when he looked in her eyes.

"Not to me, it wouldn't be."

She looked at him finally. No one had ever asked her the question outright before—except the shrinks and social workers who were paid to ask but rarely listened to the answers. She was so used to lying about her past, either for shock value or to paint a pretty picture for Kelly, that she'd almost forgotten how much it hurt to tell the truth. Their faces were close, close enough to kiss, and the thought of it filled her with longing. "It's so ugly. If you knew the things I've done ..."

He made a soft sound that might have been a laugh or a sigh or a combination of the two. "Look who you're talking to, Lainie. I'm an outlaw. I've lied, I've cheated, I've stolen. I've pointed guns at innocent women and taken their money. I've killed men who probably had more right to live than I do. And none of that is the worst of my crimes."

She laughed shakily and glanced up at him. "Aren't we a lovely pair."

"We could be. Maybe . . ."

For a second it felt as if her heart had stopped. Her smile faded. She leaned toward him, drawn to his unspoken words by a powerful, intuitive force. "Maybe what?"

"Maybe together we could be more than we are separately. I know it sounds ridiculous, but . . ." He shrugged.

"It doesn't sound ridiculous."

"Maybe . . . maybe this is what ordinary people feel every day, and it's just new to us."

"Is that possible?" she whispered, afraid to let herself hope.

"I don't know what's possible anymore. Do you?"

She thought about that. In the past week, she'd flown back in time, reexperienced her own past life, and kissed a figment of her own imagination . . . and liked it.

No, she didn't have a real good handle on what was possible.

"I know this, Lainie. You matter to me. And I haven't said that to a woman in fifteen years."

She reeled at the simple declaration. *And I haven't heard it in a lifetime.*

She pulled back slightly and squeezed her eyes shut. She couldn't look at him right now, because if she did, if she looked in his eyes and saw the emotion that matched those words, she'd lose control.

"Lainie?"

Reluctantly she opened her eyes. He gave her an understanding smile. "Come on, let's go to sleep. Tomorrow's gonna come awful early."

"I don't sleep much."

"Come here."

She sidled cautiously toward him and lay stiff, her breathing uneven, her fingers clenched around the sleeping bag.

He leaned down toward her, so close she could feel the soft strains of his breathing against her face. She slammed her eyes shut.

"I'm right here, Lainie. Remember that."

Then he did the most amazing thing. He kissed her on the temple. His lips lingered against her skin, brushing, touching, while his fingers moved soothingly through her hair.

She let out a small sigh. All her life she'd waited for someone to help her sleep, to tell her bedtime stories and stroke her brow and sing soft lullabies. Everything she imagined a mother would do. She'd waited first as a child, alone and friendless and trapped in the foster care system, then as a young girl living on the cold, hard streets, and finally as a woman, searching for love in dark alleys and blind corners, from men who didn't know the word. Never once had she found even a hint of honest caring. Until now, until she met an impossible man from an impossible place and time.

Until Killian. He could say whatever he wanted. He could rant and rave and tell her he was no good for her, but she knew the truth. Deep down, where it mattered, he was a decent, honorable man. And if she let herself, she could fall in love with him.

He slid one arm beneath her neck and gently turned her, drawing her against his body. His other arm circled her waist and held her tightly. His breath rustled the back of her hair.

The world spiraled down to the two of them, locked together in a small tent in the center of a huge, darkened desert. The rain hammered on, wind nudged the canvas walls, but inside they were warm and cozy and dry.

And safe.

For the first time in her life, sleep came easily.

The shadows twisted in on themselves and rolled forward, menacing, ugly shapes that rumbled with laughter and lowered voices.

"No." The plea slipped from her mouth. With some part of her mind, she heard herself speak, but it sounded far away, so far away. "Please ... don't ..."

An impenetrable, suffocating blackness descended on her. She gasped and tried to breathe. The sharp smell of ammonia exploded in her nostrils, made her gag and sputter. Cold, clammy sweat crawled across her forehead.

Leather straps spiraled through the darkness, slid toward her with a snapping, familiar sound. She writhed to get away from them and brought her hands up to cover her face. Hands pushed her down, pinned her until she couldn't move. Voices clattered around her in unintelligible monosyllables.

Footsteps pounded through the darkness, got fainter and fainter.

"No!" she screamed. *"Don't go!"*

Something or someone nudged her side. "Lainie, wake up. Lainie."

She snapped upright. Panting, gasping, she looked around, trying to make sense of her surroundings. She was sitting in light, pale, golden-green light that seemed to come from all around her. Walls wavered, pressed in on her.

Panic swelled in her chest. Where was she? Oh, Jesus, where was she?

"Lainie?" The voice came at her from the light, warm and comforting and familiar.

Relief washed through her in a shudder. *Killian.* She twisted around to see him. He was sitting beside her, the sleeping bag bunched around his hips. He was looking at her with concern, his silver-gray hair glinting in the strands of sunlight that pulsed through the tent's green canvas walls.

"Killian." Without thinking, she threw herself in his arms.

His arms curled around her, gave her shelter from the horror of the dream. "It's okay, Lainie," he murmured, stroking her sweat-dampened hair.

A shuddering, desperate breath escaped her. She squeezed her eyes shut, reveling in the warmth of his body. Never in her life had she been comforted after the nightmare, and the luxury of it flooded her senses. She curled her arms around him, pressed her cheek to his chest.

"It's okay. You're safe."

At the quiet, comforting words, Lainie burst into tears. She felt a moment's confusion at her reaction, stupid and childlike, and then, almost magically, she forgot herself, lost herself in the comfort of his arms. And suddenly she was crying for all of it, for the lost years that should have been a childhood, for the parents who'd run away and left a little girl alone, for the daughter she missed more than life itself.

She shuddered at the force of her tears and snuggled closer to him. He stroked her hair, whispered soothing, nonsensical words that mattered less than the gentle sound of his voice. It was the touch she'd waited for all her life, first from her mother, then from her father, and then from every two-bit hood she'd ever met.

The tears flowed until there were no more tears inside her, until she was depleted and spent and suffering from a pounding headache.

She sniffled and wiped her runny nose on her sleeve. She knew she should feel ashamed of her weakness, that she should pull away and smile up at him and pretend it didn't matter. But for once, she didn't want to apologize for something she'd done, something she was. And she felt better. It was as if those tears had been trapped inside her chest for years, a cold, solid block of ice against her heart.

Sniffing, she drew back and looked up at him. What she saw made her draw in a shaky breath. There was a sad tenderness in his gaze, as if her pain had somehow become his.

It felt impossibly familiar, that look, as if she'd seen it on his face a hundred times. Once again all the crazy things Vi had said seemed . . . not so crazy.

She looked up at him. "You're not lying, are you?"

"About what?"

"You . . . c-care about me."

He grazed her cheek with the roughened pad of his thumb. "Yeah, I do."

"Why?"

"Jesus, Lainie." His voice was so soft, she could scarcely hear it. "Wasn't *anyone* ever good to you?"

She gazed up at him, achingly aware of how much she was beginning to care for him, and even more aware of how desperately she wanted to kiss him again. The memory of every kind word he'd ever uttered, every quiet promise he'd ever made, came back, filling her with a warmth she'd never imagined feeling.

"You," she said softly. "You've been good to me."

He sighed. "That only proves how bad your life has been."

She barely heard him. She felt light-headed, caught up in a confusing kaleidoscope of emotions.

But through it all, a constant, was the knowledge that this moment of time was an impossible gift. For the first time, she saw the magnitude of the miracle, and it filled her with awe. She felt like a person who'd died and seen the light and would never be afraid of death again.

God had given her this gift, this moment. For years she'd railed at Him, demanded retribution and recompense for her own failings and pain. She had Kelly, and her daughter meant so much to her. But so often, when Kelly was asleep, Lainie had felt achingly, depressingly alone. She'd lain in her solitary bed, praying, praying for someone to come into her life to stay.

She'd thought that no one was listening to her prayers, then she'd thought He didn't exist, but she'd been so wrong.

He'd heard her every prayer, every whispered little-girl dream, and He'd answered them in a more stunning, more miraculous way than she'd ever imagined. And after this, no matter what happened in her life from now on, she'd never be the same again.

God had given her Killian and let her know what it felt like to fall in love.

Love.

The word caught her off guard. She felt a sharp flare of terror, and instinctively she tried to call back the thought. But it wouldn't go; it was lodged in her heart like a shard of glass. She felt it with every breath, piercing and pinching.

A sob caught in her throat. She stared up at Killian. Why did it hurt so much to realize that she loved him?

It shouldn't feel this way. She should have felt exultant, excited . . . instead of lonelier and scared. Jesus, so scared . . .

She looked up at him, saw the perplexed look in his eyes, and knew that she'd been silent too long. Her heartbeat sped up. A ragged sense of panic clogged in her chest, made her breath come in short, sharp gasps.

She had to tell him how she felt about him. Now, before it was too late, before she locked the feelings back in her heart and never found the courage to release them again.

"Killian, I . . ." She froze, unable to say the words. What if he laughed? What if he didn't say it back? It had happened so often in her youth, back when she'd thrown the special words around like cheap trinkets. Never once had she heard them in return.

He touched her cheek with his thumb. "What, Lainie?"

She stared at him, gave a tiny, hesitant shake of her head.

"What were you going to say?"

I love you. I love you. I love you. The words chased themselves around in her head until she was breathless and dizzy. She felt the moment slipping away, felt the opportunity God had given her begin to dissolve. She had to do something now to keep it together.

Her body. She could use her body to show him how much she cared.

She felt a heartbeat's hesitation. She'd tried this very same tactic a hundred times in her life, tried to get what she needed from a man by giving him what he wanted, the only thing of value she had to offer. Her body. But it had never worked.

This time will be different, she thought desperately. Killian hadn't asked for anything from her. This time, for the first time, she was giving herself to a man because she loved him. Maybe it wouldn't matter even if he didn't love her in return. Maybe, just this once, it would be enough that _she_ loved him. . . .

She came at him like a runaway train. Killian barely had time to brace himself before her body slammed into his. He skidded back against the tent pole.

She landed sprawled on top of him and curled her arms around his body, clutching him.

"Jesus, La—"

Her lips hit his in a punishing kiss. He tried to regain his balance, but she was all over him, kissing him, holding him, molding her body to his.

She kissed his mouth, his cheeks, his eyes, anywhere and everywhere. He heard the broken, ragged strains of her breath, felt the erratic thumping of her heart against his chest. Her kisses were fast and furious and without any intimacy at all.

He held himself back from her, but she didn't seem to notice. She was like a drunkard, consuming compulsively, without regard for the taste of the liquor at all. Someone desperate to get drunk.

He took hold of her shoulders. "Slow down, Lainie."

She made a choked, sobbing sound and pressed her lips to his forehead. "Don't push me away," she whispered hoarsely.

He touched the back of her head, held her to him. "I'm not pushing you away, Lainie. But you're not . . . you're not letting me in."

She drew back. "If I was doing it wrong, I can do it differently. Give me a chance." Her voice was raw, steeped in a pathetic desperation that tore through him, made him ache for the life that had done this to her.

He tightened his hold on her shoulders. "This isn't what I want from you, Lainie."

"You . . . you don't want to have sex with me?" Her lower lip trembled. He could see that she was fighting back tears.

"Not this way."

She looked away, stared hard at the tent's shimmering canvas wall. "This is the only way I know."

"I know that." He touched her cheek gently. "Will you trust me?"

She laughed; it was a watery, hiccuping sound. "Does it involve handcuffs?"

"Lainie," he said quietly, waiting an eternity for her to look at him. When she did, the fear and uncertainty in her gaze almost broke his heart. "Trust me," he said again, more softly.

She went so still that for a moment, she appeared to have stopped breathing. Then, slowly, she nodded. "I do trust you, Killian."

At her softly spoken words, he felt a surge of love so raw, so elemental, that for a second he couldn't breathe. He knew that whatever happened in his life, whatever twists and turns it took, he would never forget this moment, never forget the courage of this woman who was so desperately afraid and yet strong enough to go beyond that fear. It gave him a sense of coming home at last, of finding the woman he'd searched for all his life. It wouldn't be like it had been with Emily. Lainie would always survive.

His throat felt tight when he spoke. "I won't hurt you. I swear to God I won't."

She gave him a sad, knowing look. "You know, Killian, Viloula said I was here because I had a lesson to learn, and I think I've just learned it."

"What is it?"

"You might hurt me. Even if you don't mean to. But ... I'm willing to take that risk." She looked down at him, and this time there was no fear or uncertainty in her eyes, there was only the reflection of her inner strength and her determination. She gave him a quick, nervous smile, then bit down on her lower lip. "I've never taken it before, but with you ... I want to."

Their gazes met, held, and he felt for a dizzying second as if he were falling. The darkened world spiraled away from them, left them alone in a universe all their own. He stared up into her face, seeing the courage it took for her to trust him, and the truth of how he felt about her washed over him in a sudden, unexpected wave. He loved her.

He wanted to say the words to her, ached to say them, but something held him back. Maybe it was the look in her eyes, the sadness and fear and uncertainty, maybe it was his own troubled past. He didn't know, and for the moment, he didn't care.

For now, it was enough simply to be with her, to see her tenuous smile and know it was for him. For now, it was enough simply to love her.

Chapter Twenty-three

She leaned forward slowly, with a virginal hesitancy that made his blood race. The amethyst caught what little light there was and reflected it in a thousand purple and white shards.

At the touch of her lips, so soft and uncertain, Killian felt a rush of heat through his body. He cupped her small-boned face in his big, rough hands and marveled at the texture of her skin, at the velvety feel of the hair that brushed his fingertips.

Gently he drew her onto his lap and pulled her legs around his body. Her bare feet locked behind him, her arms coiled around his neck. He felt the heaviness of her butt pressing into his groin, and he wanted to caress her, explore her body, but he didn't allow himself to. Not yet. He wanted to give Lainie everything there was in him to give, and to do that, he had to let her take it as she would.

He sat perfectly still, ignoring the throbbing heat of desire, letting her control the kiss.

She made a small sound like an indrawn breath and kissed him harder. Her arms tightened around him, drew him against the round softness of her breasts. The dust and sunshine scent of her filled his nostrils, reminded him with every breath that he was with Lainie, only

Lainie, and it seemed as if he'd been waiting a lifetime for her.

He buried his hands in her cropped hair, feeling the short, silky strands push between his fingers. He deepened the kiss, drove his tongue into the moist sweetness of her mouth, tasting, exploring. A hot flame speared through his heart, made it difficult to breathe. His groin swelled and ached. He made a sound like a low, throaty groan of pain.

She drew back. "D-Did I do something wrong?"

The look she gave him was so innocent, he wanted to burst out laughing. The truth of her past was right there in her face, in the hint of a frown that pulled at her brow, in the hesitant downturned corners of her mouth. She could say she'd been "bad" from now until forever, but after this moment, he'd always know the truth. In her soul, where such things mattered, Lainie was as virginal as a girl. Her body may have been used and abused and violated, but no man had ever reached beyond her body and touched her spirit.

"You didn't do anything wrong," he said softly, kissing her. Her lips clung to his as he pulled back. He stayed just close enough to feel her breath against his mouth. "What should we do now?"

She yanked backward. "Jesus, don't tell me you're a virgin."

He chuckled. "Yeah, Lainie, I was saving myself for you."

"Ha. Ha. Well, what do you mean, then? *You* know what to do."

"Maybe I want to do what you want to do."

"I-I don't know what to do." She blushed. "I mean, beyond the basics, you know. Tab A into slot B. The . . . men I've slept with were bigger on time reduction than technique."

"Not this time, Lainie. We have all the time in the world. Why don't we start by getting undressed?"

Her eyes bulged. "It's daylight. I . . . I was thinking we could just unbutton our jeans this morning. Then, tonight—"

He kissed her into silence and eased the sweater off her shoulders. The thick red fabric slid down her arms and puddled across her lap. She shivered and tried to draw back.

He held her in place. "Uh-uh, Lainie. Relax."

"I am relaxed."

"I don't think so."

"I-I never was any good at this."

He slid the sweater back up her body, slowly, his hands gliding along the smoothness of her skin. She raised limp arms and closed her eyes as he pulled it off her head and tossed it beside him. Then she crossed her arms and stiffened.

He took hold of her wrists and drew her arms toward him. She resisted for a heartbeat, then shivered violently and let her arms drop to her sides. And still she didn't open her eyes.

Early dawn filtered through the dark green canvas of the tent walls and touched her skin, twined through her black hair in shimmering blue waves. Her flesh looked almost translucent in the glow. The slender curve of her throat was all softness and cream, touchable. So touchable.

"Look at me, Lainie."

She opened her eyes slowly, stared down into his. The thick darkness of her lashes cast shadows on her cheeks. He traced a finger up the naked expanse of her stomach, between her bound breasts, and up the curl of her throat, feeling the fluttering beat of her pulse. Using only the tip of his finger, he traced the outline of her black undergarment. What had she called it—a bra?

She shivered and closed her eyes again.

A thousand gentle words rose in his throat. He wanted to tell her how beautiful she was, how easy it was to lose himself in her eyes and her touch and her kiss, but he wasn't a man who'd used those words in his life, and he found now that they were difficult to say. There was a breathlessness in him, a building need that made him want to hold her and feel himself inside her.

"Jesus, Lainie," he said in a cracked, hoarse voice. "You're so goddamn beautiful." He winced at his words, wishing he knew how to be poetic, how to do justice to the emotion that swelled in his heart and made it burst wide open.

She sat there like a frightened virgin, trusting and yet afraid. He knew that she wanted him, wanted him perhaps as much as he wanted her right now, but her life had been as hollow and empty as his had been, and she was still, even now, afraid to reach for what she wanted.

If only she knew how much he needed her. Not as a body beneath him or even as a woman beside him. He needed her in the darkness of his soul to put a light where none had ever been before.

He leaned forward and kissed her. He tried to make it gentle and loving, but when his lips touched hers, something inside him exploded. He wrapped his arms around her and dragged her against him, wanting to merge their bodies, their souls. A low, gravelly groan lodged in his throat.

She met his kiss, coiled her slim arms around his neck. His tongue pushed past her lips, parting them. She made a quiet, gasping sound and let him in, tightening her arms around him. Her fingers were trembling against his back; he felt the flutter softness of the movement against his shirt. Using his tongue and hands, he coaxed her, urged her to feel some hint of the desire that flooded his senses.

She responded, shyly at first, then with the first strains of passion. The flicker of her moist tongue against his wrenched through his self-control.

"Take off my shirt, Lainie," he whispered harshly against her lips.

She hesitated, then brought her trembling fingers to his shirt and unbuttoned it. He shrugged out of it and tossed it aside. They came together again, harder, naked flesh against near naked flesh. The damp heat of her body melted against his, until he couldn't tell where she ended and he began. The peaks of her breasts pushed through the stretchable fabric of her bra, the hardened tips scored his chest in pinpricks of fire.

He dragged her against him and rolled her over, pressing her into the fleecy pile of the sleeping bag. She lay on her back, looking up at him through dazed, passion-darkened eyes. He kissed her again, deeply, letting his tongue communicate all the poetic, romantic notions he couldn't speak.

She made a soft, breathy sound and curled her arms around him, arching up against him. Again he felt the teasing hardness of her nipples brush his chest.

Slow down, Killian. He took a ragged breath and fought for control. He wanted to wrench her bra off and bury himself in the softness of her breasts, lose himself inside her.

Shaking, he pulled back and kissed her chin, her cheeks, her temples. His lips lingered at the velvety curve of her ear, nibbled at the lobe. She quivered at the moist contact and moved restlessly beneath him. The artless, seductive movement jolted him, sent a new spear of desire shooting to his groin.

With effort, he confined his kisses to her throat, tasting, dragging the tip of his tongue down her neck, along the golden chain of the necklace. He kissed her pulse, feeling the throb of her life against his sensitive lips.

He moved downward, letting his face glide between her breasts, but not touching them, to the warm surface of her stomach. He kissed the hard, pronounced lines of her ribs and tickled her navel with his tongue.

She clutched his head, tried to draw him up. He resisted her pressure and moved downward, flicking open the copper rivets of her Levi's.

She squirmed a little, tried harder to draw him up. "No ... Killian, no ..."

He took hold of her pants and dragged them down her thighs, easing them off her feet. Tossing them away, he removed her knee-length stockings. He kissed his way back up her calves, over the hard ball of her knee, up the tender softness of her inner thigh. She moved restlessly beneath him, making breathy, gasping sounds above his head.

He skimmed his lips across the strange cotton drawers that clung to her body like a second skin. A dark shadow of hair made a mound in the taut fabric, taunting him with images of what lay beneath. He eased the skimpy drawers down her legs. They were as light as air and he flung them over his shoulder like a flag of surrender.

A small bluish design marked the pale skin beside her pelvic bone. He frowned, looking at it.

"It's a tattoo," she said in a breathy voice, trying to cover it with her hands.

He pushed her hands away, fascinated. It was a small blue figure eight lying on its side. "What is it?"

She forced a thin laugh. "It's the symbol for infinity. I got it when I was about thirteen. Another mistake."

He leaned over and kissed it, trailed his tongue along the swirling ink marks. "Maybe not."

She shivered and clutched his shoulders, driving her short, sharp nails into his flesh. Her body stiffened, her legs slammed together. "Come up now."

He lifted his head to look at her.

She lay tense and still, breathing fast. Her eyes were wide with a remnant of some old, never forgotten fear; they looked deep and dark and fathomless next to the fragile porcelain of her skin. Her lips were puffy and swollen from his kisses.

He gave her a slow, steady smile and waited for one in return.

Nervously she wet her lower lip and tried to smile. It was a quick, wobbly curving of the mouth that vanished almost before it existed. She stared at him, her gaze focused and intense, her arms pressed against her sides. Her breasts dipped and rose with each quick, ragged breath she took.

He moved up and kissed her collarbone, trailing hot, moist kisses along the hollow of flesh beneath. Gently he slipped two fingers underneath the remarkably resilient fabric of her bra, gliding his fingers along her skin. Goose bumps followed his caress, giving her skin a new, erotic texture. He eased the fabric over her head and dropped it beside her.

She swallowed hard and stared up at him.

He looked down at her, let his gaze slide down her throat and loiter at the round swell of her breasts, the pebbly pinkness of her nipples.

She was so beautiful, she took his breath away. Deep

inside, a longing started, swelled into an ache. He knew with sudden certainty that they had been brought together for a reason, this reason, and that he would love this woman all the days of his life.

He swept her into his embrace and kissed her deeply, wrapping his arms around her naked body and dragging her close. He felt the softness of her skin against his, the tentative touch of her fingers at his back.

Desire surged through him like a lightning bolt, electrifying his body. He made a sound that was half frustrated groan, half sigh, and cupped her bottom with his hands, molding her body to his. Her feet slipped around his legs and locked. The moist heat of her mound pressed against his hardness.

Their kiss turned as hot and fevered as their bodies. He pulled back slightly, breathlessly, and trailed desperate kisses down her throat to her breasts. At the touch of his tongue, she shivered and arched toward him. He brought one hand up and kneaded her firm breasts, suckled one hard, pink tip, drawing it deeper and deeper into his mouth.

She made a quiet, gasping sound of pleasure and fell back from him, stretching out on the sleeping bag. He played with her breasts, taunting, teasing, bringing the nipples to straining hardness with his teeth and tongue. Then he moved his hand over the soft curve of her stomach to the silky triangle of hair between her legs.

She tried to squeeze her legs together.

"Relax, Lainie," he whispered hoarsely, "trust me."

She let out a shuddering breath and let her legs relax.

His fingers pushed through her hair, dropped lower, searching, seeking.

She moaned and moved restlessly against him. "Oh, God, Killian."

At the sound of his name, so drugged with passion, Killian felt himself swell with need. It was a sharp, driving pain in his groin. He drew her nipple into his mouth and sucked it hard.

His fingers moved against her mound, through the thick thatch of damp hair, against the velvet-soft core of her desire. With a groaning sigh, he slipped his finger inside, felt the slick moisture of her need and the tight grip of her body.

She let her legs fall open farther and arched against his hand. Her hips ground into his palm, matching the fast, circular motion of his hand. She writhed and moaned and twisted her hands in his hair.

Lainie had never felt anything like this in her life. Her whole body trembled, ached. Deep inside, deeper than she'd even known existed, a fire had started, slow at first, just leaping flames, but with each stroke of his hand it burned hotter, until now she was damp with perspiration and writhing with need. It seemed as if everything she was lay beneath his questing finger, as if she'd magically dwindled to a speck of throbbing, painful desire. She threw her head back and closed her eyes, floating, straining, reveling in the heat of his touch.

She wanted to reach for him, to hold him in her arms and tell him what she felt, but her arms felt heavy and drugged. She couldn't move, couldn't draw a breath. "Killian," she whispered, tossing her head and thrusting her hip against his hand. "What are you doing to me?"

He pulled back from her nipple. Cold air rushed across the hardened peak, made her shiver at the sudden chill. Straining toward her, he pressed hot, moist kisses along her throat. "Loving you," he drawled, kissing her again on the mouth.

The simple words exploded in her heart. She threw her arms around him and clung to his sweaty back, returning his kiss with an abandon she'd never experienced before, never even imagined. His huge body angled atop hers, pressed her deeper into the fleecy bedroll.

And still his hands worked their magic on her body, building her desire to a throbbing, aching crescendo. Her heart was pounding against her chest, drowning out every sound except for the ragged hiss of her breathing. It felt as if it would explode any second.

A frustrated sigh escaped her. "Now, Killian," she murmured. *"Now . . ."*

In a sweeping motion, he wrenched off his pants and rolled on top of her completely, covering her body with his. The hot, hard length of him pressed into her, drove her deeper in the bedding. She moaned softly at the contact and tightened her hold on his back. His legs slid down along hers.

She felt the heat of him everywhere, scalding her flesh. His hardness pressed the sensitive, aching spot between her legs and made her breathing shatter into weighty gasps. She waited for him to push inside her, but he didn't.

It drove her crazy with need. She clutched him, said his name on a broken sob. He kissed her, teased her until she couldn't think for wanting him.

She arched up and kissed him, losing herself in the heady taste of him. No one had ever kissed her like this before, and she knew suddenly why. This was the taste of love, the feel of it, the smell of it. Love wasn't about wedding rings and fairy tales and knights in shining armor. It was sweet-tasting and smelled of sweat and hurt so badly sometimes, you wanted to die.

And it was about pleasure. She squeezed her eyes shut. Jesus, the pleasure. Never again would she mistake lust for something else. This was desire, this was passion. She felt it surging through her body like electrical current, singing and burning the forbidden corners of her body and soul.

He filled her with a scorching heat, a throbbing need that made it difficult to think about love or lifetimes or everlasting. Even about children in other times. For a heartbreakingly perfect moment, she felt suspended, poised in a darkness where nothing mattered except the sweet ache between her legs and the hardness pressed against her body.

Then he slipped inside her and she couldn't think of anything at all. He moved slowly forward, stretching her body until she thought she'd burst from the exquisite torture. She said his name in a shuddering, moaning little voice and clung to his damp back.

He squeezed his eyes shut and angled himself onto his elbows. His face, drawn and lined by restraint, loomed above her, filled her vision. Tiny, sparkling droplets of sweat clung to his forehead, dampened the silvery hair that stuck to his face.

He moved slowly, rocking in and out of her body in a timeless, ageless rhythm that brought her past pleasure to the aching, desperate precipice of pain.

"Oh, God," she whimpered, hooking her nails into his back and riding the motion of his body, matching it with desperate, bent-kneed thrusts of her own.

She responded with an abandon she'd never known before. Nothing mattered, nothing but the painful ache between her legs. She clung to him, arching, driving her hips up to meet his downward thrusts. Their bodies merged, melded together in a scalding coil of fire.

She arched against him, quivering, clutching him against her, grinding her hips against his. Suddenly it hurt to want him so much. She couldn't stand it, couldn't breathe. A low, throaty moan escaped her. She groaned, tossed her head from side to side. Her body was poised, straining toward release. She needed it, oh, Jesus, she needed it now. Panting, almost weeping, she arched toward him.

"Oh, Killian," she groaned. "Oh, God . . ."

It exploded through her all at once, a violent, shuddering release that left her gasping. She screamed out, clung to him as wave after wave of intense pleasure washed through her body, leaving her weak and trembling.

Killian felt her release. It throbbed around his hardness in an erotic, pulsing tide that drove him mad with wanting her. He thrust into her one more time, deep and hard, burying himself in the hot, wet sheath of her, losing himself in her moist sweetness. His need erupted, spilled itself into her welcoming warmth with a force that made his body jerk. He closed his arms around her slick, trembling body and clung to her like a drowning man.

When the shudders subsided, he drew her close and buried his face in the crook of her neck. They lay there a long time, neither one speaking, neither one needing to. The crisp, cool air hung heavy with the scent of their passion.

Killian let out his breath in a long, low sigh. A remnant of their electricity tingled through his body, left him full of strange, lingering sensations that were unlike anything he'd ever experienced before. He felt . . . complete, as if the empty years had been washed away and forgotten.

He'd never felt this before, not even with Emily. Sex with Emily had been loving and gentle and caring, but if he was honest with himself, there'd always been something missing. Even after all their years together, she'd somehow remained virginal, untouchable and untouched. He'd thought that was how ladies were, all that they could be.

Lainie had begun like that; she'd touched him reluctantly if at all, she'd squeezed her legs together and been afraid of the intimacy of his touch. But the fire had swept her fear away, and without it, she was as bold and sensual and needy as he.

He smiled. The world and all of its possibilities opened up to him suddenly, offered him a future he'd never allowed himself to imagine. A new beginning for a man who'd thought life was a dead end.

He stroked the line of her back, feeling the sheen of moisture that clung to her flesh. Turning slightly, she opened her eyelids. There was a dazed look in her eyes. Then not so dazed. A slow smile curved her lips as a blush spread up her cheeks. One quick spurt of a giggle shot from her mouth before she bit down on her lower lip. "So *that's* what all the hoopla's about," she said.

He grinned down at her, knowing it was a wolfish, predatory smile and not caring in the least. Christ, he *felt* predatory right now, and territorial, too. He wanted her again, damn it, wanted her in a way he'd never wanted another woman, and never would again. He wanted her body, her soul, her heart, and he wanted them for a lifetime. "Not quite, darlin'."

She gave him a slow, sensual smile that made his blood race. "There's more that feels that good?"

He laughed softly, pulling her close. "You can't imagine what I can do with my tongue."

"You're wrong," she whispered hoarsely, twining her legs around his, locking her ankles behind his. "I'm imagining it right now."

He gave her a slow smile and slid his hand down

her stomach. "Ah, but fact is so much better than fiction."

She trembled beneath his touch. "I'll never doubt that again."

Chapter Twenty-four

Sunlight shot through the trees and gilded the dirt, played on the water in a shifting, magical pattern. The faint, familiar aromas of coffee and bacon and powdery dirt filled the air.

Killian tossed the last of their supplies into the saddlebags and turned to look back at Lainie. She sat beside the fire, her head bowed, her sweater sagging off one shoulder. She was poking a stick into the dirt, swirling it around to create a puffing cloud of dust. The last hardy flames of the near-dead fire flickered light against her face, cast her in dancing shadows.

At the sight of her, he felt a painful swell of emotion. He shook his head, sighing. Christ, he'd made love to her for hours, and he was still aching with the need to touch her again. Grinning, he strode toward her.

"Hi," she said softly, without looking up.

He sat down beside her, leaning close. "I know we should head out, but I can think of a better idea, if you're willing."

She turned to him slightly, trying to smile. Her eyes were sparkling with tears.

His smile faded. "Regrets?"

She shook her head. It was a flutter of soft movement against his shoulder. "Never."

"Then what?"

"I was just thinking about Kelly." She sighed, sagged tiredly against his body.

He stroked her hair and said nothing.

"She's my life. . . . She has been from the moment I conceived her. Until Kelly, I was . . . lost."

Silence fell in after her words, broken only by the crackling hiss of the small fire and the far-off whisper of a breeze. He knew instinctively that she had more to say, so he remained quiet, waiting, offering her the wordless comfort of his arm.

"For a while, you made me forget everything," she said softly. "And I can't tell you what that meant. I've spent a lifetime unable to forget anything. I carry around my past like some dark anchor around my throat, dragging me forever downward. But this morning . . . none of that mattered."

"Maybe if you talked about it . . ."

"Killian, I've had so much therapy, I could tell the plumber my past. It's not talking that helps you forget something; it's having another moment, another memory to replace it." She turned to him, looked at him through huge, bright eyes. "That's what you gave me just now, Killian. And I'll treasure it forever."

He touched her face, wishing he could simply accept her words and let the matter drop. But he needed her suddenly, needed to soak her up inside him and know everything about her. Before he could ask, though, she leaned toward him, so close that he could see the pain in her eyes.

"I . . ." She looked down, bit her lower lip. "I . . . want to tell you about my life now." She forced a hollow laugh. "You should know who you're sleeping with."

"Lainie—"

She pressed a finger to his lips and shook her head.

"Don't stop me, Killian. I've never done this before, not really. I've told, but I've never shared. With you . . ." She looked up, met his gaze. "With you I want to be different."

He stilled. "Okay."

"I hate to be predictable, but it starts with my folks." She shivered violently and looked away, gazing at the pond in the distance. "They were young, and they never should have had children. Heroin addicts, both of them. I was in withdrawal for the first week of my life." She gave another bitter laugh. "What chance did I have, right? Anyway, they tried to take care of me, but of course, they couldn't, and one day when I was ten years old, they just left."

He frowned. "Jesus . . ."

"My mom was found dead of a drug overdose a few months later, but Dad . . ." She shrugged. "He never came back. After that, the state stepped in and moved me from one foster home to another. That went on for years. At first I really tried to fit in, but after a while you stop caring." She looked up at him, staring at him through eyes that were heartbreakingly honest. "That's when I started partying pretty heavy. For years I moved in a drug-induced haze, not caring, not being cared about. Just one of the millions of kids who drift on city streets at night. Alone . . .

"It was on one of those nights that I was . . . raped. It was a bad scene, really stupid. I was at a party, pretty loaded up, way too young, and I met a couple of older guys. We . . . got high and they . . ." She looked away, her eyes glazing with tears that didn't fall. Her voice fell to a whisper. "They didn't think a girl like me had a right to say no."

He stared at her, feeling a young girl's pain and fear wash over him in a chilling wave. He wanted to say something, offer some comfort, but it would have sounded so cheap and hollow. So he said nothing at all.

After a long silence, she went on. "For a long time, I believed them. It sent me into a suicidal tailspin, a downward spiral that ended behind bars. But strangely, it was the bars that saved me. Finally I found a place where I belonged, or thought I did. Oh, at first I fought the orderlies like a wildcat . . . but they had . . . ways of keeping you down.

"Then one day, everything changed." She smiled, a sad, wistful curving of the lips that reached her overbright eyes. "Dr. Gray—the institution's head shrink—told me that it wasn't my fault, that every woman has the right to say no. It took a long time, a *long* time, but after a while I started to believe her. She helped me take control of my life and start over. I got my GED and started writing in the hospital. I tried never to look back, but sometimes, at night . . ."

She turned to him, met his gaze, and he could see the challenge in her eyes. She was waiting for him to pull away, to tell her that she wasn't good enough for him.

"Lainie," he said quietly, shaking his head. "I love you."

She gave him a trembling smile. "You don't know how long I've waited to hear that." She squeezed her eyes shut. "It's so damned unfair."

"What is?"

She opened her eyes. "That I would find you *now*, one hundred years in the past."

It struck him like a blow. Suddenly he thought about all the things she'd said—heroin addicts, withdrawal, foster homes, shrinks, GEDs—and the information took on a new, horrifying meaning. The words that before had meant so little, now meant everything. He stared down at her, speechless. It felt as if a huge, unforgiving weight were pressing against his lungs, suffocating him.

Jesus, it was true.

"What is it, Killian?"

He couldn't breathe, couldn't think. He could only stare at her in horror. "It's real, isn't it? Every crazy thing you've said. You really are from the future and you have a daughter waiting for you at home."

She nodded. "It's true."

He sagged forward, buried his face in his hands. "Oh, Jesus . . ."

She touched his back. "Killian?"

He wrenched away from her and stumbled forward blindly. *It's true. It's true.* The damning words circled through his mind and stabbed his heart with every breath. He'd finally found the woman of his dreams and she was only that . . . a dream. She was here for a moment, a second—just long enough to wrench his heart out of his chest and slice it in half—and then she was going away.

Leaving him. He squeezed his eyes shut, remembering in a horrifying flash what his life had been for the last fifteen years. And how goddamn different it had been since Lainie stumbled into it. She'd brought a light with her, made him examine the ugliness of his soul and try to change it. But he'd changed for her, damn it, for her. And now she expected him to go back to his old life without her.

He couldn't imagine how much that would hurt.

Yes, he could, he realized dully. He knew exactly how much it would hurt. He'd done it before . . . when Emily died.

He glanced back at her, saw her still sitting by the fire, her face streaked with tears, her mouth trembling and sad.

The image of her burned through him, lodged in his soul. He would never forget this moment as long as he lived. It would be one of those memories of which she spoke, one of the anchors that would mire him forever in the love he'd found too late.

Desperately he spun around, looked east.

Somewhere, not more than thirty miles away, the rock that lightning struck thrust up from the desert floor. The twisting, ragged red stone wall that would take her away from him.

Could he do it? he wondered suddenly. *Should* he do it?

The answer came to him on the sly voice of the wind, filling him with a wild, unreasonable hope. All he had to do was miss the Rock, or get them there too late on Sunday. Anything . . .

She materialized beside him. Through a haze, he saw her hand, pale and small, against the worn blue of his shirt. Her touch was everything he'd dreamed of all his life, gentle and loving and soft.

"We should get going," she said quietly, looking up at him. "We have a long ride ahead of us."

He answered distractedly. "Yeah, sure."

"Do you mind if I ride in front today? I . . . I want to feel your arms around me."

"Sure," he said, touching her chin, seeing the telltale silver tracing of her tears. He knew in that instant what he would do. There was only one thing he could do, and he didn't care if it damned his soul to hell. He wasn't meant to be a hero. "I'll hold you all day. And I won't let you go."

Lainie stared out at the desert, barely seeing anything beyond the hairy, curved tips of the horse's ears. Beyond, the world was a smear of gold and brown and red, floating beneath a cloudless blue sky. Hot sunlight burned her face, made the heavy sweater feel damp and scratchy against her skin. She was so tired that she imagined a small, welcoming cabin in the midst of the nothingness before them.

She closed her eyes and leaned back, letting Killian's embrace soothe her. But there was no comfort, not really, not even in his arms. There was only a crushing sense of loss.

She was leaving him. So soon . . . when she'd only just found him . . .

It was so damned unfair, and she wished she could dredge up some remnant of the anger that had always buoyed her through the bad times. If she could be mad, really, really mad, she could straighten her spine and scream at God and come out swinging.

But there was no anger in her anymore, no strength of spirit, no blacken-your-eye belligerence. There was only this sinking sense of despair, of having lost what she'd never even hoped to find.

God was asking of her the one thing she'd never imagined, asking her to make a choice no woman should ever have to make. She could have Killian or she could have her child, but she couldn't have both. And as much as she loved Killian, and she loved him with every ounce of her soul, she couldn't stay here, couldn't choose him over her baby.

Jesus, it was so unfair. . . .

Killian's hands moved slowly up her body. His fingers hooked around her sagging neckline and tugged. The sweater slid down her arms and landed across her lap in a heap of red yarn.

She shivered at the sudden change in temperature and glanced around. "Killian—"

"Ssh," he whispered against her ear, his breath as hot as the sunlight overhead.

His hands moved back up, with deliberate slowness, up the flat surface of her stomach, over the damp fabric of her bra. The roughened tips of his fingers curled under the wide straps, flipped them down onto her shoulders, where they tapped lightly against her skin. Then his hands disappeared for a split second and reappeared beneath her arms. The bra pulled taut against her breasts as he took hold of it.

He pushed the elasticized fabric down to her waist. She leaned back against him, her breasts free and bare beneath the hot sun. The feeling was deliciously forbidden, and made her forget everything except the moist heat of his breath on the back of her neck and the strong certainty of the arms around her waist.

His fingers grazed up her naked stomach, setting off a flurry of goose bumps. His palms cupped her breasts, holding them as his thumbs breezed across her nipples, coaxing them instantly to hardness.

She closed her eyes, reveling in the feel of him. It felt so good to be touched and held like this, to be stroked and cared for and protected. There was a wickedness to it, too, that added to her excitement. Out here all alone in the middle of nowhere, naked and vulnerable . . .

His hands slid out from underneath her breasts and moved to her nipples, only her nipples. Fingers closed around the pink tips, tugging, teasing. A fiery twinge of desire clutched her between the legs, sent the blood racing through her veins. She let out a breathy little half laugh that sounded more like a sigh.

He kissed the back of her neck and trailed the hard, wet tip of his tongue along her flesh. She shivered at the strange mix of feelings: the hot sun on her naked flesh, the moisture of his tongue along her skin, the rough fabric of his shirt against her back, the cool weight of the amethyst. His hands moved more ardently on her breasts, pulling and plucking and twirling her nipples until she was breathless.

He made a quiet, clicking sound behind her, and the horse leapt into a slow trot.

Lainie slammed down into the saddle, the leather curved around her crotch. She made a moaning sound of pleasure at the contact.

She arched into his hand, drove her body against the hard leather of the saddle. Beneath her, the horse's gait moved in tandem with Killian's hands on her breasts. Sensations exploded in her body, so suddenly she was left dizzy and light-headed.

"Oh, God, Killian," she groaned, feeling a hot surge of moisture between her legs.

"Whoa," he whispered hoarsely.

The horse stopped and Lainie immediately twisted around to reach for Killian. She grabbed air. She opened her eyes, blinking slowly. Her body felt drugged, aching with need for his touch. "Wha—"

"Down here."

He was standing beside her, his hands upheld. She swung her leg around and slithered down into his arms. He embraced her, held her close. The damp, sweaty smell of him filled her senses. She couldn't help herself. The need was a burning fire between her legs. Wantonly she arched forward, rubbed against him, feeling the evidence of his own desire.

He threw an arm around her and dragged her close. Her breasts pressed against his upper arm, her head lolled back. He tied the reins around a hitching post.

A hitching post?

Lainie glanced around suddenly, noticing for the first time the little cabin in front of them. It sat huddled against a sheer rock wall, its front door hanging awkwardly on broken hinges. Broken bricks lay scattered around the base of a serrated chimney.

"Home sweet home for the night," Killian growled against her ear, sweeping her into his arms. She laughed and threw her arms around his neck. In an instant, all thoughts of where they were vanished, buried beneath an avalanche of awakening desire. The need for him returned, surged through her blood, and left a painful ache in its wake.

He kicked the sagging door open. It swung inward with a creaking whine and slammed against the wall. Dust showered down from the rafters, pattered the debris-strewn floor. The sour, dank smell of mold and old dirt filled the little room.

They came together for a hard, desperate kiss that drove the cool metal of the necklace against her hot flesh. His hands seemed suddenly to be everywhere, rubbing, feeling, stroking, bringing her nipples to aching hardness. She leaned toward him, pressed her heavy, tingling breasts against his chest. The rough fabric of his shirt abraded her nipples, teased and taunted them.

He made a low, groaning sound at the contact and wrenched the fly of her Levi's open. The copper rivets popped free, the worn denim gaped across her abdomen. Cool air rushed in to graze her skin, made her flesh pucker with goose bumps.

She felt a shudder of raw, almost violent need. She grabbed his shirt collar and fumbled furiously with his buttons, ripping one off in her haste to feel his skin against hers, to taste the sweet, salty tang of it. He shrugged out of the shirt and tossed it aside. Dimly she was aware of the pale blue fabric flying through the air; it landed on a skinned log bedpost and flagged downward.

He backed her against the wall. She hit with a thud and reached for the buttons of his trousers. Wrenching them from their buttonholes, she shoved his pants down the long, hard length of his legs.

Still kissing, their hands urgently exploring each other's bodies, they kicked out of their cowboy boots and pulled off their socks and pants, flinging them wherever. Then his hands were at her breasts again, doing marvelous, tingling things that made her throb with need.

He pulled back slightly, breathing hard. "Do you want to use the bed?"

She glanced behind him to the sagging, unmade wooden bed. The mattress was yellowed and dusty and completely uninviting. They'd have to get out their bedrolls to use it. "No," she said throatily, reaching down for him. "I can't wait that long."

At her touch, he shuddered hard. "Jesus, Lainie . . ." He ripped her panties off in a hiss of tearing fabric and flung them over his shoulder. She clutched at his shoulders, dragging him against her. They staggered backward and hit the wall again. The splintery log wall scratched her skin and banged her head, but she barely noticed. All she could feel was the cresting ache of need. It swelled and throbbed and sent feelers of fire through her blood.

His hands slid down the curve of her back and settled at her bottom. He lifted her off her feet. She threw her arms around him and curled her legs around his thighs, lowering herself onto his sleek hardness.

He forced her back against the wall and thrust deeper inside her, impaling her. His body pressed against hers, grinding against the secret, sensitive core of her desire. Sensations exploded in her body, left her writhing and breathless.

A scream tore up her throat, stunning her. She tried to hold it back, but her will was gone. All she could think about was her body, and the forbidden, sensual things he was making her feel. She clung to him, riding him, scratching his sweaty back with her fingernails. At every thrust, she gasped and arched and matched his movement, driving her slick, shaking body against his. The wall behind them cracked and shuddered, raining dirt on their hair. The smell of the dust and sweat mingled, joined the sweet scent of passion, and thickened the air.

They rocked and writhed and thrust in a frantic rhythm that brought Lainie to the brink of madness. She clung to him, riding the rocking motion of his buttocks as he slid in and out of her, thrusting harder, deeper. She responded wantonly, meeting him move for move, her legs locked behind his thighs, her arms curled around his neck.

For a second, everything dwindled down to that place where their bodies were joined, sealed skin to skin. Her skin burned, and she couldn't breathe suddenly for wanting him, needing him. The ache between her legs intensified, turned from something sweet and heavy to a throbbing, desperate pain.

"Oh, God, Killian . . ." She threw her head back and closed her eyes.

He kissed down her throat, hot, moist kisses that landed everywhere, burning her flesh. Then he took one nipple in his mouth, drawing it deep, flicking the hardened tip with his tongue.

The release burst upon her like before, only a thousand times more intense. She stiffened and shuddered and cried out his name in a hoarse, breathy voice. Her body seemed to spiral into some great, black void.

Weightlessly she floated back to earth. Tears stung her eyes and slipped down her temples.

Finally, shaking with the aftermath of their passion, she lifted her head and met his gaze. The sad, loving look in his eyes almost broke her heart. Everything that stood between them was in that look, the love, the passion . . . and beneath it, hovering and dark, the impossibility of there ever being any more between them than there was right now.

She felt a swelling sense of despair. All her life she'd waited for this moment, this emotion. She'd wanted to revel in it, savor it like a glass of fine, aged wine. But now she couldn't. She had to grab at it greedily, clutch whatever remnant of it she could before it turned to smoke.

They should be cuddling and talking and laughing like new lovers. There were so many things she wanted to say to him, so many questions she wanted to ask about his life. But none of it really mattered; things like that only mattered to couples building a future together. She and Killian were just reliving a past. There was nowhere for them to go.

With a quiet sigh, she rested her head against his damp chest and closed her eyes. They stood locked together, the sweet scent of their passion heavy in the dank air, and already it felt as if they were miles apart. There wasn't a heartbeat of joy between them, just this grave, depressing realization that it was going by too fast, that it wouldn't last.

She swallowed the lump in her throat and pushed the damp, curly tendrils of hair from her face. His hold on her buttocks loosened and she slid down the length of his body. Her bare feet hit the floor with a muffled thud.

She lifted her head, though it felt impossibly heavy. Their gazes met, and in his dark eyes she saw the mirror of her own pain and regret. She tried to smile. "You're turning me into a real slut, Killian."

She could tell that he wanted to smile, but he couldn't. "Give me a lifetime and there's no telling how you'll turn out."

The words pierced her heart. "Don't," she said softly. "Don't ask that of me, Killian. I have a baby at home who needs me."

"I need you."

The despair increased, seeped through her body until she felt deflated and limp. It took almost more energy than she possessed to speak. "I need you, too, but all we can do is make the best of the time we have. There's nothing more for us."

She started to turn away, to walk past him and get her clothes. The moment of their intimacy was gone, shattered. She felt alone suddenly, maybe more alone than ever before in her life.

She took a step, perhaps two, before he stopped her. The touch of his hand on her arm was all she needed. A small, desperate sound escaped her lips as she swirled around and threw herself into his arms. He embraced her so tightly, she couldn't breathe, but it didn't matter.

"Jesus, Lainie," he whispered hoarsely against her ear. "What in the hell are we going to do?"

She clung to him, her face pressed into the crook of his neck, his skin slick with her tears. "I don't know."

They stood that way for what seemed like forever, naked, clasped in each other's arms. Neither one of them wanted to be the first to turn away, but even now, in his arms, Lainie felt as if he were light-years away. As if she couldn't actually touch him if she reached out.

Finally, as if on some unspoken cue, they both pulled apart. Lainie immediately felt a chill against her flesh, and she wondered fleetingly if she'd ever really be warm again. She reached down for her jeans, which lay in a heap at the foot of the bed. "I'll get this place picked up and start a fire. You go ahead and see to the horse."

"Yeah." The word slipped out on a heavy sigh as he reached for his own drawers and trousers.

Lainie scooped the jeans into her arms and reached down for her socks. One lay beside the jeans and the other hung from the rickety headboard. She moved right up against the bed, her shins against the wooden frame, and reached for the sock.

She heard a whispered rustling, like the crinkling of cellophane. She stopped, frowning, her hand hovering above the sock. "Did you hear—"

A sharp pain, like a quick pierce of a needle, flared near her ankle. She yelped and stumbled backward.

"What happened?"

She bent down and peered under the bed. "Something bit me."

Deep shadows lay heaped beneath the bed. She heard the scurrying sound again. Something moved.

Killian leapt toward her and flung her away from the bed. She stumbled back.

A slender, straw-colored insect crept out from the cover of the shadows. It moved slowly, six legs working as one, with two dangerous-looking pincers poised above its head. A long, jointed tail curved up over its body, ending in a sharp, hairy stinger.

"Oh, Jesus," Killian breathed. "A scorpion." He wrenched sideways and picked up his cowboy boot, slamming the heel down on the deadly insect.

Before she could say a word, Killian yanked a dirty blanket off the bed and wrapped it around her. The musty scent of old wool filled her nostrils, sickening and sour. Sweeping her into his arms, he carried her through the broken door. Racing across the untended yard, he skidded to his knees alongside the stream and shoved her foot into the cool water. "Stay here." He leapt to his feet and started to turn away from her.

She grabbed his wrist so tightly, her nails gouged his skin. He paused and glanced down at her. "Was it the deadly kind?" She had to force the question up her throat. It sounded weak and desperate and afraid. Exactly the way she felt.

The look on his face was all the answer she needed. "Stay here," he said in a gruff voice. "I'll get the cabin ready for you."

"I think I'll stay out here, thanks."

"You'll need the bed," he answered softly, and in the words she heard the ringing echo of a thousand unspoken ones.

Suddenly Viloula's prophecy came back to her. *There will be a death.* Lainie shuddered and wrapped her arms around her naked body, staring down at the foot shimmering beneath the mirror of the water. It felt, strangely, like someone else's foot, someone else's problem.

Then the pain began, a low, dull throbbing at the base of her ankle, and she knew she was in trouble this time. She'd done a lot of research on the American Southwest, and she knew that scorpions were considered the most deadly animals in the desert.

Adults rarely die, she reminded herself.

Rarely.

She closed her eyes and bowed her head, clutching the rough woolen blanket more tightly around her shoulders. The statistic wasn't quite as comforting as she'd like.

"Never," she said with a laugh that sounded a little hysterical. "Adults *never* die would be good."

She breathed deeply, trying to keep calm. She could handle pain. Hell, she'd been through childbirth. She could handle anything.

Time sort of slipped away from her for a second. She looked up suddenly, blinking hard. It felt as if she'd fallen asleep, but she didn't think she had. She stared out at the desert's blurry wash of sand and stone. Overhead the sky was so blue, it hurt her eyes. She shielded her gaze with a shaking hand and glanced back at the cabin.

How long had he been gone? Five minutes, ten? An hour? Suddenly she had no idea. She swallowed hard, fighting to keep her fear at bay.

The pain in her ankle had dwindled. She tried to draw her leg out of the water to examine the sting mark, but she couldn't move. Her leg felt numb, as heavy as stone.

Paralyzed. The word smashed through her, set off a terror so deep and dark and primal, she couldn't breathe. Her heart seemed to explode within her chest, setting off a pounding rush of blood through her veins.

"C-Calm down," she told herself firmly. "It's just the c-cold water."

She grabbed her ankle and dragged it onto the dirt. Two angry red marks spotted the tender skin in the hollow beneath her anklebone, but there was almost no inflammation or swelling.

That was probably a good sign, she thought. Probably a really good sign.

Paralyzed.

She shoved the horrifying thought aside with a shudder. But it wouldn't stay gone, it kept coming back, seeping through her thoughts and filling her with a formless terror. Suddenly she couldn't stay here anymore, couldn't sit here like a lump of clay; she had to move, had to force herself to walk.

She scooted back from the shore and staggered to her feet. Her leg was numb, but not paralyzed. If she really concentrated, she could make herself walk. The realization calmed her somewhat. *Thank God.*

Clutching the blanket around her throat, she limped back toward the cabin, dragging her hurt foot like some Victorian Quasimodo. "Killian!" She tried to scream his name, but couldn't manage it. Her tongue felt heavy now, as useless and numb as her leg.

God, what's happening to me?

Shivering violently, she limped forward. Just as she reached the cabin, the door banged open again and two men appeared in the doorway.

She frowned, wondering who the second man was.

"Layyynee?" The word—was it her name?—seemed to come at her from an endless darkness, drawn out and lingering like the last echoing strains of music. The voice was familiar.

The two watery men merged back into one, a tall, silver-haired man wearing jeans and nothing else. It took her a second to recognize him. Her mind felt strangely disconnected. *Killian.*

She tried to smile, but didn't know if her face had moved or not. "Help me" slipped from her mouth, though it hadn't been what she'd intended to say. She didn't know what she'd meant to say.

He spoke. She heard the rich, gravelly rumble of his voice, but the words were meaningless. She blinked, tried to make sense of what was happening, what she was feeling. Her heart was racing so hard, she couldn't hear anything else. She had a sudden, ridiculous image of it exploding out of her chest like the thing in *Alien.*

She couldn't breathe. It felt as if invisible hands were

coiling viciously around her throat. She gasped and tried to gulp air, but all she could draw were shallow, panicked breaths.

He moved toward her; the movement seemed lightning fast. She wanted to meet him, find comfort in his arms, but she was rooted to the spot, helpless and paralyzed.

He touched her arm, and the pain was so intense, so unexpected, that she screamed. He drew back immediately. "Follow me," he said in a long, drawn-out voice that seemed to take forever.

He led her to the bed, where two bedrolls lay side by side. She dragged herself to the bed and collapsed on top of it, letting her legs dangle over the side.

Very gently he lifted her legs onto the bed, but even that simple touch was excruciating. Her skin felt as if it were on fire, burning slowly, inch by inch, up her legs. Every whisper of his breath on her flesh hurt, every movement of the air was agony.

Biting her lower lip against the pain, she leaned back into the pillows he'd pulled from somewhere. The dank smell of long-unwashed linen filled her nostrils.

"This is going to hurt," he said.

He touched her calf and the sensitive skin exploded in pain. She gritted her teeth and squeezed her eyes shut. Beside her, she heard the wrenching hiss of fabric being ripped. Then he slid something beneath her knee, pulled it taut, and tied it down.

She whimpered and tried not to cry. Fire seemed to race through her body, burning her skin. She tossed restlessly from side to side, moaning softly.

He leaned down beside her. She felt the warm, moist strains of his breathing against her forehead. "You're going to be okay. . . ."

It was a lie. She could hear the fear in his voice; it

matched her own. For some absurd, illogical reason, she wanted to assure him that she would be all right.

She opened her eyes to look at him.

And saw nothing but blackness.

She blinked, tried again.

Same thing.

Icy fear shuddered through her, left her gasping and terrified. "Oh, my God . . . Killian, I can't see you."

"It's okay, Lainie. It's okay. The blindness is temporary."

"No." She meant to scream the denial, but couldn't manage it. The word slipped from her dead mouth, cracked and too soft.

His hand was on her forehead, and even though it hurt to be touched, it soothed her.

He was beside her, right beside her. She heard the tinkling splash of water, then the comforting feel of a cold, damp rag on her fevered forehead.

She sank into the warm bedding. Darkness curled around her, threw her into an impenetrable void where nothing existed, where even her pain was lessened. It beckoned her, that darkness, drew her forward with a sly, seductive voice. She didn't want to go. She'd been in that darkness before, and she wasn't sure she could find her way out again.

But everything seemed so far away now, so small and meaningless. Nothing made sense, nothing mattered, and she was so tired. She just wanted to go to sleep. . . .

"Don't leave me, Lainie." She heard the voice, heard the ragged edges of fear in it, and she frowned. Who was talking to her? Where was she?

The darkness lured her into its cool shade again. Once she was there, the fire in her skin dwindled into nothingness, the jagged pain in her abdomen and legs lessened. From somewhere came an even in-and-out whisper of sound, like an evening tide washing on a sand beach. It was soothing, that sound. So soothing . . .

She closed her eyes, letting herself drift into the painless darkness, letting herself forget.

Chapter Twenty-five

The night was cold and black and filled with whispered sounds. Somewhere an animal howled. The billowing, reedy sound pierced the darkness, left a lingering edge of disquiet in its wake. Everything had taken on a hazy, unreal quality. Killian felt like a shadow himself, walking woodenly through a foreign, unearthly landscape.

"Jesus," he cursed, and dumped the now tepid water on the ground. He was acting like a tenderfooted fool who'd never been in the desert's darkness before, instead of a man who'd lived alone and on the fringes of danger for half his life.

Bending slowly, knees creaking, he dipped the tin bowl into the cold creek. Cool water sucked his fingers and spilled over the back of his hand. He glanced up. Moonlight slithered across the rippling water, turned it into a snakelike silver chain against the black earth.

He straightened and turned back toward the cabin. He took a few heavy steps, then stopped. Suddenly and without warning, he was overwhelmed by it all. For the past three or four hours, as Lainie lay in the rickety bed, writhing in pain at the slightest touch, her brow beaded with sweat, her face a pale, deathly blue, he'd managed to focus on the simple acts of caring for her and nothing else. Each task, from dressing her to repairing her torn

330

underwear to bathing her hot face, had occupied his thoughts so completely that nothing else had penetrated his dazed mind.

But now there were no tasks, no needs to be met, nothing between him and a wrenching sense of fear.

He stared at the squat little cabin. It sat low to the ground, huddled against the darkened mesa. Stray remnants of moonlight caught on the broken windows, glazed their jagged peaks. Torn, dirty curtains hung limply behind the craggy mountains of glass. The acrid smell of smoke rode the crisp nighttime air.

They shouldn't be here.

That was the thought he'd kept at bay through sheer force of will since Lainie was stung.

It came at him now hard, crippling in its intensity. Guilt exploded in his chest, left him reeling and sick to his stomach.

This cabin was miles off course. Around noon, he'd turned them slightly south, so slightly she hadn't even noticed.

Of course she hadn't noticed. She'd trusted him, and because of that, she lay dying in a seedy cabin in the middle of nowhere.

A low, agonized moan slipped into the night.

The sound jerked Killian out of his stupor. Cursing silently, he raced toward the cabin and flung the door open. It crashed into the wall behind him, rattling the timbers, raining dust from cracks in the sod roof.

"I'm right here, baby," he murmured, sloshing the bowl of water down on the wobbly bedside table.

She thrashed weakly on the bed, twisting the covers around her body. Her eyes were closed. Damp, spiked black lashes fluttered against ashen, blue-tinged cheeks. Her lips were pale, the color of sun-bleached bones. A lilac-gray tinge darkened the hollows beneath her eyes.

He plunged the dishrag in the water and twisted the excess moisture from the fabric, then gently pressed it to her brow. His fingertips brushed her skin, felt the fire-hot temperature. God, she was so hot. . . .

She made a throaty, choked sound of pain.

He stared down at her, feeling utterly, desperately hopeless. The emotions swamped him, left him weak and shaking and more afraid than ever before in his life. It was all because of him that she was here, that she was dying.

He'd turned away from the Rock. God help him, he'd wanted her all to himself. . . .

He squeezed his eyes shut and bowed his head. Pain twisted his heart until every breath hurt. "Take me instead, God. Please . . . don't let her die. . . ."

He took her hand; it lay limp and unresponsive, the skin painfully hot against his. He had a sudden, desperate urge to sweep her into his arms and hold her tightly, so tightly she could never get free. Instead, he leaned forward and kissed her fevered temple, lingering, breathing in the scent of her.

She didn't respond, and gradually he drew back. With a tired sigh, he remoistened the washrag, barely hearing the splash of the water on the metal bowl. Pressing it to her brow again, he closed his eyes. "Jesus, Lainie," he whispered harshly, "don't leave me. I'll get you to the Rock. I'll get you home, just don't die on me."

He hunched forward, pressing an elbow into the flimsy, dust-scented mattress, rubbing his tired face. Tears scalded his eyes. Suddenly the brevity of their time together overwhelmed him. He'd fooled himself somehow into thinking he could steal some portion of her life, that he could purloin time that wasn't meant to be.

But God had answered him with devastating speed. Lainie wasn't supposed to be his. He wasn't meant to find this kind of love and caring in his life. He'd given up that right a long time ago, when another woman had died, all alone, waiting for the man who'd promised to love, honor, and cherish her, waiting for the husband who wouldn't return in time.

How had he forgotten? He'd known that Lainie was the only chance he'd have to redeem his lost soul ... and he'd thrown it away, been exactly the worthless, selfish man he'd always been.

The realization sickened and shamed him. He hadn't changed. After all the talk of redemption and second chances, he'd proven himself to be unworthy of the opportunity. The woman of his dreams, of his heart, had asked only one thing of him, and he'd cheated her.

Why had he turned away from the goddamn Rock?

"I wouldn't do it again."

Silence answered him, black and mocking.

He sat that way forever, hunching and shaking beside her bed, mired in a haze of self-loathing and regret. He mouthed an endless series of prayers, offered a continual stream of penances to the Almighty in exchange for just a word from Lainie, just a word.

She coughed. It was a whisper of sound, barely more than a ripple of hot breath.

It took him a moment to realize that he hadn't dreamed it. He brought his head up slowly, staring at her through gravelly, aching eyes. She lay perfectly still, staring up at the ceiling, her face drawn and tight, her mouth curved in a heartbreaking frown. Shallow breaths shuddered through her chest, made the blankets rise and fall too quickly. She coughed again, a harsh, rattling hack that sounded like music to his ears after so many hours of bone-jarring silence.

Her eyes were open. Sweet Jesus ...

He leaned closer, feeling the rapid thudding of his

heart. Hope flared in the darkness, gave him a shimmering ray to reach for. "I'm right here."

She said something; at least he thought she did. It was a rustling flutter of breath that might have been *you stayed.*

He drew the washrag from her forehead and gently eased back the sleeping bag. Heat radiated from her body in a rush. He moved slowly, so as not to disturb her, and climbed onto the bed beside her. The old wooden bed planks creaked and groaned beneath his weight.

He stretched out on top of the covers, molding his body to hers, curling an arm protectively around her waist. "I'm right here, Lainie," he breathed against her ear, kissing the hot, damp swell of her earlobe. Very gently he rocked her, whispering an endless stream of loving words in her ear, hoping against hope that somewhere she heard, that somehow she knew.

"C-Can . . ."

The sound of her voice brought his rocking to a sudden stop. Time seemed for a heartbeat to hang suspended, waiting. He tightened his hold on her and didn't dare to breathe.

"C-Can't see . . ."

"I'm right here, Lainie. Right here beside you." He stroked the moist side of her face, eased his fingers through the damp curls at her temple.

"Talk," she whispered brokenly.

Talk. He racked his mind for something to say, but he knew it didn't matter what he chose. She just wanted to hear his voice, wanted to know that she wasn't alone in the darkness.

"You asked me once about Emily," he said quietly, still stroking her hair, still pressing his lips against her face. "She wasn't murdered. She . . . she killed herself."

Images, stark and cold and terrifying, whirled through his mind in a heartbeat. The grave he'd come home to, the empty house in the middle of an unprotected prairie, the note ...

He squeezed his eyes shut. *Jesus, the note.* He hadn't thought about that in fifteen years, hadn't let himself remember. But now it was back, riding in the forefront of his mind, reminding him with sharp, undisputable proof of his failure. *I needed you, Johnny. I waited so long. . . . Where were you?*

Where were you Where were you Where were you? The horrible question circled through his mind and stabbed his heart. It flung him back in time, so long ago, made him remember.

"I wanted to get back to you, Emily. I tried. . . ." His voice cracked, broke on the clog of tears in his throat. What did it matter now that he'd been in some stinking hellhole of a Mexican jail? What difference did excuses make? He'd promised to be beside her always, until death, and he'd broken that vow.

Beside him, Lainie twisted slightly and made a quiet, breathy sound that might have been his name. He drew back.

She turned slightly and met his gaze. Her eyes were wide and vacant, the skin beneath them bruised and swollen. Tears glazed her hazel eyes. Slowly she brought a hand up and reached for him.

His breath caught, his pulse thundered in his ears. He leaned toward her, let her hand mold to his unshaven cheek. The hot, moist column of each finger burned through his skin. "I forgive you, Johnny."

Killian froze. For a single beat of his heart he couldn't breathe or think or move. He could only feel, a stunning, mind-boggling combination of hope and fear.

"Emily?"

"Johnny . . ." She whispered his name and fell back into the fleecy covers, her eyelids fluttering shut again. The warmth of her touch slid away from his cheek, leaving his skin icy cold.

Killian looked down at Lainie, too shocked to do anything but stare. It felt for a moment as if the world had shifted on its axis, as if a heady, dizzying magic had sprinkled down on him. Warmth seeped through his body, heating places that had been cold and dead for more than a decade.

He stared down at the necklace, mesmerized by the hidden light caught in the purple stone. He remembered everything that Viloula had said about lessons and second chances and destiny. It all made sense. Emily had finally learned to survive.

And Killian had betrayed her again. But Viloula was wrong about one thing. It wasn't Lainie who needed to learn something, it was Killian. And he'd failed.

"Oh, Jesus . . ." He took her in his arms and dragged her close, burying his face in the pale crook of her neck. "I've learned my lesson, God," he whispered harshly. "Please . . . don't let it be too late."

Tears scalded his eyes. He squeezed them shut and kissed her throat, breathing in the humid, feverish scent of her, losing himself in the sweetness that was hers alone. Love welled through him, mixed with the acrid sharpness of grief and fear and guilt.

His hand slipped through hers, fingers threaded. There were so many things he wanted to say, but he knew they didn't matter right now. All that mattered was loving her, needing her like air, and letting her know that he was here.

He squeezed his eyes shut and felt tears slip past his lashes. The hot moisture slid along her skin, dampened flesh that was hot and too dry. Prayers swirled through his mind, whispered, desperate pleas he didn't have the strength to actually voice.

Please, God, just make her get well. I'll do anything. Please . . .

That was all that mattered, only that. He'd get her to the Rock and walk away. He swore he would, swore it to God with every breath. He'd get her there—like he'd promised—and he'd walk away, and though it would break his heart, it would be worth it. He'd live the rest of his life without her, knowing that he would collapse into a lifeless, heartless shell without her. Knowing that without Lainie, there was nothing for him; nothing but a lifetime's worth of endless, empty days and lonely nights. It didn't matter. All that mattered was her, and getting her back to her child.

"Please, God . . ." he whispered in a throaty, cracked voice that sounded like the rustling of dead leaves. "Please don't let her die. . . ."

Lainie drew in a shaky breath and tried to open her eyes. Light stabbed her, swirled inside a world that was cold and gray and distant. She slammed her eyes shut against it.

Her whole body hurt. There was a painful sensitivity in her skin, as if her flesh had been scrubbed by sandpaper. She wedged her elbows beneath her and tried to force herself upright, but her arms were limp and shaking and she collapsed back into the pile of smelly pillows.

She let out a weary, exhausted sigh. Jesus, she felt bad. She rested awhile; it could have been ten seconds or ten hours, she didn't know. Then, slowly, she opened her eyes again.

The world swam before her. She blinked hard, tried

to focus, but it was impossible. Everything was washed in gray, shadows within shadows, shifting, moving.

"Thank God," came a ragged, torn voice from beside her.

At the voice, so painfully familiar, it all came back to her in a rush. The sting, the journey, Killian, *Kelly*. She struggled to sit up. Breathing hard, heart pounding, she looked around, trying to see through the shadows that surrounded her. "What day is it?"

"Saturday morning. You haven't missed it," he said in a soft, weary voice.

Relief flooded her. Slowly, aware again of the pain, she sank back onto the bed. Her heartbeat slowed. Then she turned slightly, and the simple movement seemed to take forever. His shadow filled her vision, wavered. After endless minutes, he started to come into focus. Silver-gray hair lay in curled, matted disarray, framed a sun-darkened face that was creased with worry. His mouth was colorless, drawn tight-lipped and set off by deeply etched lines. In his eyes, so dark and bloodshot, she saw a resignation that broke her heart. He looked, inexplicably, as if he were about to say good-bye.

He squeezed his eyes shut for a moment, and when he opened them, she would have sworn she saw the sheen of tears. "I thought I'd lost you again."

At the look in his eyes, so gentle and loving and filled with longing, she almost started to cry herself. She gave him a smile and hoped it reached her eyes, hoped it didn't look as brittle and false as it felt. "I have an irritating way of surviving."

"Don't make light of this, Lainie. Jesus Christ . . ." He reached for her and swept her into his arms, burying his face in the crook of her neck.

She swallowed hard, feeling the sting of tears. She curled her arms around him, breathing in the warm, familiar scent of him, feeling the coarse softness of his hair against her cheek. She wished fleetingly, desperately, that this moment would never end, that somehow she could lose herself in him. "You're right," she said quietly. "I should have said what I feel. It's just that I'm unused to it."

He pulled back slowly and gave her a look that was razor-sharp in its pain. "You're going to have to get used to it fast, Lainie. Our time is running out."

The words struck her like a slap, brought it all back in crystalline clarity, the pain, the knowledge that this was all they would ever have, all they would ever share. She looked away from him, stared at the log wall through a blur of hot tears.

She drew in a deep, shuddering breath. The words, the emotion she'd hoarded all her life, filled her suddenly, swelled in her heart until she felt it would burst. She looked at him and tried to smile. It was a feeble, trembling failure. "I love you, Killian."

He smiled, but it was so sad and bittersweet that it broke her heart all over again. "I know you do, but . . ." His words trailed off. He looked away, stared at the wall.

It's not enough. She heard his words as clearly as if he'd spoken them aloud. She shivered at the intensity of her reaction. It was an agony unlike any she'd ever known before, so different from the vague pain of never having loved at all. "It's all there is, Killian," she said quietly, forcing the bitter words up her throat.

"Three little words," he said, and there was a caustic edge to his voice that cut through her heart like a jagged blade.

She touched him, made him look at her. "It's more than either one of us ever expected."

The moment spilled out, steeped in silence. She

waited, breathless and afraid, to hear what he would say, wanting desperately to hear something, *anything*, that would make the unbearable pain of looking at him go away.

But he said nothing. She deflated, sagged against him, clutching him in shaking arms. There was nothing to say.

Finally he cleared his throat and looked away. "We'd better get going. We're going to have to ride hard to make the Rock by sunset tomorrow."

"Will we make it?"

"Yeah." He shoved a hand through his hair and nodded. The sun-etched lines in his face deepened suddenly, made him look old and beaten. "We'll make it."

Chapter Twenty-six

They rode hard until nightfall. Even after so many bone-rattling hours in the saddle, Killian sat stiff and erect. Lainie's arms were around him, holding him tightly, though he knew she was exhausted and hurting.

He didn't want to stop, didn't want to face the evening that lay ahead. Thoughts of it swirled through his mind, left him feeling hollow inside. This would be their last night together.

He grimaced and yanked back on the reins, wrenching the bit into the soft sides of Captain's mouth. The horse stumbled to a halt and stood there, panting and wheezing. Sweat was a stinking white foam on the animal's cooper-colored neck.

"We'll make camp here," Killian said.

She pressed against him, tightening her hold until he could barely breathe, and he knew without looking at her that she felt it, too, this debilitating, suffocating sense of nearing the end.

His strength left him in a rush. He bowed his head, sagged forward, molding a big, gloved hand around hers.

They sat that way for what felt like hours. Cold, black night curled around them, spilled out across the desert in an endless cloud of nothingness.

"I don't want to let you go," she murmured against his ear.

He straightened, tapped her hand a little too roughly. He couldn't fall into this trap, couldn't do this to either one of them. "Come on," he said gruffly, dismounting.

She waited a heartbeat and then sighed, slipping slowly to the ground beside him.

In utter silence, they prepared the campsite. He set up the small tent, cursing under his breath at every pound of the spikes into the hard ground. Behind him, he heard the clanging clatter of supper being started, the crackling hiss of a fire.

He stayed with the horse longer than necessary, brushing the animal's coat, cleaning his hooves, hobbling him down for the night. But finally he couldn't put off the inevitable anymore. Hesitantly he turned.

She sat beside the fire, crouched down, stirring a pot of something. The baggy sweater lay slipped off one shoulder, revealing a milky soft curve that sparkled with moonlight. The firelight illuminated her profile, gave it the ethereal, impossibly pale perfection of a cameo against the surrounding darkness. She looked sad and alone, her full lips drawn in a limp frown.

His heart clutched. Emotion moved through his chest in a tightening wave. He battled the sudden depression, shoved it aside. There was no point to it now. She was right. This was all they had, all they could hope to have, and he wouldn't mourn it now, before it was gone. He'd have a lifetime to grieve at the loss. Now he had to enjoy whatever seconds they'd been given.

Forcing a smile, he strode toward her. She flinched at every step he took, hunched over a little more. The edges of her mouth quivered, tears glittered in her downcast eyes, clung to the tips of her lashes. Beside her, he sat down.

The pungent aroma of coffee hung in the air, gave the campsite a false homeyness. "We can't do this, Lainie," he said softly.

She leaned against him. "I know. I keep telling myself we need to enjoy the time we have, but ... it's so hard. Every time I look at you I want to cry."

He curled an arm around her shoulder and brought her close. He wanted to crush her against him and smother her with kisses and ask her to make an impossible choice. But he loved her too much to do it. He had to be strong now, strong enough for both of them.

"Is that food ready?" he asked after a while.

She shrugged. "It's beans. What difference does it make?"

They lapsed into silence again, but it was laced with undercurrents, unspoken thoughts, unvoiced wishes. He thought about how he felt when she lay in that rickety bed, writhing with fever, screaming in pain at his touch. When he hadn't thought she'd live. It seemed so far away now, that fear, buried beneath the fresh wounds of their impending separation.

But he'd made a decision then, come to a realization. She had a life somewhere else, a child to care for, and he couldn't take that away from her. God had granted him the gift of her life; the price was good-bye.

He had to let her go. He knew that, even though the very thought of it broke his heart. He wished he had more of her to keep with him, memories to cherish in the long, cold darkness of the days without her.

Tomorrow would be here so quickly, and they knew so little about each other. Not nearly enough. They needed the one thing they didn't have. Time.

He sighed and picked up a stick, poking it into the fire. "Tell me about it ... your home, your life."

"You mean about Kelly," she said, and there was a

sad wistfulness in her voice that told him so much. And suddenly he was grateful for her daughter, more grateful than he could have imagined. She would need that kind of love and caring after this was over. "She's such a beautiful child, Killian. Well, I guess she's not a child anymore. She's a young lady."

Killian felt an unexpected stab of longing. For half his life, he'd told himself that he didn't want children, didn't need them. But now, hearing the love in Lainie's voice, he envied her. He wondered about parenthood, wondered what kind of moments he'd missed. "What's she like?"

She shrugged. "I don't know, like other kids, I guess, only . . . more so maybe. She deals with life head-on. She doesn't hide her feelings or her hurts."

He smiled, trying to lighten the moment, to make it ordinary. "Not like her mom, huh?"

She laughed quietly. "I raised her to be self-confident and unafraid . . . everything that I tried to be and never was."

"You're wrong, Lainie. You're stronger than anyone I've ever known."

"I was so afraid she'd turn out like me, and so afraid I'd turn out like my folks." She turned, gazed up at him with eyes so bright and pain-filled, it hurt to look at her. "Until you, I was afraid of everything. Now . . ." She glanced away, giving a small, almost unnoticeable shrug. "Now I'm only afraid of not feeling this anymore. Of not being with you, not holding you, not knowing that you're beside me."

"I'd stay beside you forever if—" Killian stopped.

Of course. Why hadn't he thought of it before? It was so simple, so damned obvious.

She frowned up at him. "What is it?"

He looked down at her, and for a minute he couldn't speak. His thoughts were a confused, electrified jumble.

"Killian . . . you're scaring me."

"Did Viloula tell you how it would take place, this going through time?"

She shook her head, frowning slightly. "No. She doesn't know."

"How did it happen last time?"

"I was sitting at my computer—" At his confused look, she waved airily. "I'll explain 'computer' later. Anyway, I was working at my terminal late one night. All of a sudden a storm started, lightning struck, and I woke up face-first in the Arizona dirt."

"So now you're planning to be at the Rock at midnight, hoping to ride some cosmic bolt of lightning back through time."

Her frown intensified. "Are you making fun of me?"

A grin burst across his face. He couldn't help it. He suddenly felt like a kid again, full of hope. The heavy veil of depression had ripped a little, let in a steady stream of light, and it warmed him. "Of course not. I'm just trying to understand."

"Why? All that matters is that I'm there. I have to count on fate to get me back."

"Or destiny." He said the words softly, feeling an unexpected shiver move through him. The moment he said the word, *destiny*, the pieces came together in his mind and formed a whole. *Destiny*.

She stared up at him, a hard, no-nonsense look in her eyes. "You're building up to something. What is it?"

He leaned toward her, his gaze as earnest as hers. "Do you think we're soul mates?"

"It doesn't matter. All I know is that I love you in this life . . . more than I ever thought possible."

"Well, *I* believe it."

"You do?"

I forgive you, Johnny. Lainie's words came back to him, swollen with meaning. Emily had always called him Johnny; only Emily. No one else called a gruff-talking, gray-haired giant of an outlaw Johnny. Yet the name had slipped from Lainie's mouth, an endearment from another woman, another time. But the same soul, a soul he'd loved once, and now believed he'd love for all time. "Yeah," he said softly. "I do. And that's why I'm thinking maybe we're not looking at this right."

"What do you mean?"

"We're seeing tomorrow night as an end. But maybe . . . maybe it could be a beginning."

"I don't understand, Killian. Tomorrow—"

"I could go with you."

Her mouth snapped shut. She stared up at him, un-blinking. For a split second, she went so still, she appeared to stop breathing. "Wh-What do you mean?"

He twisted around a little, clutched her shoulders, and drew her close. "Who's to say it's not possible? I mean, *none* of this is possible. What if I just held your hand and wouldn't let you go?"

She bit down on her lower lip. He could see that she was battling hope, trying not to let the potent emotion overtake her. She was afraid of it, afraid to believe in something that would break her heart. "You could be hurt. You could . . . die."

"Nothing could hurt me more than losing you."

"But if something went wrong, if it wasn't possible—"

"I'd die," he said simply. "And I wouldn't have a second's regret."

She swallowed convulsively, her wide-eyed gaze fixed on his. "You'd do that . . . for me?"

Though he should have expected it, her question

filled him with an inestimable sadness. He touched her gently, breezed a callused finger along the velvety underside of her chin. "When will you understand how much I love you?"

She tried to laugh. "Maybe when we're sixty I'll finally believe it."

"Will you let me try it tomorrow?"

"*Let* you?" She gave another laugh, this one trilling and a bit hysterical. "Will I let you risk your life to be with me? What kind of question is that? A nice person, a *heroine*, would say no. She'd make the ultimate sacrifice and be happy knowing the man she loved was alive."

A smile quirked one corner of his mouth. "And is that you, Lainie?"

She smiled in spite of her obvious intention not to. "Damn you, Killian. When did you get to know me so well?"

A lifetime ago. "I don't know. So will you let me try to come with you?"

Her smile faded. She gazed up at him with a painful honesty. "Really?"

He nodded, saying nothing.

"I'd do it for you, you know."

He smiled. "Yeah, I know."

"The twentieth century is a pretty wild place," she said, almost smiling.

"What will I do there?"

"I don't know. Your facts and my words would be a great combination. We could write killer westerns together. Or maybe a movie screenplay."

He didn't even bother asking what she was talking about. He didn't care. All he cared about was planning a future. "Sounds good," he murmured.

"I have a mystery writer acquaintance who could

help us get you an identity." She snuggled against him and sighed. "Kelly will love you."

He heard the enthusiasm in her voice, and knew it was strained, forced. "Will it work?" he asked quietly.

It took her a long time to answer, and when she did, her mouth was trembling slightly. "I don't know."

He turned to her, took her face in his hands, and gazed down at her, loving her more in that moment than he would have thought possible. "If there is a God, Lainie, I'll come back with you."

She nodded, but in her eyes he saw the truth she tried to hide. The desperate sadness that caused the tears.

She didn't believe it was possible, not really. Not in her heart and soul, where such things mattered. She'd spent a lifetime not believing in anything, and it was too late to change now. Too late to start believing in God and destiny and second chances.

"Don't worry, Lainie," he whispered, rolling her over and pressing her down on her back for a tender kiss. "I'll believe enough for both of us."

The angry sky boiled. Rain drizzled downward, pattering the ground in a ceaseless staccato that formed a thin layer of mud. A storm was coming, moving across the desert in a kaleidoscope of shadows and light.

Killian and Lainie stood at the crumbling edge of a mesa, staring down at the washed-out gray coverlet of the desert floor. Towering rock walls outlined the huge box-shaped canyon below.

Behind them, Captain stood motionless and exhausted, his tired head hung low to the ground. The wheezing snort of his heavy breathing was a steady sound amidst the marching rain.

Killian pointed at a monolithic slab of stone that towered in the distance. Rain thumped on his oilskinned sleeve. "That's the rock that lightning struck."

She squinted, trying to see through the watery blur. A great red obelisk thrust up from the earth in the canyon's corner, its top an immense, jagged crown of stone. "How far away is it?"

"Six, maybe seven miles." He tented a hand over his eyes and squinted at the weak sun. It hung low to the ground, suspended amidst the thick gray shroud of the coming storm. "We're going to have to hurry to reach it before sunset."

Sunset. She shivered at the word, wishing he had said something else. It was so final. The single word that held together all her hopes and fears and prayers. *Sunset.* Whatever would happen to them—a taste of eternity or a plunge straight to hell—would happen when that pale yellow globe ducked into the darkening earth.

She slipped her hand through his, squeezed the damp leather of his glove. Fear was a cold, hard stone in the pit of her stomach, but she refused to give in to it.

He squeezed her hand. "Let's go."

She nodded, her throat too thick to force a sound. Wordlessly she climbed back into the saddle.

With a sigh, he climbed up alongside her and settled wearily into the leather seat. Drawing back on the reins, he maneuvered Captain off the jutting precipice of rock and headed down the winding, narrow trail that led to the gorge.

For more than an hour, they picked their way through the narrow crevasse that led down to the canyon floor. The horse's hooves splashed on the slippery mud. Every now and then his heaving flank smacked against the moist sandstone walls. Rain hammered their heads, streaming down the sides of Lainie's face in icy, squiggling lines. She blinked against the wetness and tried to stay alert, but all she wanted to do was close her eyes and hold Killian. Hold him and never let him go.

Finally they reached the end of the trail and came into the open space of the canyon floor. Wind whipped down the rock walls and smacked into them, yanking the hat from Killian's head. He reached for it and missed. Lainie watched the black dot of a hat spiral away from them, dancing and twirling above the muddy redness of the ground.

The rain picked up, turned from a drizzle to a drenching, icy cold downpour. Nickel-sized droplets hammered her head, plunked on the puddles and rivulets that grew suddenly from the dirt. Wind and water spiked her eyes, made it hard to see anything.

"Can you see it?"

She heard his voice, reedy and thin against the wind's howling laughter.

"Yeah," she yelled back, drawing in a mouthful of sweet, fragrant rain. She sputtered and coughed and pressed her lips together. Though she couldn't see the sun anymore, she knew it had dipped farther in the hour they'd spent winding through the mesa's unforgiving walls.

Killian spurred Captain to a gallop. The horse gave a mighty effort. He lurched into a jarring trot, then wheezed and shuddered and staggered sideways. His trot melted back into a slow, methodical, plodding walk.

Killian shook his head and patted the animal's sweat-foamed neck.

Lainie leaned around Killian, trying to see Captain's big head. "What's the matter?"

"He doesn't have any more to give."

Lainie's gaze shot to the horizon, where the hidden sun lurked behind a gray armada of clouds. "Are we going to make it?"

"We'll make it." There was a steely determination in his voice that reassured Lainie. She settled back into her seat and tightened her hold on him, resting her damp cheek against the wet oilskin of his duster.

They picked their way across the desert floor, moving with agonizing slowness. The wind was a constant stinging slap against their cheeks, the rain a hammering stream in their eyes. Suddenly Killian drew Captain to a stop.

"What—"

He held a gloved hand up for silence. "Something's not right." He stiffened, drew the gun from his belt.

Lainie glanced to the left and saw something. A shadow of movement, a glitter of light where no light was possible.

"Kil—"

The deafening roar of a shotgun blast severed her sentence.

Captain let out a groaning, wheezing grunt and staggered sideways. His head dipped. Stumbling forward, he sank to his knees in the soft, wet earth.

"*Shit!*" Killian clutched Lainie around the waist and jumped out of the saddle.

She landed face-first in the mud, felt the cold ooze splatter her face as Captain floundered in the mire, grunting, wheezing, trying to get back onto his feet. The acrid smell of gunpowder chased away the sweet fragrance of the rain. All Lainie could smell now was wet earth and sweat and sulfur.

And blood.

She saw the dark smear of red that stained the Appaloosa's huge flank. The animal gave one last, shuddering breath and collapsed.

She stared at the horse for a heartbeat, unable to comprehend, and then, in a flash, it came to her.

"Oh, my *God*," she screamed in a panic. All at once she knew what was happening, knew why it was happening. She clutched Killian's sleeve and yanked hard. "Where are we?"

"Bloody Gorge." He inched forward on his elbows and peered over the dead horse's swelling stomach, using the now silent animal as a barrier between them and the snipers.

The world fell away from her for a second. *Bloody Gorge*. What the hell were they doing here?

Viloula's prophecy came crashing back to her. *There will be a death.*

"Killian!" a male voice yelled, echoing above the driving rain. "Surrender or we'll shoot you."

Lainie slogged through the mud and plastered herself alongside him. Taking Killian's face in her wet, dirty hands, she forced him to look at her. "You have to get out of here. That's Joe Martin."

"I'm not leaving you. We're gonna make it to the Rock."

Lainie shook her head. Tears scalded her eyes and fell down her cheeks, mingling with the cold rain. "You don't understand. This is— Oh, God . . ." For a second she couldn't talk, couldn't move, couldn't do anything except look into Killian's eyes and feel a drenching, desperate sense of regret.

"What, Lainie, for Christ's sake—"

She shook him hard, glared up at him through the stinging veil of tears. "This is where you die, damn it. Get the hell out of here."

She saw the dawning realization in his eyes, the understanding. "Bloody Gorge," he said softly. "Yeah, I remember you saying that now. . . ."

"*Now* you remember," she said hysterically. "Couldn't you have remembered yesterday?"

"There's no other way to the Rock. This is it." He frowned suddenly. "How did Joe Martin know I'd be here?"

"Mose," she said without hesitation. "He sent Joe Martin to kill you at Bloody Gorge. After your ... death, Mose takes your place with the outlaws."

"Bastard," he hissed.

"Come on out, Killian. Don't make me kill the lady, too."

Killian shot a glance at the horizon. He couldn't see the sun, but knew it was fading fast. "We've got to make a run for it. Now."

She grabbed his chin, forced him to look at her. "Not you. No way."

He clutched her by the shoulders and drew her close, giving her a hard shake. "We're in this together, damn it."

"But you *die* here, Killian." She was screaming now, screaming and crying, and she didn't care.

He gave her a hard, desperate kiss. "Don't you get it?" he whispered against her lips, his voice a thread of sound above the thumping of the rain on their bodies. "I'm dead either way. Now, get your beautiful ass up to a crawl. I'm heading for the Rock, and I'll get you there if I have to drag you."

He maneuvered onto his hands and knees and peered over the spotted swell of the horse's hindquarters. Lainie followed, keeping close. In the distance, not more than one hundred feet away, she saw the shadowy outline of three men on horseback.

She glanced to the west again, saw the sun. They had mere minutes left.

He slipped his hand in hers. She felt the solid, comforting squeeze of his fingers. "On the count of three we get to our feet and run as fast as we can to the Rock. Okay?"

"Okay." The word hurt, felt as if it had been wrenched from her soul.

"One . . . two . . ."

"Now, Killian," Joe Martin yelled. "You got thirty seconds to give yourself up."

"Three." Killian and Lainie lurched to their feet and spun around, racing for the Rock.

"Son of a bitch!" Martin shrieked. "They're makin' a run for it."

Lainie and Killian lurched forward. The thick, viscous mud sucked at their feet and splashed up their pants. Rain slashed against their faces, blinded them. Still they ran, their threaded fingers a lifeline in the shifting world. Behind them came the thundering heartbeat of horses' hooves.

Gunfire exploded again, sprayed all around them. She heard the thudding impact of bullets on the crumbling rock walls, smelled the sharp, acrid scent of gunpowder.

Suddenly Killian arced forward, his chest curving outward. His fingers spasmed around hers, clamped hard. He stumbled and slid forward, crashing to his knees.

She clung to his hand, ignoring the painful snapping of her bones. "Killian?" she screamed, wiping the rain from her eyes, trying futilely to see him.

He staggered to his feet and kept running, dragging her alongside him. "Keep running, damn it."

She glanced backward. The three horsemen were gaining ground; their tall, silhouetted forms shimmered in the silver curtain of the rain.

Thunder boomed across the darkening sky, shook the ground beneath their feet. Lightning flared, its white light bright enough to hurt Lainie's eyes. She blinked, trying to see where they were going. A huge, snaking bolt of lightning shot out of the clouds and hit a gnarled old tree. The branches exploded in a shower of golden sparks, a fire billowed up from its core. The scent of smoke was all around.

"Here." Killian yanked her sideways into a crack in the Rock. Huge, wet sandstone walls curled around them, protected them from the howling wind. He pulled her into his arms and collapsed against the Rock, breathing hard.

She clung to him, her cheek pressed to the slick, soaking wet oilskin of his duster.

"This is it," he said in a tired voice.

There was a finality in his voice that surprised her. She looked up at him, blinking against the rain. "Killian?"

"Sorry, Lainie. I thought maybe . . ."

She pulled back. "What—" Then she saw it. Wide-eyed, disbelieving, she stared at the dark blotch that spread across his chest.

Blood. He'd been shot.

She couldn't breathe. Horror shuddered through her in a wave that left her icy cold. She launched forward and pressed her hands over the wound in his chest, applying a steady pressure. Blood seeped through his shirt and squished between her fingers, running over the back of her hands. Rain diluted the blood, turning it a pathetic pink and washing it away.

"You're going to be okay," she said, breathing hard. "You'll be fine. . . ." Her voice cracked on a sob. Tears burned her eyes and turned him into a watery blur.

"Don't cry," he whispered.

"I love you," she said in a hoarse, hiccuping voice. "I love you." Her words took on a strident desperation, rose shrilly above the hammering of the rain on the rocks around them. "I love you."

"I love you, too." He winced, drew in a shaking breath that seemed to hurt. "Remember that."

"Don't do it, Killian," she said, pressing harder on his wound. "Don't you die on me. I won't let you."

He wheezed and clutched his hand over hers, wincing at the pain. The look he gave her was so sad, so filled with love, it broke her heart. "I knew . . . I . . . wouldn't be . . . there for . . . you. . . ."

"Don't you say that. Don't . . ." She threw her arms around him and clung to him, breathing in the rainy, bloody scent of him, trying to memorize everything about him in a single, aching touch. "I won't let you go, Killian. I won't. You're coming with me."

He stroked her hair for a second, then his hand wavered, drew back from her head. She heard it thump softly against his thigh. A fluttering sigh escaped him.

Shaking, she drew back. The sight of him was like a sharp blow to the chest. She drew in gasping gulps of air and tried to keep breathing. But she didn't want to, she wanted to curl up alongside him and die. Just die . . .

Racking, aching sobs clutched her chest, burned her eyes. With cold, shaking fingers, she pushed the wet hair from his eyes.

He sat slumped against the Rock, his head cocked at an unnatural angle. His face was ash gray, his mouth colorless and slack. He was staring at her through bleak, resigned eyes. "I . . . love . . . you," he said again, more softly, his voice cracking on the last word. He let out a groaning sigh and reached for her.

She waited for the touch, but it never came. Halfway there, his hand stopped, slid lifelessly downward. He breathed her name, only her name.

"Killian." She clutched his shoulders, shaking him hard.

He slumped against her, his head fell forward.

"Noooo!" She threw her arms around his lifeless body, throwing herself on top of him, as if her warmth could somehow bring him back to life. Blood seeped through his shirt and stuck to her skin. The smell of it was everywhere. "Don't leave me," she whispered against his ear again and again, tasting the salty moisture of her own tears. "You said you'd hold on to me. . . . You promised. . . ." She reached for his hand, threaded her wet fingers through his limp, lifeless ones, clinging to him. Sobbing, she brought his hand to her chest, plastered it to her heart. "You said you wouldn't let go. You promised. . . ." Her voice caught, shattered into a great, inhuman howl of pain.

Suddenly she remembered the necklace and Viloula's words. *Use it wisely.* Lainie had been wrong. *She* didn't need the necklace to get back. He did.

"Oh, God . . ." She wrenched backward and fumbled with the latch at the back of her neck, willing her shaking, ice-cold fingers to function. She couldn't do it, couldn't open the catch. Frustration welled through her, and with a scream, she ripped the necklace from her throat and pressed it to Killian's chest.

It slid downward.

Sobbing, she grabbed his limp hand and pressed the stone against his flesh, forcing his fingers to curl around it. "Take it, damn it. Hold on. You promised. . . ."

Thunder rumbled again, a sound so loud, it vibrated in the rock walls around her. Lightning ripped through the darkness, for a split second turning the world into a burning ball of white-hot light. She blinked against the brightness and buried her face in the wet crook of his neck, her fingers coiled around his.

As she lay there, sprawled on top of him, rocking him in shaking arms, a tingling sensation spread through her body. She felt tired suddenly, as if all the fight and fire had drained out of her, leaving only a broken, lifeless shell. Lightning flashed again, hit the rock above her head in a spray of fire-bright sparks. The impossible aroma of roses floated on the wind, mingled with the acrid scent of smoke.

And then she couldn't feel Killian anymore.

Terrified, she withdrew her face from the crook of his neck and stared down at him. He was sitting there, slumped just as before, his eyes closed, his skin deathly pale.

But she couldn't feel him, couldn't feel the wetness of the rain on his still warm skin, couldn't feel the stiff fabric of his duster.

With a sob, she reached for him, tried to touch him again, but her arms and fingers were hazy and unreal, shimmering and insubstantial. Ghost's arms, ghost's fingers.

She was floating away from him, her invisible ghost's body riding on the swelling rise of the wind. She screamed his name, sobbing, and fought the motion, but the more she fought it, the farther she pulled away from him.

Dimly she was aware of the three riders who appeared in the crack of the Rock beside Killian. She watched in horror as the riders approached.

Joe Martin slid out of the saddle and moved cautiously toward Killian, his shotgun pointed at the man slumped against the Rock. He jabbed Killian in the shoulder with the tip of his rifle.

Killian slid sideways and lay in a heap in the thick mud.

"He's dead," Martin said.

The man beside him laughed quietly. "The re-ward said dead or alive. Hey, what's that in his hand?"

In Killian's hand, the amethyst started to glow, lightly at first, then in pulsing, radiant purple rays. A pale white light crept through his fingers and up his arm, moving slowly.

"He probably stole it from some widow," Martin said, shoving his rifle back into its long leather holster on his saddle. "Let's get him onto a horse."

Lainie screamed Killian's name, but the sound was no more than an echoing sharpness on the wind. She reached out and scooped an armful of air, holding it to her chest, pretending that she could still feel him, still touch him.

An uncomfortable pulling sensation filled her stomach and radiated through her limbs to her fingertips and toes. She spiraled end over end—at least it *felt* as if she were spinning. She couldn't tell anymore, she was so dizzy.

The sounds of the night died. She couldn't hear anything but the gasping spurts of her own panicked breathing. She seemed to fall into the darkness and float there, alone except for a million floating golden-bright sparks.

And then, just as suddenly as before, there was nothing.

Chapter Twenty-seven

Lainie came awake slowly. She had a moment's peace, a wonderful, relaxing sensation of everything being right with the world. She stretched lazily and opened her eyes. A white wall cluttered with tacked-up photographs and pictures filled her field of vision.

It took a second for things to register.

She lurched backward. The metal wheels on her chair legs screeched across the hardwood floor. She slammed into the open door and stared around, blinking hard, unable for a second to breathe.

She was sitting in her own chair, in her own office. Her computer sat in front of her, its blank, empty screen mocked her.

She squeezed her eyes shut to block out the reality, but it didn't help. Her breathing fractured into great, wheezing gulps, her heart pounded so loud she couldn't hear anything else.

Except the thunder. *Thunder.*

She forced her eyes open and looked out her window. Rain clattered against the Thermopane glass, slid down in opaque, sparkling streams. Wind rattled the gutters and shook the maple trees huddled in her yard.

The storm was still raging . . . exactly as it had been. As if she'd never really left at all.

Panic surged through her. She shook her head in denial. *It couldn't be true. It couldn't be ...*

"I'm not that crazy," she cried.

But she was. Goddamn it, she was that crazy. . . .

She yanked a handful of sweater and brought it to her nose, sniffing, breathing in the warm, yarny scent.

There was no hint of a dust smell, no sharp odor of blood and sweat and mud. Nothing but Tide laundry soap and a lingering trace of Fendi perfume.

It had all been a dream. She'd never left this house. "Noooo," she screamed. She wouldn't believe it. *Couldn't* believe it. Killian had been real. She'd touched him, loved him, let him into her soul.

He had to be real.

If he wasn't real, she was crazy ... too crazy to be a mother, too crazy to be free. . . .

She stumbled out of her chair, spinning away from her desk and hurtling through her house. Panic and fear and desperation pumped through her in heart-stopping bursts of adrenaline. Her fingers shook, her mouth trembled, her heartbeat thundered in her ears. She moved in jerky, awkward motions, searching for something to do, to think, to feel. Anything but this paralyzing sense of terror.

Calm down, Lainie. Get a grip. It was real. It *was*. She had to prove it. Had to know for sure. But how? *Judith.*

She surged to the phone and yanked the receiver off its hook, punching out Jude's home phone number in New Jersey.

The buzzing drone of a busy signal exploded in her ears.

She slammed the phone back into its cradle. Pacing back and forth across her small, wooden-floored kitchen, she waited exactly ten seconds, then grabbed the phone and dialed again.

This time the phone rang. Judith picked up on the second ring. "Hello?"

Lainie let out a quick breath and tried to sound normal. "Jude?" she said, barely able to hear her own voice over the thudding beat of her heart. *Calm down, Lainie. Breathe.*

"Lainie, is that you?"

"Yeah, it's me. Jude, I was wondering . . . wh-when did I leave New York?"

There was a long silence before Jude answered. "Have you been drinking?"

Lainie laughed sharply, bitterly. "Unfortunately, I'm sober as a judge."

"Thank God," Jude said with a breathy laugh. "Well, you left JFK about ten hours ago. So, with the time change and all, you've been home, what—three hours? Why?"

The answer hit her like a sharp blow to the heart. She reeled backward, her fingers spasmed around the phone. She went from panic to devastation in a heartbeat, and realized a second too late that panicked was better. With panic, there'd been hope. Now, she had nothing, nothing but a yawning, desperate emptiness.

She'd thought she was lonely before she met Killian, but she hadn't known what lonely was until this instant.

"Three hours," she repeated the words in a wooden, lifeless voice. Long enough to make dinner, pour a stiff drink, and talk to Kelly. Exactly what she'd done before she sat down at the computer.

Mumbling good-bye, she set the phone down. Her hands were shaking so badly she missed the phone's cradle. The handset clattered to the floor and emitted a low, whining buzz.

Lainie moved like an automaton through her little house, staring sightlessly past her own belongings. Finally she came to the piano. She trailed a finger along the cool, ivory keys, barely hearing the trilling scale of the music. Photographs cluttered the shiny black surface, framed in dozens of textures and designs. All of them Kelly, all of them smiling.

Memories. The word cut like a knife.

There were no pictures of Killian to hold to her breast at night, no photographs to remind her what she'd felt for him.

She looked up at the ceiling, feeling the sharp sting of tears. *Where are you, Killian? What's it like there?*

What if he was afraid? What if he needed her? She didn't want him ever to be alone again; they'd both been lonely for too long. . . .

She stumbled back from the piano, seeing the pictures through a blur of tears. She knew she should call Dr. Gray, should check herself back into the hospital. The thought caused a shudder of revulsion.

She drifted into her bedroom and crossed to the window. Wind clattered against the glass, rain turned it into a rectangle of squirming silver threads. She hugged herself and stared, dazed, at the display of nature's power. Strangely, she was unafraid. For the first time in her life, the storm didn't scare her.

Another lesson learned, she thought bitterly. Another demon exorcized.

And she didn't care. She'd gladly live with fear again for just one more second with Killian. Just one more kiss.

For a heartbreaking second, she felt him beside her, felt the warmth of his arms around her, saw his sexy smile as he reached toward her. *One kiss, Lainie. Just one . . .*

With numb fingers, she flicked the metal latch and shoved the window open. Cold, fresh air hit her in the face, rustled her dirty hair. It smelled of pine and cedar and rain, just like it always did.

It hurt, that ordinary, everyday smell. Hurt more than she could have imagined. Tears blurred her vision, turned the backyard into a wash of shadows. Droplets splashed down from the trees and splattered the muddy green of her lawn, running along the fence line in a moonlit, silver rivulet.

Lightning struck in a white-hot bolt. The electric tip smacked into a dogwood tree, setting off a fiery shower of sparks. Thunder vibrated through the house, rumbled in the floorboards. The thick, acrid smell of smoke wafted through the open window. Another bolt exploded through the night and caused a brilliant, unearthly white glow.

Then everything went black.

"Damn." She sagged, too tired right now to deal with another power outage. Turning away from the window, she felt her way across her bedroom and reached for the stash of thick white emergency candles she kept in the box beneath her bed. Lighting a dozen or so, she placed them around her room, on every flat surface, until the walls glowed with a rose-gold sheen. Overhead, the Day-Glo stars twinkled against the dark blue paint.

It looked like a night sky in the Arizona desert.

Don't think about it. Don't . . . But she couldn't think of anything else.

Sagging onto the bed, she drew the soft blue coverlet around her and lay down, curling into the smallest, tightest ball she could. The fleecy folds of the blanket coiled around her and should have been warm. If only she weren't so cold inside ... so cold ...

A quiet, desperate little sound caught in her throat. Tears burned behind her eyes and ached in her chest, but she couldn't release them. She was afraid that if she cried, she'd feel better, and she didn't want to feel better, she wanted to hurt just like this for the rest of her life. As long as she was in pain, it was all real.

She drew her knees tighter against her chest and closed her eyes. *Come to me, Killian. I'm here.*

She waited, breath held, for an answer, but there wasn't one.

The magic was gone.

No, she thought dully. It wasn't gone.

It had never existed at all.

Tears scalded her eyes and shuddered through her aching chest. She didn't try to stop them this time, couldn't. Sobbing, shaking, she curled even smaller, tried desperately to disappear.

You're safe now. I love you. Lean on me, Lainie.

She tried to bring forth an image of him before his death, but she couldn't do it, couldn't remember his smile, his laugh, his sexy eyes. All she could see were the last moments, the gasping, quiet way he'd said her name, the deathly pallor of his skin.

I knew I wouldn't be there for you.

"Oh, God," she moaned.

Suddenly a gust of wind smacked the house, rattled the windows. Her curtains billowed against the wall. Icy air swept into her room, bringing a flurry of leaves with it. Downstairs, the door banged open with a crash. The house clattered and shook and moaned at the onslaught.

Lainie ignored it until shards of rain started pattering her bedroom floor, puddling on the wood. With a tired sigh, she pushed to a stand. She closed her window, then reached for a candle and walked tiredly through the house toward the front door.

A burst of wind extinguished her light, left her in a solid blackness. Leaves swirled at her feet, riveted to her shins. The open door thumped against the wall, rain hammered the wooden floors, collected in a silvery puddle.

She dropped her useless candle and tried to close the door. It wouldn't budge. Frowning, she gripped the brass knob more tightly and tried again.

Nothing. She couldn't move it.

Thunder cracked across the heavens and a white-hot bolt of lightning snaked through the clouds and hit Kelly's swing set in a shower of sparks.

Something caught Lainie's eye. Almost involuntarily, she moved into the doorway. Wind smacked her in the face, tangled in her hair. Rain slashed her cheeks and plastered her sweater to her skin.

Lightning struck again, illuminated the backyard in a series of jerking, staccato bursts.

There was something beside the swing set, a huge, hulking shadow.

She felt a sudden burst of fear and thought about slamming the door shut. Yesterday, she would have done just that, would have hidden beneath her bed and called the police. But today she was different. Stronger, somehow.

She took a tentative step forward, moved into the pulsing vortex of the storm. Whooshing wind yanked at her clothing, pulled her hair, and made her eyes water. Rain blurred her vision, but still she moved forward.

The shadow moved. A low, throaty growl came from that direction.

It was an animal in pain.

Lainie ran toward the swing set, her booted feet sliding through the rain-soaked grass.

The first thing she saw when she got close was the black hump of an oilskin duster, then a flash of lavender light.

Her breath caught. Hope slammed through her body, brought her to a dead stop. Her bones melted and she dropped to her knees. "K-Killian?" she whispered his name, so softly even she couldn't hear it above the droning whine of the rain.

He groaned and rolled over. Rain pattered his face, ran in rivulets down his cheeks.

Magically, the storm stopped. Dark gray rain clouds scudded across the sky. A full, blue-white moon peered down at them, cast them in sparkling light. Raindrops clung to the grass like a million fallen stars.

His eyes fluttered open. Their gazes locked, and in his eyes she saw it all, everything she'd ever wanted and needed and prayed to find.

She couldn't talk past the lump in her throat. She made a quick sobbing sound and bit down on her lower lip, afraid to believe in him, terrified not to.

"I'm real, Lainie."

Tentatively, she reached out. At the first touch of fabric against her fingertips, relief moved through her in a shuddering wave.

With a broken sob, she ran her hands across his chest, feeling for the stickiness of the blood, waiting for the wheezing pull of a pain-filled breath. He felt so strong and solid and *real*. She couldn't get enough of touching him.

"It's gone," he whispered, and she could hear the wonder in his voice. "I might be dead in 1896, but I'm alive now." He gave her a slow, crooked grin. "There is a God."

"I'll never doubt that again." She threw her arms around his huge, wet body and molded herself to him, kissing every patch of skin she could find.

Laughing softly, he pushed her back and stood up, drawing her beside him. Then he lifted his hand. In the callused palm lay the amethyst, its oval surface glowing with magical, iridescent light. As they watched, the light diminished, sank back into the faceted surface of the gem. Then the golden filigree lost its color, faded into the flesh tone of his hand.

In a puff of smoke, the necklace vanished.

Killian turned to her. "I was wrong," he said softly. "I'm here for you, baby. And I'm not going anywhere this time."

She stared into the hard, life-worn face of the man she loved more than life itself. At the sight of him, grinning and dripping wet, a sunburst of emotion exploded in her chest, filled her heart. Before she knew it, she was crying, happy, joy-filled tears that cleansed the last remnant of sorrow from her soul.

He kissed her, and she clung to him, losing herself in the sweetness of his mouth. "Oh, Killian . . ." she whispered against his lips.

He laughed. It was a rich, rumbling sound that slid into her heart in a warm, steady stream. "I think you can call me John now."

She drew back, gazed up at him. "John . . ." She tried the name out, liked it, and smiled. Emotion swelled in her throat, made it difficult to breathe. Suddenly it was important that she tell him the truth, everything that she felt. He'd given that to her, given her the freedom of honesty, and she'd never go back to what she'd been before. Never. "I love you so much. So much . . ."

He stared down into her eyes, and slowly his smile fell. His eyes darkened, took on an edge of sadness that seemed inestimably old. Lainie felt a stirring of memory, a recollection of what it had been like always to be alone, always to be separate. He took her face in his big, rough hands and tilted her chin up, bringing her close enough for a kiss, but not kissing her. "Lainie," he whispered in a gruff, emotional voice. "I've been waiting for you all my life."

Then he kissed her—a fierce, passionate kiss that set off a flurry of butterflies in her stomach. In a single gesture, he swept her into his arms. Laughing, she threw her arms around his neck. "Where are we going?"

"I want to see our house." He surged across the doorway and kicked the door shut.

"This is the entryway. That's a painting by—"

He didn't stop in the entryway, just pushed through to the kitchen. "This is the kit—"

They were in the dining room. Lainie didn't even bother saying anything, they were through the dining room and upstairs to the bedroom so quickly.

The magical blue room curled around them, cast them in the flickering light of a zillion candlelights. "So, outlaw," she said, grinning up at him. "Are you going to ravish me?"

He tossed her on the bed and landed beside her, drawing her close. He grinned down at her, a wolfish, predatory smile that made her blood race. She knew then that no matter how long she lived, no matter how often she died, she would remember this moment, this man, forever.

You got to believe, child. Viloula's scratchy, singsongy voice came back to her.

She smiled up at Killian, offering him everything with that smile—her heart, her soul, her life.

All at once, she understood what Viloula had said. She'd learned the lesson of her past; without even knowing it, she'd learned how to love and trust and believe. She wasn't afraid of being abandoned anymore.

"I love you, Johnny," she said quietly, and the name seemed suddenly the most natural thing in the world. As if she'd never called him anything else.

He stilled, then gave her a slow, seductive smile that filled her soul with light. "You always have," he answered, brushing a thick curl of hair from her eyes.

And she always would.

Forever.

Miracles do not happen
in contradiction to nature,
but only in contradiction
to what we know of nature.
—Saint Augustine

Dr. Bloom waited impatiently for an answer.

Meghann Dontess leaned back in her seat and studied her finger-nails. It was time for a manicure. Past time. "I try not to feel too much, Harriet. You know that. I find it impedes my enjoyment of life."

"Is that why you've seen me every week for four years? Because you enjoy your life so much?"

"I wouldn't point that out if I were you. It doesn't say much for your psychiatric skills. It's entirely possible, you know, that I was perfectly normal when I met you and you're *making* me crazy."

"You're using humor as a shield again."

"You're giving me too much credit. That wasn't funny."

Harriet didn't smile. "I rarely think you're funny."

"There goes my dream of doing stand-up."

"Let's talk about the day you and Claire were separated."

Meghann shifted uncomfortably in her seat. Just when she needed a smart-ass response, her mind went blank. She knew what Harriet was poking around for, and Harriet knew she knew. If Meghann didn't answer, the question would simply be asked again. "Separated. A nice, clean word. Detached. I like it, but that subject is closed."

"It's interesting that you maintain a relationship with your mother while distancing yourself from your sister."

Meghann shrugged. "Mama's an actress. I'm a lawyer. We're com-fortable with make-believe."

"Meaning?"

"Have you ever read one of her interviews?"

"No."

"She tells everyone that we lived this poor, pathetic-but-loving exis-tence. We pretend it's the truth."

"You were living in Bakersfield when the pathetic-but-loving pre-tense ended, right?"

Meghann remained silent. Harriet had maneuvered her back to the painful subject like a rat through a maze.

Harriet went on, "Claire was nine years old. She was missing sev-eral teeth, if I remember correctly, and she was having difficulties with math."

"Don't." Meghann curled her fingers around the chair's sleek wood-en arms.

Harriet stared at her. Beneath the unruly black ledge of her eye-brows, her gaze was steady. Small round glasses magnified her eyes. "Don't back away, Meg. We're making progress."

"Any more progress and I'll need an aid car. We should talk about my practice. That's why I come to you, you know. It's a pressure cooker down in Family Court these days. Yesterday, I had a deadbeat dad drive up in a Ferrari and then swear he was flat broke. The shithead. Didn't want to pay for his daughter's tuition. Too bad for him I videotaped his arrival."

"Why do you keep paying me if you don't want to discuss the root of your problems?"

"I have issues, not problems. And there's no point in poking around in the past. I was sixteen when all that happened. Now, I'm a whopping forty-two. It's time to move on. I did the right thing. It doesn't matter anymore."

"Then why do you still have the nightmare?"

She fiddled with the silver David Yurman bracelet on her wrist. "I have nightmares about spiders who wear Oakley sunglasses, too. But you never ask about that. Oh, and last week, I dreamed I was trapped in a glass room that had a floor made of bacon. I could hear people crying, but I couldn't find the key. You want to talk about that one?"

"A feeling of isolation. An awareness that people are upset by your actions, or missing you. Okay, let's talk about that dream. Who is crying?"

"Shit." Meghann should have seen that. After all, she had an undergraduate degree in psychology. Not to mention the fact that she'd once been called a child prodigy.

She glanced down at her platinum and gold watch. "Too bad, Harriet. Time's up. I guess we'll have to solve my pesky neuroses next week." She stood up, smoothed the pant legs of her navy Armani suit. Not that there was a wrinkle to be found.

Harriet slowly removed her glasses.

Meghann crossed her arms in an instinctive gesture of self-protection. "This should be good."

"Do you like your life, Meghann?"

That wasn't what she'd expected. "What's not to like? I'm the best divorce attorney in the state. I live—"

"—alone—"

"—in a kick-ass condo abouve the Public Market and drive a brand-new Porsche."

"Friends?"

"I talk to Elizabeth every Thursday night."

"Family?"

Maybe it was time to get a new therapist. Harriet had ferreted out all of Meghann's weak points. "My mom stayed with me for a week last year. If I'm lucky, she'll come back for another visit just in time to watch the colonization of Mars on MTV."

"And Claire?"

"My sister and I have problems, I'll admit it. But nothing major. We're just too busy to get together." When Harriet didn't speak, Meghann rushed in to fill the silence. "Okay, she makes me crazy, the way she's throwing her life away. She's smart enough to do anything, but she stays tied to that loser campground they call a resort."

"With her father."

"I don't want to discuss my sister. And I *definitely* don't want to discuss my father."

Harriet tapped her pen on the table. "Okay, how about this: When was the last time you slept with the same man twice?"

"You're the only one who thinks that's a *bad* thing. I like variety."

"The way you like younger men, right? Men who have no desire to settle down. You get rid of them before they can get rid of you."

"Again, sleeping with younger, sexy men who don't want to settle down is not a bad thing. I don't want a house with a picket fence in suburbia. I'm not interested in family life, but I like sex."

"And the loneliness, do you like that?"

"I'm not lonely," she said stubbornly. "I'm independent. Men don't like a strong woman."

"Strong men do."

"Then I better start hanging out in the gyms instead of bars."

"And strong women face their fears. They talk about the painful choices they've made in their lives."

Meghann actually flinched. "Sorry, Harriet, I need to scoot. See you next week."

She left the office.

Outside, it was a gloriously bright June day. Early in the so-called summer. Everywhere else in the country, people were swimming and barbecuing and organizing poolside picnics. Here, in good ole Seattle, people were methodically checking their calendars and muttering that it was *June, damn it.*

Only a few tourists were around this morning; out-of-towners recognizable by the umbrellas tucked under their arms.

Meghann finally released her breath as she crossed the busy street and stepped onto the grassy lawn of the waterfront park. A towering totem pole greeted her. Behind it, a dozen seagulls dived for bits of discarded food.

She walked past a park bench where a man lay huddled beneath a blanket of yellowed newspapers. In front of her, the deep blue Sound stretched along the pale horizon. She wished she could take comfort in that view; often, she could. But today, her mind was caught in the net of another time and place.

If she closed her eyes—which she definitely dared not do—she'd remember it all: the dialing of the telephone number, the stilted, desperate conversation with a man she didn't know, the long, silent drive to that shit-ass little town up north. And worst of all, the tease she'd wiped from her little sister's flushed cheeks when she said, *I'm leaving you, Claire.*

Her fingers tightened around the railing. Dr. Bloom was wrong. Talking about Meghann's painful choice and the lonely years that had followed it wouldn't help.

Her past wasn't a collection of memories to be worked through; it was like an oversize Samsonite with a bum wheel. Meghann had learned that a long time ago. All she could do was drag it along behind her.